Books by Jude Deveraux

The Velvet Promise
Highland Velvet
Velvet Song
Velvet Angel
Sweetbriar
Counterfeit Lady
Lost Lady
River Lady
Twin of Ice
Twin of Fire
The Temptress
The Raider
The Princess
The Awakening
The Maiden
The Taming
A Knight in Shining Armor

Published by POCKET BOOKS

JUDE DEVERAUX

A KNIGHT in SHINING ARMOR

POCKET BOOKS

New York   London   Toronto   Sydney   Tokyo

This book is a work of fiction. Names, characters, places and incidents are either the product of the author's imagination or are used fictitiously. Any resemblance to actual events or locales or persons, living or dead, is entirely coincidental.

POCKET BOOKS, a division of Simon & Schuster Inc.
1230 Avenue of the Americas, New York, NY 10020

Quality Printing and Binding by:
Orange Graphics
P.O. Box 791
Orange, VA 22960 U.S.A.

*I dedicate this book with love
to my editor and, more importantly,
to my friend,
Linda Marrow.*

PROLOGUE
England, 1564

Nicholas was trying to concentrate on the letter to his mother, a letter that was probably the most important document he would ever write. Everything depended upon this letter: his honor, his estates, his family's future —and his life.

But as he wrote he began to hear her. Softly at first, but growing louder. It was a woman weeping, but not weeping as from pain or even from grief but from something deeper.

He gave his attention back to the letter but he could not concentrate. The woman needed something but he could not tell what. Comfort? Soothing?

No, he thought, she needed hope. The tears, the weeping, were the tears of a person who no longer had any hope.

Nicholas looked back at the paper. The woman's problems were not his. If he did not finish this letter and soon give it to the waiting messenger, his own life would be without hope.

He wrote two more lines then stopped. The crying increased. It wasn't louder, but it seemed to grow more in size until it filled the room.

"Lady," he whispered, "give me peace. I would give my life to help you but my life is pledged."

He picked up the pen and wrote, with one hand over his ear, trying to block out the woman's need.

1

England, 1988

Dougless Montgomery sat in the back seat of the car, Robert and his pudgy thirteen-year-old daughter, Gloria, in the front. As usual, Gloria was eating. Dougless shifted her slim legs to try to make herself more comfortable around Gloria's luggage. There were six large pieces of matched, expensive luggage to hold Gloria's belongings and since they wouldn't fit in the trunk of the rented car, they were piled in the back with Dougless.

"Daddy," Gloria whined, sounding like an invalid four-year-old, "she's scratching the pretty suitcases you bought me."

Dougless clenched her fists, her nails biting into her palms. *She.* Never a name given to her. Just *She.*

Robert glanced over his shoulder at Dougless, her auburn hair just visible. "Really, I think you could be more careful."

"I didn't scratch anything, okay? I'm having a hard time sitting back here. There isn't much room."

Robert sighed wearily. "Dougless, do you have to complain about everything? Can't you even allow a vacation to be pleasant?"

Dougless swallowed her anger, then rubbed her stomach. It was hurting again. She didn't dare ask Robert to stop to get something to drink so she could take a Librax to calm the upheaval. She glanced up to see Gloria smirking at her in the makeup mirror on the sun visor. Dougless looked away and tried to concentrate on the beauty of the English countryside.

There were green fields, old stone fences, cows and more cows, picturesque little houses, magnificent mansions and . . . and Gloria, she thought. Gloria, everywhere. Robert kept saying, "She's just a child and her daddy has left her. Show some sympathy for her. She's really a sweet kid."

A sweet kid. At thirteen, Gloria wore more makeup than Dougless did at twenty-six—and she spent hours in the hotel bathroom applying it. Gloria sat in the front of the car. ("She's just a kid and it's her first trip to England.") Dougless was supposed to read the road map and follow the signs, but the fact that she could hardly see around Gloria's head didn't seem to count for much.

Dougless tried to concentrate on the scenery. Robert said Dougless was jealous of Gloria, that she didn't want to share him with anyone else, but if she'd just relax they'd be a very happy threesome. ("A second family for a little girl who has lost so much.")

Dougless had tried to like Gloria. In the year she and Robert had been living together, she'd taken Gloria shopping and spent more money on her than her small elementary-school teacher's salary allowed her to spend on herself. Night after night Dougless had stayed at Robert's house with Gloria while Robert went to cocktail parties and dinners. ("It'll be time for you two girls to get to know each other.")

Sometimes Dougless thought it was working because she and Gloria were cordial, even friendly to each other when they were alone. But the minute Robert appeared, Gloria changed into a whining, lying brat. She sat in Robert's lap, all five foot two inches, one hundred and forty pounds of her, and wailed that *She* was mean. At first Dougless had denied Gloria's accusations, had pointed out that she loved children, which is why she had chosen to teach school—it certainly wasn't for the money. But Robert always believed Gloria. Robert said Gloria was an innocent child and wasn't capable of the treachery Dougless accused the poor kid of. He said he couldn't understand how an adult like Dougless could have it in for a little kid.

During these lectures of Robert's, Dougless wavered between guilt and rage. She had a classroom of children who adored her yet Gloria seemed to hate her. *Was* Dougless jealous? Was she somehow unconsciously letting this child know she didn't want to share Robert with his own daughter? Every time Dougless's thoughts took this turn, she vowed to try harder to make Gloria like her, which usually meant she went out and bought Gloria an expensive gift.

Her other emotion was rage. Couldn't Robert just once—ONE time— take Dougless's side? Couldn't he do something like tell Gloria that Dougless's comfort was more important than his daughter's blasted suitcases? Or maybe tell Gloria that Dougless had a name and wasn't always to be addressed as *she* or *her?* But so far, Robert hadn't seemed to consider the possibility of siding with Dougless.

And Dougless didn't dare anger Robert. If she angered him, she wouldn't get from him what she wanted so much: a marriage proposal.

Marriage was what Dougless wanted most in life. She'd never been burning with ambition like her older sisters. She just wanted a nice home and husband, a few kids. Maybe someday she'd write children's books, but she had no desire to fight her way up a corporate ladder.

She'd invested eighteen months of her life in Robert, and he was such perfect husband material. He was tall, handsome, well-dressed, an excellent orthopaedic surgeon. He was neat, always hung up his clothes, he didn't chase after women, always came home when he said he would. He was reliable, dependable, faithful—and he needed her so much.

Robert hadn't been loved very much as a child and he told Dougless that her sweet, generous heart was what he'd been looking for all his life. His first wife, whom he'd divorced over four years ago, was a cold fish, a woman incapable of love. He said he wanted a "permanent relationship" with Dougless—which she took to mean marriage—but first he wanted to know how they "related" to each other. After all, he'd been hurt so badly the first time. In other words, he wanted them to live together.

So Dougless had moved into his big beautiful expensive house and done everything she could to prove to Robert that she was as warm and generous and loving as his mother and first wife had been cold.

With the exception of dealing with Gloria, living with Robert was great. He was an energetic man and they went dancing, hiking, bicycle riding. They entertained a great deal and often went to parties.

Robert was so much better than any of the other men Dougless had dated that she forgave him his little quirks—most of which revolved around money. When they went to the grocery he always "forgot" his checkbook. At the ticket window of theatres, and when the check was presented in restaurants, he almost always found he'd left his wallet at home. If Dougless complained, he'd talk to her about the new age of liberated women and how most women were fighting to pay half the expenses. Then he'd kiss her sweetly and take her somewhere expensive for dinner—and he'd pay.

Dougless knew she could stand the small problems, like Robert's penny-pinching, but it was Gloria that sent her screaming. According to Robert, the fat, ill-mannered, lying brat was perfection on earth, and because Dougless didn't see her that way, Robert began to see Dougless as the enemy. When the three of them were together, it was Robert and Gloria on one team and Dougless on the other.

Now, in the front seat Gloria offered her father a piece of candy from the box on her lap. Neither of them seemed to think of offering any to Dougless.

Dougless looked out the window and gritted her teeth. Perhaps it was the combination of Gloria and money that was making her so angry. Maybe her anger about the money was making itself felt to Gloria.

When Dougless had first met Robert they had talked for hours about their dreams and they'd talked often of a trip to England. As a child, she had often traveled to England with her family, but she hadn't been back in years. When she and Robert had moved in together the previous September, Robert had said, "Let's go to England one year from today. By then we'll know." He hadn't elaborated on what they would "know," but Dougless knew it would be whether they were compatible for marriage.

For a whole year, Dougless had worked on planning the trip. Reservations at the most romantic, most exclusive, most expensive small hotels. Robert had said, winking at her, "Spare no expense for *this* trip." She had ordered brochures, bought travel books and read and researched until she knew the names of half the villages in England. Robert had said he wanted an educational trip so she'd listed many things to do that were close to each of their lovely little hotels—which was easy to do since Great Britain is like a Disneyland for history lovers.

Three months before they were to leave, Robert started saying that he had a surprise for her on this trip, a very, very special surprise that was going to fill her with joy. Dougless worked harder on the trip plans. She hoped a marriage proposal was forthcoming. Three weeks before they left, she was balancing Robert's household accounts, when she saw a canceled check for five thousand dollars made out to a jewelry store.

"An engagement ring," she'd whispered, tears in her eyes. That it had cost so much was proof that, even though Robert was a tad stingy on small things, when something really counted, he was financially generous.

For weeks she'd walked on clouds. She cooked wonderful meals for Robert, had been especially energetic in the bedroom, doing everything she could think of to please him. It hadn't bothered her at all when he'd complained bitterly that she hadn't ironed his shirts properly. After they were married she'd send them out.

Two days before they were to leave, Robert punctured her bubble a bit— not enough to burst it, but it was deflated. He asked to see the bills for the trip, plane tickets, advance reservations, whatever she had. He then added the amounts and handed her the calculator tape.

"This is your half."

"Mine?" she'd asked stupidly.

"I know how important it is to you women today to pay your own way. I don't want to be accused of being a male chauvinist pig," he'd said with a smile.

"No, no, of course not," Dougless had mumbled. "It's just that I don't have any money."

"Really, Dougless! Do you spend *everything* you make? You ought to learn to budget yourself." His voice softened. "Your family has money."

Dougless's stomach had begun to hurt. Six months before a doctor had told her she was trying to give herself an ulcer and had prescribed Librax to quieten it. She had explained to Robert about her family a hundred times. Yes, her family had money—lots of it—but her father believed his daughters should support themselves. Dougless was on her own until she was thirty-five and then she'd inherit. If there was an emergency, she knew her father would help her, but a pleasure trip to England hardly counted as an emergency.

"Come on, Dougless," Robert had said tauntingly, "I keep hearing what a paragon of love and support that family of yours is, can't they help you now?" Before she could speak, he had changed. He'd raised her hands to his lips. "Ah, baby, try to get the money. I so much want you to go. I have such a very, very special surprise for you."

In the end Dougless couldn't bear to ask her father for money. It would be admitting defeat to him. She'd called a cousin in Colorado and asked him for a loan. The money had been given to her freely—no interest—and she'd only had to endure her cousin's lecture. "He's a surgeon, you're an underpaid teacher, you've been living together for a year, and he wants you to pay for half of an expensive trip?" She'd wanted to explain about her hopes for a marriage proposal but it would have made her sound too Victorian. "Just send the money, will you?" she'd snapped.

During the few days remaining before they left, Dougless told herself that it was only fair that she pay her own way. Robert was right: It *was* the day of the liberated woman. Her father, by not dropping millions in her lap before she could handle them, was teaching her to take care of herself and, now, so was Robert. She told herself she was an idiot for not realizing beforehand that she was supposed to pay her own way.

For the most part, she recovered her good humor and by the time she'd packed Robert's three leather bags and her one old suitcase she was again looking forward to the trip. She filled her tote bag with necessary toiletries and travel books.

In the taxi on the way to the airport, Robert had been especially nice to her. He'd nuzzled her neck until she'd pushed him away in embarrassment when she saw the taxi driver watching.

"Have you guessed the surprise yet?" Robert asked.

"You won the lottery."

"Better than that."

"You've bought us a castle and we'll live in it forever as lord and lady."

"*Much* better than that," he'd said. "Do you have any idea what the upkeep is on one of those places? I'll bet you can't guess anything as good as this surprise."

Dougless had looked at him with love. She knew just what her wedding dress would look like. Would their children have Robert's blue eyes or her green? His brown hair or her dark red? "I have no idea what the surprise is," she said, lying.

Robert leaned back against the seat and smiled. "You'll soon find out," he'd said enigmatically.

At the airport Dougless dealt with checking the luggage while Robert kept looking restlessly about the airport. As Dougless tipped the porter, Robert threw up his hand to wave to someone. At first Dougless was too busy to realize what was happening.

She looked up at the cry, "Daddy!" and saw Gloria running across the terminal, behind her porter with a hand truck carrying six new suitcases.

What a coincidence, Dougless thought, to meet Gloria at the airport. She'd watched as Gloria flung herself on her father. Moments later they broke apart, Robert with his arm tightly around his precious daughter's plump shoulders. Gloria was wearing a fringed jacket and cowboy boots; she looked like an overweight stripper from the sixties.

"Hello, Gloria," Dougless said. "Are you going somewhere?"

Gloria and her father nearly collapsed with laughter. "You haven't told her," Gloria squealed.

Robert sobered himself. "*This* is the surprise," he said, pushing Gloria forward as if she were an ugly trophy Dougless had just won. "Isn't it a *wonderful* surprise?"

Dougless still didn't understand—or maybe she was too horrified to want to understand.

Robert put his arm around Dougless. "*Both* of my girls are going with me," he said.

"Both?" Dougless whispered.

"Yes. Gloria is the surprise. She's going with us to England."

Dougless wanted to scream, to yell, to refuse to go. She did none of those things. "But all the hotel rooms are for two," she'd managed to say at last.

"So we'll have a roll-away bed brought in. We'll manage. We'll have love going for us and that's enough." He dropped his arm from Dougless's shoulder. "Now for business. Dougless, you won't mind getting Gloria checked in while I get reacquainted with lambikins, will you?"

Dougless could only shake her head. Numbly she went off to the ticket counter. She had to pay two hundred and eighty dollars overcharge for Gloria's four extra bags; she had to tip the porter. On the plane, Robert set Gloria between them so Dougless ended up on the aisle. During the flight, smiling, Robert handed Dougless Gloria's ticket. "Add this to our common list of expenses, will you? And I'll need a penny by penny—or should I say shilling—count of all money spent. My accountant thinks I can deduct this whole trip."

"But it's a pleasure trip, not business."

Robert frowned. "You aren't going to start nagging already, are you? Just keep records and when we get home, you and I'll split the expenses in half."

Dougless looked at Gloria's ticket. "You mean in thirds, don't you? Me one third, two thirds for you and Gloria."

Robert gave her a look of horror and put his arm around Gloria protectively, as if Dougless had tried to hit the kid. "I *meant* in half. Gloria is for you to enjoy, too. Money spent is nothing compared to the joy you'll receive from her company."

Dougless turned away. For the rest of the long, long flight, she read while Gloria and Robert played cards and ignored her. Twice Dougless took Librax to keep her stomach from eating itself.

◇ ◇ ◇

Now, in the car, Dougless rubbed her aching stomach. She'd tried to enjoy herself in the four days they'd been in England. She'd tried not to complain the first night in their beautiful hotel room when Gloria had moaned so about the trundle bed the hotel had put in the room—after the owner had lectured Dougless about not having expected Gloria—that Robert had asked Gloria to get into their four-poster with them. Dougless had ended up sleeping on the trundle bed. Nor had Dougless complained when Gloria ordered three entrees at the expensive restaurant so she could have "a taste of everything." "Stop being so stingy. I always thought you were a generous person," Robert had said, then handed Dougless the enormous bill that she was to pay half of.

Dougless managed to keep her mouth shut, because she knew that somewhere in Robert's baggage was a five-thousand-dollar engagement ring. The thought of that made her remember that he did love her. And all the things he did for Gloria were done out of love, too.

But after last night, Dougless's feelings were beginning to change. Last night, at another hundred-and-fifty-dollar dinner, Robert had presented Gloria with a long blue velvet box. Dougless had a sinking feeling as she watched Gloria open it.

Gloria's eyes lit up as she looked inside. "But it's not my birthday, daddy," she'd whispered.

"I know, Muffin," Robert said softly. "It's just to say I love you."

Gloria withdrew from the box a bracelet that dripped diamonds and emeralds.

Dougless gasped, for she knew that her engagement ring was being fastened about Gloria's chubby wrist.

Gloria held it up triumphantly. "See?"

"Yes, I see," Dougless said coolly.

Later, in the hall outside their room, Robert was furious with her. "You didn't show much enthusiasm about the bracelet. Gloria was trying to show it to you. She was *trying* to make overtures of friendship to you but you snubbed her. You've hurt her deeply."

"Is that what you paid five thousand dollars for? A diamond bracelet for a *child?*"

"Gloria happens to be a young woman, a very beautiful young woman, and she deserves beautiful things. And besides, it's *my* money. It's not as if we were married and you had any legal rights to *my* money."

Dougless put her hands on his arms. "*Are* we going to get married? Is it ever going to happen?"

He jerked away from her. "Not if you don't start showing us a little love and generosity. I thought you were different but now I see you're as cold as my mother. I have to go comfort my daughter. She's probably crying her little eyes out after the way you treated her." He angrily went into their room.

Dougless slumped against the wall. "Emerald earrings should dry her tears," she whispered.

◇ ◇ ◇

So now, in the car, she sat with her body twisted around Gloria's suitcases and knew no marriage proposal or ring was going to be given to her. Instead she was going to spend the month-long trip acting as a secretary-valet for Robert Whitley and his obnoxious daughter. At the moment she wasn't sure what she was going to do, but the thought of taking the first plane home appealed to her.

Even as she thought it, she looked at the back of Robert's head and her heart lurched. If she left him, would he feel as betrayed by her as he had by his mother and his first wife?

"Dougless!" Robert snapped. "Where is this church? I thought you were going to watch the road maps. I can't drive *and* navigate."

Dougless fumbled with the map and looked around Gloria's big head to try to see the road signs. "Here!" she said. "Take a right."

Robert turned down one of the narrow English lanes, bushes on either side nearly covering the road, and drove toward the remote village of Ashburton, a place that looked as if it hadn't changed in hundreds of years.

"There's a thirteenth-century church here containing the tomb of an Elizabethan earl." Dougless checked her notebook. "Lord Nicholas Stafford, died 1564."

"Do we have to see another church?" Gloria wailed. "I'm sick of churches. Couldn't she find something better to look at?"

"I was told to search out historic sights," Dougless snapped.

Robert stopped the car in front of the church and looked back at Dougless. "Gloria's statement was valid and I see no call for your temper. You are making me begin to regret bringing you."

"*Bringing* me?" Dougless said, but he'd turned away, his arm around Gloria. "I'm paying my own way," she whispered to no one.

Dougless didn't go inside the church with Robert and Gloria. Instead she stayed outside, walking around the lumpy graveyard, absently looking at the ancient gravemarkers. She had some serious decisions to make and she wanted time to think. Should she stay and be miserable, or should she leave? If she left she knew Robert would never forgive her, and all the time and effort she'd invested in him would have come to nothing.

"Hello."

Dougless jumped as she looked to see Gloria just behind her. Her diamond bracelet flashed in the sun.

"What do you want?" Dougless asked suspiciously.

Gloria stuck her lower lip out. "You hate me, don't you?"

Dougless sighed. "I don't hate you. Why aren't you inside looking at the church?"

"I got bored. That's a pretty blouse. It looks expensive. Did your rich family buy it for you?"

Dougless just looked at the girl, then turned on her heel and walked away.

"Wait!" Gloria cried, then, "Ow!"

Dougless turned back to see Gloria in a fat heap beside a rough-surfaced tombstone. Sighing, Dougless went back to help her up and to her consternation Gloria burst into tears. Dougless couldn't quite bring herself to hug Gloria but she managed to pat her shoulder. Gloria's arm was raw where she'd hit the stone. "It couldn't hurt that much," Dougless said. "Put your new bracelet on that arm and I'll bet the pain'll stop."

"It's not that," Gloria said. "It's that you hate me. Daddy said you thought my bracelet was going to be an engagement ring."

Dougless dropped her hand and stiffened. "What made him think that?"

Gloria looked at her out of the corner of her eye. "Oh, he knows everything. He knows you thought his surprise was going to be a marriage proposal and you thought the check to the jeweler was for an engagement ring. Daddy and I laugh about it a lot."

Dougless was standing so rigid that her body began to tremble.

Gloria smiled maliciously. "Daddy says you're a real nuisance, always hanging around, looking at him with cow-eyes. Daddy says that if you weren't so good in bed, he'd get rid of you."

At that Dougless slapped Gloria's smug, fat face.

Robert appeared from inside the church just in time to see the slap. Gloria went screaming into her father's arms.

"She hit me over and over," Gloria screamed, "and she scratched my arm."

"My God, Dougless," Robert said, horrified. "I can't believe this of you. To beat a child, to—"

"Child! I've had enough of that *child!* I've had enough of the way you baby her. I've had enough of the way you two treat *me!*"

Robert glared at her. "We have been kind and thoughtful to you this entire trip while you have been jealous and spiteful. We have gone out of our way to please you."

"You haven't made any effort to please me. Everything has been for Gloria." Tears came to Dougless's eyes. "You two have laughed at me behind my back."

"Now you're fantasizing. Since you're so unhappy with us, perhaps you'd rather do without our company." He turned, Gloria huddled against his side, and started for the car.

"Yes, I want to go home," Dougless said and bent to pick up her purse. It wasn't there. She looked behind a few tombstones but there was no sign of her purse. She looked up as she heard a car start.

Robert was driving away and leaving her!

She ran toward the gate as the car pulled away. To her horror, Gloria stuck her arm out the window—dangling from her hand was Dougless's purse.

Dougless ran after the car for a bit but it was soon out of sight. Dazed, numb, she walked back toward the church. She was in a foreign country with no money, no credit cards, no passport. But worst of all, the man she loved had just walked out on her.

The heavy oak door of the church was standing open and she walked inside. It was cool and damp and dim in the church, and the tall stone walls made the place feel calm and reverent.

She had to think about this, had to consider what to do. She'd have to call her father, collect, and have him send her money. She'd have to tell him that his youngest daughter had once again failed at something, that she couldn't even so much as go on holiday without getting herself into trouble.

Tears started in her eyes as she imagined hearing her oldest sister, Elizabeth, say, "What has our little scatterbrained Dougless done now?" Robert had been Dougless's attempt at making her family proud of her. Robert wasn't like the other stray-cat men Dougless had fallen for—he was so respectable, so very suitable, but she'd lost him. Maybe if she'd just held her temper with Gloria . . .

Tears blurred Dougless's eyes as she looked toward the end of the church. Sun was streaming through the old windows high above her head, and sharp, clear rays lit the white marble tomb in the arch to the left. Dougless walked forward. Lying on top of the tomb was a full-length white marble sculpture of a man wearing the top half of a suit of armor and an odd-looking pair of shorts, his ankles crossed, helmet tucked under his arm. "Nicholas Stafford," she read aloud, "Earl of Thornwyck."

She was congratulating herself on holding up so well under the awful circumstances, when suddenly everything hit her and her knees collapsed. She fell to the floor, her hands on the tomb, her forehead resting against the cold marble.

She began to cry in earnest, cry deeply from inside herself. She felt like a failure, completely, totally a failure. It seemed that everything she'd ever touched in her life had failed. Her father had bailed her out of hundreds of scrapes. There was the "boy" she'd fallen in love with when she was sixteen. He turned out to be twenty-five years old and to have a prison record. They broke up when he was arrested for grand theft. There was the minister she'd fallen for at twenty. He turned out to be using church funds to play craps in Las Vegas. There was . . . The list seemed to be endless. Robert had seemed so different, so ordinary and respectable, but she hadn't been able to hold on to him.

"What is wrong with me?" she cried.

Through her tears, she looked at the face of the man on the tomb. In the Middle Ages marriages were arranged. When she was twenty-two and had just found out her latest love, a stockbroker, had been arrested for insider trading, she'd crawled into her father's lap and asked him to choose a man for her.

Adam Montgomery had laughed. "Your problem, sweetheart, is that you love men who need you too much. You ought to find a man who doesn't need you, one who just wants you."

Dougless had sniffed. "Sure, a Knight in Shining Armor to swoop down off his white horse and want me so much he carries me back to his castle and we live happily ever after."

"Something like that. Armor's okay but, Dougless, if he's wearing a black leather jacket and riding a motorcycle, or if he gets mysterious phone calls in the night, get out, okay?"

Now Dougless cried harder, as she remembered the times she'd had to go to her family for help. And now she was going to have to ask for their help again, once again admit she'd made a fool of herself over an unsuitable man.

"Help me," she whispered, her hand on the marble hand of the sculpture. "Help me find my Knight in Shining Armor. Help me find a man who wants me."

She sat back on her heels, her hands over her face and began to cry harder.

After a long while, she came to realize someone was near her. She turned her head and the sunlight hitting metal so blinded her she sat back on the stone floor with a thud. She put her hand up to shield her eyes.

Standing before her was a man. A man who appeared to be wearing . . . armor.

He stood utterly still, glaring down at Dougless. She stared up at him in open mouthed astonishment. He was an extraordinarily good-looking man, wearing the most authentic-looking stage costume she'd ever seen. There was a small ruff about his neck, then armor to his waist. But what armor! It looked almost as if it were made of silver, and there were many rows of etched flower designs filled in with a golden-colored metal. From his waist to mid-thigh he wore a type of shorts that ballooned about his body. His legs—big muscular legs—were in stockings that looked to be knitted of silk.

He wore a garter tied above his left knee. His feet were covered with odd, soft shoes that had little cuts in them.

"Well, witch," he said in a deep baritone, "you have conjured me, what do you ask of me?"

"Witch?" she said, sniffing.

From inside his ballooned shorts, he pulled a handkerchief and handed it to her. Dougless blew her nose noisily.

"Have my enemies hired you? Do they plot against me more? Is not my head enough for them? Stand, madam, and explain yourself."

Gorgeous, but off his rocker, Dougless thought. "Listen, I don't know what you're talking about." She stood. "Now, if you'll excuse me—"

She didn't say more because he drew a thin-bladed sword that had to be a yard long and held the sharp point against her throat. "Reverse your spell, witch. I would return!"

It was all too much for Dougless. First Robert and his lying daughter and then this mad Hamlet. She burst into tears again and slumped against the cold stone wall.

"Damnation!" the man muttered, and the next thing Dougless knew she was being picked up and carried to a church pew.

She couldn't seem to stop crying. "This has been the worst day of my life," she wailed. The man stood scowling down at her like something out of a Bette Davis movie. "I'm sorry," she managed to say. "I don't usually cry so much but to be abandoned by the man I love and attacked—at sword point no less—all in the same day, sets me off." She looked at the handkerchief. It was very large and had an inch and a half border of intricate silk embroidery around the edge. "How pretty," she choked out.

"There is no time for trivialities. My soul is at stake—as is yours. I tell you again: reverse your spell."

Dougless was recovering herself. "I don't know what you're talking about. I was having a good cry all alone, and you, wearing that absurd outfit, come in here and start yelling at me. I've a good mind to call the police—or the bobbies or whatever they have in rural England. Is it legal for you to carry a sword like that?"

"Legal?" the man said. He was looking at her arm. "Is that a clock on your arm? And what manner of dress is it that you wear?"

"Of course it's a clock and these are my traveling-to-England clothes. Conservative. No jeans or tee shirts. Nice blouse, nice skirt. You know, Miss Marple-type clothes."

He was frowning at her. "You talk uncommonly strangely. What manner of witch are you?"

Dougless threw up her hands in despair, then stood. He was a good deal taller than she was. He had black curling hair just reaching the stiff little ruff he wore, black mustache and a trim, pointed, short beard. "I am not a witch and I am not part of your Elizabethan drama. I'm going to leave now, and if you try anything fancy with your sword I'll scream the windows out. Here's your handkerchief. Sorry it's so wet but I thank you for its loan. Goodbye, and I hope your play gets great reviews." She turned on her heel and walked out of the church. "At least nothing else horrible can happen to me," Dougless murmured as she left the churchyard.

There was a telephone booth at the corner, within sight of the church door. It was early in the morning in Maine, and a sleepy Elizabeth answered the phone.

Anybody but her, Dougless thought. She'd rather talk to anyone in the world but her perfect older sister.

"Dougless, is that you?" Elizabeth asked. "Are you all right? Not in trouble again, are you?"

Dougless gritted her teeth. "Of course not. Is Dad there? Or Mom?" Or a stranger off the street, she thought. *Anybody* but Elizabeth.

Elizabeth yawned. "No, they went up to the mountains. I'm here house-sitting and working on a paper."

"Think it'll win the Nobel Prize?"

Elizabeth paused. "All right, Dougless, what's wrong? Has your surgeon stranded you somewhere?"

Dougless gave a little laugh. "Elizabeth, you do say the funniest things. Robert and Gloria and I are having a wonderful time. So many things to see and do. Why just this morning we saw a medieval play. The actors were *so* good."

Again, Elizabeth paused. "Dougless, you're lying. I can hear it over the phone. What's wrong? Do you need money?"

Dougless could not make her lips form the word yes. Her family loved to tell what they called Dougless-stories. About the time Dougless got locked out of her hotel room wearing only a towel. About the time Dougless went to the bank to deposit a check and walked into a bank robbery where the robbers carried toy guns.

Now she imagined Elizabeth's laughter as she told all the Montgomery cousins how funny little Dougless went to England and got left at a church with no money and how she'd been attacked by a crazed Shakespearean actor.

"No, I don't need money," Dougless said at last. "I just wanted to say hello. I hope you get your paper done. See ya."

"Dougless—" Elizabeth said, but Dougless had hung up.

Dougless leaned back against the booth. The tears were starting again. She had the Montgomery pride but had no reason for being proud. She had three older sisters who were paragons of success: Elizabeth, a research chemist; Catherine, a professor of physics; and Anne, a criminal attorney. Dougless seemed to be the Montgomery jester, a source of endless material for laughter among the relatives.

As she was leaning there, her eyes blurred with tears, she saw the man in the knight-suit leave the church and walk down the path toward the gate. He looked at the ancient gravestones without much interest, then headed down the path toward the gate.

Coming down the lane was one of the little English buses, as usual doing about fifty miles an hour on the narrow street.

Dougless stood up straight. Somehow, she instinctively knew the man was going to walk in front of the bus. Dougless started to run. Just as she took flight, the vicar came from behind the church, saw what Dougless did and began to run also.

Dougless reached him first. She made her best flying tackle that she had learned from playing football with her Colorado cousins and landed on top of him, the two of them skidding across the graveled path on his armor as if it were a little rowboat. The bus swerved and missed the two of them by inches.

"Are you all right?" the vicar said, offering his hand to help Dougless up.

"I . . . I think so." Dougless stood and dusted herself off. "You okay?" she said to the man on the ground.

"What manner of chariot was that?" he asked. "I did not hear it coming. There were no horses."

Dougless exchanged looks with the vicar.

"Perhaps I'll get a glass of water," the vicar said.

"Wait!" the man said. "What year is this?"

"1988," the vicar said, and when the man lay back on the ground as if in exhaustion, the vicar looked at Dougless. "I'll get the water," he said and left them alone.

Dougless offered her hand to the man on the ground, but he refused it and rose to his feet.

"I think you ought to sit down." She motioned to an iron bench inside the low stone wall. He wouldn't go first but followed her through the gate, then wouldn't sit until she had, but Dougless pushed him to sit down. He looked pale and bewildered.

"You are dangerous, you know that? Listen, you sit right here and I'm going to call a doctor. You aren't well."

She turned away but his words halted her.

"I think perhaps I am dead."

She looked back at him. If he was suicidal, she didn't want to leave him alone. "Come with me," she said softly. "We'll find you some help."

He didn't move from the bench. "What manner of conveyance was it that nearly struck me down?"

She went to sit by him. If he was suicidal, maybe what he needed most was someone to talk to. "Where are you from? You sound English but you have a strange accent."

"I am English. What was the chariot?"

"All right," she said with a sigh. She could play along with him. "That was what the English call a coach. In America, it's a minibus. It was going entirely too fast but it's my opinion that the only thing of the twentieth century the English have really accepted is the speed of motor vehicles. What else don't you know about? Airplanes? Trains? Look, I really need to go. Let's go to the rectory and have the vicar call a doctor. Or maybe we'll call your mother." Surely the town knew of this crazy man who ran about in armor and pretended he'd never seen a watch or a bus.

"My mother," the man said and his lips formed a little smile. "I would imagine my mother is dead now."

"I'm sorry. Did she die recently?"

He looked up at the sky. "About four hundred years ago."

Dougless started to rise. "I'm getting someone."

He caught her hand. "I was sitting . . . in a room at a desk, writing my mother a letter when I heard a woman weeping. The room darkened, my head swam and then I was standing over a woman—you." He looked up at her.

Dougless thought that leaving this man alone would be so much easier if he weren't so utterly divine-looking. "Maybe you blacked out and don't remember dressing up and coming to the church. Why don't you tell me where you live? I'll walk you home."

"When I was in the room it was the year of our Lord 1564."

Delusional, Dougless thought. Beautiful and crazy. My luck.

"Come with me," she said softly, as if speaking to a child about to step over a cliff. "We will find some help for you."

The man came out of his chair quickly and his blue eyes blazed. The size of him, the anger of him, not to mention that he was steel-covered and carried a sword that appeared to be razor-sharp, made Dougless step back.

"I am not yet ready for Bedlam, mistress. I know not why I am here or how I came to be here, but I know who I am and from whence I came."

Suddenly, laughter began to rumble deep inside Dougless. "And you came from the sixteenth century. Queen Elizabeth, right? This is going to be the best Dougless-story ever. I'm jilted in the morning and an hour later a ghost holds a sword to my throat." She stood. "Thanks a lot, mister. You've cheered me up immensely. I am now going to call my sister and ask her to wire me ten pounds—no more, no less—and then I'm catching a train to Robert's hotel where I'll get my plane ticket home. After today the rest of my life will seem uneventful."

She turned away from him but he moved in front of her. From inside his balloon shorts he withdrew a leather pouch, looked in it, took out a few coins and pressed them into Dougless's hand, closing her fingers over them.

"Take the ten pounds, woman, and be gone. It is worth that and more to be rid of your spiteful tongue. I will beseech God to reverse your wickedness."

She was tempted to throw the money at him but her alternative was to call her sister again. "That's me, Wicked Witch Dougless. I don't know why I want a train when I have a perfectly good broomstick. I'll send the money back, care of the vicar. So long and I hope we never meet again."

She turned on her heel and left the churchyard just as the vicar came back with the man's water. Let someone else deal with his fantasies, she thought. The man probably had a whole trunk full of costumes. Today he's an Elizabethan knight, tomorrow he's Abraham Lincoln—or Horatio Nelson since he's English.

It was easy to find the train station in the little village and she went to the window to purchase her ticket.

"That'll be three pounds six," the man behind the window said.

Dougless had never been able to figure out the English money. There seemed to be so many coins that had the same value. She shoved the coins the man had given her under the cage window. "Is this enough?"

The man looked at the three coins one by one, turning them over carefully, then excused himself.

Now I'll probably be arrested for passing counterfeit money, Dougless thought. It would be a fitting end to a perfect day.

After a few minutes a man with an official-looking hat came to the window. "We can't take these, miss. I think you ought to take them to Oliver Samuelson. He's just around the corner to your right."

"He'll give me train fare for them?"

"I 'spect he will that."

"Thank you," Dougless murmured. She was tempted to call her sister and forget about the coins. She looked at them. They looked as foreign as all foreign coins did. With a sigh, she turned right and came to a shop. Oliver Samuelson, Coin Dealer.

A bald-headed little man was sitting behind a desk, a jeweler's loupe about his shiny forehead. "Yes?" he said when Dougless entered.

"The man in the train station sent me to you. He said I might get train fare from you for these."

The man took the coins and looked at them under the jeweler's loupe. After a moment he began to softly chuckle. "Train fare, indeed. Train fare."

He looked up. "All right, miss," he said. "I will give you five hundred pounds each for these, and this one is worth about, say, five thousand pounds. But I don't have that much money here. I will have to call some people in London. Can you wait a few days?"

Dougless couldn't speak for a moment. "Five *thousand* pounds?"

"All right, six, but not a shilling more."

"I . . . I . . ."

"Do you want to sell them or not? They're not ill-gotten, are they?"

"No, at least I don't think so," Dougless whispered. "But I have to talk to someone before I sell them. They are genuine?"

"As a rule medieval coins aren't so valuable, but these are rare and in mint condition. Are there more?"

"I believe so."

"If you have a fifteen-shilling piece with a queen in a ship on it, let me see it. I can't afford it but I can find a buyer."

Dougless started backing toward the door.

"Or a double," he said. "An Edward the Sixth double."

Dougless nodded at him as she left his shop. In a daze, she walked back to the church. The man was not in the churchyard and she hoped he hadn't left. She went into the church. He was there, on his knees before the white tomb of the earl, his hands clasped, his head bowed in prayer.

The vicar moved beside her. "He has been there since you left. I cannot get him to stand. Something is troubling him deeply." He turned to her. "He is your friend?"

"No, I just met him this morning. He's not from here?"

The vicar smiled. "My parishioners seldom wear armor." He looked at his watch. "I must go. You'll stay with him? For some reason, I hate to see him left alone."

Dougless said that she would and the vicar left her alone with him.

Quietly, she walked toward him and put her hand on his shoulder. "Who are you?" she whispered.

He didn't open his eyes or unclasp his hands. "Nicholas Stafford, Earl of Thornwyck."

It took Dougless a moment to remember where she'd heard that name before, and then she looked at the tomb. Carved deeply in Gothic letters was the name, Nicholas Stafford, Earl of Thornwyck.

She took a deep breath. "I don't guess you have any identification, do you?"

He lifted his head, opened his eyes, and glared at her. "Do you doubt my word? You, the witch who has done this to me? If I did not fear being accused of sorcery myself I would denounce you and stay to watch you burn."

She stood there and watched as he began to pray again.

2

Nicholas Stafford stood and stared at the young woman before him. Her manner, her dress, her speech were so strange to him he could hardly keep his thoughts together. She looked to be the witch he knew her to be: as beautiful as any woman he'd ever seen, uncased hair flowing to her shoulders, and wearing an indecently short skirt, as if she dared the contempt of man and God alike.

In spite of the fact that he felt dizzy and weak, he did not allow himself to waver from his firm stance. He returned her straightforward glare with one of his own.

He still could not believe what had happened to him. At the lowest point in his life, when there seemed to be no hope, his mother had written him that at last she had discovered something that would once again give them hope. He had been writing to her, questioning her, giving her advice, making suggestions when he'd heard a woman weeping. The sound of tears in the place where he was was not so unusual, but something about this woman's weeping made him put down his pen.

He called out for someone to go to the woman, but no one answered and the woman's sobs grew louder until they filled the little room, echoing off the stone walls and ceiling. Nicholas had put his hands over his ears to shut out the sound but he could still hear her. Her weeping grew louder and louder, until he could no longer hear his own thoughts. He felt as if his head might burst from the sound.

He tried to stand, to call out for help, but when he got to his feet, the floor seemed to fall away from under him. He felt light, almost as if he were floating, then he held out his hand and saw, to his horror, that his hand seemed to lose substance. He could see through his hand. He staggered toward the door, tried to call out but no sound came from his mouth. The door seemed to fall away, then the room. For a moment he appeared to be standing on nothing. There was a void around him, his body naught but a shadow through which he could see the darkness of nothing.

He had no idea how long he drifted in the nothingness, feeling neither hot nor cold, hearing nothing but the woman's weeping.

One moment he was nowhere, was but a shadow, and the next he was standing in the sunlight in a church. His clothes were different. Now he was wearing demi-armor, the armor he wore only for the most auspicious occasions, and his emerald satin slops.

Before him, weeping before a tomb was a girl or woman, he could not tell which, for her hair was hanging slovenly before her face.

It was the tomb that made him step backward. It was a white marble sculpture of . . . himself. Carved beneath was his name and today's date. They have buried me before I am dead? he wondered in horror.

Feeling sick with his experience and at seeing his own tomb, he looked about the church. There were burial plaques set in the walls. 1734. 1812. 1902.

No, he thought, it could not be. But as he looked at the church he could see that everything was different. The church was so *plain.* The beams were unpainted; the stone corbels were unpainted. The altar cloth looked as if it had been embroidered by a clumsy child.

He looked down at the sobbing woman. A witch! A witch who had called him forth to another time and place. He had demanded that she return him —he *had* to return, his honor, the future of his family depended upon his returning—but she had once again collapsed into helpless sobbing.

She was as vile-tempered and sharp-tongued as she was evil. She was bold enough to say she had no knowledge of how he came to be in this place, that she knew nothing of why he was there.

He was relieved when she'd gone. He was feeling steadier and was beginning to believe he had dreamed that flight through the void. Perhaps this was all a dream of remarkable reality.

He'd left the church and felt stronger to see that the churchyard looked the same as all churchyards—but he did not pause to examine the dates. One in the church had been 1982.

He had left through the church gate and walked into the silent road. Where were the people? The horses? The carts carrying goods?

What happened next happened too quickly for him to remember clearly. There was a sound to his left, a loud, fast sound such as he'd never heard before and to his right came the witch, leaping on him. He was weaker than he realized because the frail weight of the girl knocked him to the ground.

Close by him roared an obscene horseless chariot. Weakly, Nicholas allowed the witch to lead him inside the churchyard. Was this his fate, to die alone in a strange place . . . in a strange time?

He had tried to explain to the witch that he needed to return but she persisted in sneering at him, pretending she knew nothing of how or why he was in this place. He had difficulty understanding her speech and that, combined with the ordinariness of her dress—no jewels, no gold, no silver—told him she was of peasant stock. It took him a while to understand she was begging money from him. She wanted the outrageous sum of ten pounds. He dared not refuse her for fear of her other spells.

She took the money and turned away, as Nicholas went back inside the church. He'd touched the marble tomb, run his fingers in the carving of the death date. Had he died when he'd traveled through the void? When the witch had conjured him forth to this time—the churchman had said 1988, four hundred and twenty-four years later—had she killed him in 1564?

He *must* return. If he had died on 6 September 1564, then he can have proved nothing. Too much was still undone. What may yet happen to the people he had left behind?

He dropped to his knees on the cold stone floor and began to pray. Perhaps if his prayers were as strong as the witch's magic, he could overrule her power and return himself.

But as he prayed, his mind raced. Phrases ran through his head: *The woman is the key. You need to know.*

After a while he stopped reciting prayers and opened his mind to his thoughts. Witch or no, the woman had brought him forward and she was the only one who had the power to return him.

Why had he come forward? Was he to learn something? Was this witch to teach him something? Could it be possible that she was as innocent as she claimed to be? Had she been weeping over some base lovers' quarrel and, for some reason unknown to either of them, she had called him forward to this dangerous time when chariots drove at unimagined speeds? If he learned what he needed to know, would he return to his proper time?

The witch was the key. The phrase kept repeating itself. Whether she had brought him forth through malicious intent or by unhappy accident, she held the power to return him—and no doubt teach him what he was to learn in this time.

He *must* bind her to him. No matter the cost to his peace, no matter if he had to lie, slander, blaspheme, he had to bind the woman to him and see that she did not leave until he discovered what he needed to know from her.

He remained on his knees, praying for God's guidance, asking advice, and pleading with God to stay with him as he did what he must.

The woman came back to him while he was still praying, and as she complained about the money Nicholas had given her, he offered God his thanks.

◇ ◇ ◇

"Who are you?" Dougless asked the man wearing the ridiculous costume. "And where did you get these coins?" She watched him stand, and from the ease with which he wore the heavy armor, she knew he must have been rehearsing with it for a long time. "Are they stolen?"

She saw his eyes ignite, then he calmed.

"Nay, madam, they are my own."

"Well, I can't accept them," Dougless said. "They're quite valuable."

"They are not enough for your needs?"

Dougless looked at him suspiciously. A few minutes ago he was attacking her with a sword and now he was giving her a look as if he meant to . . . seduce her. The sooner she got away from this crazy man, the better off she would be.

When the man made no effort to take the coins, she put them on the edge of the tomb. "Thanks for the offer, but no thanks. I'll make do some other way." She turned to leave the church.

"Pause, madam!"

Dougless clenched her fists at her sides. This man's pseudo-Elizabethan grammar was getting on her nerves. She turned to face him. "Look, I know you have problems. I mean, maybe you cracked your head and can't remember who you are, but that's not *my* problem. I have problems of my own. I don't have a penny to my name, I'm hungry, I don't know anyone in this country and I don't even know where I'm going to sleep or how I'm going to get a bed tonight, even if I could afford one."

"Nor do I," the man said.

Dougless sighed. Needy men, she thought, the bane of my life. But *this* time she wasn't going to make any effort to help an insane man who, when angry, pulled a sword on her. "Go outside the church, take a right—watch out for cars—walk two blocks, take a left. Three blocks past the train station is a coin dealer. He'll give you lots for your coins. Buy yourself some clothes and check into a good hotel. Miss Marple says there are few problems in life that can't be solved by a week in a good hotel. Take a long, hot bath and I'll bet your memory returns in no time."

Nicholas could only stare at her. Did this woman speak English? What was a block? Who was Miss Marple?

At his blank look, Dougless sighed again. "All right, come with me to the telephone and I'll point you on your way."

Quietly Nicholas followed her, but he paused as they stepped outside the gate. What he saw was too horrifying to believe.

Dougless took a few steps forward and realized the man wasn't behind her. She turned to see him gaping at a young girl on the opposite side of the road. She was dressed in the current English idea of chic: all in black. She wore tall black high heels, black hose, a tiny black leather skirt, a huge black sweater. Her short hair was sprayed purple and red and stuck up like a porcupine's.

Dougless smiled. The punk rocker-influenced fashions were a shock to anyone, much less to a crazy man under the illusion he was from the sixteenth century. "Come on," she said good-naturedly. "She's ordinary. You should see the people attending a rock concert."

They walked to the phone booth and Dougless again gave him directions, but to her consternation he refused to leave her. "Please go away," she begged, but he wouldn't move. "If this is an English pickup, I'm not interested. I already have a guy. Or did have. *Do* have. In fact, I'm going to call him now and he's going to come and get me."

The man didn't speak and watched with great interest as Dougless called the operator to place a collect call to Robert at their hotel. There was a moment's hesitation as the hotel operator informed her Robert and his daughter had checked out an hour ago.

Dougless slumped against the telephone cubicle.

"What is this?" the man asked. "You talked to this?"

"Give me a break, will you?" she half-yelled, taking her anger out on him. She jerked the phone up, got information for the number of the hotel that was next on the itinerary she'd made for Robert. The second hotel operator informed her that Robert Whitley had canceled his reservation only moments before.

Dougless leaned against the phone cubicle and, in spite of herself, tears came to her eyes. "So where's my Knight in Shining Armor?" she whispered. As she said the words, she looked at the man standing near her. A fading ray of sunlight struck his armor, a shadow fell across his blue-black hair, a jewel in his sword-hilt twinkled. This man had appeared the last time she'd cried and begged for a Knight in Shining Armor.

"You have had bad news?" he asked.

She straightened. "It looks as though I've been abandoned," she said softly, looking at him. No, it couldn't be and she wasn't going to even consider it. It was a one-in-a-million chance that this actor who believed his role should appear at the exact moment she'd asked for a man in armor, but then she seemed to be a magnet who attracted strange men.

"I too seem to have lost all," he said.

"Someone around here must know you. Maybe if you asked at the post office."

"Post office?"

He looked so genuinely lost that she could feel herself softening toward him. No, Dougless, no, she told herself. "Come on and I'll take you to the coin dealer to exchange your coins."

They walked together and his erect, perfect carriage made Dougless straighten her shoulders. None of the English people they passed stared at them (as far as Dougless could tell, the English stared only at people wearing sunglasses), but they passed a couple of American tourists and their two children. The whole family was wearing brand-new clothing that they had no doubt "saved for vacation." The man had two cameras about his neck.

"Lookit that, Myrt," the man said and while the adults rudely gaped at Nicholas, the children laughed and pointed.

"Ill-mannered louts," Nicholas said under his breath. "Someone should teach them how to behave in the presence of their betters."

Things happened very quickly after that. A bus stopped and out stepped fifty Japanese tourists, cameras clicking. Nicholas drew his sword and stepped forward. The American woman tourist screamed; the Japanese pressed closer, cameras clicking like cicadas on a hot summer night.

Dougless did the only thing she knew worked: she flung herself against the armor-clad man, the edge of his sword cutting the upper sleeve of her blouse and drawing blood. Startled by the pain, Dougless tripped and nearly fell but the knight caught her, lifting her in his arms and carrying her back to the sidewalk. Behind them the Japanese cameras still clicked and the Americans applauded.

"Gee, daddy, this is better than Warwick Castle," an American kid said.

"It's not in the guidebook, George," the woman said. "I think they should put things like this in the guidebook or otherwise a body could think it was *real*.'"

Nicholas set the woman down. Somehow—he did not know how—he had made a fool of himself. Did this century allow a nobleman to be defamed? What manner of weapon were the odd black machines? For that matter what manner of little people were they who held the machines?

He did not ask his questions. Questions seemed to annoy the witch-woman. "Madam, you are injured."

"Only a flesh wound," she said, parodying the TV Westerns. But the man didn't smile. In fact, he looked embarrassed. "It's not anything," she said, looking at the bloody place on her arm. She took a tissue from her skirt pocket and pressed it to her arm. "The coin shop is down there."

When Dougless entered the little shop the dealer smiled at her in welcome. "I hoped to see you again. I—" He broke off at the sight of Nicholas. Slowly, without a word, the man came forward and began to examine Nicholas's clothing. He dropped the jeweler's loupe down over his eye and looked at the armor, murmuring, "Mmm-hmm" over and over. He looked at the jewels on the sword hilt, on Nicholas's hand which rested on the sword, on the dagger in his belt—which Dougless hadn't noticed before. The man went to his knees and examined the embroidery on the garter about Nicholas's knee, then looked at the knitting of his hose and last of all at his soft slippers.

The coin dealer straightened and peered at Nicholas's face, examining his beard and hair.

Throughout this perusal Nicholas had been standing stiffly, enduring this tradesman's scrutiny with ill-concealed distaste.

At last the coin dealer stepped back. "Remarkable. I have never seen anything like it. I must get the jeweler from next door to see this."

"By your leave, but you will do no such thing!" Nicholas snapped. "Do you think I wait all day here to be inspected like a hog at a fair? Will you do business or do I go elsewhere?"

"Yes, sir," the coin dealer muttered, scurrying back behind his counter.

Nicholas dropped a sackful of coins on the counter. "What do you trade me for these and remember, man, I take care of those who cheat me."

Dougless found herself cowering to one side. This armored man had a way of giving orders that could frighten one into doing his bidding. After he'd dropped the coins, he went to stand before the window while the dealer, with trembling hands, opened the bag. Dougless went to the dealer. "Well," she whispered, "what did you see when you looked at him?"

The dealer glanced at Nicholas's back. "His armor is silver and it's etched with gold. Those emeralds on his sword are worth a fortune, as are the rubies and diamonds on his fingers." He glanced at her. "Whoever made his costume spent a lot. Oh my," he said, holding up a coin. "Here it is."

"A queen in a ship?"

"Just so." He held the coin in a caressing way. "I can find a buyer but it will take a few days." His voice was that of a lover.

Dougless took the coin out of his hand and slipped it and all but one of the others back into the bag. Before these were sold, she wanted to do a little research and compare prices. "You said you'd give me five hundred pounds for that one."

"And the others?"

"I'll . . . we'll think about it."

The man went to the back of the store and a few moments later counted out five hundred pounds' worth of the large, pretty English money.

"I'll be here if you should change your mind," the dealer called as Nicholas and Dougless left the shop.

On the street, Dougless stopped and handed Nicholas the bag of coins and the modern bills. "I sold one coin for five hundred pounds. The rest of them are worth a fortune. In fact, it seems that everything you are wearing is worth a king's ransom."

"I am an earl, not a king," Nicholas said, puzzled, looking at the paper money with interest.

She peered closely at his armor. "Is that really silver and is the yellow actually gold?"

"I am not a pauper, madam."

"It wouldn't seem so." She stepped back from him. "I guess I better go now." She realized she had wasted most of the day with this man and she still had no money nor any place to go. Robert and his daughter had checked out of one hotel and canceled at the next one.

"You will help me choose?" the man was saying.

"I'm sorry, I didn't hear you."

The man seemed to be trying to say something that was very difficult for him. He swallowed as if his own words were poison. "You will help me choose clothes and find lodging for the night? I will pay you for your services."

It took Dougless a moment to understand. "You're offering me a *job?*"

"Employment, yes."

"I don't need a job, I just need . . ." She trailed off and turned away. Her tear ducts seemed to be attached to Niagara Falls.

"Money?" he offered.

She sniffed. "No. Yes. I guess I do need money. I also need to find Robert and explain."

"I will pay you money if you will help me."

Dougless turned to look at him. There was something in his eyes, something lost and lonely that made her sway a little toward him. No! she told herself. You cannot hook up with a man who you are dead certain is crazy. There's no doubt with this one. He's undoubtedly rich but insane. He's probably a rich eccentric who had his costume made and he goes from village to village hitting on lone females.

But then there were his eyes. What if he *had* lost his memory?

And what were her alternatives? She could just hear her sister Elizabeth's derisive laughter if she called asking for money. Elizabeth would never even consider taking a job from a man wearing armor. Elizabeth would know exactly what to do, how to do it, when to do it. Elizabeth was perfect. As were Catherine and Anne. In fact, all the Montgomerys seemed to be perfect—except for Dougless. She'd often wondered if she'd been put in the wrong crib in the hospital.

"All right," she said abruptly. "I might as well lose the rest of the day as well. I'll help you get some clothes, find you a place to stay and then that's it. And I'll do it for, say, fifty dollars." That should be enough to get her bed and breakfast for the night, and tomorrow she'd screw up her courage to call Elizabeth again.

Nicholas swallowed his rising anger and gave the woman a curt nod. He understood her meaning, if not her words. He had made her agree to stay with him for a few more hours. He would have to find something else to keep her by his side until he discovered how to get back to his own time. And when he found what he needed to know, he would rejoice to leave this woman.

"Clothes," she was saying. "We'll get you clothes, and then it'll be tea time."

"Tea? What is tea?"

Dougless stopped in her tracks. An Englishman who apparently didn't know about tea? This man was more than she could bear. She'd help him until she got him checked into a hotel and then she would be glad to be rid of him.

3

They walked together down the wide sidewalk in silence, the man looking at everything. His handsome face wore such an expression of astonishment that Dougless could almost believe he had never seen the modern world before. He asked her no questions but often halted to stare at cars or women in short skirts.

It was only a block to a small clothing store for men. "Here's where we can buy you something less conspicuous to wear."

"Yes, a tailor," he said, looking up over the door and frowning as if something were missing.

"No tailor, just clothes."

Inside the little shop, the man stood and gaped at the shirts and trousers hanging from the racks. "These clothes have been made," he said.

Dougless turned to the clerk who'd come forward. "We need some clothes from the skin out. And he'll have to be measured for size." Even if the man did remember his sizes, he'd no doubt pretend he didn't.

Dougless took a chair and waited while the clerk dealt with the armored man. She pretended to look at a magazine but surreptitiously she watched him. He raised his arms for the clerk to unlatch his armor. Under it he wore a big-sleeved linen shirt that was plastered to his body with sweat.

And what a body! He was indeed as broad-shouldered and muscled as she'd suspected, given the size of the armor.

The clerk brought several shirts for him to try on but the earl liked none of them. The clerk at last looked to Dougless for help.

"What is wrong?" she asked Nicholas.

"There is no beauty in these clothes," he said, frowning. "There is no

color, no jewels, no needlework. Perhaps a woman could ply her needle to
one of these and—"

Dougless laughed. "Women don't sew today. At least not like this." She
touched the cuff of his shirt which had been thrown across a clothing rack.
The cuff was embroidered in black silk thread in a design of birds and
flowers, a lovely hand-done trim of black cutwork on the edge.

Dougless caught herself. Of course women—some women somewhere—
still sewed like that, because someone in this century had sewn that shirt,
hadn't she?

She picked up a beautiful cotton shirt from the discarded heap. The
English weren't like Americans in wanting something new every five minutes, so the clothing in English stores tended to be of the best quality, made
to last for years. If one could afford the outrageous prices, the quality was
worth the cost.

"Here, try this one again," she said, finding herself coaxing him. She
wondered if there was a woman alive who hadn't experienced shopping
with a man and trying to persuade him to like something. "Look at this
fabric, how very soft it is."

Reluctantly, he bared his upper body and Dougless held the shirt while
he tried it on. He had a broad, tanned back, with muscles playing under his
skin.

"Now, step over to the mirror and have a look."

She was not prepared for his reaction to the three full-length mirrors. He
looked at them, touched them.

"They are glass?" he whispered.

"Of course. What else are mirrors made of?"

From inside his balloon shorts he withdrew a round little wooden object
and handed it to her. On the other side of the wood was a metal mirror, and
when Dougless looked into it her image was distorted.

She glanced up at the man, saw the way he was studying his reflection.
Was it the first time he'd ever seen a full-length view of himself? Of course
not, she told herself. He just didn't remember the last time.

She looked at her own reflection behind him. What a mess she was! Her
eye makeup was *under* her eyes, instead of above them, as a result of all her
crying. Her blouse was cut on the sleeve and hanging out of her belt. Her
navy blue tights were bagging at the ankle. Her hair, tangled, droopy, was
too awful to contemplate.

She turned away and mumbled "Trousers." She moved away as the clerk
measured the man, ushered him to a dressing room, then left to bring him

several pair of trousers. All was quiet for a moment until Dougless saw the dressing room door open a crack and the man peep out. She went to him.

"I cannot manage," he said softly and opened the door wider so she could enter. "What manner of fastening is this?"

Dougless tried not to think of this situation. She was squashed into a dressing room with a strange man who couldn't figure out how to work a zipper. "Here, like . . ." She started to show him on the trousers he wore, but then took a pair hanging from a hook. She showed him the zipper, then the snaps, and watched while, like a child, he zipped and unzipped, snapped and unsnapped. She started to leave.

"Wait. What is this wondrous substance?" He held up a pair of undershorts, stretching the waistband.

"Elastic." His face was so alight with discovery she couldn't help feeling good.

"Wait until you see Velcro," she said, smiling and backing out of the dressing room. "If you need more help, let me know."

She was still smiling as she closed the door. She looked at the clothes around her. How plain they must look to a man who was used to wearing silver armor. The clerk had carefully placed the armor, and the sword and dagger, in a large, sturdy shopping bag to the left of the dressing room door. Dougless could hardly lift the bag.

After a moment the man came out. He was wearing a soft white cotton shirt and slim gray cotton trousers. The shirt was of the current voluminous style, while the trousers were snug. He looked utterly divine.

She watched him walk to the mirror and glower at his image.

"These . . . these," he said, tugging at the ease of the trousers at the back of his leg.

"Trousers. Pants," she supplied.

"They do not fit me. They do not show my legs. I have fine legs."

Dougless laughed. "Men don't wear stockings now, but you look great."

"I am not sure. A chain perhaps."

"No chain," she said. "Trust me. *No chain.*"

She chose a leather belt for him, then socks. "We'll have to go elsewhere for shoes."

They went to the cash register while the clerk totaled the tags he'd cut from the clothes, and Dougless was horrified as Nicholas reached for his sword. Thankfully, it was in the shopping bag and he couldn't get to it quickly.

"He means to rob me!" the earl bellowed. "I can hire a dozen men for less than he asks for these unadorned clothes."

Dougless put herself between Nicholas and the counter while the clerk huddled against the opposite wall. "Give me the money," she said firmly. "Everything costs more now than it did. I mean, you'll remember soon enough. Give me the money."

Still angry, he handed Dougless the leather bag full of coins, then they had to search through the shopping bag and his other clothes for the paper money.

"He will take paper for clothes?" the earl whispered, then smiled. "I will give him all the paper he wants. He is a fool."

"It's paper *money* and it's backed by gold," she said as they left the shop. "You can exchange the paper for gold."

"Someone will give me gold for paper?"

"Any bank will."

"What is a 'bank'?"

"A bank is where you put your money. Money you aren't using, that is. Where do you put your money?"

"In my houses," he said, perplexed.

"Oh, I see," she said, smiling. "Dig a hole and hide it. Well, today it's put in a bank and it earns interest."

"What is interest?"

Dougless groaned. "Here's a tea shop. Are you hungry?"

"Yes," he answered and opened the door for her.

Afternoon tea was a custom Dougless had taken to readily. It was heaven to sit down at four o'clock and sip delicious hot tea and eat a scone. Or five scones as Gloria did.

Her fists clenched when she thought of Gloria. Did Robert know she had Dougless's purse? Did he know he'd left Dougless completely stranded, alone at the mercy of crazy men?

She couldn't believe he did know. Robert wasn't a bad person. If he were he wouldn't love his daughter so much. Dougless knew that Robert felt so bad because he'd left his child when he'd divorced that he wanted to make it up to her, so he'd brought her on vacation. And it was natural for Gloria to fight for her father's love. It was natural for the child to be jealous of Dougless.

Dougless knew that if Robert were to walk into the tea shop at that moment, she would fall to her knees and beg his forgiveness.

"May I help you?" the woman behind the counter asked.

"Tea for two," Dougless said. "And two scones please."

"We have clotted cream and strawberries also," the woman said.

Dougless nodded and in moments the woman passed a tray across the counter to her. She paid, then picked up the tray and looked at the earl. "Shall we eat outside?"

He followed her to a little garden with vines growing over the brick walls. She set the tray down and began to pour. She'd tried the English custom of adding milk to tea the first day they'd arrived and found it delicious.

The earl was walking about the little garden, studying the walls and the plants. She called him to the picnic table and handed him his cup of tea and a scone.

He gave the tea a tentative look then sipped cautiously. After two sips he looked at Dougless with such naked joy on his face that she laughed as he downed the tea. She poured him another cup and handed him a scone.

He picked up the scone and looked at it. It was very much like a Southern American biscuit but it had sugar in the dough, and these were fruit scones so they had raisins in them.

She took the scone from him, broke it in half and slathered it with the thick, clotted cream. He bit into it and as he chewed he looked like a man who had fallen in love.

In minutes he had drunk all the tea and eaten all the scones. Dougless went back into the shop and bought more of everything. When she returned, he looked at her.

"What caused you to weep in the church?"

"I . . . I really don't believe it's any of your business."

"If I am to return—and I *must* return—I need to know what brought me forth."

Dougless put down her half-eaten scone. "You aren't going to start that again, are you? You know what I think? I think you're a graduate student in Elizabethan history, probably Ph.D. level, and you just got carried away with your research. My father said it used to happen to him, that he'd read so much medieval script that after a while he couldn't read modern handwriting."

Nicholas looked at the woman with distaste. When he thought of all the wonders he had seen that day, the chariots, the marvelous glass, the clean streets, the riches of goods to purchase, he was amazed at how little faith this woman had in the mystery and magic of the world. "I know from whence I came," he said evenly, "and you, witch—"

Dougless left the garden at that, but he caught her before she reached the door to the shop, his hands cutting into her arm.

"Why were you weeping?" he demanded.

She jerked out of his grip. "Because I'd just been left behind," she said angrily. To her shame, tears began again.

Gently he slipped her arm in his and led her back to the table where he sat beside her, poured her another cup of tea, added milk, and handed her the pretty porcelain cup.

"Now, madam, what plagues you so that tears pour forth from your eyes as from a waterfall?"

Dougless didn't *want* to tell anyone what had happened, but to her consternation she found herself telling this odd man everything.

"He left you alone? At the mercy of ruffians and thieves?"

Dougless blew her nose on a paper napkin and nodded. "And men who believe they're from the sixteenth century too. Oh, sorry," she added.

But the man didn't seem to hear her. He was pacing the garden. "You merely knelt by the tomb—my tomb—and asked for a . . ." He looked at her.

"A Knight in Shining Armor."

He smiled a bit, his lips hidden in his beard and mustache. "I was not wearing armor when you called me forth."

"I *didn't* call you. It's customary to cry when you get left in a church. Especially when a fat brat of a girl steals your purse. I don't even have a passport. Even if my family wired me money for a ticket home I couldn't leave. I'd have to apply for another passport."

"Nor can I get home," he said. "But if you brought me forth you can send me back."

"I am *not* a witch. I do not practice black magic and I certainly don't know how to send people back and forth in time. You've imagined all of this."

He raised an eyebrow at her. "No doubt your lover was justified in leaving you. With your vile temper he would not want to remain with you."

"I was *never* vile-tempered with Robert. I loved him. *Love* him, so I was always sweet. I did whatever he wanted and I shouldn't have complained about Gloria. It was just that her lying was beginning to get to me."

"And you love this man who left you, who allowed his daughter to steal from you?"

"I doubt if Robert knows Gloria took my purse, and Gloria is just a kid. She probably doesn't even realize what she did. I just wish I could find them and get my purse back and go *home.*"

"It seems we have kindred goals."

Suddenly she knew where he was leading. He wanted her to help him on a permanent basis. She was *not* going to saddle herself with a man with amnesia.

She set her empty cup down. "Our goals aren't alike enough that we should spend the next few months together while you try to remember that actually you live in New Jersey with your wife and three kids, and every summer you come to England and put on armor and play some little sex game with an unsuspecting tourist. No thank you. Now if you don't mind, we have an agreement. I'll find you a hotel room and then I'm out."

When she finished she could see the flush of anger through his beard. "Are all the women like you now?"

"No, just the ones who have been hurt over and over again." She calmed. "If you really have lost your memory, you should go to a doctor, not pick up a woman in a church. And if this is all an act, then you should definitely go to a doctor. Either way, you don't need me." She put the tea things on the tray to carry them back into the shop, but he stood between her and the door.

"What recourse have I if I tell the truth? Have you no belief that your tears could have called me from another time, another place?"

"Of course not," she said. "There are a thousand explanations as to why you *think* you're from the sixteenth century, and not one of them has to do with my being a witch. Now, will you excuse me? I need to put these down and then I'll find you a hotel room."

Docilely, he followed her out of the tearoom, his head down as if he considered some great problem. If he had lost his memory, the worst thing Dougless could do was to stay with him and keep him from seeing a doctor.

She asked the woman in the tea shop where the nearest bed and breakfast was and the two of them walked quietly along the street. The man did not speak, nor did he look about as he had all afternoon.

"Do you like your clothes?" she asked, trying to make conversation. He was carrying the shopping bag of armor and his satin shorts.

He didn't answer but kept on walking, his brow furrowed.

There was only one room available at the bed and breakfast, and Dougless started to sign the register. "Do you still insist that you're Nicholas Stafford?"

The woman behind the little desk smiled. "Oh, like in the church." She took a postcard of the tomb in the church from a rack and looked at it. "You do look like him, only a bit more alive." She laughed at her own joke. "First door on the right. Bath's down the hall."

Dougless turned to look at the man and suddenly felt as if she were a cruel mother abandoning her child. "You'll remember soon," she said. "This lady can tell you where to get dinner."

"Lady?" he said. "Dinner at this hour?"

"All right," she said, frustrated. "Woman and it's supper. I'll bet you that after a good night's sleep you'll remember everything."

"I have forgot naught now, madam. You cannot leave. Only *you* know how to return me."

"Cut me some slack, will you? If you'll just give me the fifty bucks, that's . . ." To her horror that was only about thirty pounds. A room in this bed and breakfast had cost forty pounds. But a deal was a deal. "If you'll give me thirty pounds I'll be on my way."

She had his paper money, and she gave it back to him except for the thirty pounds. "Take the coins to the dealer." She turned to go. "Good luck," she said and gave one last glance at his blue eyes that looked so sorrowful.

When she left the house she did not feel jubilant at leaving the man, but rather as if she were missing something. She forced herself to put her shoulders back and her head up. It was getting late and she had to find a place to spend the night—a cheap place—and she had to decide where to go from here.

◇ ◇ ◇

Nicholas found the room to the right of the stairs and he was at first appalled. It was small, there were two tiny, hard beds with no hangings, and the walls were very bare. But upon closer examination he saw the walls were painted with thousands of tiny blue flowers. He thought that perhaps with a few borders and some order to the paintings they might look all right.

There was a window with that marvelous glass in it, with side hangings of painted cloth. There were framed pictures on the walls and when he touched one he felt the glass—so clear he could hardly see it. The pictures were of half-clothed women, and men wearing their hair too long and in a beribboned tail.

There was a door that led to a press that had no shelves in it. It had only a round stick going from one side to the other and strange steel shapes hung from it. There was a cabinet in the room, but such as he'd never seen before. It was entirely full of drawers! He tried but the top of the cabinet did not lift up. He pulled the drawers out one by one and they worked marvelously well.

After a while he began to look for a chamber pot, but one was not to be found, so he went downstairs and out to the back garden to find a privy. There was none.

"Have things changed *that* much in four hundred years?" he mumbled as he relieved himself in the rose bushes. He fumbled with the zipper and snaps but managed rather well, he thought.

"I will do well without the witch," he said to himself and went back into the house. Perhaps tomorrow he would wake and find this all to be a dream, a long, bad dream.

No one was about downstairs so Nicholas looked into a room with an open door. There was strange furniture in the room that was covered with fine, woven fabric. There was not one inch of the chair showing. He sat in the chair and the softness enveloped him. He thought of his mother and her old, frail bones and how she'd like a chair like this, covered in softness and fabric.

Against one wall was a tall, wooden desk with a stool beneath it. Here was something that looked somewhat familiar. He went to it and after examining it, saw the hinge and lifted the top. It was not a desk but a type of harpsichord. When he touched the keys, the sound was different. There was written music in front of him and for once something looked familiar.

Nicholas sat down on the stool, ran his fingers over the keys to hear the tone of them, then, awkwardly at first, began to play the music before him.

"That was beautiful."

He turned to see the landlady standing behind him.

" 'Moon River' always was one of my favorites. How do you do with ragtime?" She searched inside a drawer in a little table that had an extraordinary plant on top of it and withdrew another piece of music. "They're all American tunes," she said. "My husband was an American."

The most extraordinary piece of music called "The Sting" was put before Nicholas, and it took him some time before he played it to the woman's satisfaction, but once he understood it, he played it with enjoyment.

"Oh my, you are good. You could get a job in any pub."

"I will consider the possibility," Nicholas said as he stood. "The need of employment might arise yet." Suddenly he felt dizzy and reached out to catch himself on a chair.

"Are you all right?"

"Merely tired," Nicholas murmured.

"Traveling always wears me out. Been far today?"

"Hundreds of years."

The woman smiled. "I feel that way too when I travel. You should go up to your room and have a bit of a lie-down before supper."

"Yes," Nicholas said softly and started for the stairs. Perhaps tomorrow he would be able to think more clearly about how to get himself back to his own time. Or perhaps tomorrow he'd wake up in his own bed and *all* of it would be over, not just this twentieth-century nightmare but all of it.

In his room he undressed slowly. There were no pegs for his clothes so he put them neatly on the other bed. Where was the witch now? Was she back in the arms of her lover? She was powerful enough to have called him forward over four hundred years so he had no doubt she could conjure an errant lover back across mere miles.

Nude, he climbed into bed. The sheets were smooth beyond believing and they smelled of what he didn't know but it was good. Over him, instead of coverlets, was a fat, soft, fluffed blanket.

Tomorrow, he thought as he closed his eyes. Tomorrow he would be home.

He was asleep the instant he closed his eyes. He slept harder than he ever had before and he heard nothing when the sky opened and it began to rain.

It was hours later when he was awakened, thrashing about in the bed. He sat up. The room was black-dark and at first he didn't know where he was. He could hear the rain pounding on the roof. He fumbled at the table beside the bed for flint and candle but there were none.

"What manner of place is this?" he exclaimed. "No privies, no lights."

As he was grumbling, his head came up sharply. Someone was calling him. Not in words. He couldn't hear the actual sound of his name, but he could feel the urgency and the desperate need.

He had no doubt it was the witch-woman. Was she bent over a cauldron of snakes' eyes, stirring and cackling and whispering his name?

There was no use fighting her call. As he lived and breathed, he knew he had to go to her. He had difficulty dressing himself in the strange modern clothes, and when he fastened the zipper he discovered parts of his body that were most susceptible to being caught in zippers. He put on the flimsy shirt and felt his way out of the room.

In the hall was light. There was a glass-enclosed torch on the wall but the flame was encased in a round glass sphere. He wanted to examine this further, but there was a crack of thunder outside and the call came to him more forcefully.

He went down the stairs, across lush carpets, and out into the rain. On poles, high above his head, were more flames that the blowing rain did not extinguish. Nicholas put his head down in his collar. These modern clothes had no substance! No capes, no jerkins, nothing to protect him from the driving rain.

He struggled against the rain down streets that were unfamiliar to him. Several times he heard strange noises and reached for his sword only to find it wasn't there. Tomorrow he would sell more coins and hire guards to accompany him. Tomorrow he would force the woman to tell him the truth of what she had done to bring him to this strange land.

He struggled down street after street, making several wrong turns, but then the call would come again. He left the streets that had the torches on poles and entered the darkness of the countryside. He walked for several minutes along a road, then stopped and listened, wiping rain from his face. He turned right and started across a field, climbing over a fence and at last coming to a small shed.

He flung the door open and a flash of lightning showed her, drenched, curled into a ball on some dirty straw. She was once again weeping.

"Well, madam," he said, "you have called me from a warm bed. What is it you want of me now?"

"Go away," she sobbed. "Leave me alone."

His anger left him. Her teeth were chattering and she was obviously freezing. He bent and lifted her into his arms. "I do not know who is the more helpless—you or I."

"Let me go," she said but made no real struggle to get away from him. Her sobbing started harder. "I couldn't find any place to stay. Everything in England costs so much, and I don't know where Robert is and I'll have to call Elizabeth and she'll laugh at me."

He adjusted her in his arms as he swung over the fence and kept walking. She kept crying as her arms slipped around his neck. "I don't belong anywhere. My family is perfect but I'm not. All the women in my family are married to wonderful men, but I can't even *meet* any wonderful men. Robert was a great catch but I couldn't hold on to him. Oh, Nick, what am I going to do?"

"First, madam, you may *not* call me Nick. You may call me Colin if you must, but not Nick. Now, since we seem destined to know one another, what is your name?"

"Dougless," she said, clinging to him. "Dougless Montgomery."

"Ah, a good, sensible name."

"It's after Dougless Sheffield who bore the Earl of Leicester's illegitimate child."

Nicholas halted. "She what?"

"Bore the Earl of Leicester's child."

He set her on the ground and glared at her, the rain hitting them both hard in the face. "And who is the Earl of Leicester?"

"Robert Dudley, the man who loved Queen Elizabeth."

Rage filled Nicholas's face as he turned and started to stomp away. "The

Dudleys are traitors, executed, every one of them. And Queen Elizabeth is to marry the King of Spain."

"Well, she *won't*," Dougless shouted, running after him, then screamed with pain as her ankle collapsed under her and she fell forward, scraping her hands and knees.

Nicholas turned back to her. "Woman, you are a bloody great trouble," he said and lifted her into his arms again.

She started to speak again but he told her to be quiet and she was.

He carried her back to the house where he was staying, and when he pushed open the door he found the landlady sitting in a chair and waiting for him.

"There you are," the landlady said. "I heard you leave and I knew something was wrong. Oh, poor dears, you both look done in. Bring her upstairs and give her a nice, hot soak."

Nicholas followed the woman up the stairs, carrying Dougless but managing to ignore her, to a room Nicholas had not seen before. It had strange, pottery vessels in it, one of which was a bathtub. But he saw no buckets of water.

He nearly dropped the girl when the landlady turned a knob and out poured water. A fountain *inside* the house!

"It'll be hot in a minute. Get her undressed and put her in the tub. I'll get fresh towels. You look like you could use a soak too." She left the room.

Nicholas looked down at Dougless with interest.

"Don't even think about it," Dougless warned. "Get out of here while I take a bath."

He set her down and looked about. "What manner of room is this?"

"It's the bathroom."

"I see the bathing pot, but what is this? And this?"

Dougless restrained herself from asking what he'd been using if he didn't know what a toilet was. He must have been studying very, very hard to have forgotten something so basic. She demonstrated the basin, then the toilet, turning brilliant red at demonstrations of seat up, seat down. "And you never, never, *never* leave the seat up," she said and felt as if she were doing her part for womankind if she could teach one man this simple thing.

The landlady returned with more towels and on top a flowered cotton robe. "I noticed you didn't have much luggage."

"The airlines lost it all," Dougless said quickly.

"I thought as much. Well, good night."

"Thank you," Dougless said as the door closed, leaving her alone with this man. "You go too now. I won't be long." When she was alone,

Dougless slipped into the hot water and lay back. The water stung her scraped knees and elbows, but already it was beginning to warm her.

How had he found her? she wondered. After she'd left him she'd wandered all over the village, trying to find a place to stay for thirty pounds but there was nothing. She'd spent six pounds on a meal in a pub and started walking. She thought perhaps she could make it to another village and find shelter there. But the rain had come, it had grown dark, and all she could find was a tool shed. She'd curled up and gone to sleep but then woke to find herself crying—which seemed to be her normal state for the last twenty-four hours.

While she'd been crying he had appeared—and she hadn't been surprised to see him. It had seemed perfectly natural that he'd known where to find her and come out into the rain for her. It had also seemed natural when he'd picked her up into his strong arms.

She got out of the tub, dried, and put on the flowered robe. A glance in the mirror showed her to have on no makeup and her hair . . . The less thought about that the better.

Shyly, she knocked on the door that was half open. Nicholas, wearing only his trousers, opened it for her. "The bathroom is yours."

There was no softness in his face. "Get into that bed and stay there. I do not intend to go bat-fowling again."

She only nodded at him as he passed her on the way to the bathroom. Wearing the thin robe, she slipped under the comforter. When he returned they would talk. She would find out how he had known where she was, how he had found her in the dark, in the rain.

She meant to talk to him when he returned, but she closed her eyes for a moment and the next thing she knew it was morning. Sunlight hit her full in the face and she opened her eyes slowly.

There was a man standing before the window, his back to her. He had a fine, muscular back that tapered down to a small slim waist, then straight hips that were draped with a small white towel. His legs were thick and muscular as if he used them for heavy work.

Slowly, Dougless came awake and began to remember who this man was, from their first meeting in the church when he'd drawn a sword on her, to last night when he'd carried her back in the rain.

She sat up and he turned to look at her.

"You are awake," he said flatly. "Come, get up, there is much to do."

She turned away as he dressed, grabbed her own wrinkled clothing and went to the bathroom to dress. She didn't have so much as a comb to run through her hair. She looked into the mirror and thought that if all women had to face the world with the face God gave them, there would be a great increase in female suicides.

She straightened her hair and left the room. Nicholas was waiting for her in the hall.

"First we eat and then, madam, we talk," he said as if it were a dare.

Dougless merely nodded as she went ahead of him down the stairs to the dining room.

There are two meals that should be eaten in England: breakfast and tea. They sat down at a small table while the landlady brought in platters full of food: fluffy scrambled eggs, three types of bread, bacon that was like the best American ham, grilled tomatoes, sliced, fried potatoes, golden kippers, cream, butter, marmalade. And a large pretty porcelain pot of brewed tea. The English loved their tea and loved exquisite china to put it in.

Dougless ate until she could hold no more, but she couldn't come close to competing with Nicholas. He ate nearly all the food that was on the table. When Dougless finished, she caught the landlady watching Nicholas curiously. He ate everything with his spoon or his fingers. He used his knife to cut the bacon while holding it with his fingers, but he never once touched his fork.

When he was finished he gave his compliments to the landlady, took Dougless's arm, and ushered her outside.

"Where are we going?" She ran her tongue over her teeth. She hadn't brushed them in twenty-four hours now and they felt fuzzy. Also, her scalp itched.

"To the church," he said. "There we will plan."

They walked quickly to the church, with Nicholas only stopping once to gawk at a small pickup truck. Dougless thought about telling him about eighteen-wheelers and cattle trucks but thought better of it.

The old church was open and empty, and Nicholas led her to a pew at a right angle to the tomb. She was quiet while he looked again at the marble sculpture and ran his hands over the date and name.

At last he turned away, clasped his hands behind his back, and began to pace. "As I see it, Mistress Montgomery, we need each the other. It seems God has put us together for a reason."

"I thought I did it with a spell," she said sarcastically.

"I believed that at first, but I have not slept since you called me into the rain and I have had time to consider."

"I *called* you? I never even thought about you, and if I had there weren't any telephones and I certainly couldn't shout loud enough for you to hear me."

"Nonetheless, you did call me. You woke me with your need."

"Oh, I see," she said, starting to get angry. "We're going back to your belief that I *somehow*, through hocus-pocus, brought you here from your grave. I can't take this anymore. I'm leaving."

Before she could move, he was on her, one hand on the high bench arm, the other on the back, his big body pinning her to her seat. "It matters not to me whether you believe or not. Yesterday morn when I woke it was the year of our Lord 1564 and this morn it was . . ."

"1988," she supplied.

"Aye," he said, "over four hundred years later. And you, witch, are the key to my being here and to my returning."

"Believe me, I'd send you back if I could. I have enough problems without having to take care—"

He leaned close to her face. "You could not dare to say that you must care for me. I must pull you from fields in the dead of night."

"One time only," she said, then quietened. "How did you hear my . . . need, as you call it?"

He stood and went back to look down at the tomb. "There is a bond between us. An unnatural, unholy bond, but it is there. I heard you calling me. As clearly as if I'd heard the words I heard you calling me. The . . . feel of the call woke me and I followed it to find you."

Dougless was silent for a moment. She knew what he said was true because there was no other explanation for how he'd found her. "You think there's some kind of mental telepathy between us?" When he looked puzzled, she explained. "Thought transference. We read each other's thoughts."

"Perhaps," he said, looking at the tomb. "I seem to hear your need of me."

"I don't need anyone," Dougless said stubbornly.

He glared at her. "I do not understand why you are not still in your father's house. I have yet to see a woman who needs care more than you."

Dougless started to stand but a look from Nicholas made her sit back down. "All right, you heard me 'call' as you say. What does it mean?"

"I have come to this time and this fast, strange place for a reason, and you are to help me find the answer."

"I can't," Dougless said quickly. "I have to find Robert and get my passport and go home. I've had all the vacation I can stand. Another twenty-four hours like the last one and somebody better start carving *my* tombstone."

"My life and death are a jest to you, but they are not so to me."

"But you aren't dead, you're here, you're alive."

"No, madam, there am I," he said, looking at the tomb.

Dougless threw up her hands in exasperation. She should leave, maybe scream for help, but she couldn't. But then he'd been awfully nice to her and even if she didn't believe he was from another time period, he certainly seemed to believe it. "What do you plan?" she asked softly.

"I will help you find your lover, but you must help me find the reason I am here."

"How can you help me find Robert?"

"I can feed, clothe, and shelter you until he is found."

"Ah yes. How about eyeshadow, too? Okay, only kidding. So, supposing 'we' do find Robert, what do you want me to do to help you find your, ah, way back?"

"Last night you talked to me of Robert Dudley and Queen Elizabeth. You seemed to know who she will marry."

"She doesn't marry anyone. She's known as the Virgin Queen. In America there're a couple of states named for her: Virginia and West Virginia."

"Nay! This cannot be true. No woman can rule alone."

"She not only rules alone, but does a damn fine job of it. *Did* a great job of it. She made England the ruling power of all Europe."

"This is so?"

"You don't have to believe me, it's history."

He was thoughtful for a moment. "History, yes. All that has happened is history and is perhaps recorded somewhere?"

"I see," Dougless said, smiling. "You think maybe you were sent forward to find something out? How intriguing." She frowned. "I mean if it were possible for a person to have been sent forward, it would be intriguing. But since it isn't, it's not."

His look of puzzlement was beginning to become familiar to her.

"Perhaps there is something you know that I must find from you." He moved to stand over her. "What do you know of the Queen's decree? Who has told her I raise an army to overthrow her?"

"I have no idea what you're talking about. All of that happened a long time ago. Look, why don't you stay here? Why go back at all? You could get a job. You'd be *great* as an Elizabethan teacher. You might have enough to live on after the sale of the coins if you invested carefully. My father could help you or my Uncle J.T. Both of them know a lot about money."

"I *must* go back," Nicholas whispered, his right fist clasped in his left hand. "My honor is at risk. The future of the Staffords is at stake. If I do not go back, all will be forfeit."

"Forfeit?" Dougless said. She knew enough about medieval history to have some idea what he was talking about. "Usually a nobleman forfeited his estates to the king, or queen, when he was accused of . . ." She trailed off, then he turned to look at her. "Treason," she whispered. "How . . . how did you die?"

"I assume I was executed."

4

Dougless forgot about whether he was or was not from the sixteenth century. "Tell me," she whispered.

He paced a moment longer, stopped and stared at the tomb, then came to sit by her. "I have lands in Wales," he said softly. "I learned my lands were under attack, so I raised an army. In my haste I did not petition the queen for permission to raise this army. She was . . ."

He stopped and looked into the distance, his eyes angry and hard. "She was told the army was to join forces with the young Scots queen."

"Mary Queen of Scots," Dougless said and he nodded.

"I was tried hastily and condemned to be beheaded. I had three days left when you . . . when you called me here."

"Then you're lucky!" Dougless said. "Beheading. Disgusting. We don't do that now."

"You have no treason? How do you punish the nobility?" He put up his hand when she started to answer. "Nay, I must continue. My mother is a powerful woman and she has friends. She has worked to prove my innocence. If I do not return and save myself, she will lose all. She will be a pauper."

"The queen would take everything?"

"All."

Dougless thought about this. Of course, none of this was real but if it were, perhaps there was something to be learned today from the history books. "Do you have any idea who told the queen your army was going to be used to take her throne?"

"None," he said and put his head in his hands in despair.

Dougless almost reached out to touch his hair, perhaps to rub his neck. She withdrew. This man's problems weren't her own. There was no reason she should be singled out to help this man find the answer to being unjustly accused of treason.

But the idea of injustice made her skin crawl. Maybe it was in her blood. Her grandfather, Hank Montgomery, had been a union organizer before he came home to run Warbrooke Shipping. To this day, her grandfather hated any type of injustice and would risk his life to stop it.

"My father is a professor of medieval history," Dougless said, "and I've helped him do some research. Maybe you were, ah . . . assigned to me because I could help with the research. And, too, how many females have been abandoned so completely that they'd even consider helping a man wearing a sword and balloon shorts?"

Nicholas looked puzzled, then angry as he stood. "You refer to my slops? You jest at my clothing? These . . . these . . ."

"Trousers."

"Trousers. They bind a man's legs. I cannot bend. Here, these." He put his hands in his pockets. "I can carry nothing. And last night I was cold in the rain and—"

"But cool today," she said, smiling.

"And this." He pulled back the fly to show the zipper. "This can hurt a man."

Dougless began to laugh. "If you *wore* your underwear instead of leaving it on the bed, maybe the zipper wouldn't hurt."

"Underwear? What is that?"

"Elastic, remember?"

"Ah yes," he said and began to smile.

Dougless suddenly thought, what else do I have to do? Cry some more? Six of her women friends had taken her out to dinner before she left to wish her bon voyage on her romantic five-week holiday. Yet here she was wanting to go home after five days.

If she were honest with herself would she rather spend four and a half weeks with Robert and Gloria, or helping this man research what might or might not be his past life? The whole thing reminded her of a ghost story where the heroine goes to the library and reads about the curse on the house she's rented for the summer.

"Yes," she heard herself say. "I will help you."

Nicholas sat by her, took her hand in his, and fervently kissed the back of it. "You are a lady at heart."

She was smiling at the top of his head, then her smile disappeared. "At heart? Meaning I'm not a lady elsewhere?"

He gave a little shrug. "Who can fathom why God has joined me with a commoner?"

"Why you—" she began. It was on the tip of her tongue to tell him that her uncle was the King of Lanconia and she often spent summers playing with her six cousins, the princes and princesses. But something stopped her. Let him think what he wanted. "Should I address you as your lordship?" she asked archly.

Nicholas frowned thoughtfully. "I have considered that question. I can move about unharmed now. These clothes, they are like all others. I cannot understand your sumptuary laws. I must hire retainers, yet now a shirt costs a man's yearly wage. I do not understand your ways. Often I . . ." He looked away. "I make a fool of myself."

"Oh well, I do that and I've grown up in this century."

"But you are a woman."

"First of all, let's get one thing straight, and that is, in this century women aren't men's slaves. We women say what we want, do what we want. We aren't put on this earth for your pleasure only."

Slowly, Nicholas turned to look at her. "Is this what is believed today? That women of my time were for pleasure only?"

"Obedient, docile, locked away in a castle somewhere, kept pregnant, not allowed to go to school."

Nicholas began to laugh. "I will tell my mother this. My mother who has buried three husbands. King Henry said my mother's husbands wished themselves into the grave because they weren't half the man she is. Docile? Nay, lady, not docile. No schooling? My mother speaks four languages and argues philosophy."

"Then your mother is an exception. I'm sure most women are—were—downtrodden and brutalized."

He gave her a piercing stare. "Today men are noble? They do not abandon lone women, leaving them to the mercy of the elements?"

Dougless turned away, blushing. Maybe this wasn't such a good time to argue about this. "Okay, you've made your point." She looked back at him. "All right, let's get down to business. First we go to a drugstore, or chemist as it's called here, and we buy toiletries." She sighed. "Eyeshadow, blush, I'd kill for a tube of lipstick right now. Toothbrushes, toothpaste, floss." She stopped and looked at him. "Let me see your teeth."

"Madam!"

"Let me see your teeth." If he were an overworked graduate student,

he'd have fillings, but if he were from the sixteenth century no dentist
would have touched his mouth.

After a moment, Nicholas obediently opened his mouth and Dougless
moved his head this way and that to look inside. He had three molars
missing and there looked to be a cavity in another tooth but there was no
sign of modern dental work. "We need to get you to a dentist."

Nicholas pulled away from her. "The tooth does not pain me enough to
have it pulled."

"Is that why you have three teeth missing? They were pulled?"

He seemed to think this was obvious, so Dougless showed him her fillings
and tried to explain what a dentist was.

"Ah, there you are," said the vicar from the back of the church. "I
wondered if you'd patched things up."

"We weren't . . . " Dougless began, then stopped. "Yes, we've patched
it up." She stood. "We have to go. We have a great deal to do. Nicholas, are
you ready?"

Smiling at her, he offered her his arm and led her from the church.
Outside, Dougless paused and looked at the enclosed graveyard. It had been
just yesterday that Robert had left her here.

"What shines there?" Nicholas asked, looking at one of the
gravemarkers.

It was the gravestone where Gloria had fallen, then lied to Robert about
her scrapes, saying Dougless had hurt her. Curious, Dougless went to the
stone. At the bottom, hidden by grass and dirt, was Gloria's five-thousand-
dollar diamond bracelet. Dougless picked it up and held it to the sunlight
for a moment.

"The quality of the diamonds is excellent," Nicholas said. "The emeralds
are but cheap."

Dougless laughed and clasped the bracelet in her hand. "I'll find him
now," she said. "He'll come back for me now." She went into the church
and told the vicar that should Robert Whitley ask about the bracelet, to tell
him Dougless had it. She told him the name of the bed and breakfast where
she and Nicholas were staying.

When she left the church she felt jubilant. Everything was going to work
out now. Robert would be so grateful that she'd found the bracelet that
. . . who knows? Maybe she'd leave England with a marriage proposal yet.

"Let's go shopping," she said happily to Nicholas. As they walked she
made a list in her head of the things she needed, so she'd be looking her
best when she saw Robert again. Face, hair, clothes, certainly a new blouse
that didn't have a cut sleeve.

First they went to the coin dealer and sold another coin, this one for fifteen hundred pounds. Dougless called the bed and breakfast to reserve their room for three more nights, while the dealer found a buyer for Nicholas's rarer coins. And to give Robert time to find me, Dougless thought.

Then they went to a chemist's shop.

"What is this?" Nicholas whispered, looking at rows and rows of gaily wrapped packages.

"Shampoo, deodorant, toothpaste, all the usual stuff."

"I know not those words."

Dougless's head was full of Robert and the bracelet in her pocket, but suddenly she looked at the products as an Elizabethan man might see them —if Nicholas were from the past, which of course he wasn't. She knew from school that until recently, people made the products they needed at home.

"This is shampoo to wash your hair." She opened a bottle of papaya-scented shampoo. "Smell."

Nicholas smelled it and smiled at her in delight.

"Cucumber," she said, opening another bottle. "And this is strawberry." She showed him shaving lotion after that. "You wouldn't consider shaving that, would you?"

Nicholas ran his hand over his beard. "I have seen no man with a beard now."

"There're some, but it's not the fashion actually."

"Then I will find a barber and shave it." He paused. "You have barbers now?"

"We still have barbers."

"And he is the one you will have put silver in my sore tooth?"

Dougless laughed. "Nope. Barbers and dentists are separate now. Pick out a shaving lotion and I'll get cream and razors." She picked up a portable shopping basket and filled it with shampoo, cream rinse, combs, toothbrushes, toothpaste, floss, and a small electric travel set of hair rollers. She was happily looking over the makeup when she heard a noise behind her. Nicholas was trying to get her attention.

When she went around the corner she saw he'd opened a tube of toothpaste and squirted it down the front of the racks.

"I but meant to smell it," he said rigidly, and Dougless felt his deep embarrassment.

She grabbed a box of tissues, opened it, took out a handful, and began to clean the counter and some off his belt.

He took a tissue from the box. "This is paper," he said and there was wonder in his voice as well as awe. "Here, stop that! You cannot waste paper. It is too valuable, and this has not been used before."

Dougless didn't understand what he was talking about. "You use a tissue once and throw it away."

"Is your century so rich?"

Dougless still had trouble understanding him, but then remembered that in the sixteenth century all paper was handmade. "I guess we are rich in goods," she said after a moment. She put the opened tissue box in her basket and continued choosing items for purchase. She bought face cream, shaving cream, razors, deodorant, wash cloths (because the English hotels didn't supply them) and a full set of cosmetics.

Once again she took charge of Nicholas's paper money. He could not bear to hear the cost of things. "I can buy a horse for what this bottle costs," he mumbled when she read a price to him. She paid and lugged the shopping bag full of goods out of the store. Nicholas did not offer to take the bag from her.

"Let's take this back to the hotel," she said, "then we can—" She broke off because Nicholas was standing in front of a shop window. Yesterday he'd had eyes only for the street, gaping at cars, once kneeling and feeling the pavement, at other times staring at the people. Today he was noticing the shops, marveling at the plate-glass windows, touching the lettering of the signs.

He was looking in the window of a bookstore/stationers at a big, beautiful coffee-table edition of a book on medieval armor. Beside it were books on Henry the Eighth and Elizabeth the First.

"Come on," she said, smiling, and pulled him inside. Whatever troubles Dougless had, she soon forgot them when she saw the wonder and joy on Nicholas's face as he reverently touched the books. She left her shopping bag at the counter and walked with him. The biggest, most expensive books were lying face up on a table and he ran his fingertips over the glossy photos.

"They are magnificent," he whispered.

"Here's your Queen Elizabeth," Dougless said, lifting a large color volume.

As if he were almost afraid to touch the book, he took it from Dougless. He had no words to explain what he felt at the sight of so many books. Books were precious and rare, prized possessions owned by only the richest of people. If they had pictures, they were woodcuts or hand-colored illuminations.

He opened the book he held and ran his hand over the colored illustrations. "Who has painted these? Do you have so many painters now?"

"They're done by a machine."

Nicholas looked at the picture of Queen Elizabeth. "Look at her gown. Is this the new fashion? My mother would know of this."

Dougless looked at the date. 1582. She took the book from him. "I'm not sure you should look at the future." What was she saying?! 1580 the future? "Here's a nice book." She handed him *Birds of the World.*

But Nicholas almost dropped the book because the music system, which had been silent until then, suddenly began to play. Nicholas looked about him. "I see no musicians. And what is that music? Is it ragtime?"

Dougless laughed. "Where'd you hear of ragtime? No, I mean, your memory must be returning." But even as she said it she didn't believe it.

"Mrs. Beasley," he said, referring to the woman who ran the bed and breakfast. "I played it for her from her music."

"Played it on what?"

"It is like a large harpsichord but it sounded most different."

"Probably a piano."

"You have not told me what is the source of this music."

"It's classical—Beethoven, I think, and it comes from a cassette in a machine."

"Machines," he whispered. "Again machines."

Dougless was beginning to see how new this world was to him. His being a man who'd completely lost his memory, not a man from the sixteenth century, she reminded herself. Perhaps music would help bring his memory back.

Along one wall was a selection of cassette tapes. She chose Beethoven, excerpts from *La Traviata,* Irish folk music, and she started to choose the Rolling Stones but thought she'd get something more modern, then laughed at herself. "Mozart is new to him," she said, taking the Stones tape. She also bought a cheap cassette player with earphones so he could hear the music.

When she went back to Nicholas, he was in the stationery section touching the papers gingerly. Dougless showed him felt-tip pens, ballpoints, and mechanical pencils. He made a few squiggles on the testing paper but they weren't words. Dougless wondered if he could read and write, but she didn't ask him.

They left the store with a second shopping bag full of spiral notebooks, felt-tips of every color imaginable, cassettes and player, and six travel books. Three were on travel in England, one of America, and two about the world.

On impulse she'd purchased a set of Winsor Newton watercolors and a block of watercolor paper for Nicholas. She somehow felt he might like to paint. She also tucked in an Agatha Christie.

"Could we take this back to the hotel now?" Dougless asked. Her arms were starting to ache from the weight of the bags.

But Nicholas had stopped again, this time in front of a women's clothing store. "You will purchase yourself new clothing," he said and it was an order.

Dougless didn't like his tone. "I have my own clothes and when I get them, I—"

"I will travel with no beldame," he said stiffly.

Dougless wasn't sure what the word meant but she could guess. She looked at her reflection in the glass. If she thought she looked bad yesterday, she had surpassed herself today. She handed him the bag with the books. "Wait for me over there," she said, pointing to a wooden bench set under a tree.

Dougless took the bag with the cosmetics in it and went into the shop.

It took her an hour, but when Dougless returned to him she didn't look like the same person. Her auburn hair, wildly unkempt from days without care, was now pulled back off her face and, neatly combed, it fell back in soft waves to the silk scarf she'd used to tie it at the nape of her neck. Softly applied cosmetics brought out the beauty of her face. She was not a beauty of the type that looked fragile and overbred, but Dougless was healthy and wholesome-looking, as if she'd grown up on a horse ranch in Kentucky or on a sailboat in Maine—which she had.

She'd chosen clothes that were simple but exquisitely made: a teal Austrian jacket, a paisley skirt of teal, plum and navy, a plum silk blouse, and boots of soft navy leather. On impulse she'd also purchased navy kid gloves and a navy leather purse.

Carrying the shopping bag, she crossed the road toward Nicholas, and she was pleased by his expression when he saw her. "Well?" she said.

"Beauty knows no time," he said softly, rising, then kissing her hand.

There were advantages to Elizabethan men, she thought.

"Is it time for tea yet?" he asked.

Dougless groaned. Men were timeless, too, she thought. It was always: you-look-great-what's-for-dinner?

"We are now going to experience one of the worst aspects of England, and that is: lunch. Breakfast is great; tea is great. Dinner is great if you like butter and cream, but lunch is . . . indescribable."

He was listening to her with concentration, as one does when learning a new language. "What is this lunch?"

"You'll see," Dougless said and led him to a pretty little pub. Pubs were one of the things Dougless liked best about England. They settled their bags into a booth and Dougless ordered two cheese salad sandwiches and a couple of pints of beer for them both, and she proceeded to tell Nicholas the difference between a bar in America and a pub in England.

"There are more unescorted women?" he asked.

"More than me? I think most women today are independent," she said. "Most of them have their purses and credit cards, but they don't have men to take care of them."

"But what of cousins and uncles? What of sons?"

"It's not like that now. It's—" She stopped as the waitress put the sandwiches before them. They were not sandwiches as Americans know them. A cheese sandwich was a piece of cheese between two pieces of buttered white bread. A cheese salad sandwich had a small piece of lettuce on it.

Nicholas watched her as she picked up the strange-looking food and began to eat it, then he followed her lead.

"Do you like it?"

"It has no flavor," he said. "Nor does the beer."

Dougless looked about the pub and asked if it were anything like the public houses in the sixteenth century.

"Nay," he answered. "There is gloom and quiet here. There is no danger here."

"But that's good."

Nicholas shrugged. "I prefer flavor in my food and flavor in my public houses."

She smiled. "Are you ready to go? We still have lots to do."

"Leave? But where is dinner?"

"You just ate it."

He raised one eyebrow at her. "Where is the landlord?"

"The man behind the bar seems to be in charge and the woman over there cooks. Wait a minute, Nicholas, don't make a fuss. The English don't like a fuss. I'll go and—"

But he was on his feet. "Food is food, no matter what the year. No, madam, stay where you are and I will procure us a proper dinner."

Dougless watched as he went to the bartender and they talked earnestly for a few moments. Then the woman was called over and she listened to Nicholas. As Dougless watched, it occurred to her that if Nicholas learned his way around the twentieth century he might be a bit of a problem.

In moments he came back to the booth and moments after that dishes of food began to appear: chicken, vegetables, salad, beef, pork pie and for Nicholas a nasty-looking dark beer.

"Now, Mistress Montgomery," he said when the table was loaded with food, "how do you propose to find my way home?"

First Dougless gave him a lesson on the use of a fork (he almost pierced his tongue), then she withdrew a spiral notebook and a pen from a bag, and began to make notes. "I have to know all about you before we can start research." Perhaps now, with dates and places, she'd trip him up.

But nothing she asked him even slowed him down as he ate plateful after plateful of food. Born sixth June, 1537.

"Full name, or, I guess, title in your case."

"Nicholas Stafford, Earl of Thornwyck, Buckshire and Southeaton, Lord of Farlane."

Dougless blinked. "Anything else?"

"A few baronetcies but none of great importance."

"So much for barons," she said and asked more questions. As she wrote, he began to list the properties he owned. Estates from East Yorkshire to South Wales. More land in France and Ireland.

After a while she closed her notebook. "I think we'll be able to find something about you—him," she said.

After "lunch" they stopped in a barber shop and Nicholas was shaved. When he sat up in the chair, clean-shaven at last, Dougless took a moment to catch her breath. Black, black hair, deep blue eyes.

"I will do, madam?" he asked, softly chuckling.

"Passable," she said, smiling back at him.

They took the shopping bags back to the bed and breakfast, and the landlady told them she had a room with a private bath available. A sane, sensible part of Dougless's brain told her she should ask for a separate room but she didn't open her mouth. When Robert came for her, she thought it might be good for him to see her with this fabulous-looking man.

Afterward they went back to the church, but there was no word for her from Robert, nor any inquiries about the bracelet. They went to a grocery and bought cheese and fruit, to a butcher for meat pies, to a baker for bread, scones, and pastries, and to a winery for a bottle of wine.

By tea time Dougless was exhausted.

"My purse-bearer looks sinking-ripe," Nicholas said, smiling at her.

Dougless felt exactly the way "sinking-ripe" sounded. Together they walked back to their little hotel.

At the hotel they took the bag of books to the garden, their landlady made them a pot of tea, and brought them a blanket. They sat on the blanket, drank tea, ate scones, and looked at the books. It was heavenly English weather, cool yet warm, sunny but not brilliant. The garden was green and lush, the roses fragrant. Dougless was sitting up, Nicholas stretched before her on his stomach, as he ate scones with one hand and carefully turned pages with the other.

The cotton shirt was stretched across his back muscles, the trousers clung to his thighs. Black curls brushed his collar.

"It is here!" Nicholas said, rolling over and sitting up so abruptly that Dougless's tea splashed out. "My newest house is here." He shoved the book at her as she put down her cup.

"Thornwyck Castle," she read, "begun in 1563 by Nicholas Stafford, Earl of Thornwyck . . ." She glanced at him. He was lying on his back and smiling angelically, as if he'd just found some proof of his existence. ". . . Was confiscated by Queen Elizabeth I in 1564 when . . ." She trailed off.

"Go on," Nicholas said softly, no longer smiling.

". . . When the earl was found guilty of treason and sentenced to be beheaded. There was some doubt of his guilt but all investigation stopped when . . ." Dougless's voice lowered. ". . . When three days before his execution the earl was found dead at his desk over an . . ." She looked up and whispered, ". . . An unfinished letter to his mother."

Nicholas watched the clouds overhead and was silent for a while. "Does it mention what became of my mother?" he asked at last.

"No. It just describes the castle, says it was never finished, and what there was of it fell into disrepair after the Civil War—your Civil War, not mine—and was renovated in 1824 for the James family and—" She stopped. "And now it's an exclusive hotel with a two-star restaurant!"

"My house is a public house?" Nicholas asked, obviously disgusted. "It was to be a center of learning and intelligence. It was—"

"Nicholas, that was hundreds of years ago. I mean, maybe it was. Don't you see? Maybe we can get reservations. We can possibly stay at your house."

"I am to pay to stay in my own house?"

She threw up her hands in despair. "Okay, don't go then. We'll stay here and go shopping for the next twenty years."

"You have a sharp tongue on you."

"I stand up for myself."

"Except to men who abandon you."

She started to get up, but he caught her hand.

"I will pay," he said, looking up at her. He didn't release her hand but kept caressing her fingers. "You will stay with me?"

She pulled her hand away. "A bargain's a bargain. We find out what you need to know and you can perhaps clear your ancestor's name."

Nicholas smiled. "So now I am my own ancestor."

She got up and went into the house to call Thornwyck Castle. At first the reservations clerk haughtily told her that reservations needed to be made a year in advance, but there was a commotion and the clerk came back to tell her that their best suite was unexpectedly available. Dougless took it.

As she hung up, Dougless realized she wasn't surprised by the coincidence. It seemed that some kind of wish therapy was at work. Every time she wished for something, she got it. She wished for a Knight in Shining Armor and he appeared (a crazy one who thought he was from the sixteenth century, but a man in armor no less); she wished for money and he has a bag of coins worth hundreds of thousands of pounds. Now she needed reservations to an exclusive hotel and of course they had a vacancy.

She took Gloria's bracelet from her pocket and looked at it. It looked like something some rich, fat old man would give his twenty-year-younger mistress. What could she wish for with Robert? That he'd come to realize that his own daughter was a lying thief? She didn't want any parent to despise his own child. So where did that leave her? She wanted Robert, but his daughter and his love for his daughter came with him.

She called the vicarage and no one had called about the bracelet. She asked the vicar to recommend a dentist and was able to make an appointment, again due to cancellation, for the next morning. As she started back outside, she saw several American magazines, *Vogue, Harper's Bazaar, Gentleman's Quarterly,* on a table and she took them outside to Nicholas.

There were some exclamations on his part when she explained that these beautiful "books" were actually disposable goods. He started looking through the magazines, studying the ads and the clothes of the people with the intensity of a general studying battle campaigns. At first he hated the clothes, but by the end of the first magazine he was nodding his head as if he were beginning to understand.

Dougless picked up her Agatha Christie and began to read.

"You will read to me?" he asked.

From the way he merely looked at the pictures of the books and magazines, she thought perhaps he couldn't read. She read aloud to him as he looked at the photos in *Gentleman's Quarterly.*

At seven they opened the bottle of wine and ate cheese and bread and fruit, while Nicholas insisted she read more of the mystery.

As the time flew by, it seemed more and more natural to spend all her time with this gentle man. Watching him look at the world through wonder-filled eyes was a joy to her. With each passing hour, her memory of Robert was becoming less distinct.

When it grew dark, they went upstairs to their room and the intimacy of sharing a room began to dawn on Dougless. But Nicholas didn't allow her to feel awkward. After examining the bath in their room, he demanded to know where the tub was. To Dougless's American delight, there was a shower stall in the bathroom. Before she could get into the room, Nicholas had turned on the taps and sprayed himself with cold water. Laughing, he bent over while she toweled his hair.

She showed him shampoo, cream rinse, and how to brush his teeth. "Tomorrow I'll show you how to shave," she said, smiling at his mouth full of toothpaste lather.

She showered and washed her hair, put on the plain white nightgown she'd bought and slipped into one of the twin beds. She and Nicholas had a somewhat heated "discussion" about his bathing every day. The idea seemed to appall him but at last he gave in. He took a long shower, so hot that steam came rolling from under the door, and he came out wearing only a towel, rubbing his hair with another towel.

There was an awkward moment when he looked up at her, fresh-faced, wet hair slicked back, and Dougless's heart jumped into her throat.

But then Nicholas saw the table lamp, and Dougless spent fifteen minutes demonstrating electric lights. Nicholas nearly drove her crazy with turning switches on and off until, to make him go to bed, she promised to read more to him. She looked away as he dropped his towel and climbed into his own bed. "Pajamas," she murmured. "Tomorrow we buy pajamas."

She read for only about thirty minutes before she realized that he was asleep, and, turning off the light, she snuggled under the covers to go to sleep. She was just dozing off when thrashing from Nicholas made her sit up in alarm. The room was just light enough that she could see him flailing at the covers, rolling back and forth as he moaned in the grip of a nightmare. She put her hand on his shoulder. "Nicholas," she whispered, but he didn't respond, just kept thrashing. She shook his shoulder, but he still didn't wake.

She sat on the edge of the bed and leaned over him. "Nicholas, wake up. You're having a nightmare."

Immediately, his strong arms reached out for her and he pulled her to him.

"Let me go!" she said, struggling against him but he didn't release her.

Instead he calmed his thrashing and seemed to be perfectly content to hold her to him.

Using all her strength, Dougless pried his arms from around her and went back to her own bed. She was no more under the covers than he began thrashing and moaning again. She went back to stand over his bed. "Nicholas, you have to wake up," she said loudly but it had no effect on him.

Sighing in resignation, she pulled back the covers and slipped in beside him. Immediately he clasped her like a scared child with a doll and calmed. Dougless told herself she was a true martyr, that she was doing this for him, but somewhere inside she knew she was as lonely and as scared as he probably was. She put her cheek in the hollow of his warm shoulder and went to sleep.

She woke before dawn, smiling before she woke to feel Nicholas's warm, big body next to hers. Her impulse was to turn in his arms and kiss that warm skin.

She opened her eyes quickly, then eased out of bed and went to her own. She lay there alone and looked at him, sleeping so quietly, black curls on the white pillow case. Was he her own Knight in Shining Armor? Would he eventually get his memory back and realize he had a home somewhere in England? Would he perhaps want her to share that home? What if she had to choose between Robert and this man?

Feeling a bit devilish, she tiptoed out of bed, quietly pulled the new tape recorder from a bag, and took out the Stones tape. Putting it right by Nicholas's head, she put the tape in, turned it up, then pressed PLAY.

Nicholas came bolt upright in bed to the tune of "Can't Get No Satisfaction." Laughing at the expression on his face, Dougless turned it off before she woke the other guests.

Nicholas sat there in shock, his eyes wide. "What chaos was that?"

"Music," Dougless said, laughing, but as he continued to look shocked, she said, "It was a joke. It's time to get up."

He looked at her but said nothing and Dougless quit smiling. She guessed Elizabethan men didn't like practical jokes. Correction: modern men who thought they were Elizabethan men.

It was twenty minutes later that Dougless came sputtering out of the bathroom. "You put shampoo on my toothbrush!"

"I, madam?" Nicholas said, a look of innocence on his face.

"Why, you—" she said and tossed a pillow at him. "I'll get you for this."

"More of your 'music' at dawn?" he said, fending off the pillow.

Dougless laughed. "All right, I guess I deserved it. Are you ready for breakfast?"

At breakfast Dougless told him of his dental appointment, and she saw Nicholas grimace but paid no attention to it. Everyone grimaced at the thought of going to the dentist. While he was eating, she got him to give her the names of some of his other estates, besides Thornwyck, so she could go to the local library and see what she could find out about them, if perhaps some of them were open to the public.

He was quiet as they walked to the dentist and in the waiting room he didn't look at the plastic-covered chairs. Dougless knew he was really worried when he wouldn't even look at the plastic plant she pointed out to him. When the receptionist called him, Dougless squeezed his hand. "You'll be all right. Afterward I'll . . . I'll take you out and buy you ice cream. That's something to look forward to." But she knew he had no idea what ice cream was—didn't remember what ice cream was, she corrected herself.

Since she'd booked him for a checkup, at least one filling and a cleaning, she knew he'd be in there awhile so she asked the receptionist to call her at the library when he was nearly finished.

As she walked to the library, she felt as a mother must feel at having left her child behind. "It's only the dentist," she told herself.

The library was very small, oriented toward children's books and novels for adults. Dougless sat on a stool in the British travel section and began searching for any mention of the eleven estates Nicholas said he'd owned. Four were now ruins, two had been torn down in the 1950s (it made her sick to think they'd survived so long and been torn down so recently), one was Thornwyck, one she couldn't find, two were private residences, and one was open to the public. She copied down the pertinent information about the estate open to the public—hours, days open—and looked at her watch. Nicholas had been in the dentist's an hour and a half now.

She went through the card catalog but could find nothing on the Stafford family. Another forty-five minutes went by.

When the telephone on the desk rang, she jumped. The librarian told Dougless it was the dentist and Nicholas was nearly finished. Dougless practically ran back to the dentist's office.

The dentist came out to greet her and asked her to come to his office. "Mr. Stafford puzzles me," the doctor said and put Nicholas's X-rays on a wall-lit machine. "I usually make it a policy to never give an opinion as to another doctor's work, but as you can see here, Mr. Stafford's previous dental work has been . . . Well, I can only describe it as brutal. The three teeth that have been extracted look as if they were literally torn from his mouth. See, here and here the bone was cracked and grew back crooked. It must have been extremely painful. And too, I know it's impossible but I don't believe Mr. Stafford has ever seen a hypodermic before. Perhaps he was put under when he had those teeth removed."

The doctor turned off the light. "Of course, he *had* to have been put under. In this day and age we can't imagine the pain that extractions such as these must have caused him."

"But it wasn't the case four hundred years ago?"

The doctor laughed. "Four hundred years ago I imagine that everyone had extractions like his—but without anesthetic or pain killers afterward."

"How were his teeth otherwise? How was he as a patient?"

"Excellent on both counts. Very relaxed in the chair, laughed when the hygienist asked if she'd hurt him. I filled one cavity, checked his other teeth." The doctor looked puzzled for a moment. "He has some slight ridging on his teeth. I've only seen that in school textbooks, and it usually means hunger for a year or so as a child. I wonder what could have caused it? He doesn't strike me as a man whose family couldn't afford food."

Drought, Dougless almost said. Or flooding. Something to make the crops fail in a time of no refrigeration or frozen food or fresh food flown in from around the world.

"I didn't mean to keep you," the doctor said. "I was concerned about his previous dental work. He . . ." The doctor chuckled. "He certainly asked a lot of questions. He isn't by chance thinking of going to dental school?"

Dougless smiled. "He's just curious. Thank you so much for your time and your concern."

"I'm glad I had the cancellations. He has a most interesting set of teeth."

Dougless thanked him again and went into the reception room to see Nicholas leaning across the counter, flirting with the pretty receptionist.

"Come on," she snapped at him. Everything and everyone was conspiring against her to force her to believe that this man actually was from the sixteenth century.

"That is not the barber I have been to," Nicholas said, smiling, rubbing his still-numb lip. "I should like to take that man and his machines back with me."

"They're all electric," Dougless said gloomily.

He caught her arm and turned her to face him. "What ails you?"

"Who are you?" she cried. "Why do you have ridges on your teeth? How did your jawbone get cracked when your other teeth were pulled?"

Nicholas smiled at her, as he saw that at last she was beginning to believe him. "I am Nicholas Stafford, Earl of Thornwyck, Buckshire and

Southeaton. Two days ago I was in a cell awaiting my execution and the year was 1564."

"I cannot believe it," Dougless said. "I *will* not believe it. It cannot be true."

"What would make you believe?" he asked softly.

5

As Dougless walked with him toward the ice cream shop, she pondered the question. What *would* make her believe? She could think of nothing. There were explanations for everything. He could be a fabulous actor, merely pretending that everything was new to him. His teeth could have been wrenched out while playing high school football (his being a jock would make sense because he seemed unable to read). Since she could verify everything he'd told her, that meant he could find the information to learn to use in his charade.

So what could he do to prove to her that he was from the past?

In the ice cream parlor she absently ordered herself a single cone of mocha ice cream, and for Nicholas she ordered a double cone of French vanilla and chocolate fudge. She was considering her question so hard that she was startled when he leaned over and kissed her quickly and firmly on the mouth.

Blinking, she looked up at him and saw the look of sublime happiness on his face as he ate his ice cream. Dougless couldn't help laughing.

"Buried treasure," she said at last.

"Mmm?" Nicholas asked, his attention one hundred percent on his ice cream.

"To prove to me that you're from the past you have to know something no one else does. Something that isn't in a book."

"Such as who the father of Lady Sydney's last child was?" He was down to the chocolate scoop and looked as if he might melt from happiness. She ushered him to a table.

Looking at those blue eyes and thick lashes as he licked his cone, she wondered if he looked at a woman like that when he made love to her.

"You gaze at me most hard," he said and looked at her through his lashes.

Dougless cleared her throat and looked away. "I do *not* want to know who fathered Lady Sydney's kid." She didn't look back at Nicholas's laugh.

"Buried treasure," he said as he crunched the cone. "Some hidden valuable that is still there after four hundred and twenty-four years?"

Dougless looked back at him. "It was just a thought." She opened her notebook. "Let me tell you what I found out." She read her notes about his houses.

When she looked up, Nicholas was wiping his hands and frowning. "A man builds so that something of himself lives on. It pleases me not to hear what was mine is gone."

"I thought children were to carry on your name."

"I left no children," he said. "I had a son but he died in a fall the week after my brother drowned."

Dougless watched pain shoot across his face, and suddenly felt how easy and safe the twentieth century was. Sure, America had rapists and mass murderers and drunk drivers, but Elizabethans had plague and leprosy and smallpox. "Have you had smallpox?"

"Neither small nor large," he said with some pride.

"*Large* pox?"

He glanced about the room. "The French disease."

"Oh," she said, understanding. Venereal disease. For some reason she was glad to hear that—not that it mattered, but they did share a bathroom.

"What is this 'open to the public'?" he asked.

"Usually the owners couldn't afford the houses so they gave them to the National Trust and now you pay money and a guide takes you through the house. They're great tours. This one has a tea shop and gift shop and—"

Nicholas suddenly sat up straight. "It is Bellwood that is open?"

She checked her notes. "Yes, Bellwood. Just south of Bath."

Nicholas seemed to be calculating. "With fast horses we can be to Bath in about seven hours."

"With a good English train you can make it in two hours. Would you like to see your house again?"

"See my house sold to a company, with tallow-faced apron-men marching through it?"

Dougless smiled. "If you put it like that . . ."

"Can we go on this . . ."

"Train."

"Train to Bellwood?"

Dougless looked at her watch. "Sure. We can go now, have tea there, and see Bellwood. If you don't want to see the tallow-faced . . ."

"Apron-men," he said, smiling.

"Marching through, then why go?"

"There is a chance, a small chance, that I might give you your buried treasure. When my estates were confiscated by your . . ."—he looked at her mockingly—". . . your Virgin Queen . . ."—he let Dougless know what he thought of the absurdity of that idea— ". . . I do not know if my family was given permission to clear the estates. Perhaps there is a chance . . ."

The idea of an afternoon looking for buried treasure excited Dougless. "What are we waiting for?"

The train system was another thing Dougless loved about England. Nearly every village had a station and—unlike American trains—they were clean, with no graffiti, and well kept. A connecting train to Bath was just about to leave the station when Dougless bought their tickets, not an unusual occurrence since the trains were wonderfully frequent.

Once seated, Nicholas's eyes bulged at the speed of the train. After a few nervous moments, though, like a true Englishman, he adjusted to the speed and began to walk around, studying the ads high up on the walls, pointing out one for Colgate to her as he recognized the toothpaste she'd purchased. Perhaps it wouldn't be so difficult to teach him to read, she thought.

They stopped in Bristol and changed trains. Nicholas was aghast at the number of hurrying people, and he was fascinated with the ornate ironwork of the Victorian station. She purchased a fat guidebook to the castles of southern England and on the ride to Bath started to read to Nicholas about his houses that were now in ruins, but she soon saw that it made him sad, so she stopped.

He looked out the big windows, and now and then would say, "There's William's house," or "Robin lives there," when he saw one of the enormous houses that dotted the English countryside almost as frequently as the cows and sheep.

Bath, beautiful, beautiful Bath was a wonder to Nicholas. To Dougless it was old, since the architecture was all eighteenth century, but to him it was very modern. Dougless thought that New York or Dallas with their steel and glass buildings would look like outer space to him. He would *act* as if they looked weird, she corrected herself.

They had lunch at an American-type sandwich shop and Dougless ordered club sandwiches and potato salad and iced tea for both of them. He thought the meal was tasty but lacking in quantity. Dougless managed to drag him out before he started demanding a boar's head or whatever.

He was so fascinated with Bath that Dougless hated to get a taxi and take him away from the place. But getting into an automobile took Nicholas's mind off the buildings. The taxi drivers in England are a different breed from those in America. English drivers don't yell when someone takes too long to get into a car. Nicholas examined the door, the door lock, opening and closing it three times before getting in, and once in, after examining the back seat, he leaned forward and watched the driver steer and shift gears.

When they arrived at Bellwood, the tour was already started so they had time to walk around the gardens. Dougless thought they were beautiful but Nicholas curled his lip and barely looked at them. He walked around the big, sprawling house and told her what had been added, what had been changed. He thought the additions were architecturally dreadful and minced no words in telling her so.

"Is the treasure buried in the gardens?"

"Ruin a garden by putting gold at the roots of my plants?" he asked, horrified.

"But if you didn't have banks, where did you put your money? Where did *they* put their money, I mean?"

Nicholas clearly didn't understand her question so she dropped it. The gardens seemed to be making him angry so she led him to the gift shop. For a while he was happy in the shop, as he played with pens and plastic change purses and he laughed aloud when he first saw a tiny flashlight with "Bellwood Castle" stamped on it. But he didn't like the postcards and Dougless couldn't figure out what upset him about them.

He looked at the rack of tote bags with silk-screened photos of Bellwood on the front. "You will need one of these." He smiled at her, then leaned forward and whispered, "For the treasure."

Dougless bought the tote bag and the flashlight and wanted to look at the postcards but Nicholas would not let her. He forcibly clamped his strong fingers on her arm and led her away every time she got near the rack.

The next tour was called and he and Dougless, after buying tickets, went into the house with a dozen other tourists. The interior of the house looked like the set for a play about Elizabeth I. It was paneled in dark oak, there were Jacobean chairs about, carved chests, and armor hanging on the wall.

"Is this more like what you're used to?" Dougless whispered up to Nicholas.

There was an expression of disgust on his handsome face, his upper lip curled. "This is not my house. That it should come to this is most unpleasing."

Dougless thought the place was beautiful but didn't say so because the guide had started her lecture. It was her experience that English tour guides were excellent and knew their subject thoroughly. The woman was telling the history of the house, built as a castle in 1302 by the first Stafford.

Nicholas was quiet as she spoke—until she came to Henry the Eighth's time.

"A medieval woman was the chattel of her husband," their guide said, "to be used as her husband saw fit. Women had no power."

Nicholas snorted loudly. "My father told my mother she was his property —once."

"Sssh," Dougless hissed, not wanting to be embarrassed by him.

They moved to another room. The darkness of it was oppressive. "Candles were very expensive," the guide was saying, "so medieval man lived his life in gloom."

Nicholas started to open his mouth but Dougless gouged him in the ribs. "Where's your treasure?" she asked.

"I want to hear how your world thinks of mine," he answered. "Why do your people seem to think we had no mirth?"

"I guess with all the plague and smallpox and trips to the barber to have your teeth torn out, we think there wasn't room for fun."

"We made use of the time we had," he said as the group moved into another room. As soon as they entered, Nicholas opened a door concealed in the paneling and as soon as he did, a loud buzzer went off. Dougless slammed the door shut and gave a weak grin of apology to the tour guide, whose look made her feel like a child with her hand caught in a cookie jar.

"Behave!" Dougless hissed. "If you want to leave I'm ready."

But Nicholas didn't want to leave. He followed the guide through room after room, snorting now and then in derision but saying nothing.

"We now come to our most popular room," the guide said and, by the little smile she gave, her audience knew something amusing was coming up.

Nicholas, being taller, saw into the room before Dougless did. "We will leave now," he said, so stiffly that Dougless very much wanted to see the room.

The guide began to speak. "This was Lord Nicholas Stafford's private chamber and, to put it politely, he's what would be known today as a rake. As you can see, he was a very handsome man."

At that, Dougless pushed her way through the group to the front. There, hanging over the mantle, was a portrait of Lord Nicholas Stafford—her

Nicholas. He was dressed exactly as she'd first beheld him, wearing his beard and mustache, and he was just as handsome then as he was now.

Of course he wasn't the same man, Dougless told herself, but she was willing to admit that he had to be a descendant.

The guide, smiling at what she felt was an amusing story, began to tell of Nicholas's exploits with various ladies. "It was said that no woman could withstand his charms once he set his mind to her, and his enemies were concerned that if he went to court he might seduce the young and beautiful Queen Elizabeth."

Dougless felt Nicholas's fingers biting into her shoulder. "I will take you to the treasure now," he whispered.

She put her fingers to her lips for him to be quiet.

"In 1560," the guide said, "there was a great scandal concerning Lady Arabella Sydney." The guide paused.

"I wish to go now," Nicholas said emphatically into her ear.

Dougless waved him away.

The guide continued. "It was said at the time that Lady Sydney's fourth child was fathered by Lord Nicholas, who was some years younger than she. It was also said . . ."—the guide's voice lowered in conspiracy—". . . that the child was fathered on *that* table."

There was a combined intake of breath as everyone looked at an oak trestle table standing against the wall.

"Furthermore," the guide said, "Lord Nicholas—"

From the back of the room came a very loud buzzer. It went on, then off, on, then off, making it impossible for the guide to continue speaking.

"Would you mind!" the guide said, but the buzzer kept going on and off.

Dougless didn't have to look to see who was opening and closing the alarmed door—or why he was doing it. She began to make her way to the back of the group.

"I'm going to have to ask you to leave," the guide said sternly. "You can go out the way you came."

Dougless grabbed Nicholas's arm and pulled him away from the buzzing door and back through two rooms.

"What trivial knowledge is remembered through these hundreds of years," Nicholas said in anger.

Dougless looked up at him with interest. "Is it *true?*" she asked. "About Lady Sydney? About the *table.*"

He frowned at her. "Nay, madam, nonesuch happened on that table." He turned on his heel and started walking away as Dougless smiled and somehow felt relieved. "I gave the true table to Arabella," he said over his shoulder.

Dougless gasped as she watched him walk away, then hurriedly followed him. "You impregnated—" she began but he halted and looked down his nose at her. He had a way of looking at a person that made her believe he was an earl.

"We will see if these sottish people have violated my cabinet," he said, turning away from her again.

Dougless had to nearly run to cover the distance his long legs were eating up. "You can't go in there," she said as he put his hand on a door that had a NO ADMITTANCE sign on it. But Nicholas ignored her and Dougless held her breath, waiting for a buzzer to go off. When none did, tentatively, she followed him, expecting to walk into a room full of secretaries at typewriters.

But there were no secretaries, nor any people at all. There were just boxes stacked to the ceiling, and from the lettering they looked to be full of paper napkins and other items for the tearoom. Behind the boxes was beautiful paneling that Dougless thought was a shame to hide.

She followed Nicholas through three more rooms and got to see the difference between restored and unrestored. The rooms not open to the public had broken fireplaces, missing paneling, painted ceilings spoiled by a leaky roof. In one room some Victorian had put wallpaper over carved oak panels and Dougless could see where workmen were painstakingly removing it.

At last Nicholas led her to a small room off a larger one. Here the ceiling had leaked and the wide floorboards looked to be dangerously rotten. She stayed in the doorway, and Nicholas sadly looked about the room.

"This was my brother's room, and I was here but a fortnight ago," he said softly, then shrugged as if to block the regret from his mind. He walked across the rotten boards and went to the paneling and pushed at it. Nothing happened.

"The lock has rusted," he said, "or someone has sealed it shut."

Suddenly, he seemed to become enraged and began hammering on the paneling with both fists.

Dougless ran to him and, not knowing what else to do, she clasped him in her arms and stroked his hair. "Sssh," she whispered as she would to a child.

He clung to her, held her so tightly she could barely breathe. "It was my intent to be remembered for my learning," he said against her neck, and there were tears in his voice. "I have commissioned monks to copy hundreds of books. I began building Thornwyck. I have . . . Had. It is done now."

"Sssh," Dougless soothed, holding his broad shoulders.

He pushed away, turning his back to her, and Dougless saw him wipe away tears. "They remember a moment on a table with Arabella," he said.

He looked back at her and his face was fierce. "But if I had lived . . . ," he said. "If I had but lived I would have changed all. I must find out what my mother knew, the knowledge she believed would clear my name and save me from execution. And I must return."

Dougless looked at him and knew then that he was telling the truth. It was the way she felt about her family. She didn't want to be remembered for all the idiot things she'd done, she wanted to be remembered for things like, last summer, volunteering to help children who couldn't read. She'd spent three days a week at the center with children who, for the most part, had had very little kindness in their lives.

"We'll find out," she said softly. "If the information still exists today, we'll find it and when we have the information I'm sure you'll be sent back."

"You know how to do this?" he asked.

"No. Maybe it'll just happen once you know what you were sent here to find out."

He was frowning, but his frown changed to a smile. "You do not tell me I am lying?"

"I guess not. Nobody can act as well as you can." She didn't want to think about what she was saying. A sixteenth-century man could not come forward in time, but then again . . .

"Look," she said and touched the section of paneling he had been pounding. A little door stood open about an inch.

Nicholas pulled the door open. "My father told only my brother of this place, and Kit showed me but a week before he died. I told no one."

She watched as he stuck his hand in the hole and pulled out a roll of yellowed, brittle papers.

Nicholas's face was filled with consternation. "I but put these in here a few days ago."

Dougless took the papers and unrolled them a bit. They were covered top to bottom, side to side, no margins, with writing that was incomprehensible to her. "Can you read this?"

"I would hope so as I wrote it," he said, looking further into the hole. "Ah, here is your treasure." He handed Dougless a small yellow-white box, beautifully carved with figures of people and animals.

"This is ivory?" she said in wonder as she took the box. She had seen things like this in museums but she had never touched one. "It is beautiful. It is a wonderful treasure."

Nicholas laughed. "The treasure lies inside. But wait," he said as Dougless began to open the lid. "I find I am in need of sustenance." He took the box from her, opened the tote bag she'd purchased, and slipped the box inside.

"You're going to make me wait until you've *eaten* before I can see what's inside that box?" She was incredulous.

Nicholas laughed. "It pleases me to see the nature of woman has not changed these four hundred years."

She gave him a smug look. "Don't get too smart—or did you forget that I have your return train ticket?"

His faced changed to softness, and he looked at her through his lashes in a way that made Dougless's heart beat a little faster. He stepped forward; she stepped back.

"You have heard," he said, his voice low, "that no woman can withstand me."

Dougless was backed against the wall, her heart pounding in her ears as he looked down at her. He put his fingertips under her chin and lifted her face up. Was he going to kiss her, she thought, half in outrage, half in anticipation. Her eyes closed.

"I shall seduce my way back to the hotel," he said in a different tone that told Dougless he was teasing.

Her eyes flew open and she straightened up as he chucked her under the chin as a father might do—or as the gorgeous private eye might do to his soppy secretary.

"But women today are not as they were in my day," he said, shutting the little secret door. "This is the day of women's . . ."

"Lib," she answered. "Liberation." She was thinking about Lady Arabella on the table.

He looked back at her. "I would not be able to charm a woman such as you. You have told me that you love . . . ?"

"Robert. Yes, I do. Maybe when I get back to the States we can work things out. Or maybe when he gets my message about the bracelet he'll come for me." She wanted to remember Robert. Compared to this man, Robert seemed safe.

"Ah," Nicholas said, starting for the door.

"Just what is that supposed to mean?"

"No more, no less."

She blocked him from leaving the room. "If you want to say something, say it."

"This Robert will come for jewels but not for the woman he loves?"

"Of course he's coming for me!" she snapped. "The bracelet is . . . It's just that Gloria is a brat and she's lied and of course Robert believes her. Stop looking at me like that! Robert is a fine man. At least he'll be remembered for what he did on an operating table instead of on a—" She stopped at the look on Nicholas's face.

He pushed past her and strode ahead.

"Nicholas, I'm sorry," she said, running after him. "I didn't mean it. I was just angry, that's all. It's not your fault you're remembered for Arabella, it's *our* fault. Too much TV. Too much *National Enquirer*. Too much sensationalism. Colin, please." She stopped where she was. Was he going to walk away and leave her too?

Her head was down and she didn't hear him come back to her. Companionably, he put his arm around her shoulders. "Do they sell ice cream in this place?"

She laughed at that and he tipped her chin up and wiped away a single tear. "Are you onion-eyed again?" he asked.

She shook her head, afraid to trust her voice.

"Then come," he said. "If I remember rightly there is a pearl in that box as big as my thumb."

"Really?" she asked. She had forgotten all about the box. "And what else?"

"Tea first," he said. "Tea and scones and ice cream. Then I shall show you the box."

They walked together out of the unrestored rooms, past the next tour, and out the in door, which the guides did not like at all.

In the tea shop Nicholas took over. Dougless sat at a table and waited for him as he talked to a woman behind the counter. The woman was shaking her head about something Nicholas was asking, but Dougless had an idea he'd get whatever it was he wanted.

In minutes he motioned for her to come with him. He led her out and down stone stairs, across gardens to at last stop under the dappled shade of a yew tree with its bright red berries. When Dougless stopped and turned around, she saw a woman and a man carrying two large trays filled with tea and pastries and little sandwiches with no crusts and Nicholas's beloved scones.

Nicholas ignored them as they spread a cloth on the ground and set out the tea things. "There was my knot garden," he said, pointing, his voice heavy with sadness. "And there was a mound."

When the people left, Nicholas held out his hand to help her sit on the cloth. She poured his tea, added milk, filled a plate full of food for him, then said, "Now?"

He smiled. "Now."

Dougless dove into the tote bag and pulled out the old, fragile ivory box, then slowly, breath held, opened it.

On top were two rings of exquisite loveliness, one an emerald, one a ruby, the gold mountings cast into intricate forms of dragons and snakes. Nicholas took the rings and, smiling at her, slipped them on his fingers where they fit perfectly.

On the bottom of the box was a bit of velvet that was old and cracked, and in it was wrapped something. Gingerly, Dougless removed the velvet and slowly opened it.

In her hand lay a brooch, oval, with little gold figures of . . . She looked up at Nicholas. "What are they doing?"

"It's the martyrdom of St. Barbara," he said, as if she knew nothing.

Dougless thought it was something like that, because it looked like the gold man was about to cut the head off the gold woman. Encircling the figures was an abstract design of enamels and around the edges were tiny pearls and diamonds. Hanging from a loop below the brooch was indeed a pearl as large as a man's thumb. It was a baroque pearl, indented, even lumpy, but with a luster that no years could dim.

"It is lovely," she whispered.

"It is yours," Nicholas said.

A wave of covetousness shot through Dougless. "I cannot," she said, even as her hand closed over the jewel.

Nicholas laughed. "It is a woman's bauble. You may keep it."

"I cannot. It's too valuable. It's worth too much. It should be in a museum. It should—"

He took the jewel from her hand and pinned it in the middle of her blouse, just below the collar.

Dougless took her compact from her purse, opened the mirror and looked. She also looked at her face. "I have to go to the rest room," she said, making Nicholas laugh as she rose.

Alone in the rest room she had some time to look at the pin and only stopped when someone else came in. On her way back to Nicholas, she stopped in the gift shop and looked at the post cards. It took her a moment to see what Nicholas had not wanted her to see. There on the bottom was a post card of the notorious Lady Arabella. Dougless took one.

As she was paying, she asked the cashier if there was anything in any of the books for sale about Nicholas Stafford.

The woman smiled in a patronizing way. "All the young ladies ask after him. We usually have cards of his portrait but we're out right now."

"There's nothing written about him? About his accomplishments other than . . . than the women?"

"I don't believe he accomplished anything except to raise an army against the queen and he was sentenced to be executed for that. If he hadn't died he would have been beheaded. Quite a scoundrel of a young man."

Dougless took the single post card and started to leave, but turned back. "What happened to Lord Nicholas's mother after he died?"

The woman brightened. "Lady Margaret? Now there was a lady. Let me see, I believe she married again. What was his name? Oh yes, Harewood. Lord Richard Harewood."

"Do you know if she left any papers behind?"

"Oh my, no, I have no idea of that."

"All the Stafford papers are at Goshawk Hall," came a voice from the door. It was the guide whose tour she and Nicholas had so rudely interrupted.

"Where is Goshawk Hall?" Dougless asked, feeling embarrassed.

"Near the village of Thornwyck," the woman said.

"Thornwyck," Dougless said and nearly gave a whoop of joy but caught herself. It was all she could do to thank the women and run from the shop to the garden where Nicholas lay stretched on the cloth, sipping tea and finishing the scones.

"Your mother married Richard, ah . . . Harewood," she said breathlessly, "and all the papers are at . . ." She couldn't remember the name.

"Goshawk Hall?" he asked.

"Yes, that's it! It's near Thornwyck."

He turned his face away from her. "My mother married Harewood?"

Dougless looked at his back, and wondered what he was thinking. If he'd died accused of treason, had his mother, in her poverty, been forced to marry some despicable despot? Had his old, frail mother been forced to endure some man who treated her as his property?

When Nicholas's shoulders began to shake, Dougless put her hand on one. "Nicholas, it's not your fault. You were dead, you couldn't help her." *What* am I saying? she thought.

But Nicholas turned around and he was . . . laughing. "I should have known she would land on her feet," he said. "Dickie Harewood." He could hardly speak for laughing so hard.

"Tell me," Dougless urged.

"Dickie Harewood is a tardy-gaited, unhaired pajock."

Dougless frowned, not understanding.

"An ass, madam," Nicholas explained. "But a rich one. Aye, very rich." He leaned back, smiling. "It is good to know she was not left one-trunk-inheriting."

Still smiling, he poured Dougless a cup of tea, and as she took it, he picked up her little paper bag and opened it.

"No—" she began, but he was already looking at the post card of Lady Arabella.

He looked up at her with such a knowing look that she wanted to dump the tea over his head. "Did they not have a picture of the table too?" he mocked.

"I have no idea what you mean," she said haughtily, not looking at him. "The card is for research. It might help us . . ." She couldn't think what a picture of the mother of Nicholas's illegitimate child might help them find out. "Did you eat all the scones? You really can be a pig somctimes."

Nicholas gave a snort of laughter.

After a moment he said, "What say you we stay in this town this night? On the morrow I shall purchase Armant and Rafe."

It took Dougless a moment to understand what he meant, but then she remembered the American magazines he'd seen. "Giorgio Armani and Ralph Lauren?" she asked.

"Aye," he said. "Clothing of your time. When I return to Thornwyck I will not be one-trunk-inheriting either."

Dougless bit into a little sandwich. Unless she found Robert and her clothes soon, she would have to buy more clothes too.

She looked at Nicholas, his hands behind his head. Tomorrow shopping, the next day to Thornwyck, where they'd try to discover who had betrayed him to the queen.

But tonight, she thought. Tonight they'd once again spend alone in a hotel room.

6

Dougless sat in the back of the big taxi, luggage all around her. This is where I came in, she thought, remembering being in the back of Robert's car and trying to get comfortable around Gloria's luggage. But now, sprawled beside her, his long legs stretched out, was Nicholas. He was absorbed in a battery-powered video game they'd purchased this morning.

Dougless put her head back, closed her eyes, and thought about the last few hours. After tea at Bellwood yesterday, she had called a taxi and asked to be taken to a nice hotel in Bath. The driver took them to a lovely eighteenth-century building and Dougless was able to get a double room for the night. Neither she nor Nicholas mentioned asking for separate rooms. It was a beautiful room done in yellow chintz, with flowered wallpaper and flowered bedspreads on the two beds. Nicholas ran his hand over the wallpaper and vowed that when he got home he was going to have someone paint the walls of his house with lilies and roses.

After they checked in, they went walking to look in the windows of the wonderful shops in Bath. It was near dinnertime when Dougless saw a movie house called the American Cinema.

"We could always go to a movie and eat hot dogs and popcorn," she said, making a joke.

But Nicholas was intrigued and started asking questions, so Dougless bought tickets. She thought it was a bit ironic that an "American" Cinema was playing an English movie—*A Room with a View*—but they did have American hot dogs, popcorn, Cokes and Reece's Peanut Butter Cups. Knowing Nicholas's appetite, Dougless bought some of everything and they could hardly waddle down the aisle for the load they were carrying.

Nicholas loved the popcorn, choked on the Coke, thought the hot dog had possibilities, and nearly cried in delight over the peanut butter and chocolate. Dougless talked to him and tried to explain what a movie was and how very large the people were, but he was too interested in what was going on in his mouth to listen much.

He was fascinated when the lights went down, then nearly jumped out of his seat when the music came on. At the first sight of the enormous people, the expression on his face was so horrified that Dougless choked on her popcorn.

Throughout the film, watching Nicholas was much more interesting than watching the movie—which Dougless had already seen twice anyway.

When it was over, as they walked back to the hotel, he was full of questions. He'd been so enamored with the technical aspect of the movie that he could hardly follow the story. Also, he couldn't understand the clothes. It took some explaining to make him understand that Edwardian was "old."

Later, in the hotel, the only toiletries they had were what Dougless had in her purse and the little basket in the hotel, so they shared a toothbrush. Dougless meant to sleep in her underwear so, after a shower, she wrapped herself in the robe supplied by the hotel. She meant to go to bed but Nicholas wanted her to read to him, so she took her Agatha Christie from her purse and sat in a chair by him and read until he fell asleep.

Before she turned out the light, she stood over him, looking down at his soft black hair against the crisp white sheets and on impulse lightly kissed his forehead. "Good night, my prince," she whispered.

To her embarrassment, Nicholas clasped her fingers. "I am but a mere earl," he said softly, not opening his eyes, "but my thankings for the tribute."

Smiling, she pulled away from him and went to her own bed. She lay awake for a long while, listening carefully for any sounds from him, wondering if he'd have bad dreams as he had the night before. But he was utterly silent and at last she drifted off. When she awoke it was morning and he was already up and in the bathroom. Her first feeling was one of disappointment that she had not slept cuddled in his arms, but she reprimanded herself. She was in love with Robert, not a man who might or might not be crazy, but crazy or not, he was not hers. At any minute he could go up in a puff of smoke, leaving as quickly as he had arrived.

He came out of the bathroom, barefoot, bare-chested, wearing only his trousers and toweling his wet hair. There were much worse sights in the morning than the broad, nude chest of a beautiful man. Dougless lay back against the pillows and sighed.

At her sigh, Nicholas looked up and frowned. "Do you waste the day? We must find me a barber to shave this." He ran his hand over the black stubble.

"It's quite fashionable now," she said, but he wouldn't hear of going unshaved. In the end, she used the razor and a tiny can of lather furnished by the hotel and showed him how to shave. Before she could stop him, he ran his fingertips over the blade and sliced them. He laughed at Dougless for the to-do she made over such a little cut.

Dressed, fortified with a hearty English breakfast, they went shopping. Dougless was becoming accustomed to helping Nicholas do the most ordinary of things, but when it came to his clothes he knew exactly what he wanted. Dougless was amazed at how much he'd learned from an evening of looking at fashion magazines.

Nicholas the earl took over and Dougless merely stood in the background and watched. The English clerks seemed to recognize they were dealing with aristocracy, because it was "Yes, Sir" and "No, Sir" to him right and left.

Around Dougless's feet were piled big shopping bags filled with shirts, trousers, socks, belts, a marvelous coat of waxed cloth, caps, two Italian silk jackets, a luscious leather jacket, ties, even black evening clothes. As they were leaving the fifth store, Dougless rather audibly suggested that Nicholas help her carry some of the bags. He shot her a look of disdain and disbelief. A moment later he gave a piercing whistle and a taxi stopped. He learns quickly, Dougless thought. Nicholas arranged for the taxi to follow them the rest of the morning, as he purchased clothes and Dougless paid for them and hauled them out to the taxi.

At one o'clock she was wilted and ready to suggest lunch when he stopped before a lovely window display of women's clothes. He looked at the display, then at Dougless, and half-shoved her into the shop. It was amazing how quickly her energy revived. Nicholas was as generous as he was good at choosing clothing. She left within the hour with a dark green wool challis skirt, a matching wool jacket, and a cream silk blouse.

There was only one more stop to make and that was for shoes. Nicholas had come to love the comfort of modern clothes but hated the hard leather of modern shoes. The shoes he liked best were soft leather bedroom slippers. But after three stores Dougless persuaded him to purchase two pairs of Italian shoes that were frightfully expensive. He insisted she buy a pair of soft green leather boots to go with her new clothes.

They made one more stop for luggage to pack everything into. Nicholas
wanted leather luggage but there was little money left so Dougless talked
him into some blue canvas bags with leather trim.

By the time they were done shopping it was three P.M. and all the lunch
shops were closed. They purchased bread and cheese and meat pies and a
bottle of wine and ate in the back of the taxi as it drove them back to the
bed and breakfast. (Eating while traveling was something altogether new to
Nicholas.) Dougless had said they should go by train but Nicholas scoffed at
her idea that *he* handle luggage, so they were being driven all the way back
to the hotel.

On the trip Nicholas got his first sight of the six-lane English motorways.
She didn't know how he felt about the speed but it terrified her. The slow
lane traveled at seventy miles per hour so she couldn't imagine what the fast
outside lane was doing.

After a while he stopped staring at the trucks and asking questions and
settled back against the seat and played with the little video game she'd
bought for him. She thought of all the many things there were for him to
see and do yet. There were VCR's TV's, Ferris wheels, airplanes, space
rockets. There was all of America: Maine with its boats, the South which
would have to be experienced to be believed, the Southwest with its cowboys and Indians, California with . . . She smiled, thinking of Hollywood
and Venice Beach. She could take him to the Pacific Northwest for salmon,
to ski in Colorado, to a roundup in Texas. She could—

They arrived back at their little bed and breakfast before she could think
of all the things she'd like to show him, and before she remembered that he
was only temporarily with her. But then he was *her* Knight in Shining
Armor, wasn't he? Maybe he wouldn't return.

Nicholas directed the taxi driver in removing the many bags from the
back and setting them in the entryway, while Dougless paid the driver with
the last of the money from the sale of the coins. While she was figuring out
the tip, the landlady came hurrying down the steps.

"He's been here all day, miss," she said. "He came this morning and
hasn't left since. He's in an awful mood, said some terrible things. I thought
you and Mr. Stafford were married."

Dougless began to get a sinking feeling in her stomach and she immediately thought of her Librax. She hadn't needed any in days. "Who is here?"
she asked softly.

"Robert Whitley," the landlady said.

"Alone?"

"There's a young lady with him."

Dougless nodded and, with her stomach beginning to hurt more with each step, she went up the stairs to the entryway. Nicholas was busy ordering the taxi driver about, but he stopped when he saw Dougless's face. Calmly, she paid the driver, saying not a word, then went to the parlor where Robert and Gloria waited.

"At last," Robert said when Dougless entered. "We have been waiting the entire day. Where is it?"

She knew what he meant, but she refused to let him know she did. Hadn't he missed her at all? "Where is what?"

"The bracelet you stole!" Gloria said. "That's why you pushed me down in that graveyard, so you could take my bracelet."

"I did no such thing," Dougless said. "You fell against the—"

Robert put his arm around Dougless and cut her off. "Look, we didn't come here to quarrel. Gloria and I have missed you." He gave a little laugh. "Oh, you should see us. We get lost every few minutes. Neither one of us is good with a road map and we can't figure out the hotels at all. You were always so good at figuring out schedules and whether a hotel had room service or not."

Dougless wasn't sure whether to feel elated or dejected. He wanted her but only to read the road maps and order room service for the two of them.

Robert kissed her cheek. "I know you didn't steal the bracelet. It was just lucky that you found it."

Gloria started to speak, but Robert gave her a look to be quiet and that look made Dougless feel better. Maybe he was going to force his daughter to show her some respect. Maybe—

"Please, Lessa," Robert said, nuzzling her ear, "please come back with us. You can sit in the front half the time, and Gloria half the time. That's fair, isn't it?"

She wasn't sure what to do. Robert was being so nice, and it was wonderful to hear his apology and to think that he needed her.

"Well, madam," Nicholas said, striding into the room, "do you mean to unkiss our bargain?"

Robert jumped away from Dougless and immediately she was aware of hatred coming from him, a hatred directed toward Nicholas. Was Robert jealous? He'd never before evidenced any sign of jealousy for another man —just her time. He didn't want Dougless to spend time on anything else but him.

"Who is this?" Robert asked.

"Well, madam?" Nicholas asked.

Dougless felt like running from the room and never seeing either man again.

"Who *is* this?" Robert demanded. "Have you obtained a . . . a lover in the few days since you left me?"

"Left *you?*" Dougless said. "You left me and took my purse. You left me without money, credit cards or—"

Robert waved his hand in dismissal. "That was a mistake. Gloria picked up your purse for you. She was helping you. She had no idea you'd decide to remain here and refuse to travel with us. Isn't that right, sweetheart?"

"Helping me?" Dougless gasped. "I *decided* to remain here?"

"Dougless," Robert said, "do we have to discuss our very private problems in front of this stranger? We have your suitcase in the car. Let's go." He took her arm and started to lead her away.

Nicholas stood in the doorway, looking at her. "Do you mean to leave me?" he asked, anger in his voice. "Do you mean to go with this man who wants you for the service you do him?"

"I . . . I . . ." Dougless said, feeling confused. Both of these men were familiar to her. Robert wanted her to read road maps; Nicholas wanted her to help him research. Both men wanted her for what she could *do* for them. She didn't know what to do.

Nicholas decided for her. "This woman has been hired by me," he said. "Until I have done with her services she will remain with me." At that he clamped his hand on Robert's shoulder and began pushing him toward the door.

"Get your hands off me!" Robert shouted. "You can't treat me like this, I'll have the police on you. Gloria, call the police! Dougless, either you come with me *now* or you'll never get a marriage proposal out of me. You'll never—" His last words were cut off as Nicholas shut the door behind him.

Dougless sat on a chair, her head down.

Nicholas returned, took one look at Gloria, and said, "Out!"

Gloria ran for the doorway, then pounded down the front stairs.

Nicholas went to the window and looked out. "They are gone now and they have left your capcases on the ground. We are well rid of them."

Dougless didn't look up. How did she get herself in these messes? She couldn't even go away on a vacation without something awful happening to her. Why couldn't she have a normal, ordinary relationship with a man? Wouldn't it be nice to meet a man in a classroom somewhere, go on simple dates with him to a movie or to play miniature golf? Perhaps after a few dates he'd propose marriage over a bottle of wine. They'd have a nice wedding, a nice house, two nice kids. Her whole life would be simple and ordinary.

Instead, she met guys who had been in jail or were about to be taken off to jail, guys who were ruled by their obnoxious daughters or guys from the sixteenth century. She didn't know any other woman who had as much trouble with men as she did.

"What is wrong with me?" she whispered, burying her face in her hands.

Nicholas knelt before her and pulled her hands away. "I find I am most tired. Come upstairs and read to me that I may rest."

Like a dumb animal, she let Nicholas take her hand and lead her upstairs. But once upstairs he didn't expect her to read to him. Instead he told her to stretch out on the bed, which she did, and he began to sing to her. It was a soft, sweet lullaby that she doubted anyone else in this century had ever heard before. She drifted off into sleep.

Nicholas leaned back against the headboard and when she was asleep he stroked her hair. God, but how much he wanted to touch her! He wanted to put his hands in her thick, gloriously red hair. He wanted to run his hands over her pale skin, feel those legs of hers wrapped around him. He wanted to kiss away her tears, then kiss her mouth, wanted to kiss her all over until she smiled and laughed and was happy.

She slept bonelessly, like a child, and there was a catch in her breathing as if she'd been weeping. He'd never seen a woman cry as often as she did. He'd never seen any woman who was at all like her. She wanted love so much.

He had asked her about marriage in this strange new world, and the answers did not please him. Marriages should be a contract, made for alliances, made to breed an heir. But it seemed that in this new century marriage partners chose each other for love.

Love! Nicholas thought. It was a waste of a man's energy. He had seen men who lost all because of the "love" of some woman.

He touched Dougless's temple, stroked the soft hair there and looked down at her beautiful body of full breasts and slim legs. Look what this girl had suffered for "love." Nicholas thought of what his mother would have said to the idea of marrying for love. Lady Margaret Stafford had had four husbands and never considered loving any of them.

But as Nicholas looked down at this modern woman, he felt a softness in his heart that he'd never felt before. She wore her heart on the outside of her body, ready to give it to anyone who was kind to her. As far as he could tell, she had no ulterior motives for the help she gave, for the warmth she gave.

He put his hand to her cheek and in her sleep she snuggled her face against his hand.

What bond had brought them together? What bond held them? He had not told her as she did not seem to experience it, but he could feel her pain. From the first, when she felt pain, so did he. That first day, outside the church, she had made what he now knew was a telephone call to her sister. He had no idea what she was doing but he'd sensed that she was hurt.

Today he'd been in the hall directing the driver with the bags when he sensed the great despair of her. His first sight of the lover who had abandoned her was such a shock to him that he had had difficulty understanding the words.

At first his only reaction was that Dougless was going to leave him. How would he find the key to returning if she left him? What would he do without her?

It was still difficult for him to understand the modern speech, but he understood that her ex-lover wanted her to go with him and Dougless was having difficulty deciding what to do. Nicholas reacted out of a primitive instinct and threw the man out. How could Dougless consider leaving with a man who gave his daughter precedence over a woman? If for no other reason, Dougless deserved respect because she was older. What manner of country was this that worshipped children to the extent that they were treated as royalty?

Now Nicholas touched her shoulder, ran his hand down Dougless's arm. Three days, he thought. Three days ago he had never seen her before and now he found himself doing whatever he could to make her smile. She was so easy to please: a kind word, a gift, a smile.

He leaned over and softly kissed her hair. The woman needed caring for, needed someone to watch over her. She was like a rosebud that needed a little sunshine to make it open into a full blossom. She needed . . .

Abruptly, Nicholas pulled away from her and went to stand by the window. He could not let himself become over-concerned with her needs. Even if he could somehow take her back with him he could do no more than make her his mistress. He gave a one-sided smile. He did not think the soft Dougless would make a very good mistress. She would never ask her master for a thing, and what she had she'd give to any child who had no shoes.

There was more to this twentieth century that he did not understand than machines that produced light and pictures. He did not understand their philosophy. Yesterday he had seen an outrageous thing called a movie. It had taken him some time to be able to see it—it was so large—and the concept of flat giants who looked so round was difficult for him to understand. Dougless had told him they were normal size but like a person could be drawn small, one could be photographed large. After he got over his horror of the pictures themselves, he found he did not understand the story. A young girl was to marry a perfectly suitable man of means, but she had thrown him over for a penniless young man who had nothing more than a fine pair of legs.

Afterward, Dougless had told him she thought the story "wonderful" and "romantic." He did not understand this philosophy. If his mother had had a daughter and that daughter had refused to honor a good marriage contract, Lady Margaret would have beaten the girl until she grew tired, then she would have directed the strongest groom to beat the girl. But in this age disobedience in children seemed to be encouraged.

He looked back at her, asleep on the bed, her knees tucked up, her hand under her face.

If he remained in this age, he thought, then perhaps he could remain with her. It would be pleasant to live with such a soft female, a woman who asked if he wanted a pillow—a woman who held him when his dreams were bad. A woman who did not want him because he was an earl or because he had money. Life with her could be pleasant.

No! he thought and turned away from her to look out the window. He thought back to that hideous beldame at Bellwood, that hag who laughed at the memory of Nicholas Stafford. If he remained with Dougless, he would never change how he was remembered. The woman at Bellwood had said that after Nicholas's death, Queen Elizabeth had taken the Stafford estates and later most of them were destroyed in the Civil War. Only four of his many estates now remained.

Honor, Nicholas thought. People of this age seemed to think little of honor. Dougless did not really understand what he meant by honor. She thought the story of Lady Arabella was amusing. The idea of a man being executed for treason did not bother her. "It was so long ago," she'd said.

It wasn't long ago to Nicholas. To him it was a mere three days ago.

This thing that had happened to him had happened for a reason. God was giving him a second chance. Somewhere in this century was the answer to the question of who had hated him enough to want him killed. Who benefited by his death? Who had the queen's ear so completely that she would believe anything said by this person?

Nothing had come out at his trial. The facts were that he had raised an army and he had not sought the queen's permission. Men came from Wales to swear that they had asked for troops but the judges would not listen.

They swore they had "secret" evidence that told that Nicholas was planning to overthrow the queen and return England to the Catholic religion.

Nicholas had been condemned to death, and he had believed that was his fate until his mother sent a message saying that she had found new evidence and soon the truth would be known. Soon Nicholas would be a free man.

But before he could find out what the evidence was, he'd "died." At least that is what history wrote of him. An ignoble death to be sure. Found slumped over an unfinished letter.

Why hadn't his mother brought the evidence forth after his death and cleared his name? Instead, she had relinquished all control over the Stafford estates and married a fat-brain like Dickie Harewood.

There were so many questions to be answered. So much injustice to correct. So much honor at stake.

He had been called forward to this time to discover what he needed to know and he had been given this lovely young woman to assist him. He looked back at her and smiled. Would he have been so generous if she had come to him and told him she was from the future? He thought not. He would have lit the fires that burned her as a witch.

But she had devoted all her time to him, albeit reluctantly at first. It was not in her nature to be ungenerous.

And now she was falling in love with him. He could see it in her eyes. In his time, when a woman started to love him, he left her. Women who loved you were an annoyance. He much preferred women such as Arabella, who liked jewels or a fine piece of silk. He and Arabella understood each other. There was only sex between them.

But that was not the way with this Dougless. She would be one to give love, and to love with all her being. That man Robert had had some of her love, but he was too stupid to know what to do with it. He used Dougless, played with her love and made her miserable.

Nicholas took a step toward her. If he, Nicholas, had her love he would know what to do with it. He would—

No! he told himself and looked away. He could not let her love him. When he left she would be overcome with grief. Nicholas would not like to return and think of her here alone, think of her loving a man who'd been dead over four hundred years.

He had to find a way to make her stop loving him. He needed her knowledge of this foreign world; he could not let her go. But neither could he leave her behind in misery. He had to find a way to stop her love, and it had to be a way she could understand, a way that related to her world.

Smiling at the absurdity of the idea, Nicholas thought he could tell her he was in love with another woman. That usually set women off. But who? Arabella? He almost laughed aloud when he thought of the post card Dougless had bought. Perhaps a woman she'd not heard of would be better. Alice? Elizabeth? Jane? Ah, sweet, sweet Jane.

He stopped smiling. What about Lettice?

In love with his *wife?*

Nicholas hadn't thought of that cold-eyed bitch in weeks. When he had been arrested for treason, Lettice had started looking for a new husband.

Could he make Dougless believe he was in love with his wife? That movie had shown people marrying for love. Perhaps if he told Dougless he wanted to go back because he loved his wife so much . . . He could not believe Dougless would consider love more important than honor, but this age seemed very strange to him.

Now all he had to do was find a place and time to tell her.

He had made his decision but it didn't make him feel better. Quietly, he left the room. He'd go to the coin dealer and see about selling the coins. Tomorrow they would go to Thornwyck and start finding the answers to his questions.

With one last look at Dougless he left the room.

◇ ◇ ◇

Dougless awoke with a start and when she saw she was alone, a sense of panic gripped her, but she calmed herself. The scene with Robert came back to her. Had she done the right thing? Should she have gone with him? After all, Robert did apologize—sort of. He'd explained why he'd left her: he thought she was refusing to travel with him, and maybe Gloria *had* picked up her purse innocently.

Dougless put her hands to her head. Everything was so confusing to her. What did she mean to Robert? To Nicholas? What did these men mean to her? Why had Nicholas come to *her?* Why not to someone else? Someone who wasn't confused about everything in her life?

The door opened and Nicholas came in smiling. "I have sold but a few of the coins and we are rich!" he said.

She smiled back and remembered the way he'd pushed Robert out the door. Was this man her Knight in Shining Armor? Was he sent to her because she just plain needed him so much?

Her look seemed to annoy Nicholas for he turned away, frowning. "Shall we have supper?" he asked.

They went to an Indian restaurant and Nicholas loved the flavors of the cumin, coriander, garam masala, cinnamon. He had almost mastered the use of the fork, and Dougless saw envious looks from several women at nearby tables. She asked him about his life in 1564 and how the twentieth century was different from the sixteenth.

He talked but Dougless didn't really listen. Instead she looked at his eyes and his hair, at the way his hands moved. He wasn't going to return, she thought. She'd wished him forward and he'd come to her. He was the man she'd always wanted: kind, thoughtful, funny, strong, decisive, a man who knew what he wanted.

By the end of dinner, Nicholas had grown quiet and something seemed to be worrying him. They were silent as they walked back to the bed and breakfast. Nor did he seem to want to talk once they were in their room, nor did he want Dougless to read to him. He went to bed and turned away from her without so much as a goodnight.

Dougless lay awake for a long time, trying to puzzle out what had happened to her in the last few days. She had cried and begged for a Knight in Shining Armor and Nicholas had come to her. He was hers and she meant to keep him.

Near midnight she was startled by sounds from Nicholas. She smiled, knowing he was again having a bad dream. Still smiling, she went to him and climbed in bed beside him. At once he clasped her in his arms and slept peacefully. Dougless snuggled close, her cheek on his furred chest and contentedly went to sleep. Let what happens, happen, she thought.

When Nicholas awoke it was just daylight and when he realized Dougless was in his arms, he knew his dreams had come true. She fit his body as if they were carved from one piece of earth. What was the word she used? Telepathy. There was a feeling between them, a deep, deep bond that he'd never come close to feeling with another woman.

He put his face in her hair and breathed deeply and his hands began to touch her. He'd never felt such lust before, never even known such lust existed.

"Give me strength," he prayed, "strength to do what I must. And forgive me," he whispered.

He hoped he could do what he had to, but first he wanted to taste her, just this once, this one and only time and then never again would he allow himself to touch her.

He kissed her hair, her neck, his tongue on her smooth skin. His hand ran up her arm and then covered her breast. Nicholas's heart beat loudly in his ears.

Wakening, Dougless turned in his arms to kiss him—a kiss such as she'd never experienced before. *The other half of me,* she thought. *What I have been missing all my life is this man. He's the other half of me.*

"Lettice," Nicholas murmured near her ear.

Their legs were entwined, their arms clasping one another. Dougless smiled, her head back as Nicholas placed hot kisses on her neck and throat. "I've been called . . . Carrots"—she was breathless—"for my hair, but never lettuce."

"Lettice is . . ." He was kissing down her throat, lower and lower. "Lettice is my wife."

"Mmm," Dougless murmured as his hands caressed her breast and his lips went lower.

What he'd said hit her suddenly. She pushed away to look at him. "Wife?" she asked.

Nicholas pulled her back to him. "We care naught for her now."

She pushed away from him again. "You seem to care about her enough to say her name when you're kissing *me.*"

"A mere slip," he said, pulling her toward him.

Dougless shoved at him hard and got out of bed, straightening her unbuttoned gown. "Why don't you explain to me about this *wife* of yours?" she demanded angrily. "And why haven't I heard of her before?"

Nicholas sat up in bed, the sheet to his waist. "There was no reason to tell of Lettice. Her beauty, her talents, my love for her are my own." He picked up Dougless's watch off the table. "Perhaps today we will purchase me such as this."

"Put that down!" Dougless snapped. "This is serious. I think you owe me an explanation."

"Explain to *you?*" Nicholas said, getting out of bed, wearing only a pair of tiny briefs. He put on his trousers and turned to her, fastening them. "Pray, madam, who are you? Are you a duke's daughter? An earl's? Even a baron's? I am the Earl of Thornwyck and you are my servant, to work for me. In return I feed you and clothe you and perhaps, if you are worth it, a small stipend. I have no obligation to tell you of my personal life."

Dougless sat down hard on the bed. "But you never mentioned a wife," she said softly. "Not once have you referred to her."

"I would be a poor husband to profane my beloved's name to my servant."

"Servant," Dougless whispered. "Do you love her very much?"

Nicholas snorted. "She is the true reason I must return. I must find the truth and live to return to my loving wife's arms."

Robert yesterday and today finding Nicholas had a wife—a wife he loved madly. "I don't understand," she said, burying her face in her hands. "I wished you here. I prayed for you. Why did you come to me if you loved someone else?"

"You prayed on my tomb. Perhaps if anyone had done that—man or woman—I would have come forth. Perhaps God knew I would need a servant and you needed work. I do not know. I do know I must return."

"To your wife?"

"Aye, to my wife."

She turned to look at him. "And what of this?" she asked, motioning to the bed.

"Madam, you placed yourself in my bed. I am but a man and I have weaknesses."

Dougless was beginning to understand and to feel deeply embarrassed. Was there any woman on earth who was a bigger fool than she was? Was there any man on earth she *hadn't* fallen in love with? Let her spend three days with a guy and she began to imagine a life together. If Attila the Hun or Jack the Ripper had come forward she'd no doubt have fallen in love with them. With her luck she'd be in love with Genghis Khan in *two* days.

She stood. "Look, I'm sorry for the misunderstanding. Of course you have a wife. A beautiful wife and three lovely kids. I don't know what I was thinking of. You were on Death Row *and* married. I'm used to guys with only one major strike against them. I just seem to get luckier and luckier. I'll get my things and get out of here. You go back to Mrs. Stafford and have a swell life."

He blocked the entrance to the bathroom. "You mean to unkiss the bargain?"

"Unkiss?" she said, voice rising. "Again with the 'unkiss.' Yes, I mean to unkiss, unhug, un-whatever else it needs. You don't need me, not when you have lovely Lettice and Arabella-on-the-table."

Nicholas moved toward her and his voice lowered seductively. "If our interrupted love play annoys you, we can return to the bed."

"Not on your life, buster," she said, eyes blazing. "Put one hand on me and you draw back a bloody nub."

Nicholas put his hand over his jaw to hide a smile. "I see no cause for your anger. I have represented myself truly. I need help in searching for the person who betrayed me. I want to find the information and return to my home. I have never been false with you."

Dougless turned away. He was right. He'd never been secretive in any way. She was the one who'd imagined castles in the sky and their living happily ever after. Idiot, idiot, idiot, she told herself.

She turned back to him. "I'm sorry about all this. Maybe you should get someone else to help you. I've got my purse now and my plane ticket and I think I better go home."

"Ah yes," he said. "I see. You are a coward."

"I am no such thing. It's just . . ."

"You have fallen in love with me," he said with a sigh of resignation. "All the women do. It is a curse that plagues me much. I cannot spend three days with a woman and not have her come to my bed. Think not on it. I do not blame you."

"You don't blame me?" Anger was beginning to replace Dougless's self-pity. "You overrate your charms by a long shot. You don't know what women are like today. Any woman could live in the same house with you and not fall for you. We don't like conceited, puffed-up peacocks like you."

"Oh?" he said, one eyebrow raised. "It is just you who are different? In three days' time you are in my bed."

"For your information I was trying to settle you down after a nightmare. I thought I was comforting you. Like a mother and child."

Nicholas smiled. "Comfort? You may comfort me any morn you wish."

"Save it for your wife. Now, will you get out of my way? I need to get dressed and get out of here."

He put his hand on her arm. "You are angry at me that I kissed you?"

"I'm angry at you because . . ." She turned away. Why was she angry at him? He'd awakened and found her in his bed and he'd started kissing her. He hadn't made a pass at her, actually hadn't been anything but a gentleman. Never once had he even hinted that there was more between them than an employer/employee relationship.

It was she who'd made everything up. Out of his teasings, the laughter they'd shared and, especially, out of her hurt over Robert, she'd imagined more between them than there was.

"I'm not angry at you at all," she said. "I'm mad at myself. I guess I was on the rebound."

"Rebound?"

"Sometimes when you get jilted, or abandoned as I was, you want to jump right back on the train." He still looked puzzled. "I thought maybe you could replace Robert. Maybe I just wanted to go home with a ring on my finger. If I came home engaged, maybe I wouldn't have too many questions asked about the man I left America with and what happened to him."

She looked up at him. "I'm sorry for what I thought. Maybe you'd better get someone else to help you."

"I understand. You could not resist me. It is as the guide said, that no woman can withstand me."

Dougless groaned. "I could withstand you all right. Now that I know the true extent of your enormous ego I could *live* with you and not fall for you."

"You could not."

"I could and I'll prove it. I'll find your secret for you and even if it takes years I won't even be tempted by you." She narrowed her eyes. "You have any more bad dreams and I'll throw a pillow at you. *Now* will you let me in the bathroom?"

Nicholas stepped aside and she angrily closed the door behind her. He couldn't help grinning at the door. Ah, Dougless, he thought, my sweet, sweet Dougless. You may be able to resist me, but how will I resist you? A year together? A year without touching you? I will go mad.

He turned away to get dressed.

7

The long black car made its way south through the beautiful English countryside. In the back seat Nicholas looked across at Dougless. She was sitting stiffly upright. Her lovely, thick auburn hair was pulled tightly back to the nape of her neck and pinned up. Since this morning she had not smiled or laughed or made any comment except, "Yes, sir," or "No, sir."

"Dougless," he said. "I—"

She cut him off. "I believe, Lord Stafford, we have been through this. I am Miss Montgomery, your secretary, no more, no less. I hope, sir, that you can remember that and keep from giving people the impression that I am more than I am."

He turned away, sighing. He could think of nothing to say to her and, actually, he knew this was the better way but in just these few hours, already, he missed her.

Moments later his attention was caught by the tower of Thornwyck, and he found his heart beginning to beat a little faster. He had designed this place. He had taken what he knew and loved of his other houses, put his ideas together, and created this beautiful house. It had taken four years to cut the stone, to bring the marble from Italy. In the inner courtyard he had towers with rounded glass in them.

It had been only half finished when he had been arrested, but the half that was completed had been as beautiful as any building in the land.

He frowned as the driver turned in the drive. It looked so *old.* Just a month ago he had been here, and then it was new and perfect. Now the chimney pots were crumbling, there were broken places along the roof, some of his windows had been bricked in.

"It is beautiful," Dougless whispered, then straightened. "Sir."

"It is crumbling," Nicholas said in anger. "And were the western towers never completed?"

When the car stopped, Nicholas got out and looked around. It was a sad place to his mind, the unfinished half in ruins, the other half looking hundreds of years old—which it was, he thought with dismay.

When he turned back, Dougless already had the bags inside the hotel lobby. "Lord Stafford will want early tea at eight A.M.," she was telling the clerk. "And luncheon promptly at noon. I must be given a menu beforehand." She turned to him. "Would you like to sign the register, my lord, or should I?"

Nicholas gave her a quelling look, but she turned away before she saw it. He quickly signed the guest book, then the clerk led them to their suite.

The room was beautiful, with dark rose wallpaper, and a four-poster bed hung with rose and yellow chintz. A little couch of yellow and pale green sat at the foot of the bed on a rose carpet. Next to it was a small sitting room of rose and pale green.

"I will need a cot in here," Dougless said.

"A cot?" the clerk asked.

"Of course. For me to sleep on. You did not think that *I* would sleep in his lordship's chamber, did you?"

Nicholas rolled his eyes. He had been in the twentieth century long enough to know that Dougless's behavior was strange.

"Yes, miss," the clerk said. "I will have a cot sent up." He left them alone.

"Dougless," Nicholas began.

"Miss Montgomery," she said in a cold voice.

"Miss Montgomery," he said just as coolly, "see that my cap-cases are sent up. I plan to look at my house."

"Shall I accompany you?"

"Nay, I want no hell-kite with me," he said angrily, then left the room.

Dougless had the suitcases brought up, then asked the clerk where the local library was. She felt very efficient as she set off through the little village, notebook and pens in hand, but as she neared the library her steps slowed.

Don't think about it, she told herself. It was all a dream, an impossible, unreachable dream. Cold, she thought, think cold. Antarctica. Siberia. Do your job and remain cool to him. He belongs to another woman, to another time.

It was easy finding what the librarian called the "Stafford Collection."

"Many of the visitors ask after the Staffords, especially the ones staying at Thornwyck," the librarian said.

"I am interested in the last earl, Nicholas Stafford."

"Oh yes, poor man, condemned to be beheaded, then dying before the execution. It's believed he was poisoned."

"Poisoned by whom?" Dougless asked eagerly.

"By whoever accused him of treason. He built Thornwyck, you know. I've read that he even designed it, but no one can prove it. There are no drawings with his name on them. Well, here we are, all the books on this shelf have something in them about the Staffords."

Dougless took the books out one by one and began reading.

There was very little about Nicholas except what was told in a derogatory way. He had been the earl for only four years before he was tried for treason. His older brother, Christopher, had been the earl since he was twenty-two and the books raved about how Christopher had taken the failing Stafford fortunes and rebuilt them. Nicholas, only a year younger, was portrayed as frivolous, spending vast amounts on horses and women.

"He hasn't changed," Dougless said aloud, opening another book. This one was even more unflattering. It told at length the story of Lady Arabella and the table. It seems that two servants were in the room when Nicholas and Arabella entered, and they ducked into a closet when they heard the lord and lady. Later they told everyone what they'd seen and a clerk by the name of John Wilfred had put the whole story down in his diary—a diary which had survived until the present.

The third book was more serious. It told of Christopher's accomplishments and added that his wastrel of a younger brother squandered it all on a foolhardy attempt to put Mary Queen of Scots on Elizabeth's throne.

Dougless slammed the book shut and looked at her watch. It was time for tea. She left the library and made her way to a pretty little tea shop. She got her tea and scones, then sat down and began reading her notes.

"I have sought you most earnestly."

She looked up to see Nicholas standing over her. "Should I rise until you are seated, my lord?"

"No, Miss Montgomery, a mere kiss of my toes will be sufficient."

Dougless almost smiled but she didn't. He got himself a tray of tea but Dougless had to pay for it. He still carried no money.

"What is it you read?"

Coolly, she told him what she had found out. Except for a slight flush around his collar, he didn't seem to react.

"There is no mention in your history books that I was chamberlain to my brother?"

"None. It says you bought horses and fooled around with women." And she thought she could love such a man! It seemed that a lot of women had thought so.

Nicholas ate a scone and drank his tea. "When I return I will change your history books."

"You can't change history. History is fact, it's already made. And you can't change what the history books say. They're already printed."

He didn't answer her. "What did it say of the world after my death?"

"I didn't look that far. I only read about your brother and you."

He gave her a cool look. "You read only of the bad about me?"

"That's all there *was*."

"What of my design of Thornwyck? The queen hailed it as a monument of greatness."

"There is no record that you designed it. The librarian said some people believed you did, but there was no proof."

Nicholas put down his half-eaten scone. "Come," he said angrily. "I will show you what I did. I will show you the great work I have left behind me."

He strode out of the tearoom, and the unfinished scone was testimony to how upset he was. He walked ahead of her with long, angry strides and Dougless had difficulty keeping up with him as they went back to the hotel.

To Dougless the hotel was beautiful, but to Nicholas it was mostly ruins. To the left of the entrance were tall stone walls that she'd assumed were fences, but he showed her that they were walls to what had been nearly half of the house that had never been finished. Now there were merely two high walls with grass underfoot, vines growing down the walls. He told her of the beauty of these rooms if they had been built as he designed them: paneling, stained glass, carved marble fireplaces. High on one wall he pointed to a stone face, worn by rain and time. "My brother," he said. "I had the likeness carved of him."

As he described and they walked down long avenues of roofless rooms, Dougless began to see what he had planned. She could almost hear the lutes in the music room.

"And now it is this," he said at last. "A place for cows and goats and . . . yeomen."

"And their daughters," Dougless said, including herself in his derogatory description.

He turned and looked at her with cool contempt. "You believe what these fools have written about me," he said. "You believe my life was horses and women."

"I didn't say it, the books did, my lord," she answered him in the same tone.

"On the morrow we will begin to find what the books do *not* say."

◇ ◇ ◇

In the morning they were both at the library when the door was unlocked. After spending twenty minutes explaining the free-library system to Nicholas, Dougless got five of the books on the Staffords from the shelves and began to read. Nicholas sat across from her and stared at the pages of a book, frowning in consternation. After thirty minutes of watching him struggle, she took pity on him.

"Perhaps, sir," she said softly, "in the evenings I might teach you to read."

"Teach me to read?" he asked.

"In America I teach school and I've had quite a bit of experience teaching children to read. I'm sure you could learn."

"Could I?" he asked, one eyebrow raised. He didn't say any more, but got up and went to the librarian and asked her a few questions which Dougless couldn't hear. The librarian smiled and nodded, left the desk, and a moment later came back with several books which she handed Nicholas.

Nicholas put them on the table, opened the top one, and his face lit with joy. "There, Miss Montgomery, read that to me."

On the page was an incomprehensible typeface of oddly shaped letters, strangely spelled words. She looked up at him.

"*This* is my printing." He held the book up and looked at the title page. "It is a play by a man named Shakespeare."

"You haven't heard of him? I thought he was as Elizabethan as any man ever was."

Nicholas, starting to read, took a seat across from her. "Nay, I have no knowledge of him." Quickly, he became absorbed in his reading as Dougless dug more into the history books.

She could find very little about what happened after Nicholas's death. The estates were taken over by the queen. There were no children of either Christopher or Nicholas, and so the Stafford title and line had died with them. Again and again she read of what a wastrel Nicholas was and how he'd betrayed his entire family.

At noon they went to a pub for lunch. Nicholas was beginning to get used to the light lunches but he continued to grumble.

"Foolish children," he said, "if they had listened to their parents they would have lived. Your world fosters such disobedience."

"What children?"

"In the play. Juliet and . . ." He paused, trying to remember.

"Romeo and Juliet? You've been reading *Romeo and Juliet?"*

"Aye, and a more disobedient lot I have never seen. That play is a good lesson to children everywhere. I hope children today read it and learn from it."

Dougless nearly screeched at him. *"Romeo and Juliet* is about *romance* and if the parents hadn't been so narrow-minded and uptight, they—"

"Narrow-minded?"

They were off and running, arguing throughout the meal.

Later, as they walked back to the library, Dougless asked him how his brother Christopher had died.

Nicholas stopped walking and looked away. "I was to go hunting with him that day but I had cut my arm during sword practice." Dougless saw him rubbing his left forearm. "I still bear the scar." After a moment Nicholas turned to her, his face no longer full of pain. "He drowned. I was not the only brother who liked women. Kit saw a pretty girl swimming in a lake, and he told his men to leave him with her. After a few hours the men returned to find my brother floating in the lake."

"And no one saw what happened?"

"Nay. Perhaps the girl did but we never found her."

Dougless was thoughtful for a moment. "How odd that your brother drowned with no witnesses as to what happened, and a few years later you were tried for treason. It's almost as if someone planned to take the Stafford estates."

Nicholas's face changed. He looked at her with that expression men have when a woman says something they have not thought of—as if the impossible has happened.

"Who stood to inherit? Your dear, darling Lettice?" Dougless snapped her lips together, wishing she'd kept the jealousy out of her voice.

Nicholas didn't seem to notice. "Lettice had her marriage property but she lost all Stafford wealth at my death. I inherited from Kit but I can assure you I did not wish for his death."

"Too much responsibility?" Dougless asked. "Being the boss carries a burden to it."

He gave her a look of anger. "You believe your history books. Come," he said. "You must read more. Who betrayed me?"

Dougless read all afternoon, while Nicholas laughed over *The Merchant of Venice*, but she could find out nothing more.

In the evening Nicholas wanted her to dine with him but she refused. She knew she had to spend less time with him. Her heart was too newly broken and she could easily come to care more for him than was good for her. Looking like a sad little boy, he stuck his hands in his pockets and went downstairs to dinner while Dougless asked for a bowl of soup and some bread brought up to her room. She ate and went over her notes but could come up with nothing. No one seemed to gain anything by Christopher and Nicholas's deaths.

About ten P.M., when Nicholas had still not returned from dinner, curious, she went downstairs to look. He was in the beautiful stonewalled drawing room, laughing with half a dozen guests. Dougless stood in the shadow of the doorway and watched—and anger, unreasonable, unjust anger, flooded her body. *She* had called him forward, but here two other women were drooling over him.

She turned on her heel and left the hallway. He was exactly as the books said. No wonder someone had so easily betrayed him. When he should have been taking care of business, he was probably in bed with some woman.

She went upstairs, put on her gown, and got into the little bed the hotel had brought up for her. But she didn't sleep. She lay there feeling angry and foolish. Maybe she should have gone with Robert. At least Robert was real. He had a bit of a problem about sharing money and he did love his daughter excessively, but he'd always been faithful to her.

About eleven she heard Nicholas open the bedroom door and she saw light under the door between their rooms. When she heard him open the door, she tightly closed her eyes.

"Dougless," he whispered but she didn't answer. "I know you do not sleep, so answer me."

She opened her eyes. "Should I get my pad and paper? I'm afraid I don't take shorthand."

He sighed and took a step toward her. "I felt something from you tonight. Anger? Dougless, I do not want us to be enemies."

"We're not enemies," she said sternly. "We are employer and employee. You are an earl and I am a commoner."

"Dougless," he said, his voice pleading and all too seductive. "You are not common. I meant . . ."

"Yes?"

He backed away. "I meant what I said. On the morrow you must discover more. Goodnight, Miss Montgomery."

"Aye, aye, captain," she said mockingly.

◇ ◇ ◇

In the morning, she refused to eat breakfast with him. This is better, she told herself, do not relax for even a moment. Remind yourself that he is a scoundrel now, as he was then. She walked to the library alone and, out of the windows, she saw Nicholas laughing with a pretty young woman. Dougless buried her nose in the book.

Nicholas was still smiling when he came to sit across from her. "A new friend?" she said and immediately wished she hadn't.

"She is an American and she was telling me about baseball. And football."

"You *told* her that last week you were in Elizabethan England?" Dougless was aghast.

Nicholas smiled. "She believes me to be a man of learning, so I have had not time for such tilly-fally."

"Learning, ha!" Dougless muttered.

Nicholas continued to smile. "You are jealous?"

"Jealous? Most certainly not. I am your employee. I have no right to be jealous. Did you tell her about your wife?"

Nicholas picked up one of the books of Shakespeare's plays the librarian had left out for him. "You are frampold this morning," he said, but smiling as if he were very pleased.

Dougless had no idea what he meant, so she wrote the word down and looked it up later. Disagreeable. So, he thought she was disagreeable, did he? She went back to her research.

At three o'clock she nearly jumped out of her chair. "Look! It's here." Excitedly, she went around the table to take a chair by Nicholas. "This paragraph, see?" He did but he could read only phrases of it. She was holding a two-month-old copy of a magazine on English history.

"This article is on Goshawk Hall that we heard about at Bellwood. It says that there has been a recent find at Goshawk of papers of the Stafford family—and the papers date from the sixteenth century. They are now being studied by Dr. Hamilton J. Nolman. It further says that Dr. Nolman hopes to prove that Nicholas Stafford, who was accused of treason at the beginning of Elizabeth I's reign, was actually innocent."

Dougless looked at Nicholas, and the expression in his eyes was almost embarrassing.

"This is why I have come now," he said softly. "Nothing could be proved until these papers were found. We must go to Goshawk."

"We can't just go. We'll have to petition the owners to look at the papers." She closed the magazine. "What size of house must it be to have misplaced a trunkload of papers for four hundred years?"

"Goshawk Hall is not so large as four of my houses," Nicholas said as if he were offended.

Dougless leaned back in the chair and felt as if at last they were getting somewhere. She had no doubt that these papers were the papers of Nicholas's mother, and that the proof Nicholas needed to prove himself innocent was in these papers.

"Well, hello."

They looked up to see the pretty young woman who had explained baseball to Nicholas. "I thought that was you," she said, then gave Dougless the once-over. "Is this your friend?"

"Merely his secretary," Dougless said, rising. "Will there be anything else, Lord Stafford?"

"Lord?!" the young woman gasped. "You're a *lord?*"

Nicholas started to go after Dougless as she left, but the overexcited American, thrilled at meeting a lord, would not allow him to leave.

Dougless went back to the hotel, trying her best to think of her letter to Goshawk Hall, but actually thinking mostly of Nicholas flirting with the pretty American. It didn't matter to her, of course. This was just a job. Soon she'd be home, teaching her fifth-graders, dating now and then, visiting her family and telling them all about England—and explaining how she was ditched by one man and half fell in love with a man who was married and about four hundred and fifty-one years old.

The best Dougless-story yet, she thought.

By the time she got to the hotel, she was slamming things about. Damn all men, she thought. Damn the good ones as well as the bad. They broke your heart over and over again.

"I see your temper has not improved," Nicholas said from behind her.

"My temper is not your concern," she snapped. "I was hired to do a job and I'm doing it. I'm going to write Goshawk Hall and see when we can look at the papers."

Nicholas was beginning to get angry himself. "The animosity you bemete to me has not foundation."

"I have no animosity toward you," she said with fury. "I'm doing my best

to help you, to help you get back to your loving wife, to your own time."
Her head came up. "I just realized that there's no need for you to be here. I
can do the research. You can't read much anyway. Why don't you to go to
. . . to the French Riviera or something? I can do this by myself."

"I am to leave?" he asked softly.

"Sure, why not? Go to London and party. Meet all the beautiful women
of this century. We have lots of tables nowadays."

Nicholas stiffened. "You want away from me?"

"Yes, yes, yes. My research would go much better without you. You're
. . . you're really in my way. You know nothing about my world. You can
barely dress yourself; you still eat with your hands half the time; you can't
read or write; I have to explain the simplest things to you. It would be a
thousand times better if you left me alone." Her hands were gripping the
chair back so hard her knuckles were about to come through the skin.

She glanced up at him and the naked pain on his face was more than she
could bear. He *had* to leave, had to let her piece her mind and body back
together. Before she humiliated herself with tears, she turned and left the
room. Once in her bed-sitting room, she leaned against the door and cried
deeply.

Just to get this over, she thought, to send him away, to go back home and
never even look at another man again, that's what she needed.

She fell down on her bed and buried her face in her pillow and cried
silently. She cried for a long time, until the worst of it was over and she
began to feel better. And she began to think more clearly.

How stupid she'd been acting! What had Nicholas done wrong? She
visualized his sitting in a dungeon somewhere awaiting execution for a
crime he didn't commit, the next minute he's floating through the air and
he's in the twentieth century.

She sat up and blew her nose. And how well he'd handled everything!
He'd adjusted to automobiles, novels, a strange language, strange food and
. . . And a weepy woman suffering from the rejection of another man.
Nicholas had been generous with his money, his laughter, his knowledge.

And what had Dougless done? She'd been furious with him because he'd
dared marry another woman some four hundred years ago.

When she looked at it that way, it was almost humorous. She glanced up
at the door. Her room was dark but there was a light on under the door.
The things she'd said to him! Awful, terrible things.

She practically ran to the door. "Nicholas, I—" The room was empty.
She ran to open the door into the hall but it was empty. She turned back

into the room and saw the note on the floor where he must have slipped it under her door. Quickly, she looked at it.

Dougless had no idea what the words said but to her eyes the paper looked like an Elizabethan runaway note. His clothes were still in the closet and so were the capcases—suitcases, she corrected herself.

She had to find him and apologize, tell him he shouldn't leave, that she'd need his help. Her head seemed to ring with all the rotten, terrible things she'd said to him. He *could* read. He had lovely table manners. He—Damn, damn, damn, she thought as she tore down the stairs, out the hotel and into the rain.

She clasped her hands about her upper arms, put her head down and started running. She had to find him. He probably had no idea what an umbrella was or a raincoat. He'd catch his death. He'd probably be fighting the rain so hard he'd walk in front of a bus—or a train. Would he know a train track from a sidewalk? What if he got on a train? He wouldn't know where to get off—or how to get back if he did get off.

She ran to the train station but it was closed. Good, she thought, pushing cold, wet hair out of her face. She tried to read the dial on her watch but the rain was hitting her in the face. It looked to be after eleven. She must have been crying for hours. She shivered, thinking what could have happened to him in all those hours.

She saw a dark shape in a distant gutter and ran to it, knowing it was Nicholas lying dead in a heap. But it was only a shadow. Blinking, trying to keep her eyes open against the rain, sneezing twice, she looked at the dark windows of the village.

Maybe he had just started walking. How far could a person walk in . . . She didn't even know how long he'd been gone. Which direction had he taken?

She started running toward the end of the street, cold water splashing up the back of her legs and under her skirt. There seemed to be no lights on anywhere, and then as she rounded a corner she saw a light in a window. A pub, she thought. She'd ask there and see if anyone had seen him.

She walked in and the warmth and light hit her so that she couldn't see for a moment.

Freezing, shivering, dripping, she stood there to let her eyes adjust. And then she heard a laugh that had become familiar to her. Nicholas, she thought, and ran through the smoke-filled room.

What she saw was like an advertisement for the seven sins. Nicholas, his shirt unbuttoned to the waist, a cigar clamped between his strong teeth, sat behind a table that looked as if it might break under the weight of the food on it. There was a woman on either side of him, and there was lipstick on his cheeks and his shirt.

"Dougless," he said in delight. "Come join us."

She stood there feeling like a wet cat, her hair plastered against her head, her clothes sticking to her, a gallon of water in each shoe, a puddle at her feet that could sail a three-masted schooner

"Get up from there and come with me," she said in the voice she used to settle down unruly schoolchildren.

"Aye, captain," Nicholas said, smiling.

He's drunk, she thought.

He kissed each woman on the mouth, then leaped to the seat, bounded over the table, and swooped Dougless into his arms. "Put me down," she hissed, but he carried her through the pub and outside.

"It's raining," she said.

"Nay, madam, it is clear." Still holding her, he began to nuzzle her neck.

"Oh no you don't, put me down at once."

He did, but in such a way that her body slid over his. "You're drunk," she said, pushing away from him.

"Oh aye, I am," he said happily. "The ale here pleases me. The women please me," he said as he caught her about the waist.

Dougless pushed him away. "I was worried about you, and here you were boozing it up with a couple of floozies and—"

"Too fast," he cried, "too many words. Here, my pretty Dougless, look at the stars."

"In case you haven't noticed, I happen to be very wet and I'm also freezing." As if to emphasize the fact, she sneezed.

Once again he lifted her into his arms. "Put me down!"

"You are cold; I am warm," he said, as if that settled the matter. "You feared for me?"

She was willing to admit defeat as she snuggled against him. He was indeed warm. "I said some awful things to you and I'm very sorry. You aren't really a burden."

He smiled down at her. "Is this the cause of your fear? That perhaps I was angered?"

"No. When you were gone I thought maybe you'd walked in front of a bus or a train or something else. I was afraid of your being hurt."

"Do I appear to have no *pia mater?*"

"Huh?"

"Brain. Do I seem stupid to you?"

"No, of course not. You just don't know how our modern world works, that's all."

"Oh? Who is wet and who is dry?"

"Both of us are wet since you continue carrying me," she said smugly.

"For all your knowledge I have found what we need to know and tomorrow we ride to Goshawk."

"How did you find out anything and from whom? Those women in there? Did you kiss it out of them?"

"Are you jealous, Montgomery?"

"No, Stafford, I am not." That statement proved that the Pinocchio theory was false. Her nose didn't grow at all. "What did you find out?"

"Dickie Harewood owns Goshawk."

"But didn't he marry your mother? Is he as old as *you?*"

"Beware or I will show you how old I am." He shifted her in his arms. "Am I feeding you too much?"

"It's more likely you're weak from flirting with all the women. It saps a man's strength, you know."

"Mine has not been impaired. Now, I was telling you?"

"That Dickie Harewood still owns Goshawk."

"Yes, on the morrow I shall see him. What is a weekend?"

"It's the end of the workweek, when everyone gets off. And you can't just go riding up to some lord's house. I hope you're not thinking of inviting yourself for the weekend."

"The workers get off? But no one seems to work at all. I see no farmers in the fields, no one plowing. People now shop and drive cars."

"We have a forty-hour workweek and tractors. Nicholas, you're not answering me. What are you planning to do? You really can't tell this man Harewood you're from the sixteenth century. You can't tell anyone that, even women in bars." She tugged at his collar. "You've ruined that shirt. Lipstick never comes out."

He grinned at her and shifted her again. "You have on none of this lipstick."

She moved her head away from him. "Don't start that again. Now tell me about Goshawk Hall."

"The Harewood family owns it still. They come for the end . . ."

"Weekend."

"Aye, the weekend and—" He gave Dougless a sideways look. "Arabella is there."

"Arabella? What does the twentieth-century Arabella have to do with anything?"

"*My* Arabella was Dickie Harewood's daughter, and there seems to be a Dickie Harewood again at Goshawk Hall and he again has a daughter named Arabella, who is the same age as my Arabella was when we—"

"Spare me," Dougless said, and thought for a moment. The papers recently found, another Arabella, another Dickie. It was almost as if history were repeating itself.

8

Dougless watched Nicholas atop the stallion and held her breath. She'd heard of people riding horses like this one but she'd never seen it. Every employee, every visitor at the riding stables had stopped to watch as Nicholas worked to control the high-strung, angry, mean-tempered animal.

Last night they'd stayed up until after one A.M., while Dougless made him tell her all about his relationship to the Harewoods. There wasn't much. They'd had estates near one another. Dickie was old enough to be Nicholas's father and he'd had a daughter, Arabella, who'd married Robert Sydney. Arabella and her husband had hated one another and after she'd given him an heir they'd lived apart, although Arabella had given birth to three more children.

"One of them yours," Dougless had said, taking notes.

Nicholas had softened. "There is no reason to think ill of her. She and the child died in that childbirth."

"I'm sorry." Dougless thought with a grimace that the woman could easily have died from something as simple as the midwife not washing her hands.

Dougless tried to think of a way to get invited to the Harewood estates as quickly as possible, but she had no credentials as a scholar and although Nicholas was an earl, his title had been taken from him when he was condemned for treason. She thought until she couldn't stay awake any longer, then she'd bid Nicholas good night and gone to her own bed.

This is better, she thought as she drifted into sleep. She had her emotions under control. She was getting over Robert and she was no longer falling for a married man. She'd help Nicholas get back to his wife, help him clear his name, and she'd go home feeling good about herself. For once in her life she was *not* going to fall for an unsuitable man.

Nicholas woke her early in the morning by throwing open the sitting-room door. "Can you ride a horse? Can anyone today ride a horse?"

Dougless assured him she could ride, courtesy of her Colorado cousins, and then after breakfast she'd found a nearby riding stables. It was four miles and Nicholas insisted they walk. At the stables he'd turned up his nose at the horses for rent, but his eyes had lit up at the sight of an enormous horse in a field. It was prancing about and tossing its head as if it dared anyone to come near it. As if in a trance, Nicholas had walked toward the animal. The horse ran at him, making Dougless jump back from the fence.

"This one," Nicholas said.

"You can't really think of riding that horse. There are lots of horses here, pick one of them," she'd said.

Nothing anyone could say to him would change his mind. The owner of the stables came and thought it would be a great joke to see Nicholas break his neck. Dougless knew that in America there'd be talk of insurance, but not in England. The stallion was led into a stall, a groom saddled the horse, then led it to a pasture and gleefully handed Nicholas the reins.

Now Nicholas sat on top of it and almost easily brought it under control.

"I've never seen anyone ride like that," a groom said. "He ride a lot?"

"Always," Dougless answered. "He'll get on a horse before he'll get in a car. In fact, he's spent much more of his life on a horse than in a car."

"Must have," the groom mumbled, watching Nicholas with awe.

"You are ready?" Nicholas asked Dougless.

She mounted her sedate mare and followed him as he took off. Never had she seen a happier man, and it struck Dougless afresh how different the modern world must be from what he knew. He and the horse fit together as one being, as if he were a centaur.

Rural England is full of footpaths and horse trails and Nicholas went galloping down one of them. Dougless started to call out to him that he'd better ask directions but then she realized that it was unlikely anyone had moved Goshawk Hall in the last few hundred years.

She had trouble keeping up with him, lost him repeatedly, and once he returned for her. She had stopped at a crossroads and was looking at the ground for his tracks. When he saw her, he was very interested in what she was doing. Dougless, trying her best to control her mare that was reacting to the aggressive nearness of Nicholas's stallion, told him she'd buy him some Louis L'Amour books and read to him about tracking.

At last she came to a road and followed it until she reached a gate with a small brass plaque reading, GOSHAWK HALL. She rode down the drive to see an enormous rectangular fortress of a house set amid acres of beautiful, rolling gardens.

Dougless felt a bit embarrassed to be riding up to this house uninvited, unannounced, but Nicholas was there, already off his horse and walking toward a tall, grubby-looking man on his hands and knees in a bed of petunias.

"Don't you think we should knock on the front door first?" Dougless asked when she reached Nicholas. "Maybe ask for Mr. Harewood and tell him we'd like to see the papers."

"You are on my ground now," he said and went ahead toward the gardener.

"Nicholas!" she hissed at him.

"Harewood?" Nicholas asked the gardener.

The tall man turned and looked up at Nicholas. He had blue eyes and blond hair that was now turning gray and the smooth, pink complexion of a baby. He also didn't look especially intelligent. "Ah yes. Do I know you?"

"Nicholas Stafford of Thornwyck."

"Hmmm," the man said and stood, not bothering to dust off his dirty old trousers. "Not the Staffords with that rogue son who got himself tried for treason?"

Dougless thought the man could have been speaking of something that happened last year.

"The same," Nicholas said, his back straight.

Harewood looked from him to his horse. Nicholas was wearing a very expensive riding outfit with tall, shiny black boots, and Dougless suddenly felt grubby in her Levi's, cotton shirt and Nike's. "You ride that?" Harewood asked.

"I did. I hear you have some papers on my family."

"Oh yes, we found them," he said, smiling. "Found them when a wall fell down. Looks like somebody hid them. Come in and we'll have some tea and see if we can find the papers. I think Arabella has them."

Dougless started to follow them, but Nicholas, with barely a glance, dropped the reins of his horse in her hand and calmly strode off with Lord Harewood.

"Just a minute," she said and started after the men, leading the horses, but Nicholas's stallion started prancing and Dougless looked back at the animal. It was looking at her with a wild-eyed expression. "Just try it," she warned and the horse stopped prancing.

Now what do I do? she wondered. If she was supposed to be Nicholas's secretary and she was supposed to find out the secrets his mother may or may not have known, why was she standing here holding the horses?

"Should I rub them down, your lordship?" she muttered, then started walking to the back of the house. Maybe there were stables back there where she could get rid of the animals.

There were half a dozen buildings in the back of the house, and Dougless went toward one that looked as if it might be the stables. She was nearly there when a horse and rider came tearing past her. The horse was as large and as mean-looking as Nicholas's stallion, and on top of it was a stunning woman. She was the very picture of what all women wanted to grow up to look like: tall, slim-hipped, long, long legs, an aristocratic face, big breasts, a straight-backed carriage that would make a piece of steel envious. She had on English riding breeches that could have been painted on, and her dark hair was pulled back in a severe bun, but that only emphasized her striking features.

The woman halted her horse and turned it around. "Whose horse is that?" she demanded in a voice that Dougless knew men would love: deep, throaty, husky, and powerful. Let me guess, Dougless thought, this is the great-great-great-etc. granddaughter of Arabella-on-the-table. Just my luck.

"Nicholas Stafford," Dougless said.

The woman's face turned pale—which made her lips redder, her eyes even darker. "Is this somebody's idea of a joke?" She glared at Dougless.

"He's a descendant of *the* Nicholas Stafford," Dougless answered. Dougless tried to imagine how an American family would react if someone mentioned the name of an Elizabethan ancestor. They'd have no idea whom she was talking about, but these people acted as if Nicholas had been gone only a couple of years.

The woman dismounted beautifully and tossed Dougless the reins. "Rub him down," she said and started toward the house.

"I wouldn't hold my breath," Dougless muttered. She now held three horses, two of whom looked as if they liked to kill small females before breakfast. She didn't dare look at the horses but just kept walking toward the stables.

An older man, sitting in the sun, drinking a mug of tea and reading a newspaper, did a double take when he saw her.

Slowly, cautiously, he rose. "Just be quiet, miss," he said. "Stand very still and I'll take both of 'em."

Dougless didn't dare move while the man approached her as if approaching a wounded tiger. He stuck out his hand, not wanting to get too near, and took the reins to one of the stallions. Slowly, he led the horse away from her and took it into the stables. Moments later he repeated his performance and took Nicholas's horse away.

When the man returned he removed his cap and wiped the sweat from his brow. "How did you get Lady Arabella's horse and Sugar together?"

"Sugar?"

"The stud from the Dennison's Stables."

"Sugar. Great joke. He should be named Enemy of the People. So that was Lady Arabella?" She looked back at the house. "How do I get into that place? I'm supposed to be . . . helping."

The man looked Dougless up and down, and she knew her American clothes and accent were about four strikes against her.

"That door there's the kitchen entrance."

Dougless thanked him and went off muttering. "The kitchen entrance. Should I bob a curtsy to the cook and ask for employment as a scullery maid? Wait until I see Nicholas! We'll settle a few things right away. I am *not* his horse-tender."

A man answered her knock on the door and when she asked for Nicholas, he led her into the kitchen. It was an enormous place with new appliances, but in the center of the room was a vast table that looked as if it had been there since William the Conqueror arrived. Everyone in the room stopped and stared at her. "Just passing through," she said. "My, ah . . . employer, he, ah, needs me." She smiled weakly. Too bad I'm going to kill him, she thought, and imagined the lecture she was going to give him on modern equality.

The man she was following—who didn't speak to her—led her through several kitchen storage rooms, with everyone she saw stopping and staring at her. Nicholas is going to look forward to his execution when I finish with him, Dougless thought.

The man didn't stop until they were at the entrance hall, a big round room with magnificent staircases going up both sides, portraits hanging everywhere. Lord Harewood and Nicholas and the dashing Lady Arabella were standing together as if they were old friends. Arabella, if possible, looked even better than she had when Dougless had first seen her. Her beautiful eyes were practically eating up Nicholas.

"You have joined us," Nicholas said when he saw Dougless, acting as if she had been out taking the air. "My secretary must stay with me."

"With you?" Arabella said and looked down her nose at Dougless. Dougless knew how a grape must feel when it's being made into a raisin.

"A place for her," Nicholas clarified, smiling.

"I think we can find room," Arabella said.

"Where? In the trash compactor?" Dougless said under her breath.

Nicholas clamped down on her shoulder painfully. "American," he said, as if that explained everything. "We will be here for tea," he said, and before Dougless could say another word, he pushed her out the door before him. He seemed to know exactly where the stables were, because he headed toward them.

Dougless had to hurry to keep up with his long strides. There were sometimes disadvantages to being five feet three inches tall. "What have you done now?" she asked. "Are we staying here for the weekend? You didn't tell them you were from the sixteenth century, did you? And where do you get off calling me an American in that tone?"

He stopped on the gravel path. "What do you have to wear to dinner? They dress for dinner."

"What's wrong with what I have on?" she said with a smirk.

He turned and started walking again.

"Think Arabella will dress? Something with a cleavage to the floor, I'll bet."

Nicholas, his back to her, smiled. "What is a trash com . . . ?"

"Compactor," she filled in and explained it to him. He turned away before she saw him smile.

At the stables the groom stayed well back while Nicholas mounted Sugar. "Had I a groom that cowardly I would have beat him," Nicholas mumbled.

Dougless couldn't get a word out of Nicholas as they rode back to the public stables. They also walked back to the hotel in double time. It was lunchtime at the hotel and Nicholas, still sweaty, went into the dining room and ordered three entrées and a bottle of wine.

Only when the wine had been poured did he speak. "What would you have of me?" he asked, his eyes twinkling.

Her curiosity won over her anger about the way he'd treated her. "Who? How? What? When?"

He laughed. "A woman without guile."

He began to tell her how Dickie Harewood was the same, not too bright, wanting only to hunt and tend his gardens. "They are near as good as mine," Nicholas said.

"Stop bragging and go on." She dug into her plate of roast beef. English beef was one of the great wonders of the earth: tender, succulent, cooked perfectly.

Two months ago workmen were repairing the roof of Goshawk Hall and it seemed their hammering knocked a piece out of a wall. "They do not build today as well as they should," Nicholas said. "In my houses—"

He broke off at a look from Dougless, then continued. Inside the wall was a trunk full of papers and when examined they were found to be the letters of Lady Margaret Stafford.

Dougless leaned back in her chair. "That's wonderful! And now we're invited to their house to read them. Oh, Colin, you are beautiful."

Nicholas's eyes widened at the name she'd called him, but did not comment. "There are problems."

"What sort of problems? No, let me guess. Lady Arabella wants you served on a platter to her every morning with her orange juice."

Nicholas nearly choked on his wine. "Your language, madam," he said primly.

"Am I right or wrong?"

"Incorrect. Lady Arabella is authoring a book on . . ." He turned away and Dougless thought his face pinkened.

"On you?" she gasped.

He looked back at his food but not at her. "It concerns the man she believes to be my ancestor. She has, ah, heard the stories of . . ."

"Of you two on the table?" Dougless grimaced. "Great, now she wants to repeat history. Is she going to let you see the documents or not?"

"She cannot. She has signed a contract with a physician."

Dougless had to figure that one out. A physician? Was she ill? No, a *doctor.* "Not the doctor in the magazine? What was his name? Dr. Something Hamilton. No, Hamilton something. That guy?"

Nicholas nodded. "He arrived but yesterday. He hopes to gain something by clearing my name. But Arabella says the book will take years. I do not believe I can wait that long. Your world costs too much."

Dougless knew from her father's career how important it was in the academic world to get published. To the outside world it might not seem important to solve an Elizabethan mystery, but to a scholar, especially a young man just starting out, a book with new information could mean the difference between tenure or not, or in getting a teaching position at a large, well-paid school or at a small community college.

"So," she said, "Dr. Whatever is there and he's sworn your Arabella to secrecy so you're not going to be given access to the papers. Yet it seems that we are invited as house guests anyway."

Nicholas smiled over his wine glass. "I have persuaded Arabella to tell me what she knows of me. I hope I can persuade her to tell me all. And you," he fixed Dougless with a look, "you are to talk to this physician."

"He's a Ph.D., not a physician and . . . What! Wait a minute, are you saying what I think you are? I am not, under any circumstances, going to play up to some history nut to help you out. I signed on as a secretary, not as a . . . What are you doing?"

Nicholas had taken her hand in both of his and was kissing her fingertips one by one.

"Stop that! People are looking." Dougless's shoes came off her feet. Nicholas's lips traveled up her arm until they reached the sensitive little spot on her inner elbow. Dougless was sinking down in the chair.

"All right!" she said. "You win! Stop that!"

He looked up at her through his lashes. "You will help me?"

"Yes," she said as he kissed her arm again.

"Good," he said and dropped her arm so abruptly that it landed in her dirty plate. "Now we must pack."

Dougless, grimacing, mopped up her arm and ran after him. "Is that how you're going to persuade Arabella?" she called after him, then stopped as she saw the other diners staring at her. Dougless gave a crooked smile of apology and ran from the room.

In their suite, Dougless saw a different Nicholas. He was very concerned that his clothes weren't correct. He held up a gorgeous linen shirt and said, "It needs pluming up."

Dougless looked at her own meager wardrobe and felt like crying. A weekend at an English lord's estate, where they dress for dinner and she had nothing but a suitcase full of serviceable wool. She wished she had her mother's white gown, the one with the pearls, or the red one with—

She stopped and smiled and the next minute she was on the phone to her sister Elizabeth in Maine.

"You want me to send you two of Mother's best gowns? She will kill both of us."

"Elizabeth," Dougless said, pleading. "I take full responsibility. Just send them NOW. Overnight mail. Got a pencil?" She gave Elizabeth the address at Goshawk Hall.

"Dougless, what's going on? First I get a frantic-sounding call from you where you won't tell me anything and now you want me to ransack Mother's closet."

"Nothing much. How's your paper coming?"

"It's making me crazy. And as if it weren't bad enough I have stopped-up drains. A plumber is coming today. Dougless, are you sure you're all right?"

"I'm fine. Good luck with your paper and your plumber. Bye."

Dougless packed her suitcase, and Nicholas's—it was one of those things he wouldn't even consider doing for himself—then called a taxi. There was no suitcase large enough to hold his armor so it was put into the biggest shopping bag.

At Goshawk Hall, Arabella literally met Nicholas with open arms. "Come inside, darling," she purred. "I feel we already know one another. After all, our ancestors were *very* friendly. Who are we to be any different?" She ushered inside, leaving Dougless with a half dozen or so suitcases at her feet.

"Who are we to be any different?" she mocked in a falsetto voice as she paid the cab driver.

It didn't take Dougless five minutes to learn that she was not considered a house guest but a servant, and not a very welcome one at that. A man ushered her—Dougless carrying her own suitcase—to a small, barren, cold room not far from the kitchen. Feeling like a governess in a Gothic novel, neither servant nor family, she unpacked and hung her clothes in a grubby little wardrobe. Looking about the ugly little room she felt martyred. Here she was doing this to help some guy save his life and his family name, and she was never even going to be able to tell anyone about it.

She went into the kitchen to find that big room empty, but tea for two had been set up at one end of the worktable.

"There you are," said a large woman with graying hair.

In minutes Dougless found herself sitting at the table having tea with this woman. Mrs. Anderson was the cook and the most wonderful gossip Dougless had ever met. There wasn't a thing the woman didn't know or was unwilling to tell. She wanted to know why Dougless was there and who Lord Stafford was, and in return she wanted to tell Dougless *everything.* Dougless obliged with a complicated web of lies that she prayed she'd be able to remember.

An hour later the other servants began filtering back into the kitchen, and Dougless could see they wanted her to leave so Mrs. Anderson could tell them all the juicy news.

Upon leaving the kitchen, Dougless went in search of Nicholas. She found him with Arabella under a grape arbor, the two of them cozied up like nesting birds.

"Lord Stafford," Dougless said loudly. "You wanted to dictate letters?"

"Lord Stafford is busy at the moment," Arabella said, glaring. "He will attend to business on Monday. In the library are notes of mine you may type."

"Lord Stafford is—" *My employer,* she meant to say but Nicholas interrupted her.

"Yes, Miss Montgomery, perhaps you can help Lady Arabella."

Dougless glared at him and almost told him what she thought of him, but his eyes were pleading with her to be obedient and, in spite of what she knew she should do, that is, tell them both what she thought of them, she turned on her heel and went back to the house. It wasn't any of her business, she thought. It didn't matter to her what he did with other women. Of course, she might point out to him that his foolishness with Arabella in the past had left generations of people laughing at him, and now it appeared he was about to repeat himself. Yes, she might bring herself to point that out to him. And, also, if he was so madly in love with his wife, how come he even wanted to snuggle up with the overendowed Arabella?

It took her a while to find the library and it looked just as she thought a library in one of these big, grand houses should look: leather-bound books, leather chairs, dark green walls, oak doors. She was looking around the place and didn't at first see the blond-haired man standing in front of the bookcases, absorbed in a book. Even with his face tipped down Dougless could see he was extremely good-looking, not divine as Nicholas was, but enough to set a few hearts to beating quickly. She also took in the fact that he was only about 5'6" tall. It had been Dougless's experience that short, handsome men were as vain as bantam roosters and loved short pretty females such as Dougless.

"Hello," she said.

The man glanced up from his book, down, then up again, and ended by staring at her with unabashed interest. He put his book away and came forward with his hand outstretched. "Hi, I'm Hamilton Nolman."

Dougless took his hand. Blue eyes, perfect teeth. What a very interesting man. "I'm Dougless Montgomery and you are an American."

"Guilty," he said and there was an immediate bond between them. He stepped closer. "Can you believe this place?" He glanced around the room.

"Never. Or the people. Lady Arabella sent me in here to type and I don't even work for her."

Hamilton laughed. "She'll have you scrubbing toilets before long. She doesn't allow pretty women near her. All the maids working here are dogs."

"I hadn't noticed." She looked at him. "Aren't you the doctor who's working on the Stafford papers? The ones that fell out of the wall?"

"That I am."

"That must have been exciting," Dougless said, wide-eyed, trying to look as young and innocent and as dumb as possible. "I heard the papers contained secret information. Is that true, Dr. Nolman?"

He chuckled in a fatherly way. "Please, call me Lee. It has been rather exciting. Although I'm just getting into the papers."

"It's all about some man who was about to be beheaded, wasn't it? I . . . ." She lowered her eyes and her voice. "I don't guess you'd tell me about it, would you?"

She watched him puff out his chest in pride, and the next minute they were seated and he was lecturing her as if he were already a full professor. In spite of the fact that he was a little pompous, she found herself liking him. Wouldn't her father love having a son-in-law who was interested in medieval history?

Wait a minute, Dougless, she cautioned herself. You're swearing off men, remember? She was listening so intently to Lee that she didn't hear Nicholas enter the room.

"Miss Montgomery!" Nicholas said so loudly and sternly that her arm fell out from under her chin and she nearly fell off the chair. "Are my letters typed?"

"Typed?" she asked. "Oh, Ni . . . Lord Stafford, I'd like you to meet Dr. Hamilton Nolman, he's—"

Nicholas arrogantly walked past Dr. Nolman, ignoring his outstretched hand. He went to the window. "Leave us," Nicholas said.

Lee wiggled his eyebrows at Dougless, picked up his books, and left the room, shutting the heavy doors behind him.

"Just who do you think you are?" Dougless asked. "You're no longer some sixteenth-century lord and master now. You can't just dismiss people like that. And besides, what do you know about typing?"

Nicholas turned to look at her, and she could tell by his expression that he had no idea what she was talking about. "You were very close to that small man."

"I . . ?" Dougless trailed off. Was that jealousy in his voice? She walked over to the big oak desk. "He's very good-looking, isn't he? And a scholar at his age, imagine. How's Arabella doing? Told her about your wife yet?"

"What conversation did you have with that man?"

"The usual," she said, running her finger along the desk. "He told me I was pretty, that sort of thing."

She looked back at Nicholas and saw his face had an expression of controlled rage. Her heart swelled with happiness. Revenge, she thought, *can* be sweet. "I did find out some things though. Lee—that's Dr. Nolman—hasn't really read any of the material yet. It seems that your Arabella took her time in choosing among the many scholars who asked to look at the papers. From what I gather she chose the best-looking man from photographs. Sort of a male beauty contest. I hear she threw away the women's photos. He said she was awfully disappointed that he turned out to be shorter than she is. Lee said Arabella took one look at him and said 'I thought Americans were tall.' Lee, thankfully, seems to have his ego intact because he just laughed. He pretty much thinks Arabella is a jerk. Oh, sorry, I'm forgetting how much you adore her."

Nicholas's face was still enraged and Dougless gave him her biggest smile. "How *is* Arabella?" she asked sweetly.

Nicholas glared at her a moment, then his eyes changed. He turned and pointed to an old oak table standing against a wall. *"That* is the true table." He gave her a little smile, then left the room.

Dougless clenched her fists then went over and kicked the table. Hobbling about, holding her toe, she cursed all men.

9

Dinner was to be served at eight, and Dougless dressed in her museum-visiting clothes, hoping that Elizabeth would send the gowns to her as soon as possible. But as eight drew near and no one summoned her to dinner, she wondered what was going on. She knew the servants had eaten earlier and she hadn't been invited to eat with them, so she sat in her room and waited.

At eight-fifteen, a man came to her and told her to follow him. She was led through the maze of rooms to a long dining room with a big fireplace and a table long enough for skateboarding. Arabella, her father, Nicholas, and Lee were already seated. Arabella, as Dougless expected, was wearing a dress so low-cut it pretty much left her bare from the waist up. She was showing more than Dougless even possessed.

As unobstrusively as possible, Dougless slipped into a chair that a servant held out for her, next to Lee.

"Your boss wouldn't eat until you were here," Lee whispered as the first course was served. "What's going on between you two, and is he a descendant of *the* Nicholas Stafford, the one that was almost beheaded?"

Dougless gave Lee the same story she had given to the cook, and by now every servant probably knew that Nicholas was indeed a descendant and wanted very much to clear his ancestor's name.

"I'm glad I had ol' Arabella sign a contract because if he'd asked first I think she would have given him first access to the papers. Look at them. The way she's looking at him they just might go to it on the table—again."

Dougless choked on her salmon and had to drink half a glass of water to clear her throat.

"What is the boss to you? You two aren't . . . you know."

"No, of course not," Dougless said and looked at Nicholas as he leaned over, looking at Arabella.

When she saw Nicholas glance up, she moved a little nearer Lee. "I was thinking, Lee, since my boss seems so busy, maybe you need a secretary for the weekend. My father is a professor of medieval history and I've had some experience helping him with research."

"Montgomery," Lee said. "Montgomery. Not Adam Montgomery?"

"That's my dad."

"I heard him once present a brilliant paper on thirteenth-century economics. So, he's your father. Maybe I could use a little help."

Dougless could almost read his mind. Adam Montgomery would be in a position to help a struggling young professor. But Dougless didn't mind. Wasn't ambition good? Besides, she could let him believe whatever he wanted if it helped her find out what secret Nicholas's mother knew.

"The trunk is in my room," Lee was saying, and his looks were decidedly warmer since finding out who her father was. "Maybe after dinner you'd like to, ah . . . visit."

"Sure," Dougless said and envisioned an evening spent running around a table trying to escape his advances. At the thought of a table she glanced at Nicholas and saw he was glaring at her. She lifted her wine glass to him and drank. He turned away, glowering.

After dinner Dougless went back to her room to get her notebook and a few supplies, as well as her purse. She thought she might as well be prepared for a long night of rummaging through four-hundred-year-old documents.

Twice she got lost turning wrong corners as she looked for Lee's room. Outside one open door she halted when she heard Arabella's seductive voice. "But, darling, I get so frightened alone at night."

"Truly," Dougless heard Nicholas say, "I would have thought you past such childish fears."

Dougless rolled her eyes.

"Here, let me refill your glass," Arabella said. "And then I'd like to show you something." Her voice lowered. "In my room."

Dougless grimaced. Stupid man! According to the cook, Arabella showed *everything* in her room to every male. Then with a malicious little smile, Dougless began looking through her purse. Brightly, she walked into the parlor. Every light except one dim one was off, Arabella was pouring a waterglass full of bourbon and Nicholas sat on the sofa with his shirt half open.

"Oh, Lord Stafford," Dougless said brightly, and briskly began going about the room turning on every light. "Here is the calculator you wanted, but I'm afraid the only one I have is solar. It will only work in a very bright room."

Nicholas stared with interest at the small calculator she handed him and when she began to demonstrate it, his eyes turned to saucers. "One may add?"

"And subtract and multiply and divide. See, here's your answer. Say you wanted to subtract this year, 1988 from 1564, the year your ancestor was accused of treason and lost his family's fortune forever, you'd get a minus four hundred and twenty-four years. Four hundred and twenty-four years in which to right a wrong and keep your descendants from laughing at you—him."

"You," Arabella said, so angry she could barely speak, "leave this room at once."

"Oh. Oh," Dougless said innocently. "Was I disturbing you? I'm awfully sorry. I didn't mean to. I was just doing my job." She started backing toward the door. "Please carry on with what you were doing."

Dougless left the room, walked down the hall, then tiptoed back. She saw the shadows from the room darken.

"I need light," Nicholas said. "The machine does not work without light."

"Nicholas, for God's sake, it's only a calculator. Put it away."

"It is a most wondrous machine. What is this mark?"

"It's a percent sign but I can't see that it matters now."

"Demonstrate its function."

Dougless could hear Arabella's sigh through the walls. Smiling, quite pleased with herself, Dougless went off in search of Lee's room. He greeted her, wearing, of all things, a silk smoking jacket. Dougless refrained from giggling. One look at his face and at the martini glass he held and Dougless knew that he had no intention of talking to her about anything except why she should jump into bed with him. She took the martini, sipped it, and grimaced. She hated martinis, dry or otherwise.

Lee started by telling her how beautiful her hair was, how surprised he was to find such a stunning woman in this mouldy old house, what a great dresser she was, and how little her feet were. Dougless could have yawned. Instead, when he refilled her glass, she took two precious Librax from her purse, opened the capsules, and poured them into Lee's drink. "Bottoms up," she said cheerfully.

While she was waiting for the pills to take effect, she showed Lee the note Nicholas had slipped under her door. "What does this say?"

He glanced at it. "I think I should write the translation." He took a pen and paper and wrote:

> I think my selfe moch
> bownden unto yow.
> I am Desyrynge of yo
> assystance no further.

"Desyrynge?"

"Deserving."

She had come close to guessing what Nicholas had said that night when he'd left her, the night she'd found him in a tavern.

Lee rubbed his hand over his eyes and yawned.

He stood, went to the bed, and stretched out "for just a minute."

He was out like a light and Dougless eagerly went to the little wooden chest on the table near the fireplace.

The papers inside were old, yellow and brittle, but the writing was clear, the ink not faded as modern inks faded in a mere year or two. Dougless had eagerly grabbed the papers but her heart sank as she looked at them. They were in the handwriting of the note Nicholas had slipped under her door and she couldn't read a word.

She was bent over the papers, trying to decipher a word here and there, when suddenly the door burst open.

"Ah-ha!" Nicholas said, his sword in his hand as he charged into the room.

When Dougless's heart settled back in place from the fright he'd given her, she smiled at him. "Arabella finish with you?"

Nicholas looked from Lee asleep on the bed to Dougless bending over the papers, and began to look embarrassed. "She was off to bed," he said.

"Alone?"

Nicholas walked to the table and picked up a letter. "My mother's hand," he said.

At the tone in his voice, Dougless forgot her jealousy. "I cannot read them."

"Oh?" he said, lifting one eyebrow. "I might teach you to read. In the evenings. I believe you could learn."

Dougless laughed. "Okay, you've made your point. Now sit down and read."

"And him?" Nicholas pointed with his sword at the sleeping Lee.

"He's out of it for the night."

Nicholas put his sword across the table and began to read the letter. Since Dougless could be of no help, she sat quietly and watched him. If he was so in love with his wife, why was he jealous when another man looked at her, Dougless? And why was he fooling around with Arabella?

"Nicholas?" she said softly. "Have you ever considered what would happen if you didn't return to your time?"

"No," he answered, scanning a letter. "I *must* return."

"But what if you don't? What if you stay here forever?"

"I have been sent here to find answers. A wrong has been done my family, as well as me. I have been sent here to right that wrong."

Dougless was playing with the hilt of his sword, rolling it so the jewels reflected in the table lamp. "But what if you were sent here for another reason? A reason that had nothing to do with your being accused of treason?"

"And what would be that reason?"

"I don't know," she said, but she thought *love.*

He looked at her. "For this love you speak of?" he asked, almost reading her mind. "Perhaps God thinks as a woman and cares more for love than for honor." He was making fun of her.

"For your information, there are many people who believe God is a woman."

Nicholas gave her a look that let her know how absurd he thought that idea.

"No, really," Dougless said. "What if you don't go back? What if you find out what you need to know and you still stay here? Like say for a year or more?"

"I will not," Nicholas said, but he looked up at Dougless. Four hundred years had not changed Arabella. She was the same. She still wanted one man after another in her bed, still had a heart of stone. But this girl who made him laugh, who helped him, who looked at him with big eyes that showed everything she felt, this woman could almost make him want to stay. "I *must* return," he said sternly and looked back at the letters.

"I know it's all fiercely important but it did happen so long ago and everything seems to have worked out all right. Your mother married a rich man and lived out her days in luxury. It wasn't as if she was tossed out in the snow or anything, and I know your family lost the Stafford estates but, really, who was left? You said you had no kids and your brother died childless, so who did you deprive? The estates went to Queen Elizabeth and she built England into a great country so maybe your money helped your country. Maybe—"

"Cease!" Nicholas said angrily. "You do not understand honor. My memory is ridiculed. Arabella says she has read about me and all your world remembers is what a clerk recorded. I know the man. He was ugly and no woman would have him."

"So he wrote about you. Nicholas, I'm sorry, but it really is done. It's over. Maybe history can't be changed. I was just wondering what you'd do if you had to stay, if you weren't called back."

Nicholas didn't want to think about that. Would he tell Dougless that he'd marry her and run with her to bed? He didn't want to tell her that Arabella, once so very, very appealing, was now a bore to him.

"Montgomery, do you fall in love with me again? Come, we will take these letters to my bedchamber. I will let you make love to me."

"Drop dead," Dougless said, rising. "Stay here and read. I don't care what happens to you, whether you stay in the twentieth century or go back to the sixteenth century, or to the eighth for all I care." She left the room, shutting the door so hard Lee stirred on the bed.

Falling in love with him, indeed, she thought. She might as well fall in love with a ghost. He had about as much substance as a ghost. And, besides, if he did stay in the twentieth century he'd be a great nuisance. Always, she'd have to explain things to him. Imagine trying to teach him to drive a car! Horrendous thought. And if he did stay, what would he do? What *could* he do? All he seemed capable of was riding mean horses, handling a sword and . . .

And making love to women, she thought. He seemed to be awfully good at that.

As she made her way down to her dreary little room, she told herself she'd be quite glad to get rid of him. His poor wife. She had a great deal to put up with. Arabella was only one of the women Dougless knew about. There were probably hundreds of women the poor ugly little clerk had known nothing about.

Yes, Dougless thought as she put on her nightgown, she would be well rid of him when the time came. But as she climbed into bed she couldn't imagine not seeing Nicholas every day, not watching his delight over things she took for granted. She couldn't imagine not seeing his smile or having him tease her.

It took her a long time before she slept and when she did, she slept fitfully.

In the morning, feeling absolutely rotten, Dougless went into the kitchen to see the cook, Mrs. Anderson, and another woman staring at the work table. It was covered with opened tin cans, somewhere between twenty and thirty of them.

"What happened?" Dougless asked.

"I'm not sure," the cook said. "I opened a tin of pineapple then left the room for a moment. When I returned someone had opened all these tins."

Dougless stood frowning for a moment, then looked at Mrs. Anderson. "Did anyone see you open the can of pineapple?"

"Now that you mention it, there was someone here. Lord Stafford came through to go to the stables. He stopped and spoke to me. Very nice man, that."

Dougless tried to hide her smile. Nicholas had no doubt seen the marvel of a can opener and decided to try it out. At that moment a maid came running into the kitchen, carrying a vacuum cleaner hose.

"I need a broom handle," the maid said and sounded as if she were about to cry. "Lord Stafford asked to see the Hoover and he sucked up all of Lady Arabella's jewelry. I'll be discharged when she finds out."

Dougless left the kitchen feeling a great deal better than she had.

She didn't know where she was supposed to eat breakfast, but she wandered into the empty dining room to find a sideboard covered with silver chafing dishes. Feeling a little defiant, she filled a plate and sat down.

"Good morning," Lee said, entering the room. He filled a plate and sat across from her. "Ah . . . sorry about last night," he said. "I guess I sort of passed out. Did you see the letters?"

"I did but I couldn't read them," she said honestly, then leaned forward. "Have you read enough to find out who betrayed Nicholas Stafford to the queen?"

"Oh heavens, yes. I found that out the first time I opened the trunk."

"Who?" she asked under her breath.

Lee opened his mouth to speak, but Nicholas entered the room and Lee shut up.

"Montgomery," Nicholas said sternly. "I would see you in the library." He turned and left the room.

Lee grunted. "What's wrong with him? Get up on the wrong side of Arabella's bed?"

Dougless threw down her napkin, glared at Lee, and went to the library. She closed the door behind her. "Do you know what you did? Lee was just about to tell me who betrayed you, and you walked in and stopped him."

Nicholas had circles under his eyes, but instead of making him look bad they made him look even better, even more darkly romantic, rather like Heathcliffe. "I read the letters," he said as he sat down in a leather-upholstered chair and stared out the window. "There is no naming of who betrayed me."

There was something making him sad. Dougless went to him and put her hand on his shoulder. "What is it? Did the letters upset you?"

"The letters tell," he said softly, "of what my mother suffered after my death. She tells of . . ." He stopped and took her hand and held on to her fingers. "She tells of the ridicule of the Stafford name."

Dougless couldn't bear the pain in his voice. She went to the front of the chair and knelt before him, her hands on his knees. "We'll find out who lied about you," Dougless said. "If Lee knows I'll find out. And when we find out you can return and change things. Your being here means you're being given a second chance."

He looked at her for a long moment, then cupped her face in his big hands. "Do you always give hope? Do you never believe there is no hope?"

She smiled. "I'm almost always optimistic. That's why I keep falling in love with thugs and hoping one of them will turn into my Knight in Shining— Oh, Colin," she said and started to pull away.

But Nicholas pulled her from the floor and into his arms and kissed her. He'd kissed her before, but then he'd merely desired her, now he wanted more from her. He wanted her sweetness, her loving heart. He wanted the way she looked at him, her eagerness to please.

"Dougless," he whispered, holding her, kissing her neck.

It was when the thought crossed his mind that he didn't want to leave that he shoved her from him. "Go," he murmured in the tone of a man under great stress.

Dougless stood, her anger rising. "I don't understand you. You kiss any woman who can reach your face, you never push any of them away, but with me you act as if I have some contagious disease. What is it? Do I have terminal bad breath? I'm too short for you? My hair not the right color?"

Nicholas looked at her and all his desire for her, all his longing was flaming in his eyes.

Dougless stepped back from him, as a person might step back from a bonfire that was too hot. She put her hand to her throat and for a long moment they just looked at each other.

The door flew open and Arabella burst into the room. She was wearing what was obviously a designer-made English outdoor outfit. "Nicholas, where have you been?" She looked from Nicholas to Dougless and she didn't seem to like what she saw.

Dougless turned away, for she could no longer bear to look in Nicholas's eyes.

"Nicholas," Arabella demanded, "we are waiting. The guns are loaded."

"Guns?" Dougless asked, turning around, composing herself.

Arabella looked Dougless up and down and obviously found her wanting. Tall women often seemed to feel like that about small women, Dougless thought, and was awfully glad men didn't feel the same.

"We hunt duck," Nicholas said and wasn't looking at Dougless. "Dickie will show me a shotgun."

"Great," Dougless said, "go shoot pretty little ducks. I'll manage." She hurried past Arabella and out the door. Upstairs she looked down on the courtyard as Nicholas got into a Range Rover and Arabella drove him away.

Turning away, she realized she had nothing to do. She didn't feel free to explore Arabella's house and she didn't want to walk in Arabella's gardens. She asked a passing servant where Lee was and found he was locked in his room with the letters and was not to be disturbed.

"But he left a book for you in the library," the servant said.

Dougless went back to the library and there on the desk was a small volume with a note attached. "Thought you might enjoy this. Lee," it read. She picked up the book.

At her first sight of the book she knew what it was: it was the diary of John Wilfred, the ugly little clerk who had written of Nicholas and Arabella-on-the-table. The foreword said the book had been found in a cubby-hole behind a wall when one of Nicholas's houses was torn down in the fifties.

Dougless took the book and settled down on the settee to read it. Within twenty pages she knew it was the diary of a lovesick young man—and the woman he loved was Nicholas's wife, Lettice. According to John Wilfred, his mistress could do no wrong and his master no right. Pages listing Nicholas's shortcomings were followed by pages listing Lettice's glories. According to this drooling clerk, Lettice was beautiful beyond pearls, wise, virtuous, kind, talented . . . on and on until Dougless wanted to throw up.

The clerk had nothing good to say about Nicholas. According to the book, Nicholas spent his time fornicating, blaspheming, and making the lives of everyone around him hell. Other than the snide, spiteful story about Arabella and the table, there were no specific stories about what Nicholas had done to deserve the animosity of all (if Wilfred were to be believed) his household.

Dougless finished the book and slammed it shut. Because of the false accusation of treason against Nicholas, his estates had been destroyed and with them the true story of his life, how he'd managed the estates owned by his brother and designed a beautiful mansion.

All that was left of him was the spiteful yearnings of a whining boy. Yet people today *believed* this.

She stood, her anger making her fists clench. Nicholas was right: he had to return to his own time to right the wrong done him. She'd tell him about the book, and when he returned to the sixteenth century he could kick ol' John Wilfred out of his house. Or, Dougless thought, smiling, he could send the ugly little clerk off with the perfect Lettice.

Dougless took the book, left the library, and asked a servant where Lord Stafford's room was. She thought she'd leave the book for him to see. He was beginning to be able to read modern print now, and she was sure he'd have enough interest to read this book.

His room was next to one that a maid said was Lady Arabella's. It would be, she thought angrily.

Once in his room, her anger left her. It was done in shades of blue, with a four-poster bed draped with rich blue silk. In the bedroom were Nicholas's toiletries, all the things she'd chosen for him. She put out her hand and touched the shaving cream, the toothpaste, his razor.

Quite suddenly, it hit her how much she missed him. Since he'd appeared, they'd been together almost constantly. They'd shared a bedroom, a bathroom, a toothbrush. She turned and looked at the tub, with no shower head above it, and wondered how he dealt with the lack of a shower. Were there other things in his room that he didn't understand?

As she walked back into the bedroom she smiled, remembering the way he would come out of the bathroom wearing nothing but a towel, his hair clean. Before coming to Goshawk Hall, they'd been intimate in such a pleasant way. She'd tucked him in at night, kissed his forehead, washed out his underwear in the basin. They'd laughed together, talked together, shared together.

There was a *Time* magazine on the bedside table and on impulse she pulled out the table drawer. Inside was a little pencil sharpener and three pencils, two of which were now only an inch long, and a stapler and two pieces of paper with about fifty staples in them. There was a toy friction car on top of a colored brochure for Aston-Martin cars, and beneath that was the current issue of *Playboy* magazine. Smiling, she closed the drawer.

She walked toward the window and looked out across the rolling lawns to the trees beyond. It was odd how she had lived with Robert for over a year and had believed herself madly in love with him, but on some levels she didn't feel she'd ever been as intimate with Robert as she had with Nicholas. Maybe it was because Nicholas was so easy to be with. Nicholas never complained when she squeezed the toothpaste tube in the middle. Nicholas never whined about how she hadn't made everything absolutely perfect.

In fact, Nicholas seemed to like her just as she was. He seemed to accept what was, whether in people or things, and he found joy in them. Dougless thought of all the dates she'd had with modern men and how they complained about everything: the wine wasn't right, the service was slow, the movie had no deeper meaning. But Nicholas, faced with insurmountable problems, found joy in such things as a can opener.

She wondered how Robert would react if he suddenly found himself in the sixteenth century. No doubt he'd start demanding this and demanding that and whining when it wasn't given to him. She wondered if the Elizabethans were like cowboys of old and hanged men who were particularly bothersome.

She leaned her head against the cool glass. When would Nicholas leave? When he found out who had betrayed him? If Lee mentioned the name at dinner, would Nicholas suddenly go up in a puff of smoke?

It's almost over, she thought and felt her heart yearning for him. How would she deal with never seeing him again? If she could barely stand not seeing him for one whole day, how was she to live the rest of her life without him?

Please come back, she thought. We have so little time left. Tomorrow you might be gone and I don't want to miss this time with you. Don't spend this little bit of time we have left with Arabella.

She closed her eyes and tightened her whole body as she wished for him to return.

"If you'll come back," she whispered, "I'll make you an American lunch: fried chicken, potato salad, deviled eggs and a chocolate cake. While I'm cooking you can . . ." She thought. "You can look at plastic wrap and aluminum foil and Tupperware—if they have it in England. Please, please, please return, Nicholas."

◇ ◇ ◇

Nicholas's head came up. Arabella's arms were about his neck, her abundant breasts pressed against his bare chest. They were in a private glade where he and a past Arabella had spent an energetic afternoon. But today Nicholas had little interest in the woman. She had told him she wanted to discuss what she'd found out about his ancestor. She said she had new information, facts that had never been published before.

Her words were a lure to him and to find out what she knew he'd pay any price.

Arabella pulled Nicholas's head back down.

"Do you hear it?" Nicholas said.

"Nothing, darling," Arabella whispered. "I hear only you."

Nicholas pulled away from her. "I must go."

Seeing anger flood her haughty face, Nicholas knew he did not want to enrage her. "Someone comes," he said, "and you are too lovely to share with the prying eyes of anyone. I would keep your beauty to myself."

This seemed to mollify her as she began fastening her clothes. "I've never met a man who was more of a gentleman than you. Tonight then?"

"Tonight," he said and left her.

For the most part the hunters drove Range Rovers but there were a half-dozen horses tied near the cars. Nicholas took the best one, rode it back to the house, and mounted the stairs two at a time. He flung open the door to his bedroom.

Dougless wasn't surprised, really, when Nicholas appeared in the doorway.

Nicholas stood there for a moment and stared at her. Her face, her body, showed her wanting of him. It was the most difficult thing Nicholas had ever done but he looked away. He could not, would not touch her. If he did . . . If he did, he was not sure he would want to return to his own time.

"What do you want of me?" he asked harshly.

"*I* want you?" she asked, angry. She'd seen the way he'd turned away from her. "It looks as if someone else wanted you, not me."

Nicholas looked up at a mirror in the wardrobe door and saw that his shirt was buttoned wrong. "The guns are good," he said, refastening his shirt. "With those we could beat the Spanish."

"England beats everyone and without modern guns. Next thing you'll want bombs to take back with you. Did the guns unbutton your shirt?"

He looked at her in the mirror. "Your jealousy brightens your eyes."

Dougless's anger dissolved. "Cad!" she said. "Did it ever occur to you that you're making a fool of yourself a second time around? History has loved the story of you and Arabella, and now here you are doing it again."

"She knows what I do not."

"I'll bet she does," Dougless muttered. "Probably more experienced."

Nicholas chucked her under the chin. "I doubt so. Is that food I smell? I am hungry."

Dougless smiled. "I promised you an American lunch. Come on, let's go see Mrs. Anderson."

They walked arm in arm to the kitchen. The hunters had taken lunch with them in baskets so the kitchen was not being used now, except for a pudding steaming on the back burner of the Aga.

After getting Mrs. Anderson's permission, Dougless set to work, putting potatoes and eggs on to boil, then starting on the cake. She decided on chewy, pecan-filled brownies instead. Nicholas sat at the big table and experimented with plastic wrap and aluminum foil and opened and closed plastic containers. He peeled eggs and potatoes and chopped onions.

"Did you help Lettice cook?" she asked.

Nicholas laughed at her.

When the food was ready, Dougless cleaned the kitchen—Nicholas refused to help—and packed everything in a big basket along with a thermos of lemonade. Nicholas carried it for her out to a little walled garden where they sat under elm trees and ate.

She told him about reading the diary that morning and, as he ate his fifth piece of chicken, she asked him about Lettice. "You never mention her. You talk about your mother, your brother who died. You've even mentioned your favorite horse but you never say anything about your *wife*."

"You would have me tell of her?" he said in a tone that was almost warning.

"Is she as beautiful as Arabella?"

Nicholas thought of Lettice. She seemed farther away than a mere four hundred years. Arabella was stupid, a man could never have a moment's conversation with her, but she had passion. Lettice had no passion but she had brains—brains enough to always determine what was best for her. "No, she is not like Arabella."

"Is she like me?" Dougless asked.

Nicholas looked at her and thought of Lettice cooking a meal. "She is not like you. What is this?"

"Sliced tomatoes," she said absently and started to ask Nicholas more questions but he interrupted her.

"The man who abandoned you, you said you loved him. Why?"

Dougless immediately felt defensive and started to say that Robert was great husband material, but her shoulders slumped. "Ego," she said. "My own overblown sense of how powerful I was. Robert told me no one had ever loved him very much. He said his mother was cold to him and his first wife was cold. I thought I could give him all the love he'd ever need. So I gave to him and gave to him. I tried to do everything he wanted me to do, but . . ."

She looked up at the sky. "I guess I thought that someday he'd be like those men in the movies and turn to me and say, 'You're the best woman in the world. You give me all that I ask for.' But he didn't. Robert kept saying, 'You never give me anything.' So, dumb me, I'd try even harder to give him more. But . . ."

"Yes?" Nicholas asked softly.

Dougless tried to smile. "He gave his daughter a diamond bracelet and me half of the bills."

She looked away from him, but then she saw he was holding out a ring to her. He'd stopped wearing his big rings when he astutely saw that no other men wore such rings. This ring was an emerald the size of a beach pebble.

"What is this for?"

"Had I access to what is mine, I would shower you with jewels."

She smiled at him. "You've already given me the pin." She held her hand to her heart. She wore the pin inside her bra, afraid to wear it outside because its age and uniqueness might cause questions. "You've given me too much already. You've bought me clothes, you've . . . You've been kind to me." She smiled. "Nicholas, the past few days since I met you have been the happiest time of my life. I hope you never go back."

She clamped her hand over her mouth. "I didn't mean that. Of course you need to go back. You need to go back to your beautiful wife. You need to . . . need to make some heirs to inherit those wonderful estates you won't have to forfeit to the queen. But, did you realize that if Dr. Nolman tells us who betrayed you you might return then? Immediately. Lee says the name and you disappear. Pow! Gone, just like that."

Nicholas, who had been rummaging in the basket, stopped. "I will know tomorrow. Whether he wishes to tell me or no, on the morrow I will find out."

"Tomorrow," Dougless said and looked at him as if trying to memorize his features. She looked down at his body, at the shirt stretched across his wide shoulders, his flat belly, his muscular legs. Fine legs, he'd said, and she remembered him wrapped in a towel.

"Nicholas," she whispered, leaning toward him.

"What is this?" he asked sharply, holding a brownie between their faces.

"A brownie," she said in disgust, feeling like a fool. Who was she kidding? He'd kissed her a few times but only when she'd thrown herself at him. Yet he'd returned from a morning with Arabella with his shirt misbuttoned. "Food," she muttered. She seemed able to please him only with food and plastic wrap. She so much wanted to touch him that her fingertips ached, but he seemed to have no such feeling toward her.

"I guess we better go," she said flatly. "Arabella will be back soon and she'll want you." She started to stand but Nicholas caught her arm.

"I would rather an hour with you than a life with Arabella."

Dougless swallowed and didn't dare look at him. Was he telling the truth or just trying to make her feel better?

"Sing me a song while I eat these," he said.

"I can't sing and I don't know any songs. How about a story?"

"Mmm," was all he said, his mouth full of chocolate.

Dougless realized how many stories were new to him, stories that were part of our culture but he knew nothing of. She told him of Dr. Jekyll and Mr. Hyde.

"I have a cousin like that," he said. He finished off the plate of brownies, then, to her surprise, turned and put his head in her lap.

"You're going to get fat if you keep eating like you do."

"You think me fat?" he said, looking up at her and making Dougless's heart beat faster. He seemed to know exactly what he did to her and laughed at her for it, but he remained unaffected by her. Only when she was near another man did he show any interest in her.

"Close your eyes and behave," she said, stroking his hair, that thick, soft, curling mass, while she told him story after story.

It was nearly sundown when he opened his eyes again and looked up at her for a long while. "We must go."

"Yes," she said softly. "Tonight I will try to find out from Lee who betrayed you."

He moved so that he was kneeling before her and he put one hand on her cheek. Dougless held her breath as she thought he was going to kiss her again. "When I return," he said, "I will think of you."

"And I you," she said, putting her hand on his.

He moved his hand, picked up the emerald ring from the basket lid and put it in her hand, closing her fingers over it.

"Nicholas, I can't take this. You've given me so much already."

His eyes locked with hers and there was a faraway sadness in them. "I would give more than this to . . ."

"To?" she encouraged.

"To take you back with me."

Dougless drew her breath in sharply.

Nicholas cursed himself. He should not have said that. He should not make her hope. He did not want to hurt her, but the thought of leaving her behind was becoming an almost unbearable pain. Soon he would find out what he needed to know and then he knew he'd go back. One night more, he thought. At the most he'd have one more night with her.

Perhaps tonight he'd take her to his bed. Their last night spent in love and ecstasy.

No! he told himself, looking into her eyes, falling into them. He could not do that to her, to leave her behind, weeping harder than when he'd first seen her. Hell, he thought, he could not do it to himself. To go back to his cold wife, to the emptiness of women like Arabella. No, it was better to leave her untouched.

"Aye," he said, grinning, "to cook for me."

"Cook?" Dougless asked stupidly. "Why, you overbearing, insufferable, vain—"

"Pillicock?" he asked.

"That sounds perfect. You pillicock! If you think I'm going back to a time of no running water, no doctors, where the dentists yank out your teeth and break your jaw doing it, just to *cook* for you, then—"

He leaned forward, nuzzled his face under her hair, and licked her ear-lobe. "I will let you visit my bed."

Dougless pushed him away and started to describe his vanity, but her expression changed. She could give it out too. "Okay, I'll do it. I'll go back with you and cook for you and Sunday afternoons we spend in bed together. Or on the tables. Whichever."

Nicholas rocked back on his heels and his face seemed to drain of color. He began tossing scraps into the basket. It horrified him to think of her in his age. If she were his lover, Lettice would chop her into little pieces.

"Nicholas," Dougless said, "I was just teasing." He didn't look at her. "Here, I'll take the ring if it will make you happy."

He stopped shoving things into the basket and looked at her. "You do not know what you say. Do not wish for what should not be. When last I was home I was to face the blade. If I went back then and you came with me, you would be alone. My age is not like yours. Lone women do not fare well. If I were not there to fend for you, you—"

She put her hand on his arm. "I really was only teasing. I won't go back. I have no secrets to find out. *You* came to find out something, remember?"

"You are right," he said and quickly lifted her hand and kissed it. He stood and Dougless could see he planned to leave the basket where it was. He probably only cleaned up because he was upset. But what in the world had upset him?

She carried the basket back to the house, following behind him, neither of them speaking.

10

When they got back to the house, Nicholas barely nodded to her as he went through the kitchen and up to his room. Dougless, more puzzled than anything else, went to her room. On her bed was a large box, bearing the name of an express company. Dougless tore into it, throwing tape and paper everywhere.

Inside were two of her mother's gorgeous designer gowns.

"Thank you, thank you, Elizabeth," she breathed, holding a gown up to her. Maybe tonight Nicholas would notice someone besides the stately Arabella.

◇ ◇ ◇

When Dougless walked into the sitting room where the Harewood family was serving cocktails, she knew the two and a half hours of work of getting ready had been worth it. Lee paused with his drink halfway to his mouth, and Lady Arabella, for once, looked away from Nicholas. Lord Harewood even stopped talking about guns and dogs and his roses. As for Nicholas, Dougless thought, his reaction was worth all the effort. His eyes lit when he first saw her, grew hot as he approached, and at last he halted and scowled.

Her mother's white dress was one piece of clingy fabric that had one long sleeve but left her other shoulder and arm bare. It was covered with tiny beads and when she moved they showed off every curve she had. She had fastened Gloria's diamond bracelet about the wrist of her bare arm.

"Good evening," she said.

"Wow," Lee said, looking her up and down. "Wow."

Dougless smiled at him rather regally. "Is that a drink? Could you possibly get me a gin and tonic?"

Lee went off as obediently as a schoolboy.

It was amazing what clothes could do for a woman, Dougless thought. Last night she wanted to cower under the table in Arabella's presence, but tonight Arabella's low-cut red gown looked frumpy and tasteless.

"What do you do?" Nicholas asked, hovering over her.

"I have no idea what you're talking about," she said, blinking innocently up at him.

"You are exposed." He sounded shocked.

"A lot less than your Arabella is," she snapped, then smiled. "Do you like this dress? I had my sister ship it to me."

Nicholas's back was stiffer than usual. "Do you mean to see that physician after supper?"

"Of course," she said sweetly. "Remember that you asked me to find out what he knew."

"Nicholas," Arabella called. "Dinner."

"You must not wear that gown."

"I'll wear anything I please and you better go. Arabella is rattling your table legs."

"You—"

"Here you are," Lee said, handing Dougless a drink. "Good evening, Lord Stafford."

Dinner was a wonderful experience for Dougless. Nicholas couldn't keep his eyes off her—much to the lovely Lady Arabella's fury. Lee hovered over her so closely that his coat sleeve dangled in Dougless's soup bowl.

After dinner they went to the drawing room and, like a scene from a Jane Austen novel, Nicholas played the piano and sang. He had a rich, deep voice that she loved. He invited Dougless to sing with him but she knew she had no voice. She sat on a hard little chair and watched jealously as Arabella and Nicholas sang a duet, their heads together, their voices entwined.

At ten o'clock, Dougless excused herself and went to her room. She had no desire to spend the evening alone with Lee in his room. The secret of who betrayed Nicholas would have to wait another day.

At midnight, Dougless knew she wasn't going to be able to sleep. She kept seeing Nicholas singing with Arabella, kept remembering the way he'd returned from the fields with his shirt misbuttoned. She got out of bed, put on her robe, fluffed up her hair, and made her way through the big house to Nicholas's room. There was no light from under *his* door, but there was light and the sound of glasses clinking and Arabella's seductive laugh coming from behind *her* door.

Dougless didn't think about what she was doing. She gave a single knock, and at the same time she put her hand on the doorknob, turned it, and walked into Arabella's bedroom. "Hi, I was wondering if I could borrow a pin. I seem to have a broken strap. A very important strap, if you know what I mean."

Nicholas was stretched out on Arabella's bed, his shirt open and hanging out of his trousers. Arabella was wearing a filmy black peignoir that didn't cover much of her skin, and what little fabric there was was transparent.

"You . . . you . . ." Arabella sputtered.

"Oh, hi, Lord Stafford, did I interrupt something?"

Nicholas was looking at her with great amusement.

"Look at this," Dougless said, "a Bang and Olafson TV. I've never seen one. I hope you don't mind, I really wanted to see the late news. Ah, here's the remote control." She sat on the edge of the bed, turned on the big color TV and began flipping channels. Behind her she felt Nicholas sit up.

"A movie," he whispered.

"Naw, just TV." She handed him the remote control. "See, here's the on and off. This is volume, and these are channels. Look at that! It's an old movie about Queen Elizabeth." She flipped off the TV, put the remote control on the bedside table near Nicholas, yawned, and said, "I just remembered that I have some pins. Thanks though, Lady Arabella. Hope I didn't disturb you too much."

Dougless had to run to the door because Arabella was coming after her, her hands forming claws. Dougless barely made it through the door before it slammed on her heels. Standing outside, she listened to what went on inside the room. After a moment, she heard the unmistakable sounds of a TV western, then Arabella screeching, "Turn that off!" Smiling, Dougless went back to her room and she had no trouble going to sleep.

◇ ◇ ◇

In the morning, Lee met her for breakfast. "I thought maybe you'd come by my room last night," he said. "I was going to read the letters to you."

"Planning to tell me who betrayed Nicholas Stafford?"

"Mmm," was all Lee'd say, so after breakfast Dougless followed him up the stairs. If he told her the name, would Nicholas immediately return to the sixteenth century?

But she saw right away that getting Lee to tell her anything was going to be a problem.

"I was trying to remember. Wasn't your father on the board of directors at Yale? Maybe he'd be interested in reading my findings."

"I'd sure be glad to tell him about them. I'd especially like to tell him who betrayed Lord Stafford."

Lee stepped very close to her. "I'd tell if perhaps you made a little call."

"My father's staying in the wilds of Maine right now and can't be reached."

"Oh," he said, turning away. "I guess I can't tell you then."

"You little blackmailer," Dougless seethed before she thought. "You're playing with a single career, but the name of this traitor means a man's life to me."

He turned to her with a look of astonishment. "How can some sixteenth-century papers mean someone's life?"

She didn't know how much to explain to him. "I'll talk to my father. I'll write him a letter today. You can see the letter. He'll get it as soon as he returns."

Lee looked at her, frowning. "Why do you want this name so much? There's something fishy about all this. Who is Lord Stafford anyway? You two don't act much like secretary and boss. You act more like—"

It was at that moment that the door flew open and Nicholas entered. He was wearing his Elizabethan clothes, his legs showing all their muscularity in the tight hose, his silver and gold armor flashing in the sunlight. He held his sword and pointed it at Lee's throat.

"Just what is this?" Lee demanded. He pushed the sword away, then gasped when the sharp blade cut the side of his hand.

Nicholas advanced on him, the tip of the lethal weapon at Lee's throat.

"Dougless, get some help," Lee said, backing up. "He's gone mad."

When Lee was pinned against the wall, Nicholas spoke. "Who betrayed me to the Queen?"

"Betrayed you? You *are* crazy. Dougless, get someone before this lunatic does something we'll both regret."

"Say his name," Nicholas said, pushing the sword tip deeper into Lee's throat.

"All right," Lee said, exasperated. "It was a man named—"

"Wait!" Dougless cried and looked at Nicholas. "If he tells, you might go. Oh, Nicholas, I might never see you again."

Still holding the sword at Lee's throat, Nicholas held his arm out to Dougless and she ran to him, her mouth to his before their bodies touched.

She kissed him with all the longing, all the pent-up desire she felt. Her hands clutched his hair and pulled his head down as she kissed him. For all that Dougless thought he didn't desire her, the passion she felt coming from Nicholas made her feet come off the floor as he lifted her with one arm.

He broke away first. "Go," he said.

Tears were blurring Dougless's eyes and she could swear there were tears forming in Nicholas's eyes.

"Go," he said again. "Stand away from me."

Obediently, too limp to disobey, Dougless walked a few feet away and stood looking at him. Never to see him again, never to hold him, never to hear him laugh, never—

"The name!" Nicholas demanded but his eyes never left Dougless's. When he left this world he wanted his last sight to be of her.

Lee was bewildered by all that was going on. "The man was named—"

Everything happened at once. Dougless, unable to bear the thought of Nicholas's leaving, made a flying leap at him. If he was going, she was going too.

"Robert Sydney," Lee said as Nicholas and Dougless went sprawling on the floor at his feet. He looked down at them. *"Both* of you are crazy," he said, stepping over them and leaving the room.

Dougless kept her head buried against the silver-coated steel of Nicholas's armor, her eyes tightly shut.

When Nicholas recovered himself, he looked down at her, amused. "We have arrived," he said.

"Where? Are there cars outside or donkey carts?"

Chuckling, he lifted her face in his hands. "We remain in your time. I said you were to stand to one side."

"Well, I . . . ah, I . . ." She got off him to sit up. "I just thought it might be a wonderful experience to see Elizabethan England firsthand. I could write a book, you know, and answer all the questions that people *really* want to know, like was Elizabeth bald or not? Were the people happy? What did—"

Nicholas sat up and kissed her mouth most sweetly. "You cannot return with me." He put his hand to his back. "You are hard on my armor. There are scratches from when you last struck me down."

"You were about to step in front of a bus."

He stood and held out his hands to lift her, and when Dougless stood she wouldn't release his hands. "You're still here," she breathed at last. "You know the traitor's name and yet you're still here. Robert Sydney. Sydney? But wasn't it Arabella Sydney that you . . . That you and she . . ."

Nicholas put his arm about her shoulders and walked to the window. "He was Arabella's husband," he said softly. "It is not easy to believe he would lie to the queen about me."

"Damn you and that table!" she said fiercely. "If you hadn't been so . . . so overzealous and had Arabella on the table her husband might not have hated you. And what about your wife? She must have been pretty upset too."

"I was unmarried on that occasion when I took Arabella."

"On that occasion," Dougless muttered. "Maybe Robert got mad for all the other times, too." She turned to look at him. "If I went back with you, maybe I could keep you out of trouble."

He pushed her head down on his armored shoulder. "You cannot return with me."

"Maybe you won't return. Maybe you're going to stay here forever."

"We must go to Ashburton where my tomb lies. I will go there and pray."

She wanted to say more, to say something that would make him give up the idea of returning, but she knew there were no words. His family, his name, his honor were very important to him. "We'll leave today," Dougless said softly. "I don't guess you need to see any more of Arabella."

"Have you no more calculators or televisions to distract me?" he asked, amused.

"I was saving the stereo for tonight."

He turned her around to face him, his hands on her shoulders. "I will pray alone," he said. "If I return I go alone. You understand me?"

She nodded. Borrowed time, she thought. We are now on borrowed time.

◇ ◇ ◇

Douglass sat on the twin bed in the bed and breakfast and looked across at Nicholas in the other bed. The early morning light made his face above the light cover dim and indistinct, but it was enough for her to see him. They'd known the name of the traitor for three days now and every minute of those three days Dougless knew he was going to disappear. Every morning he went to the church and spent two hours on his knees praying before his tomb. He spent another two hours in the afternoon.

And each time he went inside the church, Dougless stayed outside and held her breath. She knew it would be the last time she ever saw him again.

At ten A.M. and four P.M. she would tiptoe into the church, and when she saw him, sharp tears of relief and joy came to her eyes. Her heart went out to him when she saw the sweat on his face and body. He prayed so hard each day that he was limp with exhaustion afterward. Dougless would help him stand, his knees painful and stiff from two hours of kneeling on the cold stone floor. The vicar, feeling pity for Nicholas, had put out a cushion for him, but Nicholas refused to use it, saying he needed the pain of his body to make him remember what must be done.

Dougless didn't ask why he needed a reminder of his duty, because she didn't want to jinx the growing seed of hope that she was beginning to cherish. Every day when she came to him in the church and he looked at her and saw that he was still with her, there was a light in his eyes. Maybe he wouldn't return, Dougless thought. She knew she too should pray for his return. She knew that honor and a family name and the future of many people were more important than her selfish wants, but every time she saw him kneeling in the church, sunlight on his big body, she whispered, "Thank You, God."

Three days, she thought, three heavenly days. When Nicholas wasn't in church, they spent every moment together. She rented bicycles and had a hilarious time teaching him to ride. Whenever Nicholas fell, he pulled her with him and they went tumbling together across the sweet English grasses. Across sweet English grasses filled with cow manure.

Laughing at how awful they smelled, they showered and shampooed and Dougless rented a VCR and a tape and they stayed in their room and watched a movie.

Nicholas was insatiable for knowledge so they purchased a card from the little local library and went through hundreds of books. Nicholas wanted to see everything that had happened since 1564, wanted to hear every piece of music. He wanted to smell, taste, touch everything.

"Were I to remain here," he said one afternoon, "I would make houses."

It took Dougless a while to realize he meant design them. She thought of the beauty of Thornwyck and knew he had talent. Before she could stop herself, a flood of words came from her mouth. "You could go to architecture school. You'd have to learn a lot about modern building materials but I could help you. I could teach you how to read modern print better and my Uncle J.T. could get you a passport. He's the King of Lanconia and we'd just say you're a Lanconian so I could take you to America, and my father could help you get into a school and in the summer we could go to my hometown of Warbrooke on the coast of Maine, it's beautiful there, and we could go sailing and—"

He turned away. "I must return."

Yes, return, she thought. To go back to his wife, the woman he loved so much. How could Dougless care so much for him and he feel nothing for her? The other men in her life had wanted something from her. Robert wanted her to worship him. A couple of men had dated her because of her family's money. A couple of men had wanted her because she was so gullible, so easy to fool. But Nicholas was different. He wasn't trying to take anything from her.

There were times when Dougless looked at him and such lust filled her that she wanted to leap on him in the library, or in a pub, or on the street. She kept having fantasies about tearing his clothes off and ravishing him.

But every time she got too close he stepped away. It seemed that he was interested in tasting, smelling, touching everything in the world except her.

She tried to interest him. Heavens but she tried. She paid—on her credit card—two hundred pounds for a red silk peignoir set that was guaranteed to drive a man wild. When she came out of the bathroom wearing it, Nicholas had barely glanced at her. She'd bought a tiny bottle of perfume called Tigress that set her back seventy-five pounds, then leaned over Nicholas so that her shirt fell away from her breasts and asked if he liked the smell. He'd barely mumbled a reply.

She put her jeans in scalding hot water in the bathtub to shrink them and when they were dry they were so tight she had to put a big safety pin on the zipper and lie on the floor to pull it up. She wore them with a thin red silk blouse and no bra. Nicholas didn't look.

She would have thought he was gay if he hadn't looked at every other female who passed them.

Dougless bought black hose, black high heels, and a tiny, tiny black skirt and wore it with the red silk blouse. She felt ridiculous riding a bicycle wearing high heels but she did it anyway. She rode in front of Nicholas for four miles but as far as she knew he never once looked. Two cars ran into ditches looking at her, but Nicholas paid no attention whatever.

The video tape she rented was *Body Heat.*

By the fourth day she was desperate, and with their landlady's help, she devised an elaborate scheme to get Nicholas in bed with her. The landlady told Nicholas she needed their room, so Dougless made reservations at a nearby lovely country house hotel. She told Nicholas the only room she could get had one large four-poster bed, but that they'd have to make do. He gave her an odd look that she couldn't fathom and walked away.

So now Dougless was in the bathroom of the hotel where she'd been for thirty minutes. She felt as nervous as a virgin bride on her wedding night. With trembling hands, she doused herself in perfume.

Ready at last, she fluffed her hair and left the bathroom. The room was dark but she could see the outline of the bed—the bed she was to share with Nicholas.

Slowly, she walked toward the bed. She could see a long shape under the covers. She reached out her hand to touch it. "Nicholas," she whispered.

But her hand didn't touch him, it was . . . Pillows!

She turned on the bedside lamp and saw that Nicholas had made a central barricade of all the pillows between them. It reached from the head to the foot of the bed. On the far side he lay with his back to her, and his broad back was like another barricade.

Biting her lip to keep tears from coming, she climbed into bed, staying on the edge, not touching the hated pillows. She didn't turn out the light because suddenly all strength left her body. Tears, hot, hot tears began rolling down her cheeks.

"Why?" she whispered. "Why?"

"Dougless," Nicholas said softly, turning toward her but not reaching over the pillows to touch her.

"Why am I so undesirable to you?" she asked and hated herself for doing so, but she had no pride left. "I see you look at other women who I know aren't as pretty as I am, but you never look at me. You had your hands all over Arabella and sometimes you kiss me but nothing more. You've made love to so many women but you refuse me. Why? Am I too short? Too fat? You hate redheads?"

When Nicholas spoke, Dougless could tell the words were from deep inside him. "I have never desired a woman as much as you. My body aches with wanting you but I must leave. I cannot return and know I leave you grieving. When I first saw you you were weeping so that I heard you across four hundred years. I cannot leave you to such grief again."

"You won't touch me because you don't want me to grieve for you?"

"Aye," he whispered.

Dougless's tears began to be replaced by laughter. She got out of bed and, standing, looked down at him. "You idiot," she said. "Don't you realize that when you leave I'm going to grieve for you every day for the rest of my life? I am going to cry so long and loud and hard that I will be heard to the beginning of time. Oh, Nicholas, you fool, don't you know how much I love you? Whether you touch me or not, you won't be able to stop my tears."

She paused and smiled at him. "While I'm grieving, why don't you let me have a memory that will knock Arabella off her table?"

As Dougless stood and watched, Nicholas just lay there, not moving, looking at her over the pillows. One second he was in bed, the next he was on her. Dougless never saw him move, she just felt his body against hers, felt his mouth on her skin, his hands holding her shoulders, then moving quickly and firmly out to her hands.

"Nicholas," she whispered. "Nicholas."

He was on her, his mouth and hands everywhere as she kissed whatever part of him came near her mouth. His hands tore at her gown and Dougless heard it ripping away. When his hot, wet mouth fastened onto her breast she screamed in ecstasy.

This was Nicholas, who she'd wanted, desired, craved for hundreds of hours. His big, hard hands moved down her sides, his thumb toying with her navel as his lips and tongue played with her breasts.

Her fingers burrowed into his hair. "Let me," she whispered. She had always chosen men who needed her, men who thought no one could give them enough. Dougless's experience with sex had been with men who expected her to give to them.

"Nicholas?" she said as his lips began moving down her belly. "Nicholas, I don't think—" His hands caressed her thighs, his thumb kneading the soft white flesh there, then he moved downward, downward.

Dougless arched her body against the carpet. No man had ever done this to her before. Passion built in her as his tongue . . . Oh God, his tongue.

"Nicholas," she moaned and began to pull his hair as her body moved under him. He nibbled at the inside of her thighs, caressing the back of her knees until she didn't think she could stand any more.

Nicholas grabbed her left leg and bent it up as he moved on top of her and entered her so hard and big she tried to push him away. But her body closed around him, her free leg wrapping about his leg as he pounded into her with hard, deep thrusts that pushed her across the carpet. She put up her hands to brace herself against the wall.

Nicholas released her bent leg, and she clasped him about the waist and her hips rose to meet his thrusts as his hands cupped her buttocks and lifted her to him. Higher, higher.

When at last she felt him arch into her for a final blinding thrust, Dougless felt her own body shuddering in answer.

It was a while before she came to herself and remembered where she was, who she was. Her head was almost against the wall, the bedside table and lamp looming over her.

"Nicholas," she murmured, touching his sweaty hair. "No wonder Arabella risked all for you."

He lifted himself on one elbow and looked down at her. "Do you sleep?" he asked, chuckling.

"Nicholas, that was wonderful," she whispered. "No man—"

He didn't allow her to finish but took her hand and lifted her to stand by him. Gently, sweetly, deeply, he kissed her, then took her hand and led her into the bathroom. He got the shower water hot, then pulled her in with him. He pinned her to the wall and kissed her, his big, hard body pressing against hers.

"I have dreamed of this," he murmured. "This water fountain was made for love."

Dougless was too absorbed in the way he was moving down to her breasts to be able to answer him. With the hot water beating on them Nicholas began kissing her body, his mouth on her breasts, her stomach, her neck. Dougless had her head back, her hands on his shoulders, shoulders so broad they nearly reached from one side to the other of the shower stall.

He came up to face her. Dougless opened her eyes and saw he was smiling at her. "Perhaps some things in this modern world do not change," he said. "I seem to be your teacher now."

"Oh?" she said and began kissing his neck, then across his shoulder, down his muscular chest, her hands kneading his back muscles. Fat, she thought. She'd said he was going to get fat but all of him was muscle, thick, hard, sculptured muscle.

The hot water beat down on her head and she went lower, her hands on his buttocks. When her mouth closed over him, it was his turn to gasp. His hands buried in her wet hair as she heard his soft moans of pleasure.

He nearly pulled her up by her hair as he slammed her against the slick wall, pulled her legs about his waist and rammed into her almost brutally. Dougless held on to his passion, fastening herself to him as his mouth took hers, his tongue thrusting just as his body did.

When the final moment came, Dougless would have screamed, except that Nicholas covered her mouth with his.

She clung to him, trembling, her body limp. She was sure that if Nicholas hadn't been holding her she would have gone down the drain.

He kissed her neck. "Now I will wash you," he said softly and set her on her own feet, but caught her when she nearly fell.

As if he had an electric switch in his body, he seemed to leash his passion as he turned her to face the shower head and began to shampoo her hair. His big, strong hands and his big body made her feel small and fragile—and protected. When he was done with her hair, he lathered his hands and began soaping her body.

Dougless leaned back against the wall as Nicholas's hands slid over her, up and down, around, in and out. Before she forgot herself, she took the soap and began to caress him with her soapy hands. He had the most beautiful body she'd ever seen on a human. He was tall, broad-shouldered, small-waisted, with heavy thighs. God, she thought, even his feet were beautiful.

She shut off the water and soaped him. Looking at him, touching him. There was a birthmark on his left hip, shaped like a figure eight. There was a scar on his right calf. "Fell off a horse," he murmured, eyes closed. There was a long scar on his left forearm. "Sword practice the day . . ." Dougless knew that the rest of the sentence was, "the day Kit died." There was an odd oval scar on his shoulder. Nicholas smiled, his eyes closed. "A fight with Kit. I won," he said.

She came back to his head. "I'm glad to see no woman has left a mark on you."

"Only you, Montgomery, have marked me," he whispered.

Dougless wanted to ask him about his wife. Did he care for her, Dougless, as much as he loved his beautiful wife? But she didn't ask, too afraid of the answer she'd hear.

Nicholas spun her around, put the water back on and rinsed them both. When they were clean, he pulled her out of the shower and began gently combing her hair. Dougless wanted to put on her robe but Nicholas wouldn't allow it.

"I have dreamed of you this way," he said, looking at her in the mirror. "You have fair driven me mad. The smell of you." He stopped combing and slid his hands down her arms. "The clothes you wear . . ."

Dougless smiled, her head against his. He *had* noticed, she thought. He had.

When her hair was combed he toweled it dry, then held up the white terry robe the hotel furnished. "Come," he said, putting on the other robe.

He led her downstairs, through the darkened hotel lobby and into the kitchen.

"Nicholas," she said, "we shouldn't be here."

He kissed her to silence. "I am hungry," he said as if that were excuse enough.

Being in the hotel kitchen when she knew they shouldn't be added excitement to this most wonderful night. She looked at Nicholas's back as he opened the refrigerator door. He was hers, she thought, hers to touch whenever she wanted. Holding his hand, she pressed her body against his and put her head in the crook of his shoulder.

"Nicholas," she whispered, "I love you so much. Don't leave me."

He turned and looked into her eyes, his face full of puzzlement and longing. He looked back in the refrigerator. "Where's the ice cream?"

She laughed. "In the freezer. Try that door." She pointed.

He wouldn't let her out of his sight or reach as he pulled her toward the freezer. There were big cardboard vats of ice cream inside. Clinging together like Siamese twins, they went about the kitchen and found bowls, spoons and a steel ladle. Nicholas scooped out an enormous amount into each bowl and slipped the vat back into the freezer. He dribbled vanilla ice cream down the front of her then licked it off, the ice cream traveling lower, just below his tongue. He licked the last just as it reached her red-gold curls.

"Strawberry," he said, making Dougless laugh.

They sat on the eight-foot-long butcher block cutting table, feet and lower legs entwined. They ate quietly for a moment but then Nicholas dropped ice cream on Dougless's foot and licked it off. Dougless leaned forward to kiss Nicholas and "accidentally" dropped ice cream on his inner thigh.

"I'll bet that's awfully cold," she said against his lips.

"I cannot bear it," he whispered.

Slowly, so her breasts raked along his bare body, she made her way to the splat of ice cream on his thigh and licked it off, and when it was gone she continued licking. The ice cream was forgotten as Nicholas leaned back against the table and pulled her up to him. As if she weighed nothing, his biceps bulging, he picked her up and set her down on top of him, his hands moving up her body to clutch her breasts as Dougless moved slowly up and down.

It was a long time before they arched together, Nicholas pulling her down to kiss her hungrily and fiercely.

"I believe, madam," he whispered in her ear, "that you have melted my ice cream."

Dougless laughed and snuggled against him. "I've wanted to touch you for so long," she said. She caressed his chest and shoulder and then reached as far as she could into the sleeve of the robe that he still wore to stroke his arm. "I've never met a man like you."

She lifted on one elbow and looked down at him. "Were you an unusual man in the sixteenth century or were they all like you?"

Nicholas grinned at her. "I am unique, which is why the women—"

She kissed him. "Say no more. I'd as soon hear nothing more about your women—or your wife." She put her head down. "I'd like to think I'm special, not just one of hundreds."

He lifted her chin to look at her. "You called me across centuries and I answered. Is that not enough to make you 'special'?"

"Then you do care for me? At least some?"

"There are no words," he said and kissed her lightly and pushed her head back down, but as he stroked her damp hair, he felt her relax against him and knew she was falling asleep. Closing her robe, he bundled her into his arms and carried her out of the kitchen and up to their room. He removed both their robes and put her into bed, then climbed in beside her. She was already asleep as he snuggled her to him, her bare bottom up against his half-swollen maleness, his leg over hers.

She asked if he cared for her. Cared for her? She was becoming all to him, his reason for living. He cared what she thought, what she felt, what she needed. He couldn't bear more than minutes away from her.

Each morning and afternoon he went to pray for God to return him, but part of his mind thought constantly of what it would be like to never see her again, to never hear her laugh, to never see her cry again, to never hold her in his arms.

He ran his hand over her shoulder and tucked the cover closer about her. Never had he met a woman like her. She had no guile, no sense of taking what she wanted, no sense of self-preservation. He smiled, remembering her protests when he'd first met her. She'd said she would not help him, but he'd seen in her eyes how she couldn't bear leaving him alone in a strange land. He thought of the women of his own time and knew of no woman who would help some poor madman.

But Dougless had, he thought. She'd helped him and taught him and . . . loved him. She'd given her love freely and completely.

Completely, he thought, smiling in memory of this night. No woman had ever responded to him with such complete abandonment. Arabella used to demand. "Here! Now!" she'd say. Other women thought they were granting him a favor. Lettice . . . He didn't like to think of his cold wife. She lay in bed stiff-limbed, her eyes open as if challenging him to do his husbandly duties. In four years of marriage he'd not been able to get her with child.

He caressed Dougless's bare arm and in her sleep she tried to move closer to him. He kissed her temple. How could he leave her? he thought. How could he go back to his other life, to his other women, leaving her alone and unprotected? So soft was she that she was at the mercy of men like the one he'd tossed into the street.

He thought of his mother and Lettice. Those two women would be able to take care of themselves no matter what befell them. But not Dougless. He feared that a week after he left she'd be back with that odious man she once had believed she loved.

He stroked her hair. How could he leave her alone? There would be no one to protect her. He did not understand the modern world. It was her father's duty to choose a husband for her. Nicholas smiled as he thought of how Dougless would fare with some man of his age, whom a father might choose for her. All her childish talk of love.

But as Nicholas looked at her, he knew he was beginning to understand what she meant. Love. Dougless said that perhaps he'd been sent to the modern world for love. Nicholas had scoffed at the idea. This cataclysmic thing had happened for love and not for honor? But they'd found the name of the traitor and Nicholas had not left this world.

He remembered Dougless saying that everything in the past had turned out all right. All right to her, perhaps. He was remembered as a fool, but then, perhaps, he had been a fool. There had been many other women, which he needed with a wife like Lettice, and perhaps cuckolding Robert Sydney had been foolish enough to cause his own death, but if he could return he would right the wrongs.

If he returned . . .

What then? He'd still be married to Lettice, and there would be women like Arabella to tempt him. Even if he could free himself from the accusation of treason, would it change him?

He turned on his back, holding Dougless tightly to him. What if he remained in this century? What if he had misjudged God's purpose? What if he had been sent forward in time, not to return, but to do something *here?*

He remembered the books he and Dougless had looked at. There were books of houses from around the world and they had intrigued him. Dougless had talked about something called architecture school, where he could learn to design houses. To learn to be a tradesman? he thought in wonder, but it did not seem to be something bad in this century. Instead, men like Harewood who were mere landowners were looked down on—by Americans anyway, Dougless had explained.

America, he thought, this place Dougless talked about constantly. She said they would go to America and "set up housekeeping" and he could go to school. School at his age? he'd asked disdainfully, not letting her see how the idea intrigued him. To live with Dougless in this modern world and design buildings? Was this the reason he had been brought forth? Perhaps

God had seen Thornwyck, liked it, and decided to give him another chance, Nicholas thought with a smile, laughing at the idea of God being so frivolous.

But what did he know of God's purpose? He hadn't been sent forward in time to find out who betrayed him. He'd found that out nearly a week ago and he was still here. So why? Why had he come to the modern world?

"Nicholas!" Dougless cried out, sitting up with a jolt.

He pulled her back into his arms as she clung to him. "I dreamed you were gone, that you weren't here, that you'd left me."

He stroked her hair. "I will not leave you," he said softly. "I will remain with you for always."

It took a moment for his words to reach Dougless. She lifted up to look at him. "Nicholas," she said slowly, questioning.

"I . . ." He took a breath. The words were hard for him. "I do not wish to return. I will remain here." He looked at her. "With you."

Dougless buried her face in his shoulder and began to weep.

He stroked her body and laughed. "Are you sad that I do not leave you so that you may return to this Robert who gives diamonds to children?"

"I'm just so happy."

He took a tissue from a box beside the bed. "Here, stop your weeping and tell me of America." He gave her a sideways look. "And tell me of your uncle who is king."

Dougless blew her nose and smiled. "I didn't think you heard that."

"What is a cowboy? What is a passport? What is the Grand Cannon? And do not move so far from me."

"It's *canyon*," she said, moving back into his arms as she began to tell him of America, of her family, of her uncle who'd married a princess and was now King of Lanconia.

As the dawn light came into the room, they began to make plans. Dougless would call her Uncle J.T. and explain as best as she could that she needed a passport for Nicholas, so he could go to America with her. "Knowing Uncle J.T. he'll want you to come to Lanconia and inspect you first. But he'll like you."

"And his queen?"

"Aunt Aria? Well, she can be a little intimidating at times, but she's really great. She used to play baseball with us kids. They have six kids of their own." She smiled. "And she has this weird friend named Dolly who runs around the palace wearing blue jeans and a crown." She looked at Nicholas, his black hair and blue eyes, and thought of the way he walked, the way he sometimes had of looking at people that made them shrivel. "You'll fit in in Lanconia," she said.

They had breakfast served in their room and over the table, Nicholas said, "I'd rather have strawberry ice cream."

In another moment they were on the floor, rolling about exuberantly as they tore at each other making love. Afterward they filled the tub and sat in it at opposite ends and planned more of their future life together.

"We'll go to Scotland," Dougless said. "While we're waiting for the passport we'll stay in Scotland. It is a beautiful place."

Nicholas had his foot on her stomach, kneading her flesh. "Will you wear the heeled shoes to ride a bicycle?" he asked.

Dougless laughed. "Don't make fun of me. Those shoes got me what I wanted."

"And I," he said.

After the bath they dressed and Dougless planned to call her Uncle J.T.

Nicholas turned away. "I must return to the church for one last time," he said softly.

Dougless felt her entire body stiffen. "No," she whispered, then ran to face him, her hands gripping his arms.

"I must," he said, smiling at her. "I have been often and naught has happened. Dougless, look at me."

She lifted her head and he smiled. "Are you onion-eyed yet again?"

"I'm just frightened."

"I must pray for forgiveness for not wanting to return to save my name and my honor. Do you understand?"

She nodded mutely. "But I'm going with you and I don't let go of you. Got that? I don't wait outside for you this time."

He kissed her. "I mean to never release you again. Now, we will go to the church for my prayers, then you will call your uncle. Does Scotland have trains?"

"Of course."

"Ah, then it has changed. In my time it was a wild place." He put his arm about her shoulders and they left the hotel.

11

At the church, Dougless wouldn't release Nicholas. He knelt to pray and she knelt beside him, both her arms tightly around him. He didn't push her away as she feared he might and she knew, in spite of his pretended amusement, he was as frightened as she was.

They knelt together on the cold floor for over an hour and Dougless's knees hurt and her arms ached from holding on to Nicholas, but she never considered relaxing her hold. The vicar came in once and stood watching them for a while, then silently walked away.

As hard as Nicholas prayed for forgiveness, Dougless prayed for God not to take him, to let him stay with her forever.

At long last, Nicholas opened his eyes and turned to her. "I remain," he said, smiling. He laughed when he stood and Dougless, almost crippled, also tried to stand, but her arms still held him.

"My arms have no blood in them," he said, chiding her gently.

"I'm not letting you go until we're out of this place."

He laughed. "It is over."

"Nicholas, stop teasing me and let's get out of here. I never want to see your tomb again."

Still smiling at her, he started to take a step but his body didn't move. Puzzled, he looked down at his feet. From his knees down, there was nothing, merely space. There was floor where his feet should have been.

Quickly, he pulled Dougless into his arms and held her as if to crush her. "I love you," he whispered. "With all my soul I love you. Across time I will love you."

"Nicholas," she said, her voice betraying her fear at his words. "Let's get out of here."

He held her face in his hands. "Only you have I loved, my Dougless."

She felt it then. His body was no longer solid in her arms. "Nicholas," she yelled.

He kissed her, so softly, yet with all the yearning and wanting and desire and need he felt for her.

"I'm going with you," she said. "Take me with you. God!" she screamed. "Let me go with him!"

"Dougless," Nicholas said and his voice was far away. "Dougless, my love."

He was no longer in her arms but standing before his tomb wearing his armor. He was faded, indistinct, like a movie seen in a bright room. "Come to me," he said, holding out his hand. "Come to me."

Dougless ran to him, but she couldn't reach him.

A streak of sunlight came in through the windows and flashed off his armor.

And then there was nothing.

Dougless stood and stared and looked at the tomb, and then she put her hands to her ears and screamed, a scream such as no human had ever uttered before. The old stone walls vibrated, the windows quivered and the tomb . . . The tomb just lay there, silent and cold.

Dougless collapsed to the floor.

◇ ◇ ◇

"Drink this," someone was saying.

She caught the hand that held the cup to her lips. "Nicholas," she said, a faint smile on her lips. Her eyes flew open and she sat up. She was stretched out on a pew in the church, just a few feet from the tomb. She swung her legs to the side, her feet on the floor. Her head swam.

"Are you feeling better?"

She turned to see the vicar, his kindly old face full of concern, a cup of water in his hand.

"Where is Nicholas?" she whispered.

"I didn't see anyone else. Should I call someone for you? I heard you . . . scream," he said. Just remembering that sound made the hair on his body stand on edge. "I came here and you were lying on the floor. Could I call someone for you?"

On weak legs, Dougless made her way to the tomb. Slowly, memory was coming back to her, yet still she couldn't believe it. She looked at the vicar. "You didn't see him leave, did you?" she asked hoarsely. Her throat was raw.

"I saw no one leave. I just saw you praying. Not many people pray today."

She looked back at the tomb. She wanted to touch it but knew it would be cold, so unlike Nicholas. "You saw *us* praying," she corrected.

"Just you," the vicar said.

Slowly, Dougless turned to look at him. "Nicholas and I were praying together. You came in and saw us. You've watched him all week."

The vicar gave her a sad look. "I'll take you to a doctor."

She moved away from his outstretched hand. "Nicholas. The man who prayed here every morning and every afternoon this week. He was the man in the Elizabethan armor. Remember? He nearly walked in front of a bus."

"A few days ago I saw you step in front of a coach. You asked me the date."

"I . . ?" Dougless asked. "But that was Nicholas. You told me this week you were amazed at his devoutness. I waited for him outside. Remember?" Her voice was urgent and she stepped toward him. "Remember? Nicholas! You waved to us as we rode by on the bicycles."

The vicar backed away from her. "I saw you on a bicycle but no man."

"No . . . ," Dougless whispered and stepped back from him, her eyes wide with horror.

She began to run, out of the church, through the churchyard, down three streets, to the left, then a right and into the hotel. She ignored the greeting of the woman at the desk and ran up the stairs.

"Nicholas," she cried and looked about the empty room. The bathroom door was closed and she ran to it, flung it open. Empty. She turned again to the room but stopped in the doorway, then looked back. She stared at the shelf below the mirror. Her toiletries were there but his were gone. She touched the empty half of the shelf. No razor, no shaving cream, no after-shave lotion. In the shower his shampoo was gone.

She ran into the room and flung open the closet door. Nicholas's clothes were gone. Only hers hung there, her old suitcase and carry-on below it. In the dresser his socks and handkerchiefs were missing.

"No," she whispered and went to sit on the side of the bed. It almost made sense that Nicholas was gone but not his clothes, not the things he had given her. She put her hand to her heart, tore open her blouse. The pin, the beautiful gold pin with the pearl hanging from it was gone.

Dougless didn't try to think after that. She tore the room apart looking for something left behind. The emerald ring he'd given her was gone; the note he'd left under her door was gone. She opened her notebooks. Nicholas had written in them in his bizarre handwriting but now the pages were blank.

"Think, Dougless, think," she said. There had to be some mark left by him. In the closet were the books they'd purchased and Nicholas had written his name inside them. They were blank now.

There was nothing, nothing of him. She even looked on her clothes for any dark hairs. Clean.

It was when she saw her red silk nightgown that Nicholas had torn from her body and saw that it was now whole that she became angry. "No!" she said, teeth clenched. "You can't take him away from me so completely."

People, she thought. If there was no physical evidence of him there were an awful lot of people who would remember him. Just because a daffy old vicar couldn't remember him, didn't mean other people didn't.

She grabbed her purse and left the hotel.

◇ ◇ ◇

Dougless opened the door to the hotel room slowly, dreading the empty room. Her body was exhausted but, unfortunately, her mind still worked.

She sat on the edge of the bed, then wearily turned and lay down. It was late and her body was empty of food, but she didn't consider eating. Her eyes were wide open, sandy-feeling, dry as she stared up at the underside of the bed canopy.

No one remembered Nicholas.

The coin merchant had no medieval coins and he didn't remember seeing Nicholas or Dougless. Didn't remember examining his clothes, said he'd never seen silver and gold armor. The clerk in the clothing store didn't remember Nicholas pulling a sword on him. The librarian said Dougless had checked out books and she'd always been alone. The dentist said he'd never seen a man with ridges on his teeth and a cracked jaw. He had no X-rays. No one at the pubs remembered him or the tea shops. They all remembered Dougless coming in alone. The bicycle shop showed her the receipt where she'd rented only one bike. Their sweet landlady at the bed and breakfast didn't remember Nicholas and said no one had played her piano since her husband had died.

Like a woman possessed, she went wherever she and Nicholas had been and asked anyone who might have seen him. She asked tourists in tea shops, residents on the street, clerks in stores.

Nothing, nothing nothing.

Weary, numb with the dawning realization of what had happened, she went back to the hotel and now lay on the bed. She didn't dare go to sleep. Last night she'd awakened from a dream that Nicholas was lost to her. Nicholas had cradled her in his arms and gently laughed at her and told her she was dreaming, that he was with her and always would be.

Last night, last night, she thought. He had touched her and loved her and today he was gone. More than gone. His body, his clothes, other people's memory of him was gone.

And it was her fault. He had stayed so long as they hadn't made love, but once he'd touched her he went away. It didn't help to know she'd been right. He'd come to her for love, not for any rightings of wrongs. He'd stayed when he found out who betrayed him but he'd slipped through her arms once he'd admitted he loved her.

She clasped her arms about her chest. Gone as irreversibly as death. Only she had no comfort of other people who remembered and loved him.

When the telephone on the bedside table rang, she didn't at first hear it. On the fifth ring, dully, she picked it up. "Hello?"

"Dougless," said Robert's voice, stern and angry. "Are you over your hysterics yet?"

She felt too numb, too empty to fight. "What do you want?"

"The bracelet, of course. If you aren't too wrapped up in Loverboy to find it."

"What?" Dougless said, slowly at first, then, "What! Did you see him? Did you see Nicholas? Of course you did. He threw you down the steps."

"Dougless, are you out of your mind? No one has *ever* thrown me down any stairs and they better not try it either." He sighed. "Now you've got me acting crazy. I want that bracelet."

"Yes, of course," she said hurriedly, "but what did you mean when you referred to 'Lover-boy'?"

"I don't have time to repeat every—"

"Robert," Dougless said calmly, "you either tell me or I flush the bracelet down the toilet and I don't believe you have insurance on it yet."

There was a pause on the other end. "I was right to ditch you. You're crazy. No wonder your family won't let you have the dough until you're thirty-five. I can't put up with you that long."

"I'm on my way to the bathroom now."

"All right! But it's hard to know what you were talking about that night. You were hysterical. You said something about having a job helping some guy rewrite history. That's all I remember."

"Rewrite history," Dougless said under her breath. Yes, that's why Nicholas had come: to change history.

"Dougless! Dougless!" Robert was shouting but she put down the telephone.

When Nicholas had come to her he had been facing an execution. What they had found out had saved him from that. She grabbed her big carry-on satchel from the closet and stuffed some clothing into it and as she closed a drawer, she glanced into the mirror and put her hand to her throat. Beheading. Today we read about it, read that some person walked upon a platform and another person struck them with an axe, she thought. But we do not think of what it really means.

"We saved you from that," she whispered.

Once she was packed, she sat down in a chair to wait for morning. Tomorrow she'd go to Nicholas's houses and hear how they had changed history. Perhaps hearing that Nicholas lived to be an old man and had accomplished great things would help her feel better. She leaned back in the chair and stared at the bed. She didn't dare close her eyes for fear she'd dream.

◇ ◇ ◇

Dougless took the first train out of Ashburton and arrived at Bellwood Castle before they opened the gates. She sat outside on the grass and waited —trying not to think.

When the gates opened she bought a ticket for the first tour. Some of her misery was beginning to leave her as she thought of how much Nicholas's name had meant to him. He'd so hated being a laughingstock and now she was going to have the comfort of hearing how he'd changed history.

The tour guide was the same one who'd led her and Nicholas the first time, and she smiled in memory of Nicholas opening and closing the alarmed door.

She didn't pay much attention to the first part of the tour or listen to the guide. She just looked at the walls and furniture and wondered what part of it Nicholas had contributed.

"And now we come to our most popular room," the guide said and there was that same little smirk in her voice as before.

The guide had Dougless's full attention now, but something in her tone puzzled Dougless. Shouldn't the guide be more respectful now?

"This was Lord Nicholas Stafford's private chamber and, to put it politely, he's what would be known today as a rake."

The crowd moved forward, eager to hear of this notorious earl, but Dougless stood where she was. Things should have changed. When Nicholas went back, he meant to change history. Dougless had once said that history couldn't be changed. Had she been terribly, horribly right?

With several firm "excuse me's," Dougless pushed to the front of the group. The guide's talk was word for word, exactly the same. She talked of Nicholas's devastating charm with the ladies and she again told the awful story of Arabella and the table.

Dougless felt as if she wanted to put her hands over her ears. Between the people in Ashburton not remembering Nicholas and now history being the same, it almost made her doubt whether any of the things she remembered had actually happened. Was she crazy, just as Robert said? When she'd so frantically asked the people of Ashburton if they'd seen Nicholas, they had looked her as if she were insane.

"Alas," the guide was saying, "poor, charming Nick was executed for treason on the ninth of September, 1564. Now, if you'll step through here we'll see the south drawing room."

Dougless's head shot up. Executed? No, Nicholas was found dead, slumped over his mother's letter.

Dougless made her way to the guide, who looked down her nose at Dougless. "Ah, the door opener," she said.

"I didn't open the door. Ni . . ." She halted. It was no use explaining if this woman remembered their last visit as her, not Nicholas, opening and closing the alarmed door. "You said that Lord Nicholas Stafford was executed. I heard that three days before the execution was to take place, Lord Stafford was found dead, slumped over a letter he was writing to his mother."

"He was *not,*" the woman said emphatically. "He was sentenced to death and the sentence was carried out on schedule. Now, if you'll excuse me, I have a tour to conduct."

Dougless stood where she was for a moment, staring up at the portrait of Nicholas hanging over the fireplace. Executed? Beheaded? Something was deeply, thoroughly wrong.

She turned and started to leave the castle. On her way out, she paused at the door with the NO ADMITTANCE sign on it. Behind that door, down a few corridors, was the room that held the secret cabinet and in it the ivory box. Could she find it? She put on her hand to the knob.

"I wouldn't if I were you." someone behind her said.

Dougless turned to see one of the guides, an unfriendly look on her face.

"A few days ago some of the tourists went in there. We've put a lock and an alarm on the door since then."

"Oh," Dougless murmured. "I thought it was a rest room." She turned away and left the castle, the guides outside frowning because she was once again going out the entrance.

She went to the gift shop and asked to buy anything they had on Nicholas Stafford.

"There's a bit on him in the tour book but nowhere else. He didn't live long enough to accomplish much," the cashier said.

She asked if they'd yet received post cards of his portrait but they hadn't. Dougless bought the tour book and went outside to the gardens. Finding the place where she and Nicholas had sat down to tea, that heavenly day when he'd given her the pin, she began to read.

In the fat, beautifully illustrated book, Nicholas rated only a short paragraph, and that was about the women and how he'd raised an army and been executed for it.

Dougless leaned back against the tree. Even knowing the name of the man who'd betrayed him hadn't helped. He hadn't been able to persuade the queen of his innocence. He hadn't even been able to destroy the diary written by that nasty little clerk that had left Nicholas's name blotted for all time. And, too, it seemed that no one doubted Nicholas's guilt. The guidebook, as brief as it was, portrayed Nicholas as a power-mad womanizer. The tour group had chuckled when they'd been told of Nicholas's execution.

Dougless closed her eyes and thought of her beautiful, proud, sweet Nicholas mounting the steps to a wide platform. Would it have been like in the movies, with a muscular man dressed in black leather holding a hideous-looking axe?

Her eyes flew open. She could *not* think of that. Could not think of Nicholas's beautiful head rolling across a wooden floor.

She stood, picked up her heavy tote bag, left the castle grounds and walked the two miles to the train station. She bought a ticket to Thornwyck. Perhaps there, in the library, in their collection of books on the Stafford family, she'd find some answers.

The librarian in Thornwyck welcomed her back and in answer to Dougless's question said she'd never seen Dougless with a man. Dispirited, Dougless went to the Stafford books and began to read. Each and every book told of Nicholas's execution. No more did they tell of his dying before the execution and poison being suspected. And every book was as disdainful of Nicholas as it had been before. The notorious earl. The wastrel. The man who had everything and threw it away.

When the librarian came to tell her the library was closing, Dougless closed the last book and stood. She felt dizzy and swayed, catching herself against the table.

"Are you all right?" the librarian asked.

Dougless looked at the woman. The man she loved had just had his head cut off. No, she was far from all right. "Yes, I'm fine," Dougless murmured. "I'm just tired and maybe a little hungry." She gave the woman a weak smile and went outside.

Dougless stood outside for a moment. She guessed she should get a room somewhere, probably should eat something, but it didn't seem to matter. Over and over and over she kept seeing Nicholas climbing the stairs to meet an executioner. Would his hands be tied behind his back? Would he have priests with him? No, when Nicholas returned, Henry the Eighth had already abolished Catholicism.

She sat down on an iron bench and put her head in her hands. He had come to her and loved her and left her. For what? He had returned to a scaffolding and a bloody axe.

"Dougless? Is that you?"

She looked up to see Lee Nolman standing over her.

"I thought that was you. Nobody else has hair that color. I thought you left town."

She stood but then swayed against the bench.

"Are you all right? You look terrible."

"Just a little tired."

He looked at her closely, at the circles under her eyes, the gray tinge to her skin. "And hungry too in my guess." He took her arm in his and shouldered her bag. "There's a pub around the corner. Let's get something to eat."

Dougless allowed him to lead her down the street. What did she care what happened to her?

Inside the pub, he escorted her to a booth and ordered a couple of beers and food. One sip of hers and it went to her head, and Dougless realized she hadn't eaten since yesterday when she'd had breakfast with Nicholas— and they'd made love on the floor.

"So what have you been doing since you left Thornwyck last week?" Lee asked.

"Nicholas and I went to Ashburton," she said, watching him.

"He somebody you met?"

"Yes," she whispered. "And what about you?"

He smiled in a Cheshire cat way, as if he knew something very important. "The day after you left, Lord Harewood had the wall in Lady Margaret Stafford's room repaired and guess what we found?"

"Rats," Dougless said, not caring about anything.

Lee leaned across the table in conspiracy. "A little iron box and in it Lady Margaret's story of the truth of why Lord Nicholas was executed. I tell you, Dougless, what's in this is going to establish my reputation forever. It's like solving a four-hundred-year-old murder mystery."

It took a while for his words to penetrate Dougless's misery. "Tell me," she whispered.

Lee leaned back against the booth. "Oh no you don't. You coaxed me out of Robert Sydney's name but not this. You'll have to wait for the book."

Dougless started to speak, but then the waitress appeared with their food. She didn't look at her cottage pie but when they were alone she leaned across the table toward Lee. With an intensity Lee had never seen before in human eyes, Dougless said softly, "I don't know if you know about my family but the Montgomerys are one of the richest families in the world. On my thirty-fifth birthday I will inherit millions. If you will tell me what Lady Margaret wrote, I will this minute sign one million dollars over to you."

Lee was too stunned to speak. He hadn't known about her family but he believed her. Nobody could have the look on her face that she did and be lying. He knew she wanted this information, look how she'd pestered him for Robert Sydney's name, and he didn't feel like asking her why. If she was willing to offer a million dollars for it and if her family had as much money and power as she said, then it was rather like having a genie offer you one wish.

"I want a chair in the history department of an ivy league school," he said quietly.

"Done," answered Dougless, sounding like an auctioneer. She'd donate a wing or a building to a college if she had to.

"All right," Lee said, "settle back and eat. This is a *great* story. I may be able to sell it to the movies. The story starts years before poor ol' Nick was executed. He—"

"Nicholas," Douglass said. "He doesn't like to be called Nick."

"Sure, okay, Nicholas then. What I'd never read in any book—I guess no historian thought it important—was that the Stafford family had an obscure claim to the throne through Henry the Sixth. They were descended directly through the male line while Queen Elizabeth was considered by some to be a bastard and, being a woman, unfit to rule. You know that for years her throne was not exactly secure?"

Dougless nodded.

"If the historians forgot that the Staffords were related to kings, there was someone who didn't. A woman named Lettice Culpin."

"Nicholas's wife?"

"You do know your history," Lee said. "Yes, the beautiful Lettice. It seems that her family also had some claim to the throne of England, a claim even more obscure than the Staffords'. Lady Margaret believes that Lettice was a very ambitious young woman and she planned to marry a Stafford, produce an heir and put the child on the throne."

Dougless considered this. "But why Nicholas? Why not the older brother? It seems like she'd want to marry the man who was earl."

Lee smiled. "I have to keep on my toes with you, don't I? You're going to have to tell me where you learned so much about the Staffords. The eldest brother . . . ah . . ."

"Christopher."

"Yes, Christopher was engaged to marry a very rich French heiress who happened to be only twelve years old. I guess he decided he'd rather have the money than Lettice, no matter how beautiful she was."

"But Kit died and Nicholas became the earl," Dougless said softly.

"Lady Margaret hinted that her eldest son's death might not have been an accident. He drowned but Lady Margaret said he was a strong swimmer. Anyway, she never knew for sure, she just guessed."

"So Lettice married Nicholas."

"Yes," Lee said, "but things didn't go the way Lettice planned. It seems Nicholas wasn't interested in furthering himself at court, or in talking conspiracy and trying to find someone who'd back him if he tried for the throne. Nicholas was mostly interested in women."

"And learning," Dougless shot at him. "He commissioned monks to copy books. He designed Thornwyck. He—" She stopped.

Lee's eyes were wide. "That's true. Lady Margaret wrote all that, but how did you know?"

"It doesn't matter. What happened after Nicholas married . . . her?"

"You sound as if you're jealous. Okay, okay. After they were married, and Lettice seems to have quickly realized Nicholas wasn't going to do what she wanted him to, she began to look around for some way to get rid of him."

"As she had Christopher."

"That was never proven. It may have been a very fortunate accident— fortunate for Lettice anyway. Lady Margaret admits that most of this is speculation, but Nicholas had some very close calls. A stirrup broke, a—"

"And he cut his calf," Dougless whispered, "when he fell from the horse."

"I don't know where he was hurt, Lady Margaret didn't say. Dougless, are you sure you're all right?"

She glared at him.

"Anyway, Nicholas proved much harder to kill than Christopher had been, so Lettice began to look for someone to help her."

"And she found Robert Sydney."

Lee smiled. "I bet you're great with detective novels, always figuring out the ending. Yes, Lettice found Robert Sydney. He was Arabella Harewood's husband and he must have been pretty mad about all of England laughing about Stafford and his wife on the table. To make matters worse, nine months later Arabella presented him with a black-haired son."

"And the child and Arabella died."

"Right. Lady Margaret thinks Sydney had a hand in those deaths."

Dougless took a breath. "So Lettice and Robert Sydney contrived to get Nicholas accused and executed for treason."

"Yes. Lady Margaret thinks Lettice just waited for an opportunity to get Nicholas for something, so when Stafford started gathering men to protect his Welsh estates, she informed Sydney, who rode hell-bent-for-leather to the queen. In a way, it's understandable that Elizabeth believed Sydney. Just months before, Mary Queen of Scots had declared herself Queen of England as well as Scotland, and here was the Earl of Stafford raising an army. Elizabeth just clapped Stafford in chains, had a mock trial with 'secret' evidence and whacked off Stafford's head."

Dougless winced. "So Lettice and Robert Sydney went free."

Lee smiled. "Sort of. Actually, what happened after Stafford's execution was rather ironic. It seems that Lettice, who had planned everything so carefully, hadn't considered Robert Sydney's ambition into her plan. Lady Margaret thinks Lettice planned to marry some English duke who was Elizabeth's cousin and start all over again, but Sydney had other plans. He threatened to tell the queen everything if Lettice didn't marry him. He wanted to put *his* kid on the throne."

"Blackmail," Dougless whispered.

"Right. Blackmail. I told you this was like a movie. Or a best seller. Maybe I should fictionalize this. Anyway, she was forced to marry Sydney." Lee gave a snort of laughter. "What's *really* ironic about this whole story is that Lettice was barren. She never conceived at all, not even to miscarry, so she sent her first husband to the blade because of what she wanted for a child she would never have. Unbelievable, isn't it?"

"Yes," Dougless said through a choked throat. "Unbelievable." She paused. "What of Lady Margaret?"

"Neither Lettice nor Sydney had any idea the old woman knew what they'd done. No doubt they'd have killed her if they had, but she was a clever old broad and kept her mouth shut. Maybe she realized she couldn't prove anything. The queen confiscated everything she owned so Sydney stepped in and offered her a choice between the pauper's farm or marrying his ex-father-in-law, Lord Harewood. Of course Sydney had an ulterior motive. Since he had three kids of Arabella's still alive, Lady Margaret's marriage made them obscurely related. It isn't much of a relationship by our standards today, but then it was enough that Queen Elizabeth gave Sydney two of the Stafford estates."

He took a sip of his beer. "After Lady Margaret married Harewood she wrote everything down, put it in an iron chest, had some faithful old servant knock out part of a wall and hid the box in there. As an afterthought she put her letters in a chest and hid them too. Then the wall was sealed up."

He paused. "It was a good thing she did it when she did. According to a letter written by a friend of hers that's survived, two weeks later Lady Margaret was found dead at the bottom of a stairs, her neck broken. I guess after Mr. and Mrs. Sydney got the two Stafford estates they had all they needed from her."

Dougless leaned back against the booth and was silent for a while. "What happened to them? To . . . Lettice and Robert Sydney?" She could hardly bear to say the names.

"Roasted in hell, I imagine. But actually, I don't know. I know they never had any kids and their estates passed into the hands of his nephew, who was a desolate little bastard and in one generation managed to bankrupt the Sydney estates. It'll take more research to find out what happened to Lettice and her husband. Historians haven't been too interested in them." He smiled. "Up to now, that is. History will change when I write my book."

"To change history," Dougless whispered. That's what Nicholas had wanted to do but all they'd managed was making his execution happen. "I have to go," she said abruptly.

"Where are you staying? I'll walk you there."

"I don't have reservations." Her head came up. "I'd like to stay at Thornwyck Castle."

"Yeah, wouldn't we all? You have to book a year in advance to get into that place. Wait a minute, don't look so sad. I'll call." He walked away and minutes later returned, grinning. "You are one lucky devil. They had a cancellation. You can check in now. I'll walk you."

"No," Dougless said. "I need to be alone. Thanks for dinner and thanks for telling me. You'll have your chair." She put out her hand to shake his, then turned and left the pub.

12

$\mathbf{A}$t Thornwyck no one remembered Nicholas. She looked back through the guest register and, where Nicholas had signed the book, an unfamiliar hand had written Miss Dougless Montgomery. Listlessly, she put her tote bag in the single room and went outside to look at the unfinished part of the castle. It had never been finished because Nicholas was executed.

As she looked at the roofless walls, the vines still hanging down them, she remembered every word Nicholas had told her of what he'd planned for this place. A center of learning, he'd said. Yet it had come to nothing.

When he'd left her yesterday, had he gone back to his cell? Had he gone back to the time when he'd been writing his mother and trying to find out who had betrayed him? What had he done in those three days before his execution? Would no one listen to him when he told of Robert Sydney's lies?

Wearily, she leaned back against a wall. *Whom* had he told about Robert Sydney? Lettice? Had his beloved wife come to visit him? Had he told her what he knew and asked for her help?

Irony, Dougless thought. Lee had said all of it was ironic. The true irony was that Nicholas had died because he was *good*. He'd refused to commit treason with his wife, refused to even consider it—and he'd died for it. Not a quick, honorable death, but a death that was public and meant to ridicule him. He'd lost his life, his honor, his name, his estates, the respect of future generations, and all because he'd refused to conspire with a power-mad woman.

"It is wrong!" Dougless said aloud. "What happened was *wrong.*"

Slowly, she walked back to the hotel, as if in a trance. She showered, put on her nightgown, and went to bed, lying awake for a long time, anger not allowing her to sleep. Irony, she thought. Treason. Betrayal. Blackmail. The words tumbled about in her head.

Toward dawn she fell into a fitful sleep and when she awoke she felt worse than she had before she went to bed. Feeling a thousand pounds heavier and very old, she dressed and went downstairs to breakfast.

Nicholas had been given a second chance, and he had asked her for help but she had failed him. She had been so jealous of Arabella that she'd lost sight of the true purpose of why they'd been at the Harewoods. When she should have been searching for information she had been worrying about whether Nicholas and Arabella were touching each other. Well, no one was going to touch Nicholas now—not in the twentieth century or in the sixteenth.

She ate, she checked out, she walked to the train station and boarded a train going back to Ashburton. Somewhere during that time her failures stopped plaguing her and she began to ask herself what could be done now. Would the publication of Lee's book help to clear Nicholas's name? Perhaps if she volunteered her services as his secretary and helped him research, she could make up somewhat for how she hadn't helped Nicholas when he was in the twentieth century.

She leaned her head against the train window. If only she had to do it over again, she wouldn't be jealous, she wouldn't waste their precious time together. When she was at Goshawk Hall, why hadn't she asked Lee if there were any other secrets hidden behind the wall? Why hadn't she looked? Why hadn't she—

The sign for Ashburton appeared out the window and she left the train. As she walked, she realized there was nothing she could do. The time to help was past. Lee could write his book himself and she knew he'd do a great job of it. Robert had his daughter and he didn't need her. Nicholas had been the one who needed her and she'd failed him.

There was nothing more for her to do but go home.

She left the train station and started toward the hotel. She'd call the airlines and see if she could get a flight home immediately. Perhaps if she went home to familiar surroundings she could begin to forgive herself.

As she walked, she went past the church that contained Nicholas's tomb and her feet seemed to turn of their own accord toward the gate. The church was empty inside, the sunlight streaming down through the stained glass windows to gently touch Nicholas's tomb. The pale white of the marble looked cold and dead.

Slowly, Dougless walked toward the tomb. Perhaps if she prayed, Nicholas would return. Perhaps if she begged God, He'd let Nicholas come back to her. For five minutes, she thought. That's all she'd need to tell him of his wife's treachery.

But as she touched the cold marble cheek she knew it wouldn't work. What had happened was a once-in-a-century happening. She'd been given a chance to save a man's life and she'd failed.

"Nicholas," she whispered and for the first time since he'd gone, tears came to her eyes. They were hot, thick tears that blurred her vision.

"I am onion-eyed again," she said, almost smiling. "I am sorry for failing you, my darling Nicholas. I don't seem to be much good at anything. Only I never had anyone *die* because of my shortcomings before now.

"Oh God," she whispered and turned around to sit on the edge of the tomb. "How do I live with your blood on my hands?"

She unzipped her bag that was still hanging from her shoulder and rummaged inside for a tissue. She pulled out a soft travel pack, then took a tissue. As she blew her nose, she saw a piece of paper fall from the tissue pack to the floor. Bending, she picked it up and looked at it.

It was the note Nicholas had written and slipped under her door.

"The note," she said, standing up straight. It was a note written in Nicholas's own hand! It was something that he had touched, something that was . . . that was *proof,* she thought.

"Oh, Nicholas," she said and the tears began then, real tears, deep, deep tears of grief. Her legs gave way beneath her and she slid slowly to the stone floor, the note held to her cheek. "I am sorry, Nicholas," she cried. "Very, very sorry that I failed you."

She leaned her forehead against the cold marble tomb, her body huddled in a knot. "God," she whispered, "help me to forgive myself."

Dougless, in her grief, was unaware of the way the light came in through the stained glass and touched her hair. The window was of an angel kneeling and praying, and the light came through the angel's halo to touch Dougless's hair and, as a cloud moved, the sun touched Nicholas's marble hand.

"Please," Dougless whispered, "please."

It was at that moment that Dougless heard laughter. Not just any laughter, but Nicholas's laughter.

"Nicholas?" she whispered and lifted her head, blinking to clear her vision. There was no one in the church.

Awkwardly, she rose. "Nicholas?" she said louder and turned abruptly when she heard the laughter again, this time behind her. She reached out her hand but there was no one, nothing, there.

"Yes," she said, standing up straight, then louder, "Yes." She raised her face to the sunlight and the angel in the window. She closed her eyes, her head back. "Yes," she whispered.

Suddenly, Dougless felt as if someone had punched her in the stomach. She doubled over in pain and fell forward onto the stone floor. When she tried to get up, she felt dizzy and as if she were going to throw up. She had to get to a rest room. She couldn't befoul the church.

But when she tried to move, nothing happened. It was as if her body were no longer obeying her brain. "Nicholas," she whispered and put out her hand toward his tomb, but the next moment everything went black and she collapsed to the floor.

◇ ◇ ◇

When she awoke, she felt dizzy and weak and not sure where she was. She opened her eyes to see blue sky overhead, a leafy tree near her.

"Now what?" she whispered. Had she wandered out of the church?

She closed her eyes. She was so weak she felt like staying where she was and taking a nap. She would figure out where she was later.

As she began to doze, she was vaguely aware of a feminine giggle nearby. Kids, she thought, kids playing.

But at the sound of a male's responding laughter, her eyes opened. "Nicholas?" Abruptly, she sat up and looked around. She was sitting on the grass under a tree in a pretty part of the English countryside. She turned about to get her bearings. When had she left the church?

She stopped turning when she saw a man in a field. He was far away and difficult to distinguish, but he seemed to be wearing a sort of short brown robe and he was plowing a field with an ox. Dougless blinked her eyes but the vision didn't change. Rural England was indeed rural.

Behind her came the woman's giggle again. "Sir Nicholas," the woman said in a dreamy sort of way.

Dougless didn't think about what she did, she merely reacted. She leaped to her feet, went to the bushes behind her, and shoved her way through them.

There on the ground, rolling about, was Nicholas. *Her* Nicholas. His shirt was half off, and his strong arms were about a plump girl whose top half was coming out of an odd-looking dress.

"Nicholas," Dougless said loudly, "how could you? How could you do this to me?" Tears were starting again. "I've been crazy with worry about you and here you are with . . . with this . . . Oh, Nicholas, how could you?" She took a tissue from her pocket and blew her nose loudly.

On the ground, Nicholas and the girl had stopped moving. The girl, with frightened movements, hastily tied the front of her dress and scurried out from under Nicholas, then ran off through the hedges.

Nicholas, a scowl on his handsome face, turned over, leaned back on one elbow and looked up at the red-haired woman. "What mean you by this?" he demanded.

Dougless's first reaction of anger left her. She stood for a moment staring down at him. Nicholas was here with her. Here!

She leaped on him, her arms about his neck, and began kissing his face. His arms went around her as they fell back against the ground.

"Nicholas, it *is* you. It is. Oh, my darling, it was awful after you left. No one remembered you. Nobody remembered us together." She kissed his neck. "You've grown your beard back but that's okay, I kinda like it."

He was kissing her neck. His hand was on her shirt front and her blouse easily parted as his lips moved down her throat.

"Nicholas, I have so much to tell you. I saw Lee after you left and he told me all about Lettice and Robert Sydney . . . and . . . Oh, that's nice, that's very nice."

"No!" she said abruptly and pushed him to arm's length. "We mustn't do this. You remember what happened the last time, don't you? We have to talk. I have so many things to tell you. Did you know that you were executed after all?"

Nicholas stopped trying to pull her back in his arms. "I? Executed? Pray, madam, for what?"

"For treason. For raising the army. For—Nicholas, don't you lose your memory too. I've had all the amnesia I can take lately. Listen to me. I don't know how long you'll stay here before you go back. Your wife planned everything. I know you love her but she only married you because you're related to Queen Elizabeth—or is it the queen's father? Anyway, Lettice wants you out of the picture because you won't play along with her and put her kid on the throne. Of course she can't have any kids but she doesn't know that."

She paused. "Why are you looking at me like that? Where are you going?"

"I make for my home, away from your Colley weston ward talk." He stood and began tucking his shirt into his balloon shorts.

Dougless rose too. "Colley weston ward. That's a new one on me. Nicholas, wait, you can't leave."

He turned back to face her. "If you desire to finish what you began"—he nodded toward the ground—"I will remain and I will pay you well, but I cannot abide this deboshed manner of speaking."

Dougless stood there blinking at him, trying to understand what he was saying. "Pay me?" she whispered. "Nicholas, what's wrong with you? You act as if you've never seen me before."

"Nay, madam, I have not." He turned on his heel and left the clearing.

Dougless was too stunned to move. Never seen her before? What was he talking about? She pushed through the bushes. Nicholas was dressed in the most extraordinary clothes of a black satin jacket that seemed to be decorated with . . .

"Are those diamonds?" she gasped.

Nicholas narrowed his eyes at her. "I do not deal kindly with thieves."

"I wasn't planning to rob you, I've just never seen anyone who had diamonds on his clothes before." She stood back and looked at him, really looked at him, and she saw that he was different. It wasn't just the clothes or that he was again wearing his beard and mustache, but there was a seriousness missing from his face. This was Nicholas but he somehow seemed younger.

How could he have grown his beard back so soon?

"Nicholas?" she asked. "When you were last home, not the first time you came to me, but this time, what year was it?"

Nicholas slipped a short cloak of black satin that was trimmed in ermine about his shoulders, and from behind the bushes he pulled a horse, an animal as wild-looking as the rented Sugar had been. Easily he vaulted into a saddle that was as big as an American cowboy saddle, but it had a tall wooden upright shelf in front of and in back of the seat. "When last I was home, this morn it was the year of our Lord 1560. Now, you, witch, get from my sight."

Dougless had to step back against the bushes to keep from getting run down by the horse. "Nicholas, wait!" she called but he was gone.

Disbelieving, Dougless stared after him until he was little more than a speck on the horizon, then she sat down on a fallen log, her head in her hands. Now what, she thought. Did she have to start all over again and explain to him all about the twentieth century? The last time she'd seen him he'd come from 1564, but this time it was four years earlier. What had happened hadn't happened yet.

Her head came up. Of course! That was it. When he'd found out about Robert Sydney he'd been in jail—or the medieval equivalent thereof—and he couldn't do much about saving himself. But this time he'd come forward four years earlier. There was time to *prevent* what had caused his execution.

Feeling a great deal more cheerful, she stood. She had to go find him before he did something dumb like walk in front of a bus again. She picked up her heavy tote bag from the ground, slung it over her shoulder and started walking in the direction Nicholas had gone.

The road was the worst she'd ever seen: deep ruts, rocks sticking up, narrow, weed-choked. The roads in rural America weren't this bad and she'd never seen anything like this in England.

She stepped to the side of the road when she heard a vehicle coming around a corner. A tired-looking donkey was pulling a cart that had two big wheels. Beside it was a man wearing a short dress that looked as if it'd been made from a burlap bag. His legs, bare from mid-calf down, had great ugly sores on them. Dougless stared at him in opened-mouthed astonishment, and the man turned and gaped at her in the same way. His face was like leather and when he opened his mouth, Dougless could see rotten teeth. He looked her up and down, his eyes fastening on her stocking-clad legs, then he leered at her, grinning and showing off his hideous teeth.

Dougless quickly turned away and started walking rapidly. The road got worse, the ruts deeper, and there was manure everywhere. "England's using manure to fill the ruts now?" she muttered.

At the top of a little hill she stopped and looked down. Below her were three little houses, tiny places with thatched roofs and bare ground in front of them, where chickens and ducks and children scratched about. A woman wearing a long skirt came out the door of one hut and emptied a round container beside the front door.

Dougless started down the hill. Perhaps she could ask directions of the woman. But as she neared the village she slowed. She could smell the place. Animals, people, rotting food, piles of manure, all reeked. Dougless put her hand to her nose and breathed through her mouth. Really! she thought, the English government should do something about this place. People shouldn't live like this.

She went to the first house, trying to keep her shoes clean but not succeeding very well. A child, about three, wearing a filthy nightgown, looked up at her. The poor thing looked as if it hadn't been washed in a year and it obviously wasn't wearing a diaper. Dougless vowed that when she got Nicholas straightened out she was going to complain about this place. It was a health hazard.

"Excuse me," she called into the dark interior of the house. It didn't seem to smell much better inside than out. "Hello? Is anybody home?"

No one answered but Dougless felt as if she were being watched. She turned and saw three women and a couple of children behind her. The women weren't any cleaner than the child she'd seen, their long dresses encrusted with food and no telling what else.

Dougless tried smiling. "Excuse me, but I'm looking for the Ashburton church. I seem to have lost my way."

The women didn't speak but one woman came toward Dougless. It was difficult to keep smiling, for the woman reeked of body odor.

"Do you know the way to Ashburton?" Dougless repeated.

The woman just walked around Dougless, staring at her, looking at her clothes, her hair, her face.

"A bunch of looney tunes," Dougless muttered. Living in filth as they did, they probably weren't too bright. She stepped away from the stinking woman and unzipped her tote bag. The woman jumped back at the sound. Dougless took out her map of southern England and looked at it, but it didn't help any, since she didn't know where she was so she couldn't figure out where she was going.

She lowered the map when she realized one of the women was very near, her head almost inside Dougless's tote bag. "I beg your pardon," she said sharply. The woman's head was covered with a cloth that was caked with dirt and grease.

The woman jumped away but not before she'd taken Dougless's sunglasses from her bag. She ran back to the other women and the three of them examined the glasses.

"This is too much." Dougless strode toward the women, her foot slipping in something but she didn't look down. "May I have those back?"

The women looked at her with hard faces. One of them had deep, pitted scars on her neck and she held the sunglasses behind her back.

Dougless put her hands to her sides. "Would you please return my property?"

"Be gone with you," one of the women said, and Dougless saw that three upper teeth were gone and two others were rotten.

It was then that she began to understand. She looked at the house before her, saw the firewood stacked, saw the onions hanging from the roof. The dirt, the carts, the people who had never heard of a dentist.

"Who is your queen?" she whispered.

"Elizabeth," one woman said in an odd accent.

"Right," Dougless whispered, "and who was her mother?"

"The witch Anne Bullen."

The women were gathering around her now, but Dougless was too stunned to notice. Nicholas had said that this morning it had been 1560 and then he'd ridden off on a horse with a funny saddle. He hadn't seemed disoriented or unsure of where he was going. He hadn't acted as he had when he'd first arrived in the twentieth century. Instead, he'd acted as if he were right at home.

"Ow!" Dougless said, for one of the women had pulled her hair.

"Be ye a witch?" one of the women asked, standing very close to Dougless.

Suddenly, Dougless was afraid. It was one thing to laugh at a man in the twentieth century for calling someone a witch, but in the sixteenth century people were burned for being witches.

"Of course I'm not a witch," Dougless said, backing away, but there was a woman behind her.

A woman pulled on Dougless's sleeve. "Witch's clothes."

"No, of course they aren't. I live . . . ah, in another village, that's all. Next year you'll all be wearing this." She couldn't go back or forward, for the surrounding women were blocking her. You'd better think fast, Dougless, she thought, or you just might be this evening's barbecue. While keeping an eye on the women, she put her hand into her tote bag, digging for she knew not what. Her hand lit on a book of matches she'd taken from a hotel somewhere.

She pulled out the matches, tore off one, and struck it. With a gasp the women moved back. "In the house," she said, holding the lit match at arm's length. "Go on, get in the house."

The women backed up and stepped inside the doorway just as the match burned down to Dougless's fingertips. She dropped the match and began to run.

She left the stinking houses and the rutted road behind and ran into the woods. When she was out of breath, she sat down on the ground and leaned back against a tree.

It appeared that when she'd passed out in the church she'd awakened in the sixteenth century. So here she was, alone—Nicholas didn't know her— in a time before soap was invented, or at least before it was used. And the people seemed to regard her as some freak of evil.

"So how am I to tell Nicholas all he needs to know if I don't even see him?" she whispered.

The first drops of rain were cold on Dougless. She pulled an umbrella from her bag and opened it. It was at that moment that she really looked at her beat-up old carry-on. She'd had the thing for years. It had traveled with her wherever she went and she'd gradually filled it with everything anyone could need while traveling. Inside were cosmetics, medicines, toiletries, a sewing kit, office kit, magazines, nightgown, airline nut packages, felt-tip pens and no telling what was in the very bottom.

She pulled the bag under the umbrella with her, feeling as if the bag were her only friend. Think, Dougless, think, she told herself. She had to tell Nicholas what he must know and then she had to get back to her own time. She could tell already that she didn't want to stay in this backward place with its filthy, ignorant people. In just this short time she missed hot showers and electric blankets.

She huddled under the umbrella as the rain started coming down harder. The ground under her was getting wet and she thought of sitting on a magazine, but who knows? She might end up selling the magazines in order to live.

She put her head down on her knees. "Oh Nicholas, where are you?" she whispered.

Then she remembered the evening of the first day she'd met him and she'd been in that tool shed crying. He'd come to her then and said he'd heard her "calling." If it worked then, maybe it would work now.

With her head down, she concentrated on asking Nicholas to come to her. She visualized his riding up to her and then she thought of all their time together. She smiled, remembering a dinner, chosen by her, that their landlady had cooked for them: corn-on-the-cob, avocados, barbecued spare-ribs, and a mango for dessert. Nicholas had laughed like a small boy. She remembered the music he'd played, his delight over the books, how critical he had been of modern clothes.

"Come to me, Nicholas," she whispered. "Come to me."

It was dusk and the rain was coming down hard and cold when Nicholas appeared, sitting atop his big black horse.

She grinned up at him. "I knew you'd come."

He did not smile, but instead glared down at her in anger.

"Lady Margaret would see you," he said.

"Your mother? Your mother wants to see *me?*" She couldn't be sure because of the rain but he seemed to be momentarily shocked at her words. "All right," Dougless said, rising, then handing him her umbrella and raising her hand for him to help her on to his horse.

To her disbelief, he took the umbrella, examined it with interest, then held it over his own head and rode off, leaving Dougless standing with rain pelting down on her. "Of all the—" she began. Was she supposed to *walk* while he rode?

She moved back to the relative dryness under the tree and after a while Nicholas came back, the umbrella held over him.

"You are to come with me," he said.

"Am I supposed to go on foot?" she yelled up at him. "You ride and I slog along in the mud and muck behind you while you take my umbrella? Is that what you had in mind?"

He seemed confused for a moment. "Your speech is most strange."

"Not as strange as your outdated ideas. Nicholas, I am cold and hungry and getting wetter by the minute. Help me on your horse and let's go see your mother."

Nicholas gave her a bit of a smile, then reached his hand down for her. Douglass took it, put her foot on his and swung onto the back of the horse —not into the saddle with him but on to the hard unsteady rump of the horse. Dougless put her arms around Nicholas's waist, but he pried her loose and pushed her hands down to the high back of the saddle, then handed her the umbrella.

"Hold this over me," he said and kicked the horse forward.

Dougless wanted to make a retort but all her attention was on holding on to the horse. She had to use two hands so the umbrella hung uselessly to the side as they sped along. Through the rain she saw more hovels, and more people working in the rain, apparently oblivious to it. "Maybe it'll wash them," she muttered, hanging on as best she could.

Because she was behind Nicholas and he was too tall to see over, she didn't see the house until they were in front of it. There was a tall stone wall before them and behind it stood a three-story stone house.

A man wearing clothes somewhat like Nicholas's—no burlap dress—came running to take the horse's reins. Nicholas dismounted, then stood impatiently by, slapping his gloves against his palm, while Dougless struggled down by herself, lugging her heavy bag and the umbrella.

When she was down, the servant opened the gate and Nicholas went through it, seeming to expect Dougless to follow. She hurried after him, down a brick path, up stairs, across a brick terrace, and into the house.

A solemn-faced servant stood waiting to take Nicholas's cloak and wet hat. Dougless closed the umbrella and Nicholas took it from her and looked inside, obviously trying to figure out how it worked. After the way he'd been treating her, she wasn't about to tell him. She snatched the umbrella from his hands and gave it to the wide-eyed servant. "This is *mine*. Remember that and don't let anyone else have it."

Nicholas looked at her and snorted. Dougless hitched her bag on her shoulder and glared at him. She was beginning to believe that he was not the man she'd fallen in love with. Her Nicholas wouldn't have made a woman ride on the back of a horse.

He turned away and started up the stairs and Dougless, dripping and cold, followed him. She had only a brief glimpse of the house but it didn't look like the Elizabethan houses she'd seen on guided tours. For one thing the wood wasn't darkened from being four hundred years old. The walls were paneled in golden oak and everywhere there was color. The plaster above the panels was painted with scenes of people in a meadow. There were bright, pretty, new tapestries and woven cloths hanging on the walls. There were silver plates gleaming from table tops. And under her feet, oddly enough, seemed to be straw. Upstairs there were carved pieces of furniture in the hall, looking as new as if they'd been made last week. On one table was a tall pitcher that had beautiful, deep fluting on it. It was of a yellow metal that could only be gold.

Before Dougless could ask about the pitcher, Nicholas opened a door and strode inside.

"I have brought the witch," she heard Nicholas say.

"Now just a minute," Dougless said, leaving the pitcher and, hurrying into the room behind him, she stopped. She had entered a beautiful room. It was large, with tall ceilings, the walls paneled with more of the beautiful oak, the plaster above painted with colorful birds and butterflies and animals. The furniture, the window seat, and the enormous bed were all draped with cushions and hangings of brilliant silk, all of it embroidered in gold and silver and bright silk thread. Everything in the room, from cups and pitchers, to a mirror and comb, seemed to be a precious object, made of gold or silver, encrusted with jewels. The whole room glittered beautifully.

"My goodness," Dougless said in awe.

"Bring her to me," said an imperious voice.

Dougless pulled her eyes away from the room to look at the bed. Behind its exquisitely carved posts, behind scarlet silk hangings that twinkled with flowers embroidered in gold thread, lay a stern-looking woman wearing a white nightgown with black embroidery on the cuffs and ruffled neck. About her eyes Dougless could see a resemblance to Nicholas.

"Come here," she commanded and Dougless moved closer.

The woman's voice, for all its command, sounded tired and stuffy, as if she had a cold.

It was when Dougless was closer to the foot of the bed that she saw that the woman had her left arm stretched across a pillow and a man, wearing a long, voluminous robe of black velvet, was bending over her and tending to . . .

"Are those leeches?" Dougless gasped. Slimy little black worms seemed to be stuck on the woman's arm.

Dougless didn't see Lady Margaret exchange looks with her son.

"I have been told you are a witch, that you make fire from your fingertips."

Dougless couldn't take her eyes off the leeches. "Doesn't that hurt?"

"Aye, it hurts," the woman said in dismissal. "I would see this magic of fire."

The distaste Dougless felt at seeing the leeches on the woman's arm overrode her fears of being called a witch. She walked to the side of the bed and put her tote bag on top of a table, pushing aside a pretty silver box that had emeralds across the top. "You shouldn't let that man do that to you. It sounds to me like you just have a bad cold. Headache? Sneezing? Tired?"

Wide-eyed, the woman stared at her and nodded.

"That's what I thought." She rummaged in her bag. "If you'll make that man take those nasty things away I'll fix your cold. Ah, here they are. Cold tablets." She held up the package.

"Mother," Nicholas said, stepping forward, "you cannot—"

"Go away, Nicholas," Lady Margaret said, "and you," she said to the physician.

The man pulled the leeches from Lady Margaret's arm and dropped them into a little leather-bound box.

"You'll need a glass of water."

"Wine!" Lady Margaret commanded and Nicholas handed her a tall silver goblet studded with rough-cut jewels.

Dougless was aware of the unnatural hush in the room and suddenly she realized how brave Lady Margaret was. Or how dumb, she couldn't help thinking, taking medicine from a stranger. Dougless handed her a cold tablet. "Swallow it and in about twenty minutes it should work."

"Mother," Nicholas began, but Lady Margaret waved him away as she swallowed the capsule.

"If she is harmed you will pay," Nicholas said into Dougless's ear and Dougless swallowed. What if the Elizabethan body wasn't ready for cold tablets? What if Lady Margaret was allergic?

Dougless stood where she was, still dripping water, beginning to shiver from cold. Her hair was plastered to her head, but no one had offered her a towel. No one in the room seemed to breathe as they watched Lady Margaret lying against the embroidered pillows. Dougless shifted nervously and became aware of another person in the room, near the bed curtains.

Dougless could just see the shape of a woman in a dress with a tight bodice and a full skirt.

Dougless coughed and Nicholas, at the foot of the bed, gave her a sharp look.

It was the longest twenty minutes of Dougless's life as she stood there, cold and nervous, and waited for the pill to take effect. When it did work, it worked quickly. Lady Margaret's sinuses cleared and she lost that awful stuffy feeling of having a cold.

Lady Margaret sat up straighter, her eyes wide. "I am cured," she said.

"Not really," Dougless answered. "The pills just mask the symptoms. You should stay in bed and drink lots of orange juice . . . or whatever."

The woman behind Dougless came bustling from the shadows, leaned over Lady Margaret, and tucked the covers around her.

"I am well, I tell you," Lady Margaret said. "You! Go!" she said to the physician and he backed out of the room. "Nicholas, take her, feed her, dry her, clothe her, and bring her to me on the morrow. Early."

"I?" Nicholas said haughtily. "I?"

"You have found her, you are responsible for her. Now go."

Nicholas looked at Dougless and curled his upper lip. "Come," he said and there was anger as well as distaste in his voice.

She followed him out of the room and in the hall she said, "Nicholas, we must talk."

He turned on her, still wearing that expression of distaste. "Nay, madam, we do not talk." He arched one eyebrow. "And I am *Sir* Nicholas, Knight of the Realm." He turned on his heel and walked away.

"*Sir* Nicholas?" she asked. "Not *Lord* Nicholas?"

"I am but a knight. My brother is lord."

Dougless stopped walking. "Brother? You mean Kit? Kit is *alive?*"

Nicholas turned to face her, his face distorted with rage. "I do not know who you are or how you come to know of my family, but I warn you, witch, you harm one person, should a hair on my mother's head change color, and you will forfeit your life in payment. Do not think to use your witchcraft on my brother."

He turned again and started walking. Dougless followed but she didn't say anything. Great, just great, she thought. She'd come all the way back across four hundred years to save Nicholas's head and all he could do was threaten to kill her. How was she going to make him listen?

They went upstairs to the top floor and Nicholas threw open a door. "You sleep here."

She stepped inside. This was no pretty room filled with treasures but a windowless cell of a place with a lumpy mattress in a corner and a filthy wool blanket on top. "I can't stay here," Dougless said, horrified. But when she turned, she saw Nicholas was gone. She heard a key turn in a lock.

She yelled and pounded on the heavy door with her hands but he didn't open it. "You bastard!" she shouted and slid down the door to the floor. "You rotten bastard," she whispered, alone in the dark room.

13

No one came to release Dougless that night or the next morning. She had no water, no food, no light. There was an old wooden bucket in a corner and she assumed this was to relieve herself in. She tried lying on the mattress but within minutes she felt little things crawling on her skin. Clawing herself, she jumped out of the bed and pressed herself against the cold stone wall.

She could tell when morning came because some light from the outside hallway came under the door. During the long night she'd scratched so much at whatever was on her skin that places were bleeding. Expectantly, she waited for someone to release her. Lady Margaret had said she wanted to see Dougless early. But no one came.

By holding her arm to the light under the door she could see her wristwatch and, if it was set correctly for Elizabethan time, at noon no one had yet come to release her.

She tried to keep her mind active and not give in to despair, so she went over again and again everything Lee had told her about the events leading up to Nicholas's execution. Somehow she had to warn Nicholas. Somehow she had to prevent Lettice and Robert Sydney from using Nicholas.

But how could she do anything at all when she was locked away in a dark, flea-ridden room? And Nicholas not only wouldn't listen to her, he seemed to hate her. She tried to remember what she'd said when she'd first seen him yesterday that had so offended him. Was it her references to his beloved Lettice?

It was cold in the room and Dougless shivered as she scratched at her itching scalp. In the twentieth century she always had the Montgomery name and money to fall back on. Even though she was years from inheriting she'd always known the money was there, that she could offer a million dollars for information she wanted.

But here in the sixteenth century she had nothing, was nothing. All she had was a tote bag full of modern wonders and her brains. Yet somehow she had to persuade these people that they couldn't just toss her into a prison and leave her to rot. The first time Nicholas had come to her she'd failed to find the information needed to stop his execution, but this time she would *not* fail. This time she was going to succeed no matter what she had to do.

She stood and energy began to replace her lethargy. Her father loved to tell his daughters stories of their ancestors, of the Montgomerys in Scotland, in England, in America. There was one story after another of heroic deeds and near escapes.

"If they can do it, so can I," Dougless said aloud. "Nicholas," she said firmly, "come release me from this hideous place." She closed her eyes and concentrated, imagining Nicholas coming to her.

It didn't take him long to "hear" her. When he flung open the door, his face was black with anger.

"Nicholas, I want to talk to you," she said.

He turned away from her. "My mother asks for you."

She stumbled after him, her legs weak from lack of use, her eyes not adjusted to the light in the hall. "You came because I called you," she said. "There is a bond between us and if you'd let me explain—"

He stopped and glared at her. "I wish to hear naught that you say."

"Will you tell me what you're so angry at me about? What have I done?"

He looked her up and down in an insolent way. "You accuse me of treason. You frighten the villagers. You besmirch the name of the woman I am to marry. You bewitch my mother. You . . ." His voice lowered. "You come into my head."

She put her hand on his arm. "Nicholas, I know I must seem strange to you but if you'd just listen to me and let me explain—"

"Nay," he said, turning away. "I have petitioned my brother to cast you out. The villagers will see to you."

"See to me?" she whispered and shuddered as she remembered those filthy women in the village. No doubt those rotten-toothed hags would stone her if given the chance. "You would do that to me? After the way I helped you?" Her voice was rising. "After all I did for you when you came forward, you'd throw me out? After the way I've come four hundred years to save you, you'd just throw me into the streets?"

He glared at her. "My brother decides." He turned and went down the stairs.

Dougless stayed close behind him and tried to control her anger enough to think. She had to do something to keep from being tossed out of the relative safety of the house and into the muck of the streets. Lady Margaret seemed to be the answer.

Lady Margaret was again in bed and Dougless knew the twelve-hour cold tablet had worn off.

"You will give me another of the magic tablets," she said, leaning back against the pillows.

In spite of being hungry, tired, and frightened, Dougless knew that now she had to use her wits. "Lady Margaret, I am not a witch. I am merely a poor humble princess set upon by thieves, and I must appeal to you for help until my uncle the king can come to me."

"Princess?" Lady Margaret said.

"King?" Nicholas half-shouted. "Mother, I—"

Lady Margaret put up her hand to silence him. "Who is your uncle?"

Dougless took a deep breath. "He is the King of Lanconia."

"I have heard of this place," Lady Margaret said thoughtfully.

"She is no princess," Nicholas said. "Look you at her."

"This happens to be the style of dress in my country," she snapped at him. "Are you going to throw me in the street and risk a king's wrath?" She looked back at Lady Margaret. "My uncle would be very generous to any-one who protected me."

Dougless could see that Lady Margaret was considering this. "I can be very useful," Dougless said quickly. "I have lots of cold tablets and I have all sorts of interesting things in my bag. And I . . ." What could she do? "I can tell stories. I know lots of stories."

"Mother, you cannot consider—" Nicholas began. "She is no better than a flirt-gill."

Dougless guessed that that was a lady of ill repute. She turned angry eyes on him. "Look who's talking. You and Arabella Sydney can't keep your hands off one another."

Nicholas's face turned purple and he took a step toward her.

Lady Margaret coughed to cover laughter. "Nicholas, fetch Honoria to me. Go! Now!"

With one more look of anger at Dougless, he obediently left the room.

Lady Margaret looked at Dougless. "You amuse me. You may remain in my care until a messenger can be sent to Lanconia to ask after your uncle."

Dougless swallowed. "How long will that take?"

"A month or more." Lady Margaret's eyes were shrewd. "Do you recant your story?"

"No, of course not. My uncle *is* King of Lanconia." Or will be, Dougless amended to herself.

"Now the tablet," Lady Margaret said, leaning back on the pillows. "Then you may go."

Dougless got a cold tablet from her bag, but hesitated. "Where am I supposed to sleep?"

"My son will tend to you."

"Your son locked me in a hideous little room and there were bugs in the bed!"

From the look on Lady Margaret's face she didn't seem to see anything wrong in this.

"I want a proper room and some clothes that won't make people stare at me and I want to be treated with the respect due to . . . to my station in life. And I want a bath."

Lady Margaret looked at her with cold, dark eyes, and Dougless saw where Nicholas got his imperious manner. "Beware you do not amuse me too much."

Dougless tried to keep her knees from knocking. Once, as a child, she'd seen a wax museum that showed a medieval torture chamber. The rack. The Iron Maiden. "I mean no disrespect, my lady," she said softly. "I will earn my keep. I will do my best to continue to amuse you." Like Scheherazade, she thought. If I don't amuse this woman, tomorrow it's off with my head.

Lady Margaret studied her for a while and Dougless knew her fate was being decided. "You shall attend me. Honoria will—"

"That means I can stay? Oh, Lady Margaret, you won't regret this, I promise. I'll show you how to play poker. I'll tell you stories. I'll tell you all of Shakespeare's tales. No, I better not do that, it might upset things. I'll tell you about . . . ah, *The Wizard of Oz* and *My Fair Lady*. Maybe I can remember some of the words and music." She began to sing, "I Could Have Danced All Night."

"Honoria!" Lady Margaret said sharply. "Take her, clothe her."

"And food and a bath," Dougless added.

"The tablet."

"Oh, sure." Dougless handed over the cold tablet and Lady Margaret took it.

"Let me rest now. Honoria will see to you. She will stay with you, Honoria."

Dougless hadn't heard the other woman enter. She looked to be the same woman who had been in the room last night, but still Dougless couldn't see her face as she kept it turned away. Dougless followed Honoria from the room.

She felt better now, knowing that she had some time before Lady Margaret found out she wasn't a princess. Was lying to a lady punished by death or merely torture? Perhaps if Dougless could entertain Lady Margaret well enough, she wouldn't care whether she was a princess or not. And, too, perhaps a month was long enough to do what she must.

Dougless clasped her tote bag to her and followed Honoria. Honoria's room was next to Lady Margaret's. It was about half the size of Lady Margaret's, but still it was large and very pretty. There was a white marble fireplace, a big four-poster bed, some stools, two carved chairs, a chest at the foot of the bed. Sun came in through a window that had small diamond-shaped panes of glass.

Looking about the pretty room, Dougless was beginning to relax somewhat. She had managed to keep herself from being thrown into the streets.

"Is there a bathroom around here?" she asked the back of Honoria.

The woman didn't turn.

"A privy?" Dougless explained.

The woman still didn't turn, but she pointed to a small door in the paneling. Dougless opened it and inside was a stone seat with a hole cut in it, the equivalent of an outhouse indoors. It stunk to high heaven. Beside the seat was a stack of paper, thick, hard paper that had writing all over it. She held one piece up. "So that's what happened to all the medieval documents," she murmured. Quickly, she used the privy and left it.

When she reentered the room, she watched as Honoria opened a chest, pulled clothes out, and laid them on the bed. She left the room and Dougless walked about exploring. This room had no silver and gold ornaments as Lady Margaret's had, but everywhere were embroidered fabrics. Dougless had seen a few examples of Elizabethan embroidery in museums but they were old and faded. Here the cushions were brilliant, undimmed by time or use.

She walked about, touching everything, marveling at the brightness of all. New antiques, she thought, scratching furiously at bites on her back.

After a while the door opened and two men came in bearing a big, deep wooden tub. The men wore tight-fitting jackets of red wool, then puffy shorts like Nicholas wore, and black knitted hose. Both men had strong, muscular legs.

There are things to be said for the Elizabethan age, Douglass thought as she admired the men's legs.

Behind the men came four women bearing buckets of steaming hot water. They wore simple, long wool skirts with tight bodices, and little caps on their heads. Two of the women had smallpox scars on their faces.

When the tub was half full of steaming water, Douglass began to undress and Honoria turned toward her. She was a plain-faced woman, neither pretty nor ugly, with pale, nondescript features. "Hi, I'm Douglass Montgomery," she said, holding out her hand to shake.

Honoria didn't seem to know what to do, so Douglass picked up her hand and clasped it. "So, we're to be roommates."

Honoria gave Douglass a puzzled look. "Lady Margaret has requested that you remain with me, yes." She had a soft, pleasant voice and Douglass could see that she was quite young, maybe only twenty-one or -two.

Douglass easily stripped off her clothes and got into the tub while Honoria picked up the modern clothes and examined them carefully.

Douglass took the soap left for her but it was like a harsh version of Lava and it lathered about as well as a stone. "Would you hand me my bag, please?" she asked Honoria. Looking quite hard at the nylon of the bag, Honoria set it on the floor by her, then watched as Douglass unzipped it. She withdrew a cake of soap—she was always saving the pretty, scented bars from hotels—and began to wash herself.

By now Honoria was making no attempt to hide her curiosity as she watched Douglass wash.

"Would you tell me about this place?" Douglass asked. "Who lives here? Tell me about Kit and Nicholas, and is he engaged to Lettice and is John Wilfred here and what about Arabella Sydney?"

Honoria sat on a chair and tried to answer questions, watching in awe as Douglass used the marvelous soap, then shampooed her hair.

As far as Douglass could tell from Honoria's words, she'd been transported back in time early enough that only Nicholas's engagement had taken place. Nicholas had not yet made a fool of himself on the table with Arabella, and John Wilfred was insignificant enough that Honoria didn't know who he was. Honoria would give Douglass any facts she wanted but would not give an opinion. She refused to gossip.

After Douglass had bathed and washed her hair, Honoria handed her a coarse, rough towel of linen, and when she was damp-dry and her hair combed, Honoria began to help her dress.

First went on a long nightgown-like garment, very plain, of finely woven linen. "What about underpants?" Douglass asked.

Honoria looked blank.

"Knickers. You know." Dougless picked up her pink lacy briefs from the chest top where Honoria had put them, but Honoria still looked blank.

"There is nothing below," Honoria said.

"My goodness," Dougless said, wide-eyed. Who would have thought that underpants were a recent invention? "When in Rome . . ." she murmured and tossed her briefs aside.

Dougless wasn't prepared for the next layer of clothing. Honoria held up a corset for her. Dougless's experience of corsets was *Gone With the Wind* and Mammy pulling Scarlett's laces, but this corset was . . .

"Steel?" Dougless whispered, holding the thing.

It was made of thin, flexible strips of steel covered in silk, with steel hooks down one side, and since it wasn't new, rust showed through the fabric. Honoria buckled her into it and Dougless thought she might faint. Her rib cage could not expand, her waist was about three inches smaller, and her breasts were pressed flat.

Dougless steadied herself against the bedpost. "And to think that I used to complain that panty hose were uncomfortable," she murmured.

Over the corset went a voluminous long-sleeved linen shirt, the ruffled collar and sleeves embroidered prettily in black silk.

Around her waist tied a Scarlett O'Hara-type crinoline, a half-slip of linen that had wire sewn inside it so it stood out in a perfect bell shape. "A farthingale," Honoria said when asked, giving Dougless an odd look for not knowing this simple fact.

"This is getting heavy. Is there more?" Dougless asked.

Honoria next put a half-slip of lightweight wool over the wired farthingale.

Over this petticoat went another one, this one of emerald green taffeta. Dougless began to cheer up. The taffeta rustled when she moved and the fabric was gorgeous.

Next Honoria picked up the dress. It was of rust-colored brocade with a huge abstract design of flowers in black. It wasn't easy to get into. Over her shoulders was a network of silk cords, done in a crisscross pattern, with a pearl at every joint. The bodice fastened in front under an embroidered band, with hooks and eyes that looked strong enough to hold Army tanks together.

There were no sleeves on the dress and Honoria attached them separately, pulling them up over the long sleeves of the linen shirt underneath. At the shoulder the sleeves were big and puffy, then they tapered to the small wrists. The sleeves weren't solid fabric but strips of hemmed emerald taffeta, fastened every few inches by a gold square set with a pearl.

Dougless touched the pearls, while Honoria hurriedly and efficiently went around Dougless, with a long hatpin type of instrument, and pulled bits of the white underblouse out the cuts in the sleeves.

By now it had taken Honoria an hour and a half to put this garment on Dougless and she wasn't finished yet.

Next went the jewels. A belt of gold links with rough-cut square emeralds went around Dougless's now-tiny waist. An enameled brooch with pearls around it was pinned in the middle of the bodice and two gold-link chains went off to either side, fastening under her arms. Honoria picked up a collar that was a soft ruffle of linen, put it around Dougless's neck, and tied it in back. (Later, Dougless found out that in 1564, Nicholas's ruff had been stiff with yellow starch, but a mere four years earlier, no one had heard of starch.) To conceal where the ruff joined the dress, Honoria slipped a third belt of square gold links about her neck.

"You may sit," Honoria said softly.

Dougless tried to walk, but she was wearing somewhere around forty to fifty pounds of clothing and the steel corset was preventing her from breathing.

Stiffly, her head up off the ruff, she made her way to a stool and collapsed. She did not, however, slump. One does not slump when wearing a steel corset.

Dougless sat rigidly while Honoria combed Dougless's thick auburn hair and pulled it back from her face and braided it, then, using bone pins, fastened the braids up. Over the braids, on the back of Dougless's head, she fastened a little cap that was like a hair net, but again, pearls were at each joint.

Honoria helped Dougless stand. "Yes," she said, smiling. "You are most beautiful."

"As pretty as Lettice?" Dougless asked without thinking.

"Lady Lettice is most beautiful also," Honoria said.

Dougless smiled. Tactful, very tactful.

Honoria had Dougless sit on the edge of the bed, put out her leg, and Honoria slipped hand-knit, fine wool stockings up to Dougless's knees, then tied them with pretty ribbon garters embroidered with bumblebees. She slipped soft leather, cork-soled shoes on Dougless's feet, then Dougless stood again.

She walked slowly toward the window and back. The clothes were ridicu-

lous, of course. They were heavy, unwieldy, terrible for your lungs and yet
. . . She put her hands to her waist. She could practically encircle it with
her hands. She was wearing pearls, gold, emeralds, satin, and brocade, and
in spite of the fact that she could barely breathe and her shoulders were
already aching from the weight, she'd never felt so beautiful in her life.

She twirled about and the skirts belled out from her prettily.

She looked up at Honoria. "Whose dress is this?"

"Mine own," Honoria said softly. "We are near the same size."

Dougless went to her, put her hands on her shoulders. "Thank you very
much for loaning it to me. It was very generous of you." She kissed Honoria
on the cheek.

Confused and blushing, Honoria turned away. "Lady Margaret wishes
you to play for her tonight."

"Play?" Dougless was looking at the sleeves of her gown. Real gold, not
fake. How she wished she had a full-length mirror! "Play what?" Her head
came up. "You mean like play an instrument? I can't play anything."

Honoria was obviously shocked. "They do not teach music in your country?"

"They teach it, but I didn't take any lessons."

"What does a woman learn in your country if not sewing and music?"

"Algebra, literature, history, things like that. Can you play an instrument? Sing?"

"Most certainly."

"Then how about if I teach you some songs and *you* play and sing
them?"

"But Lady Margaret—"

"Won't mind. I'll be the band leader."

Honoria smiled. "We shall go to the orchard," she said.

Honoria left the room and Dougless took a few minutes to apply cosmetics very lightly—she didn't want to look like a painted hussy.

Moments later, Honoria had returned with a lute, a man brought
Dougless some bread and cheese and wine, and they were on their way
outside.

Now Dougless wasn't afraid that any minute she was going to be thrown
into a dungeon, so she looked about her. There were people *everywhere*.
There were children running up and down stairs carrying things, men and
women scurrying hither and yon. Some wore coarse linen or wool, some
dressed in silks, some had jewels, some not, some wore fur, some men wore
shorts like Nicholas, some men wore long gowns. Nearly all the people

seemed young, and what surprised Dougless the most was that the people seemed to be as tall as twentieth-century people. She'd always heard that people in the Middle Ages were much smaller than modern people. But she found that, at five feet three inches, she was short in the twentieth century and short in the Elizabethan age as well. The people did seem to be a lot slimmer, though. From all the moving about they did, they probably didn't have time to put on weight.

"Where is Nicholas's room?" Dougless asked and Honoria pointed to a closed door.

Dougless had to watch her step descending the staircase in her long skirts, but the brocade in her hand made her feel elegant and rich.

They went out the back of the house and Dougless had glimpses of lovely rooms with gorgeously dressed women bent over embroidery frames. Outside they stopped on a brick terrace, a low wall around it, a stone balustrade on top, and she had her first look at an Elizabethan garden. Before her, down some steps, was a maze of deep green hedges. To her right was another walled garden of vegetables and herbs set in perfectly arranged squares. A pretty little octagonal building stood in the middle. To her left she could see another garden of fruit trees and an odd sort of hill in the middle. On top of the hill was a wooden rail.

"What is that?" she asked.

"A mound," Honoria replied. "Come, we go to the orchard."

Walking briskly down brick stairs, then across a raised walk beside a rose-covered wall, Honoria opened an oak door and they were in the orchard. Dougless found that although the gown very much constricted her upper body, from the waist down she was free. The farthingale held the weight of the skirts off her legs, and not wearing any underpants gave her the oddest feeling of being naked.

The orchard was lovely and it struck Dougless how perfectly in order it was. Everything was planted symmetrically and it was perfectly clean. She could see at least four men and two children raking and cleaning and generally making the garden beautiful. Now she could see why Nicholas had been so upset by the garden at Bellwood, but to keep a garden like this took the services of many, many people.

Honoria walked around the gravel path on the edge of the orchard to a grape arbor. As far as Dougless could see, there wasn't a dead leaf or twig on the vines and the unripe grapes hung down abundantly.

"This is very pretty," Dougless whispered. "I have never seen a garden this pretty."

Honoria smiled, sat on a bench in front of a pear tree that was perfectly espaliered against the wall, and pulled her lute into her lap. "You will teach me now?"

Dougless sat beside her and unwrapped the cloth package a man had handed her. Inside was a big piece of bread, white bread but not like modern white bread. It was heavier, and very fresh, but there were odd holes in the crust. It was delicious. The cheese was tangy and fresh. Inside a hard leather bottle was a sour-tasting wine. There was also a little silver goblet.

"Does no one drink water?"

"The water is bad," Honoria said, tuning her fat-bellied lute.

"Bad? You mean undrinkable?" She thought of the little houses she'd seen yesterday. If those people had access to the water it was sure to be dirty. How odd, she'd always thought that water pollution was a twentieth-century problem.

Dougless spent a lovely two hours with Honoria in the orchard, eating the cheese and bread, sipping the cool wine from a silver goblet, watching the jewels on her own dress and on Honoria's twinkling in the sunlight, watching the gardeners go about their work. She didn't know many songs, but she'd always loved Broadway musicals and had seen most of them on video, so when she began to think about it, she knew more than she thought. She knew "I Could Have Danced All Night" and "Get Me to the Church on Time" from *My Fair Lady*. She made Honoria laugh at the title song from *Hair*. And she knew "Call the Wind Mariah" from *Paint Your Wagon*. She also knew the theme song from "Gilligan's Island" but she didn't sing that.

Honoria put up her hand to halt. "I must write these," she said and went back to the house to get paper and pen.

Dougless was content to sit where she was, like a lazy cat in the sun. Unlike her usual life, she felt no urgency to be somewhere else or do something else.

On the far side of the orchard a little door opened and she saw Nicholas enter. Immediately, Dougless was alert and her heart raced. Would he like her dress? Would he like her better now that she looked like the other women of his century?

She started to rise but then she saw someone enter behind him. It was a pretty young woman whom Dougless had never seen before. Nicholas was holding her hand and the two of them were running down the path toward the grape arbor in the opposite corner of the garden. It wasn't difficult to see that they were lovers slipping away to somewhere private.

Dougless stood, her fists clenched at her side. Damn him, she thought.

This is just the sort of thing that gained him such an awful reputation in the twentieth century. No wonder the history books had nothing good to say about him.

Dougless's first thought was to run after them and tear the woman's hair out. Nicholas might not remember, but that didn't change the fact that Dougless was the woman he loved. But, Dougless told herself, that was neither here nor there. She owed it to the future memory of Nicholas to put an end to this cavorting.

Feeling saintly, telling herself she was doing this for Nicholas's own good, she walked toward the arbor. She was aware that every gardener in the orchard had stopped work and was watching her.

In the secret shade of the arbor, Nicholas already had the woman's skirt up her bare thigh, his hand disappearing underneath. His jacket and shirt were open, the woman's hand inside as they kissed with a great deal of enthusiasm.

"Well!" Dougless said loudly, somehow controlling her urge to spring at the two of them. "Nicholas, I don't believe this is the behavior of a gentleman."

The woman pulled away first and looked at Dougless in surprise. She started to push Nicholas away, but he didn't seem able to stop kissing her.

"Nicholas!" Dougless said sharply in her schoolteacher voice.

Nicholas turned his head to look at her. His eyelids were lowered and he had that sleepy look that she'd seen only when he had made love to her.

She drew in her breath.

Nicholas's expression soon changed to anger and he dropped the woman's skirt.

"I think you'd better leave," Dougless, her body shaking with anger, said to the woman.

The woman, looking from Nicholas to Dougless as they glared at each other, hurried out of the arbor.

Nicholas looked Dougless up and down and the anger on his face almost made her retreat, but she held her ground.

"Nicholas, we have to talk. I have to explain to you who I am and why I'm here."

He walked toward her and this time she did step back. "You have charmed my mother," he said in a low voice, "but you do not charm me. If you come between me and my wishes again I will take a batlet to you."

He shoved past her so that Dougless nearly fell against the wall and she watched with a heavy heart as he strode angrily down the path and through the door in the wall. How was she supposed to accomplish anything if he wouldn't listen to her? He wouldn't even spend ten minutes in her company. What was she supposed to do, lasso him? Right, she thought, tie him up and tell him she was from the future and she had come back through time to save his neck—literally. "And I'm sure he'll believe me," she whispered.

Honoria returned with a wooden lap desk, big feathers which she expertly trimmed into pens, ink and three sheets of paper. She plucked out the notes of the songs and asked Dougless to write the music. Her opinion of Dougless's education was further lowered when she found Dougless could neither read nor write music.

"What is a batlet?" Dougless asked.

"It is used to beat the dust from the clothes," Honoria answered, writing the notes down.

"Does Nicholas . . . ah, fool around with all the women?"

Honoria stopped playing and looked at Dougless. "You should not lose your heart to Sir Nicholas. A woman should give her heart only to God. People die but God does not."

Dougless sighed. "True, but while we're alive, people can make living worthwhile or not." Dougless started to say more but she glanced up, and standing on the terrace of the house, she saw someone's head and it looked like . . .

"Who is that girl?" Dougless demanded, pointing.

"She is to marry Lord Christopher when she is of age. If she lives. She is a sickly child and not often out."

The girl, from this distance, looked just like Gloria, just as fat, just as petulant. Dougless remembered Lee saying that Nicholas's older brother was to marry a French heiress, and that was why he'd refused Lettice's offer of marriage.

"So, Nicholas is to marry Lettice and Christopher is engaged to a child," Dougless said. "Tell me, if that girl were to die, would Kit consider marrying Lettice?"

Honoria was taken aback at Dougless's casual use of Christian names. Her country must be very different. "Lord Christopher is heir to an earldom, and he is related to the queen. Lady Lettice is not of his rank."

"But Nicholas is."

"Sir Nicholas is a younger son. He does not inherit the estates or the title. For him Lady Lettice is a good match. She also is related to the queen but distantly. Her dowry, though, is not large."

"But if Lettice married Nicholas and then, say, Christopher died, Nicholas would be the earl, right?"

"Aye," Honoria said and stopped writing notes. She looked up at the terrace and saw the fat, spotty, sickly French heiress go back into the house. "Sir Nicholas would become the earl," she said thoughtfully.

14

By the time Dougless climbed into bed beside Honoria that night, she was exhausted. No wonder she'd seen so few fat people and the women had such tiny waists. Between the steel corset and the constant activity, fat didn't have a chance to settle on a person's body.

She and Honoria had left the garden to attend Vespers in the pretty little chapel on the ground floor of the house. They'd listened to a richly dressed minister intone a service in Latin, and they'd spent a great deal of time on their knees. Dougless couldn't keep her eyes and ears on the service for looking at the gorgeous clothes of the men and women around her: silk, satin, brocade, fur, jewels.

It was in the chapel that she had her first glimpse of Christopher. He looked like Nicholas but not so young, not so handsome. There was a quiet strength coming from him that made Dougless stare. He glanced across to her and there was so much interest in his eyes that she looked away, blushing. She did not see Nicholas watching the two of them and frowning.

After chapel was supper, which Dougless took in the Presence Chamber with Lady Margaret, Honoria, and four other women. There was vegetable beef soup, a nasty bitter beer, and fried rabbit. A man, who Honoria said was the butler, chipped cinders from the crust of a loaf of bread and served it to them, and thus explained the holes in the bread of Dougless's earlier loaf.

The other women, Dougless learned, were Lady Margaret's gentlewomen and chamberers. As far as Dougless could tell, everyone in the household had a specific rank, and servants had servants who had servants. And, to her surprise, they also had specific duty hours. Her knowledge of servants was based on what she'd read of Victorian households, where the servants worked from very early to very late, but from what she learned from questioning Honoria, there were so many servants in the Stafford household that no one worked longer than about six hours at a time.

At supper, Dougless was introduced and the ladies eagerly asked about her country of Lanconia and her uncle the king. Dougless, squirming with the lie, muttered a reply, then asked the ladies about their clothes. She received some fascinating information on the Spanish style of dress, the French, the English, and the Italian fashions. Dougless became very involved in this and found herself planning a gown for herself in the Italian style, which had something called a bum roll under it instead of a farthingale.

After supper, servants cleared the tables away and Lady Margaret asked to hear Dougless's songs. What followed was an energetic and laugh-filled evening. Since there was no TV and no one had ever seen a professional performance, the gathering was not shy about singing or dancing. Dougless had never sung aloud before, because she knew she was terrible compared to the people on the radio and on records, but before the evening was over she found herself singing solos.

Christopher came to join them and Honoria taught him "They Call the Wind Mariah," which he played on the lute. Everyone seemed to play an instrument and before long Lady Margaret and all five of her ladies were playing the melodies on oddly shaped, strange-sounding instruments. There was a guitar of sorts but shaped like a violin, a three-stringed violin, a tiny piano, an enormous lute, several kinds of flutes, and a couple of horns.

Dougless found herself drawn to Kit. He was so much like Nicholas, the Nicholas she'd known in the twentieth century, not this sixteenth-century Nicholas who went from one woman to another. She sang "Get Me to the Church on Time" and Kit quickly picked up the melody. In no time they were all singing the funny song.

At one point she saw Nicholas standing in the doorway, glowering. He refused to come in when Lady Margaret motioned to him.

It was only about nine o'clock when Lady Margaret said it was time to retire. Kit kissed Dougless's hand and she smiled at him, then followed Honoria off to bed.

A maid—Honoria's maid—came to help the two women undress. Dougless took several lovely, deep breaths and, wearing the long linen undergarment she'd worn under her dress and a little cap to protect her hair, she climbed into bed. The sheets were linen and scratchy and not too clean, but the mattress was of goosedown and as soft as a whisper. She was asleep before she'd pulled the coverlet over her.

She didn't know how long she'd been asleep when she awoke. She felt as if someone were calling her. She lifted her head, heard no one, so lay back down. But the feeling that someone wanted her would not go away. The room was silent, but she couldn't get rid of the feeling that she was needed by someone.

"Nicholas!" she said, coming bolt upright.

Looking at the sleeping back of Honoria, Dougless crept out of bed. There was a heavy brocade robe on the foot of the bed and she put it on, then slipped her feet into the soft, wide shoes. Elizabethan corsets might be murder, but the shoes were heaven.

Silently, she left the room, then stood outside the closed door and listened. There was no sound and, what with the straw on the floor, she'd be able to hear any footsteps. She started walking to the right, for she felt the call strongest there. She went to one closed door, put her hand on it, but felt nothing. The same at the second door. It was at the third door that she could feel the call.

She opened the door and wasn't surprised to see Nicholas sitting in a chair wearing his tight hose, the baggy shorts, which she now knew were called slops, and a big linen shirt open to the waist. A fire burned in the fireplace and he held a silver tankard. He looked as if he'd been drinking for a while.

"What do you want of me?" she asked. She was more than a little afraid of this Nicholas. He didn't seem remotely like the man who had come to her.

He didn't look at her, just stared at the fire.

"Nicholas, I'm very tired and I'd like to go back to bed, so if you don't mind, just tell me what you want so I can leave."

"Who are you?" he asked softly. "How do I know of you?"

She went to sit in the chair next to him, facing the fire. "We are bonded somehow. I can't explain it. I cried for help and you came to me. I needed you and you heard my call. You gave me . . ." *Love*, she almost said. Somehow that seemed long ago and this man seemed like a stranger to her. "It seems to be my turn now. I've come to warn you."

He looked at her. "Warn me? Ah yes, I must not commit treason."

"You don't have to sound so cynical. If I can come all this way, the least you can do is listen. That is, if you can keep your hand from under some woman's skirt long enough."

She could see his face turning red with rage. "Callet!" he said under his breath. "You who use your witchcraft to befuddle my mother, who exhibit yourself to my brother, dare to speak ill of me?"

"I am *not* a witch. I've told you that a thousand times. All I've done is what I've had to do to get myself inside your house so I can warn you." She stood and tried to calm herself. "Nicholas, we have to stop arguing. I've been sent back to warn you, but unless you listen to me, everything's going to happen anyway. Kit will—"

He stood, cutting her off, leaning over her threateningly. "When you came to me this night, did you come from my brother's bed?"

Dougless didn't think about what she did, but she slapped him across the face.

He grabbed her against him, his body forcing hers backward as he put his mouth on hers, hard, angry.

Dougless didn't like a man using force to kiss her, and she pushed at him with all her strength, but he didn't release her. One of his hands was on the back of her head, forcing her head sideways, the other hand slipped to the small of her back and pushed her body intimately to his.

Dougless no longer fought him. This was Nicholas, the Nicholas she'd come to love, the man that even time couldn't separate her from. Her arms went about his neck and she opened her mouth under his. As she kissed him in return, her body began to melt into his. Her legs were weak and trembling.

His lips moved to her neck.

"Colin," she whispered, "my beloved Colin."

He pulled his face away from her, looking puzzled. She touched the hair at his temples, ran her fingertips down his cheeks.

"I thought I had lost you," she whispered. "I thought I'd never see you again."

"You may see all of me that you wish," he said, smiling, then put his hand under her knees and carried her to his bed. He stretched out beside her and Dougless closed her eyes as his hand went under her robe, then untied the neck of her gown. He kissed her ear, nibbling at her lobe, then ran his tongue down the sensitive cord of her neck while his hand slipped inside her gown to touch her breast.

As his thumb rubbed the peak of her breast, as his breath was on her ear, he whispered, "Who has sent you to me?"

"Mmm," Dougless murmured. "God, I suppose."

"What is the name of the god you worship?"

Dougless could barely hear him as he slipped one leg over hers. "God. Jehovah. Allah. Whoever."

"What man worships this god?"

Dougless was beginning to hear him. She opened her eyes. "Man? God? What are you talking about?"

Nicholas squeezed her breast. "What man has sent you to my house?"

She was beginning to understand. She pushed away from him and, sitting up, she tied her gown and robe. "I see," she said, trying to control her anger. "This is how you always get what you want from women, isn't it? At Thornwyck all you had to do was kiss my arm and I'd agree to do whatever you wanted. So now you've decided that I'm up to no good, so you're going to seduce it out of me."

She got off the bed and stood glaring at him. He lounged on the bed, not at all upset at his devious actions. "Let me tell you something, Nicholas Stafford, you're not the man I thought you were. The Nicholas I knew was a man who cared about honor and justice. All *you* care about is the number of women you can bed."

She stood up straighter. "All right, I'm going to tell you who sent me and why I'm here."

She took a deep breath. "I'm from the future, the twentieth century actually, and you came to me there. We spent several lovely days together."

His mouth dropped open and he started to speak, but Dougless put up her hand. "Hear me out. When you came to me the time here was September of 1564, four years from now, and you were sitting in a prison somewhere awaiting your execution for treason."

Nicholas's eyes began to twinkle in amusement as he rolled off the bed and picked up his tankard. "I see why my mother has taken you to amuse her. Tell me more. What treason had I committed?"

Dougless clenched her fists at her side. "You hadn't. You were innocent."

"Ah yes," he said patronizingly. "I would be."

"You were gathering an army to protect your lands in Wales, and you didn't petition the queen for permission to raise an army. Someone told her you were planning to take her throne."

Nicholas sat down and looked at her, his eyes filled with amazement. "Pray tell me who lied to the queen about these lands I do not own and this army I do not possess?"

She was so angry at his attitude that she wanted to leave the room. Why bother to try to save him? Let the history books record that he was a wastrel. He *was* a wastrel. "They were your lands and your army because Kit was dead, and Robert Sydney and your beloved Lettice lied to the queen."

Nicholas's face changed from amusement to cold rage. He stood and advanced on her. "Do you enter this household to threaten my brother's life? Do you think to cast your spells on me, so that I feel what you feel in the hopes that I will take you to wife and make you a countess? Do you stop at nothing? You besmirch the name of my betrothed as well as my cater-cousin to gain your desires?"

She backed away, afraid of him now. "I can't marry you. I can't even go to bed with you because I'll probably disappear and besides that I don't *want* to marry you. I came back to give you a message and that's it. So now that it's given maybe I'll disappear. I *hope* I do. I hope I never have to see you again."

She grabbed the door handle, but he slammed the door shut and wouldn't let her out.

"I will watch you. If my brother has one pain I will know it is caused by you and you will pay."

"I left my voodoo doll on the plane. Now, will you let me out or do I scream?"

"Heed me, woman."

"I understand you perfectly but I don't guess I have any fears since I'm not a witch, do I? Now open the door and let me out of here."

He stepped back and Dougless, with her head high, left the room. She was all the way down the corridor to the room she shared with Honoria before she started crying. She thought she had lost Nicholas when he had returned to the sixteenth century, but that hadn't been as complete as this. Now he wasn't even the same man she'd known and loved such a short time ago.

She didn't return to Honoria's bedroom but went to the Presence Chamber to sit on the window seat. The tiny diamond-shaped panes of glass were too thick and ripply to see out of, but Dougless didn't care about seeing out. How many times was she going to lose the man she loved? Was the Nicholas who came to her in the twentieth century the man who'd just kissed her? Other than looks, the two seemed to have nothing in common.

Once again, Dougless, she told herself, you've fallen for the wrong man. If he wasn't a man with one foot in jail, he was a man who chased after every woman around. One minute Nicholas was cursing Dougless for being a witch and the next he was kissing her.

Toward dawn she dried her tears and began to stop feeling so sorry for herself. Before, when Nicholas had gone back, because they'd not had enough information, he had been executed. She had felt that they might have gotten the information they needed if Dougless had not spent so much time being jealous of Arabella. If she had spent more time research-ing and asking questions, she might have saved Nicholas's life.

So now she'd been given a second chance and she was repeating all the same mistakes. She was letting emotion blind her to what must be done. This extraordinary, unbelievable thing of switching two people back and forth through time had been done to her and Nicholas so that lives and fortunes could be saved, and all Dougless could think of was whether Nicholas still loved her or not. She threw jealous fits like a junior high girl because a grown man was fooling around with some woman in a grape arbor.

Toward dawn, Dougless stood. She had a job to do and she had to do it without allowing petty emotion to get in her way.

She tiptoed back into Honoria's bedroom and slipped into bed beside her. Tomorrow she would start finding out what she could to prevent the treachery of Lettice Culpin.

Dougless had barely closed her eyes when the bedroom door was flung open and Honoria's maid entered. She flung back the hangings to the four-poster bed, opened the shutters to the windows, took Honoria's and Dougless's gowns and the layers of underwear from the chest at the foot of the bed and shook them. Dougless was soon caught up in the bustle of the day, of dressing, again in Honoria's second-best gown, of eating a breakfast of beef and beer and bread. Honoria started to clean her teeth with a linen cloth and some soap that Dougless did not want to put in her mouth, so Dougless loaned Honoria a toothbrush and paste and they companionably brushed their teeth, spitting into a lovely hammered copper basin.

After breakfast in their chamber, Dougless followed Honoria in a bustle of activity as she attended Lady Margaret in directing the large household. There was a morning church service to attend, then the servants to see to. Dougless stood by and watched in awe as Lady Margaret went over every problem, talked and listened to every complaint.

Dougless asked Honoria a thousand questions, as Lady Margaret competently and efficiently dealt with what seemed to be hundreds of servants: marshals of the hall, yeomen of the chamber, yeomen waiters. Honoria explained that these were only the household heads and that each of these men had many servants under him and that Lady Margaret was unusual in that she dealt personally with the household servants.

"There are more servants than these?" Dougless asked.

"Many more, but Sir Nicholas deals with them."

There is no mention in your history books that I was chamberlain to my brother? Dougless remembered Nicholas asking.

After an exhausting morning, at about eleven A.M. the servants were dismissed and Dougless followed Lady Margaret, Honoria, and the other ladies downstairs to what Honoria said was the winter parlor. Here a long table was beautifully laid with a snowy white linen cloth and place settings of a large plate, a spoon, and a big napkin. In the center of the table the plates were . . . Dougless could hardly believe her eyes, the plates were *gold*. The next plates were silver, then pewter plates, until a couple on the end were made of wood. There were chairs behind the gold plates, and stools and benches for the other diners. There was no disguising who was considered a higher rank than someone else.

Dougless was happy to see that Honoria led her to a silver plate and Dougless was pleased to find herself sitting across from Kit.

"What amusement do you plan for us this eve'n?" he asked.

Dougless looked into his deep blue eyes and thought, How about Spin the Bottle? "Ah . . ." She had been so involved with Nicholas she had given her job little thought. "Waltzing," she said. "It is the national dance of my country."

He smiled at her and Dougless smiled back warmly.

Her concentration was broken when a servant brought a ewer and basin and towel for each guest to wash his hands. Dougless saw that Nicholas was across from her, three seats down, and he was in serious conversation with a tall, dark-haired woman who wasn't beautiful exactly but very handsome. For Dougless it was odd to see women without makeup, but the women obviously took care of their skin. They didn't just get up and wash their faces and go.

On the other side of Nicholas was the French heiress who was to marry Kit. The girl sat quietly, her lower lip stuck out, a frown on her plain face. No one spoke to her and she didn't seem to mind. Behind her hovered a fierce-looking older woman who, when the girl knocked her napkin askew, straightened it.

Dougless caught the girl's eye and smiled, but the girl glowered back at her, and the hovering woman looked as if Dougless had threatened her charge. Dougless looked away.

When the food arrived, Dougless realized it was done with great ceremony. And cooking like this *deserved* ceremony. The first course of meat was brought in on enormous silver trays: roast beef, veal, mutton, salted beef. Wine, which was kept cool in copper tubs of cold water, was poured into gorgeous goblets of Venetian glass.

The next course was fowl: turkey, boiled capon, chicken stewed with leeks, partridge, pheasant, quail, woodcock. Next came fish: sole, turbot, whiting, lobster, crayfish, eels.

Each dish was served with a different sauce, all of it highly spiced and delicious.

Vegetables came next: turnips, green peas, cucumbers, carrots, spinach. Dougless did not find the vegetables as good since they were cooked to a pulp.

With every course there was a different wine, and servants rinsed the glasses before filling them with another wine.

Salads came after the vegetables. Not salads as she knew them but cooked lettuce and even cooked violet buds.

When Dougless was so full she felt like lying down and sleeping the afternoon away, dessert was brought in. Tarts and pies of quince, almond, every fruit imaginable, cheeses that ranged from creamy to hard, and fresh strawberries.

For once Dougless was thankful for her steel corset which kept her from gorging herself.

After the meal the ewer of water was brought around again, because the food had been eaten with spoons and fingers.

At last, after three hours, the group broke up and Dougless waddled up the stairs to Honoria's room and flopped on the bed. "I am dying," she said woefully. "I'll never be able to walk again. And to think I expected Nicholas to be happy with a club sandwich for lunch."

Honoria laughed at her. "Now we must attend Lady Margaret."

Dougless soon found out that the Elizabethan people worked as hard as they ate. Her hand on her full belly, Dougless followed Honoria downstairs, through a beautiful knot garden and out to the stables. Dougless was helped onto a horse with a sidesaddle, which she had a great deal of trouble holding on to, then Lady Margaret, her five women, and four men wearing swords and daggers, set off at a mad pace. Dougless had a hard time keeping up and knew her Colorado cousins wouldn't be very proud of her, because she used both hands to hold on with.

"They have no horses in Lanconia?" one of the men asked her.

"Horses yes, sidesaddles no," she answered.

After about an hour she began to feel less fearful and she could look around her. Going from the beautiful Stafford house to the English countryside was like going from a fairy castle to a slum, or maybe from Beverly Hills to Calcutta.

Cleanliness was not part of the villagers' lives. Animals and people lived in the same buildings and on the same sanitary level. Kitchen and privy slops were thrown outside the doors of the dark little houses. The people

were dirty as only years' worth of dirt and sweat could make them. Their
clothes were coarse and stiff with grease and use.

And diseases! Dougless stared at the people they passed. They were
marked with smallpox; they had neck goiter, ringworm, running sores on
their faces. Many times she saw crippled and maimed people. And no one
over the age of ten seemed to have all his teeth—and the ones left were
usually black.

Dougless's huge lunch threatened to come up. What made her feel worse
than the sights and smells was the fact that most of the illnesses could be
cured with modern medicine. As she rode, holding on to the saddle, she
could see that there were very few people past the age of thirty, and it
occurred to Dougless that, had she been born in the sixteenth century she
wouldn't have lived past ten years old, because at ten her appendix had
ruptured and she'd required emergency surgery. Maybe she wouldn't even
have been born because Dougless had been a breech birth and her mother
had hemorrhaged. As she thought this, she looked at these people with new
eyes. These people were survivors, the healthiest of the healthy.

The villagers came out of their huts, stopped working in the fields and
stared at the procession of beautifully dressed people on their sleek horses.
Lady Margaret and her attendants waved to the villagers and the villagers
grinned back. We're rock stars, movie stars, and Lady Diana all rolled into
one, Dougless thought, and she waved at the people too.

They rode for what seemed to be hours to Dougless's sore backside before they halted in a pretty little meadow that overlooked a field full of
grazing sheep. One of the grooms helped Dougless from her horse and she
limped over to where Honoria sat on a cloth on the damp ground.

"You have enjoyed the ride?" Honoria asked.

"About as much as measles and whooping cough," Dougless murmured.
"I take it Lady Margaret is over her cold?"

"She is a most energetic woman."

"I can see."

They sat in companionable silence for a while, Dougless looking at the
pretty view and trying not to think of her encounter with Nicholas the
night before. She asked Honoria what a callet was and found out it was a
lewd woman. Dougless bit her tongue on renewed anger.

"And a cater-cousin?" she asked Honoria.

"A friend of the heart."

Dougless sighed. So Nicholas and Robert Sydney were "friends of the
heart." No wonder he would believe nothing bad about him. Some friend-

ship, she thought. Nicholas rolls about on a table with Robert's wife, and Robert plots to have his friend executed.

"Robert Sydney is a pillicock," Dougless muttered.

Honoria looked shocked. "You know him? You care for him?"

"I don't know him and I certainly don't care for him."

Honoria looked so puzzled that Dougless asked what a pillicock was. "It is a term of endearment, it means a pretty rogue."

"Endearment? But—" She broke off. When Nicholas had asked her to return to the sixteenth century to cook for him and she'd been so angry, she had called him rotten names and Nicholas had supplied "pillicock" to the list. He must have loved hearing an angry woman call him a term of endearment.

She smiled. He could indeed be a pillicock.

One of the women, who was a maid to a maid to Lady Margaret, passed about little cookies made of crushed almonds.

Munching, Dougless asked, "Who was the handsome dark-haired woman sitting next to Nicholas at dinner today?"

"Lady Arabella Sydney."

Dougless choked and coughed, sputtering crumbs. "Lady Arabella? Has she been here long? When did she come? When will she leave?"

Honoria smiled. "She arrived yesterday eve and leaves early on the morrow. She journeys with her husband to France. They will not return for years and she came to bid my Lady Margaret farewell."

Dougless's mind raced. If Nicholas hadn't had Arabella on the table yet and tomorrow Arabella left, then *this* had to be the day. She had to stop it!

Suddenly, she doubled over, her hands on her stomach, and began to groan.

"What ails you?" Honoria asked, concerned.

"Something I ate. I must return to the house."

"But—" Honoria began.

"I *must.*" Dougless gave a few more groans.

Honoria stood and went to Lady Margaret and in a few minutes returned. "We have permission. I will accompany you with one groom."

"Great. Let's just go fast."

Honoria looked confused as Dougless hurried toward the horses. As a groom helped her into the saddle, Dougless didn't look at all ill.

Dougless would have thrown her leg over the idiot sidesaddle, but there was no stirrup on one side, so she tightened her leg around the big protrusion where the pommel should have been, took a little riding crop, and applied it to the horse's flanks. She leaned forward and hung on as the horse thundered down the rutted, dirty road.

Behind her came the groom and Honoria, doing their best to keep up with her.

Twice Dougless had to jump, once over a wagon tongue, once over a small wooden wheelbarrel. She reined in sharply as a child started across the road but she avoided him. She ran through a flock of geese that set up a terrible clatter.

When she reached the house she leaped from the saddle, tripped on her heavy skirts, and fell face forward. But she didn't waste a moment as she flung open the gate and ran down the brick walk and up the stairs, across the terrace and in the front door.

She stopped, staring up at the staircase. Where? Where was Nicholas? Arabella? The table?

From her left came voices, among them Kit's. She ran to him. "Do you know where there's a table, about six feet long, three feet wide? The legs are turned in a spiral."

Kit smiled at the urgency in her voice. Her face was running with perspiration, her cap was half off, and her auburn hair was falling about her shoulders. "We have many such tables."

"This one is special." She was trying to remain calm but couldn't quite do it. She was trying to breathe but the corset was constricting her lungs. "It's in a room Nicholas uses and there's a closet in the room, a place two people can hide."

"Closet?" Kit said, puzzled, and Dougless knew that a closet in Elizabethan England wasn't a place to hang clothes.

An older man behind Kit whispered something to him and Kit smiled. "The chamber next to Nicholas's bedchamber has such a table. He often—"

Dougless didn't hear the rest, but grabbed her skirt and petticoats and ran up the stairs. Nicholas's bedroom was two rooms down on the right and next to it was a door. She tried the handle but it was locked. She ran to his bedroom, ran through, but the connecting door was also locked.

She banged on the door with her open palms. "Nicholas! If you're in there, let me in. Nicholas! Do you hear me?"

She could swear she heard sounds inside the room. "Nicholas!" she screamed. "Nicholas!"

He opened the door, a lethal-looking dagger in his hand. "Is my mother well?" he asked.

Dougless pushed past him. There, against the wall, was the table she'd seen in the Harewoods' library. It was four hundred years younger but it was the same table. And sitting on a chair, trying to look innocent, was Lady Arabella.

"I will have your—" Nicholas began.

But Dougless cut him off when she flung open a little door to the left of the window. There, huddled against the shelves, were two servants. *"This* is why I wanted you to open the door," she said to Nicholas. "These two spies would have seen everything you two were about to do."

Nicholas and Arabella were gaping at her, speechless.

Dougless looked at the two servants. "If one word of this gets out we'll know who told. Do you understand me?"

In spite of Dougless's odd speech pattern, they did indeed understand. "Now get out of here," she said.

As quickly as mice, they scurried from the room.

"You—" Nicholas began.

Dougless ignored him and turned to Arabella. "I have saved your life because your husband would have heard of this. I think you'd better go."

Arabella, not used to being spoken to like this, started to protest, but then she thought of her husband's temper. She hurried from the room.

Dougless turned to Nicholas, saw the rage on his face—which was nothing new since he'd hardly looked at her any other way since she'd arrived. She gave him a hard glare and started for the door.

She didn't make it because Nicholas slammed the door in her face.

"Do you spy on me?" he asked. "Do you enjoy watching what I do with other women?"

Count to ten, Dougless thought, or better yet, twenty. She drew a deep breath. "I do not get my kicks from watching you make a fool of yourself with women," she said calmly. "I've told you why I'm here. I knew you were about . . . about to have Arabella on the table because you'd already done so. The servants told everybody, John Wilfred wrote the story, Arabella had your kid and Robert Sydney did her in. Now, may I go?"

She watched the emotions running across Nicholas's face, the anger, the confusion, and Dougless felt sympathy for him. "I know that what I'm saying is impossible to believe. When you came to me I wouldn't believe you either, but, Nicholas, I am from the future and I've been sent back in time to prevent some awful things from happening. Lettice—"

His look cut her off. "Do you accuse an innocent woman? Or are you jealous of all women I touch?"

Dougless's vow to control her emotions flew out the window. "You vain peacock! I couldn't care less how many women you bed. It's nothing to me.

You aren't the man I once knew. In fact you're half the man your brother is. I was sent back in time to right a wrong and I'm going to do the best I can, no matter how hard you try to thwart me. Maybe if I can prevent Kit's death, that will save the Stafford estates and nobody will have to try to change you from being a randy satyr. Now, let me out of here."

Nicholas didn't move from in front of the door. "You speak of my brother's death. Do you mean to cast—"

Dougless threw up her hands and turned away. "I am *not* a witch. Can't you understand that? I'm a regular, ordinary person who's been caught in very strange circumstances." She turned back to him. "I don't know all of what happened when Kit died. You said you were at sword practice and you cut your arm so you couldn't go riding with him. He saw some girl in a lake and went after her. He drowned. That's all I know." Except that Lettice might have been responsible, Dougless thought, but didn't add that.

He was staring at her, his eyes hostile.

Her voice softened. "When you came to me I didn't believe you either. You told me several things that weren't in the history books, but I still didn't believe you. Finally, you took me to Bellwood and showed me a secret door that held a little ivory box. No one, in all the years of the many different owners of the castle, had found the door. You said Kit showed you the door the week before he died." She didn't like to think of Kit dying.

Nicholas gaped at her. She *was* a witch, for Kit had shown him the hidden door at Bellwood only last week. What had she done to Kit to persuade him to tell her of this door that by right should be known only to family members?

In truth, what was she doing to his family and his household? Yesterday he'd heard a stableman singing some absurdity on a song called "Zippity Doo-Dah." Three of his mother's women now applied paint to their eyelids that they said came from "Lady" Dougless. His mother—his sane, level-headed, wise mother—took medicine from her hand with the trust of a child. Kit watched the red-haired wench with the intensity of a bird of prey.

In the few days she had been in the Stafford house she had upset everything. Her songs, her outrageous dances, the stories she told (lately the castle folk had been talking about some people named Scarlett and Rhett), even how she painted her face was affecting everyone. She was a sorceress and she was gradually putting everyone under her spell.

Nicholas was the only person who made any attempt to resist her. When he tried to talk to Kit of the power the woman was gaining, Kit had laughed. "What consequence are a few stories and songs?" Kit had said.

Nicholas didn't know what the woman wanted, but he did not mean to so easily fall under her spell as the others had. He meant to resist her no matter how difficult that might be.

Now, glaring at her, he knew that resisting her would never be easy. Her auburn hair was about her shoulders and she held the little pearl cap in her hands. Never had he seen a woman as beautiful as she. Lettice, perhaps, was more perfect-featured, but this woman, this Dougless who enraged him, had something more, something he could not name.

From the first moment he'd seen her, it had been as if she had some secret hold over him. He liked being in control with women, liked kissing them and feeling them melt against him. He liked the challenge of winning a difficult woman, liked the sense of power it gave him when he walked away from her.

But from the first this woman had been different. He watched her far more than she did him. He was aware of every time she looked at Kit, of every time she glanced at some handsome servant, of every time she smiled or laughed. Last night in his room his awareness of her had approached the point of pain, and this awareness had made him so angry he could barely speak or think coherently. Her effect on him enraged him. After she left he had not slept because he knew she wept. The tears of women had never bothered him before. Women always cried. They wept when you left them, when you would not do what they wanted, when you told them you did not love them. He liked women like Arabella and Lettice who never cried.

But last night this woman had spent the night weeping, and even though he could neither hear nor see her, he had felt her tears. Three times he had almost gone to her, but he'd managed to restrain himself. He had no intention of letting her know she had power over him.

As for her story of past and future, he did not so much as consider it. But something about her was strange. He did not for a moment believe she was a Lanconian princess—nor did he think his mother believed her, but Lady Margaret liked the odd songs and the woman's strange manner of speaking. She acted as if everything were new to her, from the food to the clothes to the servants.

". . . You'll tell me, won't you?"

Nicholas stared at her, had no idea what she'd been saying. But suddenly a wave of such desire for her flooded his veins that he stepped back against the door. "You will not bewitch me as you have my family," he said as if he meant to convince himself.

Dougless saw the lust in his eyes, saw the way his lids lowered. Her heart pounded. You touch him and you return, she told herself, and you can't leave until Kit is safe and Lettice's treachery is exposed.

"Nicholas, I don't mean to bewitch you and I haven't done anything with your family that I haven't needed to do to survive." She put out her hand to touch him. "If you would only listen to me . . ."

"Listen to your talk of past and future?" he said with a sneer. He leaned his face close to hers. "Beware of what you do, woman, for I watch you. When word comes that you have no uncle who is king, I myself will toss you from my home. Now get you from me and do not spy on me again." He turned and stormed from the room, leaving Dougless alone and feeling helpless.

She looked through his bedroom at his retreating back. "Please, God," she prayed, "show me how I am to help Nicholas. Let me do what I failed to do the first time. Please show me the way."

Feeling older than when she had entered, she left the room.

15

In the morning, Dougless saw Arabella just as she stepped on a block to mount her beautiful black horse. Near her was a man who Dougless assumed was her husband, Robert Sydney. Dougless wanted to see him, wanted to see the face of the man whom Nicholas considered his friend, yet had sent his "friend" to be executed.

Sydney turned and Dougless drew in her breath. Robert Sydney looked very, very much like Dr. Robert Whitley, the man she had once planned to marry.

Dougless turned away, her hands shaking. Coincidence, she told herself. Nothing more than coincidence. But later that day she remembered how, in the twentieth century, Nicholas, when he'd first seen Robert, had looked as if he'd seen a ghost. And Robert had looked at Nicholas with hatred in his eyes.

Coincidence, she told herself again. It could be nothing more.

During the next two days Dougless rarely saw Nicholas. When she did see him he was glowering at her from a doorway or frowning at her across a table. Dougless was kept very busy by the household, because they had come to regard her as TV, movies, carnival, and concert all in one. They wanted games, songs, stories; their demand to be entertained was insatiable. Dougless could not walk in the garden or in the house without someone stopping her and asking for one more little bit of entertainment. She was kept busy long hours trying to remember everything she'd ever read or heard. With Honoria's help, she devised a crude version of Monopoly. They played Pictionary with slate tablets. When she ran out of stories of books

she'd read, she started telling them stories about America—Lady Margaret
specially loved these.

She tried her best to stay in the entertainment field and not talk about
religion or politics. After all, just a few years earlier Queen Mary had been
burning people for being of the wrong religion. But sometimes Kit asked
questions about farming in her country and, as little as Dougless knew, she
was able to make a few suggestions about compost and how it could be used
with the crops.

Dougless knew that Lady Margaret's ladies were appalled at Dougless's
poor education, at her speaking only one language, at her not being able to
play a musical instrument, and they could not read her handwriting, but for
the most part they forgave her.

While Dougless was teaching, she was also learning. These women did
not have the pressure on them that twentieth-century American women did
to be everything to everyone. The sixteenth-century woman was not supposed to be a corporate executive, an adoring mother, a gourmet cook and
hostess, and a creative lover with the body of an athlete. If she was rich she
was to sew, look after the household, and enjoy herself. Of course she didn't
expect to live past about forty, but at least she wasn't under constant pressure to do more and be more during her few years on earth.

As the days in sixteenth-century England accumulated, Dougless remembered her time of living with Robert. The alarm went off at six A.M. and she
hit the floor running. She had to run to get a day's work done in a day.
There were meals to prepare, groceries to buy, the house to be straightened
(Robert had a cleaning woman once a week) and the kitchen to be cleaned
again and again and again. And in her "spare time" she had a full-time job.
Sometimes she had wished she could stay in bed for three days and read
murder mysteries, but there was always too much to do to consider being
lazy.

Besides, there was the guilt. If she was resting she felt she "should" be at
the gym trying to keep her thighs from spreading, or she "should" be
planning some scrumptious dinner party for Robert's colleagues. She felt
guilty when, exhausted, she served a pizza from the freezer for dinner.

But now, here in the sixteenth century, the modern-day pressures seemed
far away. People didn't live alone and isolated. This wasn't one house with
one woman to do twenty jobs, this was one house with a hundred and forty-
some people to do maybe seventy jobs. One tired, lonely woman didn't have
to cook, clean, wash, etc., and hold an outside job as well. Here one person
had one job.

Modern women had their own self-made guilt to make them miserable, but sixteenth-century people had diseases, their fear of the unknown, their ignorance of medicine, and constant and ever-present death to haunt them. People's lives in the sixteenth century were not long, and death was always nearby for the Elizabethans. There had been four deaths in the household since Dougless had arrived, and all of them could have been saved with decent emergency room care. One man died when a wagon fell on him. Internal bleeding. When Dougless saw the man, she would have given anything to be a doctor, able to stop the bleeding. People died from pneumonia, flu, or a blister that became infected. Dougless passed out aspirin, dabbed wounds with Neosporin ointment, gave out spoonfuls of Pepto-Bismol. She might help people temporarily, but she could do nothing about decaying teeth, about torn ligaments that left people crippled for life, or about appendixes that burst and killed children.

Nor could she do anything about the poverty. Once she tried to talk to Honoria about the vast difference between the way the Stafford family lived and the way the villagers lived. It was then that Dougless learned about sumptuary laws. In America everyone pretended to be equal, saying that a man who was worth millions was no better than some guy who sweated for a living. But no one believed that. Rich criminals got off with light sentences; poor men got maximum sentences.

In the sixteenth century Dougless had found that the idea of equality was a concept that met with laughter. People were not equal, and by law they were not even allowed to dress equally. In disbelief, Dougless had asked Honoria to explain these sumptuary laws. If a man had an income of a hundred pounds a year or less, he could wear velvet in his doublet but not in his gown. If he made twenty pounds a year he could wear only satin or damask doublets and silk gowns. A man making ten pounds or less a year could not wear cloth costing more than two shillings a yard. Earls might wear sable, but barons could wear only the arctic fox. Servants could not wear a gown that reached below their calves. Apprentices constantly wore blue (which is why the upper classes rarely wore the color).

On and on the rules went. They covered income, furs, colors, cloth, cut. Dougless was allowed to dress like a countess, because she was one of Lady Margaret's ladies. Honoria laughed and said that everyone wore what he could afford and if a person was found out, he paid a fine to the city coffers and continued wearing what he wanted.

In the twentieth century she'd never cared much about clothes. She liked them to be comfortable and long-wearing, but other than that she paid little attention to them. But these beautiful Elizabethan gowns were another matter! In the few days she'd been in the sixteenth century she'd found the people to be obsessed with clothes. Lady Margaret's ladies spent hours planning gowns.

One day a merchant arrived from Italy and he and his two cartloads of fabrics had been welcomed into the Presence Chamber as if he'd discovered a cure for fleabites. Dougless had found herself joining in the frenzy of pulling out bolts of narrow fabrics and holding them to herself and the other women.

Both Nicholas and Kit had joined them. Like most men, they loved being surrounded by laughing, excited, pretty women. To Dougless's consternation, Kit had chosen fabric for two gowns for her, saying it was time she wore her own clothes.

That night, in bed, Dougless had lain awake for a while and thought how different, yet how much alike these Elizabethans were from people of her own time. From reading novels set in Elizabethan times, Dougless had thought the people did nothing but discuss politics. Even with TV, radio, and weekly news magazines, the American people weren't half as well informed as the players in medieval novels seemed to be. But, like ordinary Americans, Dougless found these people much more concerned with clothes and gossip and the smooth running of the enormous and complicated household than in what the queen was doing.

In the end, Dougless decided to do what she could, but she didn't believe her job was to change sixteenth-century life. She had been sent back through time to save Nicholas and that was what she planned to concentrate on. She was an observer, not a missionary.

There was one aspect of medieval life Dougless could not tolerate, though, and that was the lack of bathing. They washed their faces and hands and feet, but a full bath was a rare occurrence. Honoria kept warning Dougless about her "frequent" bathing (three baths a week), and Dougless hated the servants having to haul the tub into the bedroom and then lug in buckets of hot water. The effort of preparing a bath was so enormous that after Dougless bathed, two more people would use the water. Once Dougless was the third bather and there were lice floating on the water.

Bathing was close to becoming an obsession with her, until Honoria showed her a fountain in the knot garden. The "knots" were hedges that had been planted in intricate designs, with bright flowers in the loops. In the center of the four knots was a tall stone fountain set in a little pool. Honoria motioned to a child weeding the garden and he ran out of sight behind a wall and, to Dougless's delight, water came from the top of the fountain down into the pool. The child had been sent to turn a wheel.

"How lovely," Dougless had said. "Just like a waterfall, or a . . ." Her eyes began to gleam. "Or like a shower." It was at that moment that a plan began to form in her mind. Privately she talked to the child who knew how to turn the wheel and arranged to pay him a penny if he'd meet her at four A.M. the next morning.

So, at four A.M. the next morning, Dougless tiptoed out of Honoria's room, down the stairs, and out to the knot garden. She carried her shampoo and rinse, a towel and washcloth. The child, sleepy-eyed but smiling, took the penny (which Honoria had given Dougless) and went to turn the wheel. Dougless hesitated for a moment about whether to remove all her clothes or not, but it was still quite dark and it would be a while before the rest of the household woke. So, she slipped off her borrowed robe and the long linen shirt and stepped under the fountain.

Never has anyone in history enjoyed a shower more! Dougless felt as if years of dirt and oil and sweat were washing off of her. She'd never been able to feel clean using a bathtub, and after weeks of not showering she felt grimy. She shampooed her hair three times then conditioned it, shaved her legs and underarms and rinsed. Heaven. Sheer, perfect heaven.

At long last she stepped out of the fountain, gave a whistle to the boy to stop turning the wheel, then dried and put on her robe.

She was smiling broadly as she started back down the path toward the house. Perhaps she was grinning too broadly to be able to see properly or maybe it was yet too dark to see well, but she ran into someone.

"Gloria!" she gasped, then realized it was the French heiress. "I mean," she said, stumbling, "I guess you're not Gloria, are you? Where's the lioness?" Dougless gasped at what she'd said. She'd rarely seen this girl and when she had, she'd always been accompanied by her tall, overbearing guardian/nurse. "I didn't mean—" Dougless began, apologizing.

The heiress didn't listen but sailed past Dougless with her nose in the air. "I am of an age to care for myself."

Dougless smiled at the girl's plump back. She sounded just like Dougless's fifth-graders. They always thought they were old enough to take care of themselves too. "Sneaked out, did you?" Dougless said, smiling.

The girl turned quickly and glared at Dougless, then her face softened. "She does snore," she said with a bit of a smile. She looked back at the fountain. "What do you here?"

Dougless looked at the fountain and to her horror saw that the little pool was full of soap bubbles. To her they were pollution but the heiress seemed to think they were wonderful. The girl lifted a handful of suds.

"I took a bath," Dougless said. "Want one?"

The girl gave a delicate shudder. "Nay, my health is most delicate."

"Bathing won't hurt—" Dougless began but stopped. No missionary work, remember? she reminded herself. She went to stand by the girl and looked at her closely in the early light. "Who told you you were delicate?"

"Lady Hallet." She looked at Dougless. "My lioness guard." There were tiny dimples in her cheeks.

Dougless considered what she was about to say, and she knew she was taking a chance, but the child looked as if she needed a friend. "Lady Hallet says you're delicate so she gets to tell you what to eat, when you can and cannot walk. She gets to keep you so much under her thumb that you have to sneak out before daylight just to see the gardens. That about it?"

The girl's mouth dropped open, then she stiffened. "Lady Hallet guards me from the lower classes." She looked Dougless up and down.

"Such as me?" Dougless asked, suppressing a smile.

"You are not a princess. Lady Hallet says a princess would not make a spectacle of herself as you do. She says you are not educated. You do not even speak French."

"That's what Lady Hallet says. What do *you* think of me?"

"That you are not a princess or you would not—"

"No." Dougless cut her off. "Not what Lady Hallet says, what do *you* think?"

The girl gaped at Dougless, obviously not knowing what to say.

Dougless smiled at her. "Do you like Kit?"

The girl looked down at her hands and Dougless thought her face turned red. "As bad as that?"

"He does not notice me," the girl whispered, tears in her voice. Her head came up and she glared in hate at Dougless, and at that moment she looked exactly like Gloria. "He looks at you."

"Me?" Dougless gasped. "Kit isn't interested in me."

"All the men like you. Lady Hallet says you are close to being a . . . a . . ."

Dougless grimaced. "Don't tell me. I've already been called that. Look . . . What's your name?"

"Lady Allegra Lucinda Nicolletta de Couret," she said proudly.

"And what do your friends call you?"

The girl looked puzzled for a moment, then smiled. "My first nurse called me Lucy."

"Lucy," Dougless said, smiling. She looked at the sky. "I guess we better get back. People will be searching for . . . us."

Lucy looked startled, then gathered her heavy, expensive skirt and started to run. She was obviously terrified of being found missing.

"Tomorrow morning," Dougless called after her. "Same time." She wasn't sure Lucy heard or not.

Dougless went back to the house, ignoring servants' looks at her wet hair and her robe. When she opened the door to Honoria's bedroom, she sighed. Now began the long, painful process of dressing, and just now she wished for the comfort of jeans and a sweatshirt.

After breakfast she sneaked away from the other women to look for Nicholas. The women were demanding new songs, and already Dougless's small store was depleted. She was down to humming tunes and persuading the women to make up their own words. But today she had to talk to Nicholas. Nothing about his execution was going to change if she didn't talk to him.

She found him in a room that could only be an office, sitting at a table surrounded by papers. He appeared to be adding a column of figures.

He looked up at her, raised one eyebrow, then looked back down at his paper.

"Nicholas, you can't ignore me. We must talk. Sometime you're going to *have* to listen to me."

"I am occupied. Do not plague me with your nonsensical chatter."

"Chatter! Nonsense!" He gave her another look to be quiet and returned to his column of numbers. The numbers made no sense to Dougless because some were Roman numerals, some written with a *j* instead of an *i*, and some numbers were arabic. No wonder he had a difficult time adding them. She opened the little embroidered pouch that hung at her waist and took out her solar calculator. She carried it with her because Honoria and the other ladies were always counting stitches in their embroidery, and Dougless often added and subtracted for them so their patterns would be accurate. She put the calculator beside Nicholas's hand.

"Has Kit shown you where the secret door at Bellwood is?" she asked.

"*Lord* Kit," he said emphatically, "is not your concern. Nor am I. Nor, for that matter, is my mother's household. Madam, you are not wanted here."

She was standing over him, looking down at him and she watched as, in his anger, he picked up the calculator and began punching the buttons. He punched in the numbers, hitting the plus key between them, then the equal at the end. Still speaking, he wrote down the total on his piece of paper.

"And furthermore—" he said, starting to add the second column.

"Nicholas," she whispered, "you remember." She drew in her breath, then louder she said, "You remember."

"I remember naught," he said angrily, but even as he spoke he stared down at the calculator in his hands. He realized he'd been using it, but now the knowledge of what it was and how it was used fled him. He dropped the thing as if it were evil.

Seeing him use the calculator was a revelation to Dougless. Somehow, what he'd experienced in the twentieth century was buried in his memory. It was four years before it happened, but now also happened to be four hundred years before Dougless's birth. So many strange experiences were happening to her that she couldn't question his knowledge of a calculator. But if he remembered that, then he remembered her.

She went to her knees beside him, put her hands on his arm. "Nicholas, you do remember."

Nicholas wanted to pull away from her, but he couldn't. What was it about the woman? She was pretty, but he'd seen women more beautiful. He'd certainly been around women more pleasing than she, but this woman . . . this woman never left his mind.

"Please," she whispered, "don't close your mind to me. Don't fight me. You might remember more if you'd allow yourself."

"I remember naught," he said firmly, looking down into her eyes. He'd like to take her hair out of the little cap, out of its braid.

"You *do* remember. How else would you know how to use the calculator?"

"I did not—" he began and glanced at the thing sitting on top of the papers. But yes, he had known how to use it, had known how to add with it. He jerked his arm from under her hands. "Leave me."

"Nicholas, please listen to me," she pleaded. "You must tell me if Kit has told you of the door at Bellwood or not. It will give us an idea of how long we have until he's . . . he's drowned." Until Lettice orders him killed, she thought. "It may be weeks yet or months, but if he's shown you the door it is a matter of days. Please, Nicholas, don't fight me on this."

He was not going to allow her to control him. He was not going to be like the rest of the household and follow her about begging for her favors. Any day he expected her to ask for a purse of gold in exchange for another song. And his mother was so enamored of her that she'd no doubt give the gold. As it was, Lady Margaret showered this woman with dresses and fans, and dug into the Stafford jewel chests to loan her all sorts of riches.

"I know of no door," Nicholas said, lying. It had been but days since Kit had shown him the door.

Dougless sat back on her heels, her green satin skirt billowing about her, and sighed in relief. "Good," she whispered. "Good." She didn't want to think that Kit was close to death. If Kit didn't die, then perhaps Lettice wouldn't have a chance to get her hooks into Nicholas, and the great injustice would be prevented. And, besides, perhaps after Kit was saved, she would be sent back to the twentieth century.

"You care for my brother?" Nicholas said, looking down at her.

She smiled. "He seems like a nice guy but he'll never be . . ." She trailed off. The love of my life, she had almost said. She looked into Nicholas's blue eyes and remembered the night they had made love. She remembered his laughter, his interest in the modern world. Without thinking what she was doing, she reached her hand out to him. He took it and raised her fingertips to his lips.

"Colin," she whispered.

"Sir," came a voice from the doorway. "My pardon."

Nicholas dropped her hand and Dougless, knowing the moment was lost, rose and smoothed her skirts. "You'll tell me about the door, won't you? We'll have to keep watch over Kit."

Nicholas didn't look at her. All the woman spoke of was his brother. She haunted his mind, but she seemed to feel no such pull toward him. Her thoughts were of Kit alone. "Go," he murmured, then louder. "Go and sing your songs to the others. It will take more than a song to enchant me. And take that." He looked at the calculator as if it were something from the devil.

"You can keep it and use it if you want."

He turned hard eyes toward her. "I know not how."

With a sigh, Dougless took the calculator and left the room. Every attempt she had made to talk to Nicholas had failed. At least now she was beginning to understand that he thought he was protecting his family from her. She couldn't help smiling at that thought because the Nicholas she'd loved so much had also put his family first. In the twentieth century he'd wanted to return to a possible execution in order to save his family's honor.

This man *was* the Nicholas she'd come to love. On the surface, what with the women on the table and in the arbor, he had seemed like the rake the history books had portrayed him to be. And of course she'd hated his anger and animosity toward her. The rest of his family couldn't be nicer to her, only Nicholas was hostile.

What if she had had an ulterior motive for wanting to be near his family? It wasn't good to be as trusting as the family was. Nicholas was the one who was right. He *should* mistrust her. Since he remembered nothing of having met her before, he had no reason to trust her, and what with the bond between them, the way he "heard" her calling him at times, he had reason to believe her to be a witch.

Remember, she thought. He said he remembered nothing but he'd remembered the calculator enough to use it correctly. She wondered if there were other things he remembered and began to think of the contents of her tote bag. What could she show him that might jog his memory?

In the Presence Chamber everyone was in a flurry. It seemed that the caterer's goods had arrived. Dougless learned that this was a man who traveled all over England and bought special foods for the Stafford family and sent them back once a month. This month he'd sent back pineapples, and chocolate that had come from Mexico to Spain to England. There was also sugar from Brazil.

Dougless stood back and watched as the women exclaimed over these delicacies and couldn't help but think how the twentieth century took food for granted. Americans could have any food at any time of the year.

As she looked at the chocolate powder, carefully wrapped in cloth, she thought of the American picnic she'd cooked for Nicholas: fried chicken, potato salad, deviled eggs, and chocolate brownies.

Suddenly an idea hit her. She'd heard that smells and flavors were some of the strongest memory generators. She knew that certain foods reminded her of her Grandmother Amanda, for there was always an astonishing variety of food in her grandmother's house. And the smell of jasmine always reminded Dougless of her mother. If she served Nicholas the same meal he'd eaten in the twentieth century, would it help him remember more of the time he had spent with her?

Dougless went to Lady Margaret and asked permission to be allowed to prepare the evening meal. Lady Margaret was pleased with the idea but horrified that Dougless wanted to work in the kitchen herself. She proposed that Dougless tell the Groom of the Pantry what she wanted and talk to the Groom of the Kitchen (the one for the mouth) and not go to the kitchen herself.

Dougless did her best to insist, besides, Lady Margaret had piqued her curiosity about the kitchen. What was a Groom of the Kitchen for the mouth?

After the long, sumptuous dinner, Dougless went downstairs to the kitchen and was awed at what she saw: room after room with enormous fireplaces, huge tables, and many people scurrying about. Each person had a job. There were two slaughtermen, two bakers, two brewers, a maltmaker, a couple of hop men, laundresses, children to do odd jobs, and even a man called a roughcaster whose job it was to patch the plaster when it fell down. There were also clerks to record every penny of expense.

Huge carcasses of beef and pork were delivered into the kitchen in wagons and passed through to the slaughtering room. There were storage rooms that were bigger than houses and they were filled with barrels. Sausages as big as an arm and several feet long hung from the tall ceilings. In two rooms set back in the wall high above the double fireplaces were tiers of beds with straw mattresses where many of the kitchen workers slept.

The head groom took her through the rooms, and after Dougless was able to close her mouth in awe at the size of the place and at the vast quantity of food prepared in the kitchen rooms, she began to tell them what she wanted.

She swallowed as she saw crates of chickens brought in, then a large woman began wringing necks. Cauldrons of water were put on to boil to scald the chickens so their feathers could be plucked. (The softest feathers were saved for pillows for the servants.)

She was surprised that potatoes were found in a sixteenth-century household but not eaten often. Women were set to peeling potatoes, others to boiling eggs that were much smaller than twentieth-century eggs.

To get the flour for the batter for the chicken and for the brownies, Dougless was taken to the bolting room. Here flour was sifted again and again through fabric sieves that were gradually of increasing fineness. Dougless began to understand why pure white bread, called manchet, was so prized. The lower the status of the person in the household, the coarser his bread. Bread that had been bolted only once still had lots of bran—and sand and dirt—in it. Only the family and their immediate retainers got bread that had been bolted until it was perfectly clean.

Dougless knew there could be enough chicken, eggs, and potatoes for the whole household, but the brownies with the precious, expensive chocolate would be for the family only. One of the cooks helped her decide how much chicken got coated with rough flour and how much got flour from the next bolting, how much the next, etc. Dougless wasn't about to give a lecture on equality, especially since she knew the finest flour had no bran in it and many of the vitamins were missing, and it was therefore not as nutritional as the flour that had been bolted fewer times. Dougless just concentrated on preparing a meal that could feed an army.

The food, which had been so easy when prepared in a modern English kitchen and done on a small scale, was not easy in the sixteenth century. Everything had to be made in vats and from scratch. There was no mustard or mayonnaise from the grocery for the eggs and potatoes. All the pepper, kept under lock and key, was whole and someone had to pick out the stones, then the peppercorns had to be crushed in a mortar the size of a bathtub.

The pecans for the brownies didn't come in a plastic bag but had to be shelled.

Dougless supervised and watched and learned. She gasped when the cake pans were lined with paper that had been written on. She saw chocolate batter being poured over a deed that she was sure had been signed by Henry the Seventh.

By the time the food was nearly ready to be served, Dougless knew that the meal had to be a picnic. She sent men into the orchard to spread cloths on the ground, then had pillows brought down.

Supper was late that evening, not served until six P.M., but from the looks on people's faces, the work was worth it. They ate their potato salad with spoons and devoured platefuls of deviled eggs. They loved the high seasoning of the chicken.

Dougless sat across from Nicholas and watched him so closely she hardly ate. As far as she could see, nothing sparked a memory.

At the end of the meal, the servants triumphantly carried out silver platters heaped high with pecan-filled chewy brownies. At the first bite there were tears of gratitude in the eyes of some of the diners.

But Dougless looked only at Nicholas. He bit; he chewed. Then slowly, he looked at Dougless, and her heart leaped to her throat. He does remember, she thought. He remembers something.

Nicholas put down the brownie and, not knowing why he did it, he removed the ring from his left hand and handed it to her.

Dougless put out a shaking hand and took the ring. It was an emerald ring, the ring he'd given her before on that day at Arabella's house when she'd first made brownies for him. She could see by his expression that he was puzzled by his action.

"You gave me this ring before," she said softly. "When I cooked this meal for you then, you gave me this same ring."

Nicholas could only stare at her. He started to ask her to explain, but Kit's laughter broke the spell of the moment.

"I do not blame you," Kit laughed. "These cakes are worth gold. Here," he said, and pulled off a simple gold ring and gave it to Dougless.

Smiling and frowning at the same time, she took the ring Kit offered. The ring was worth nothing compared to Nicholas's emerald, but had the values been reversed, Nicholas's ring still would have been worth much more to Dougless. "Thank you," she murmured and looked back at Nicholas. But he was looking away now and she knew that what he had remembered was gone.

◇ ◇ ◇

"You are too silent, brother," Kit said, smiling at Nicholas. "You should come and make merry. Dougless is to teach us a card game called poker this night."

Nicholas looked away from his brother. Something had happened tonight, something he couldn't understand. At supper he had bitten into one of the chocolate cakes the woman had prepared and he'd known, quite suddenly, without words, that she was not his enemy.

Even as he handed her his ring he told himself he was being a fool. He told himself that, when it came to this woman, he was the one sane person in his household. He was the only person who did not believe her to be a gift from God. If her good works did indeed turn out to be treachery, he was the only one who would be able to see her as she truly was.

But this evening, as he'd eaten that wonderful cake, images had flashed across his mind. He saw her with her hair loose, her legs bare, sitting on an odd two-wheeled metal frame of sorts. He saw her with water pouring down over her beautiful, nude body. And last he saw her clutching his emerald ring to her breast and looking at him with love. Without a thought, he had slipped the ring from his finger and given it to her. Somehow the ring seemed to belong to her.

"Nicholas?" Kit was saying. "Are you well?"

"Yes," Nicholas said absently. "I am well."

"Do you join us?"

"Nay," Nicholas murmured. He didn't want to be near the woman, didn't want her to cause him to see images of something he knew had not happened. If he spent time with her, perhaps he would begin to listen to her, even begin to believe her absurd stories of past and future.

"Nay, I do not go," he said to Kit. "I work this night."

"Work?" Kit asked, his voice teasing. "No women? When I think on it, have you had a woman to your bed since Lady Dougless arrived?"

"She is no—" Nicholas began. He suddenly had another image of her smiling down at him, her hair soft and full about her shoulders.

Kit laughed knowingly. "It goes that way, does it? I cannot blame you, the woman is beautiful. Do you mean to make her your mistress after your marriage?"

"Nay!" Nicholas said forceably. "The woman is naught to me. Take her away with you. I wish never to see her again, never to hear her voice again. I wish she had never come to my life."

Kit stepped back, still smiling. "So the thunderbolt has hit," he said, obviously enjoying Nicholas's agony.

Nicholas came out of his chair, ready to do battle over his brother's smirking, knowing tone. But Kit backed toward the door and when Nicholas came close, laughing loudly, Kit left the room, shutting the door in Nicholas's face.

Nicholas sat down at the table again and tried to give his attention to the accounts before him, but all he could think of was the red-haired woman. She was laughing now, amused at what she was doing. He knew he'd feel it if she weren't happy.

He stood and walked toward the window, turned the latch, opened the window, and looked down into the garden. Unwanted, an image came to him. He saw another garden. It was night and raining, and the woman was calling to him. He saw lights, strange, purple-blue lights on poles. He saw himself in the rain, clean-shaven and wearing strange clothes.

Nicholas pulled away from the window and slammed it shut, then rubbed his hands over his eyes as if to clear the vision. He would not let this woman ensorcel him. He must not let her control his mind.

He left the office and went to his bedchamber, poured himself a tall goblet of sack, and downed it. He downed a second and third helping as quickly as possible, until he could feel the warmth of the wine coursing through his veins. He would drown his images of her. He would drink until he couldn't hear her, see her, smell her . . . remember her.

For a while the wine worked and he was able to still the images in his head. Content, feeling calm, he stretched out on his bed and was asleep instantly.

The images came again in the form of dreams.

"You must tell me if Kit has shown you the door," he heard the woman saying. "Tell me if you cut your arm." "Kit died and you caused it." "What if you are wrong?" The woman's voice grew louder, urgent. "What if you are wrong and Kit dies because you won't listen?"

Nicholas awoke sweating, and the rest of the night he lay with his eyes open, afraid to go back to sleep. Something had to be done about the woman if she wouldn't let him sleep. Something had to be done.

16

At four A.M. Dougless crept out of the house to go to the fountain to take a shower. Yesterday a couple of the ladies had been talking about the suds in the fountain and Lady Margaret had looked at Dougless knowingly. Dougless had flushed and looked away, wondering if there was anything that went on in the Stafford household that Lady Margaret didn't know about.

Now, Dougless smiled in memory. If it weren't all right for her to use the fountain for a shower, no doubt Lady Margaret would have told her so.

Even in the faint light, Dougless could see Lucy waiting for her. Poor lonely kid, she thought. Dougless had asked questions and found out that Lucy and her guardian had been brought to England to the Stafford household when Lucy was just three years old. It was believed that she'd make a better wife for Kit if she knew English ways and got to know her husband's family before marriage.

But from the moment Lucy had arrived, Lady Hallet had denied anyone access to the child, who had been very ill from the voyage across the channel and then the rough journey across England. By the time Lucy was well, no one seemed to remember she was living with them.

Something Dougless had noticed about the sixteenth century was that the adults didn't idolize children the way twentieth-century Americans did. It surprised Dougless to find out that most of Lady Margaret's ladies were married and two of them had young children at their homes, one of which was a hundred miles away. The women didn't seem to be in any throes of agony over whether or not they were spending "quality time" with their children. Dougless once, over embroidery—which the other ladies did very well and at which Dougless was hopelessly clumsy—mentioned that in her country women spent whole days with their children, entertaining them, teaching them, trying never to be bored by them. The women had been horrified at this idea. They believed you should ignore children until they were of marriageable age. After all, they died easily and their souls weren't formed until they were of age.

Dougless had returned to her embroidery. Heretofore, she'd thought parents had always, throughout time, adored their children. She thought that mothers were always agonizing over whether or not they gave enough to their children. But there seemed to be differences between the twentieth century and the sixteenth, other than clothes and politics.

Now, looking at Lucy, she could feel the girl's loneliness. She was a stranger in a house where she'd lived since she was a child.

"Hello," Dougless said.

Lucy smiled broadly, then stiffened. "Good morn," she said formally. "Do you mean to do this again?" she asked as Dougless started to remove her robe.

"Every day." Dougless stepped into the fountain and gave a whistle for the boy to turn the wheel. She gasped at the icy water, but a clean body was worth some discomfort.

Lucy turned away while Dougless bathed and washed her hair, but she didn't leave and Dougless knew there was something she wanted. Perhaps it was only that she wanted a friend.

Dougless got out of the fountain-shower, dried, and turned to Lucy. "This morning we're going to play charades. Maybe you'd like to join us."

"Will Lord Christopher attend?" she asked quickly.

"Ah," Dougless said, understanding. "I don't think so."

Lucy slumped on the bench as if she were a beach ball that had suddenly been deflated. "Nay, I will not come."

Dougless toweled her wet hair and looked at Lucy thoughtfully. How did a dumpy-figured, not-very-pretty adolescent capture the attention of a gorgeous hunk like Kit?

"He talks of you," Lucy said sullenly.

Dougless sat beside her on the bench. "Kit talks about *me*? When do you see him?"

"He visits me most days."

Kit would, Dougless thought. He seemed awfully thoughtful and kind. "Kit talks to you of me, but what do you talk to him about?"

Lucy wrung her hands in her lap. "I say naught."

"Nothing? You don't say anything to him? He comes to visit you every day and you just sit there like a bump on a log?"

"Lady Hallet says it would be unseemly for me to—"

"Lady Hallet! That ogre? The woman is so ugly that the back of her head would crack a mirror."

Lucy giggled. "A hawk once went to her instead of to its master. I thought the hawk mistook her for its mate."

Dougless laughed. "With that beak of hers I can understand the mistake."

Lucy laughed aloud, then covered her mouth. "I wish I were like you," she said wistfully. "If I could make my Kit laugh . . ."

She didn't have to say more to make Dougless understand. My Kit, as in *my* Nicholas. "Maybe we could find a way to make Kit laugh. I was thinking about doing a vaudeville routine with Honoria, but maybe you and I could do it together."

"Vaudeville? Routine? I do not believe Lady Hallet will—"

"Lucy." Dougless took the girl's hands in hers. "Something I've learned that hasn't changed over time is that if you want the man you have to fight for him. Now, what you want is for Kit to notice you and what you *need* is a little self-confidence. You also need to trust your own judgment and not someone else's. So maybe we can accomplish a few of these things by putting on a show. Kit will see that you're not a little girl—and so will Lady Hallet for that matter—and we'll both have a good time. So how about it?"

"I . . . I don't know. I . . ."

"What did one duke say to the other duke?"

Lucy looked blank.

"That was no lady, that was my wife."

Lucy's mouth opened in shock, then she giggled.

"Where does a three-hundred-pound canary sit?" Dougless paused. "Anywhere he wants to."

Lucy laughed harder.

"You'll do," Dougless said. "You'll do very well. Now, let's plan. When can we rehearse? No excuses. You're the heiress, remember, and Lady Hallet works for you."

By the time Dougless got back to the house, it was full daylight. She knew that many people had an idea of what she was doing each morning, for there were no secrets in the household, but everyone politely refrained from asking her point-blank.

In the morning Lady Margaret was too busy to want any new games, so Dougless wandered into the gardens and soon found herself drawing ABCs in the dirt for three children who worked in the kitchen. It was time for dinner before she realized it.

Neither Nicholas nor Kit came to dinner. Dougless vowed that after the meal she would look for Nicholas and again try to talk to him. At least now she knew that Kit had not shown Nicholas the secret door at Bellwood, so she knew that Kit's "accident" was not imminent.

Smiling, she left the table and allowed Honoria to try again to teach her to make lace from a bit of linen. Honoria was making a beautiful cuff with the word Dougless in it, her name surrounded by odd little birds and animals.

Bent over her embroidery frame, Dougless felt at peace. She was going to be able to help Lucy, and yesterday Nicholas had remembered something about their time in the twentieth century. She glanced at the big emerald ring on her thumb. Now that his memory had been jogged, surely he'd soon remember more. She was going to be able to accomplish what she had failed to do the first time.

◇ ◇ ◇

Nicholas's head hurt and he didn't feel too steady on his feet. He'd seen no more images after he stopped sleeping last night, but this morning he was still haunted by the dreams. "What if you are wrong?" he kept hearing in the woman's voice. Wrong about what? About her being a witch? The images were proof he was right.

He lunged with his sword at the man before him, not seeing the startled look on the knight's face. He wasn't usually aggressive in sword practice but today, with his head pounding and his anger raging, he felt aggressive. He lunged again and again. The knight stepped back out of his way.

"Sir?" the man said, astonished.

"Do you mean to give me a good fight or not?" Nicholas challenged and lunged again. Perhaps if he were tired enough he wouldn't be able to hear the woman, see her.

Nicholas wore out three men before a fresh, fourth man brought him low. Nicholas went right when he should have gone left and the man's blade neatly sliced his left forearm open almost to the bone. Nicholas stood and stared at his bleeding arm and suddenly there was an image. But the image didn't just appear, he was *in* the dream.

He was walking beside the red-haired woman in a strange place and they stopped before a building with glass windows, but windows such as he'd never dreamed existed, glass as clear as if it were not there. A machine, a big, strange machine with wheels went by, but he didn't seem to be interested in it. He was intent only in talking to the woman and telling her of the scar on his arm. He was telling her that Kit had been drowned the day he'd hurt his arm at sword practice.

He came out of the dream as abruptly as he went into it, and when he returned to the present, he was lying on the ground, his men hovering anxiously over him, one of them trying to stop the flow of blood.

Nicholas had no time to give over to pain. "Saddle two horses," he said quietly, "one a woman's saddle."

"Ride?" asked one man. "You mean to ride with a woman? Your arm—"

Nicholas turned to him with cold eyes. "For the Montgomery woman, she—"

"She can ride only enough to keep from falling from the horse," said a man, contempt in his voice.

Nicholas came to his feet. "Bind my arm so the bleeding stops, then saddle two horses—men's saddles. Do it now," he said. "Waste no time." His voice was low but there was command in it.

"Should I fetch the woman?" another man asked.

Nicholas, his arm held out while a man bound a cloth tightly about it, looked up at the windows of the house. "She will come," he said with confidence.

◇ ◇ ◇

Dougless hunched over her embroidery and listened to one of the ladies telling a juicy story about a woman who'd tried to bed another woman's husband. She was listening to the story with all her attention, when suddenly a fierce, burning pain stabbed her left forearm.

She gave a cry of pain, fell back on the stool and landed on the floor. "My arm. Something has hurt my arm." She cradled her arm to her, tears of pain coming instantly.

Honoria leaped to her feet and ran to kneel by Dougless. "Rub her hands, do not let her faint," Honoria commanded as she quickly untied Dougless's sleeve at the shoulder and slipped it down. Honoria winced as she had to take Dougless's arm away from her breast to remove the sleeve. Once the sleeve was off, Honoria pushed up the linen undersleeve to look at Dougless's arm.

There was nothing wrong with it. The skin was not even reddened.

"I see nothing," Honoria said, suddenly afraid. She'd grown to care for

Dougless, but the woman was very odd. Sir Nicholas accused her of being a witch. Was this pain a manifestation of her witchcraft?

The pain in her arm was blinding, but Dougless looked down and saw that there was nothing on her forearm. "It feels as if it's been cut," she whispered, "as if someone has cut it deeply with a knife."

She used her right hand to rub her forearm but she could barely feel her own touch. "I can feel the cut," she whispered, trying not to whimper. The women around her were looking at her very strangely, as if Dougless weren't quite sane.

Suddenly, Dougless could hear Nicholas's voice in her head. They were in bed together and she'd touched the scar on his left forearm, the scar he'd received the day Kit had drowned.

Dougless was on her feet instantly. "Where do the men practice swords?" she asked, trying not to sound frantic. Please, God, she prayed, do not let me be too late.

The other women seemed to be assured of Dougless's lack of sanity, but Honoria answered. Dougless no longer surprised her. "To the back, past the maze, through the northeast gate."

Dougless nodded and used no more time for anything else. She grabbed her skirts, thanked heaven for the farthingale that held the skirts away from her legs, and began to run. In the hall she crashed into one man, and when he fell she leaped over him. A woman in the kitchen was getting something off a high shelf. Dougless crouched and kept running under her arms. A wagonload of barrels had come untied and Dougless leaped five barrels, one after another, looking like an oddly dressed Olympic hurdler. She ran past Lady Margaret outside the maze and didn't speak. When the gate in the wall at the back of the maze stuck, she lifted her foot and smashed it open.

Once outside the gardens, she ran as fast as she could.

Nicholas, his arm swathed in a bloody bandage, was sitting on a horse and looking down at her.

"Kit!" Dougless screamed, still running. "We have to save Kit."

Dougless didn't say any more because a man swooped her into his arms and dumped her onto a horse and, oh, thank all that was holy, it was a man's saddle. She jammed her feet into the stirrups, grabbed the reins and looked at Nicholas.

"We ride!" he shouted and kicked his horse forward.

The wind in her eyes stung and her arm still hurt, but most of Dougless's concentration was on following Nicholas. Behind them thundered three men trying to keep up with Dougless and Nicholas.

They ran across plowed fields, through gardens of cabbages and turnips.

They ran through the dirty, barren yards of peasants, and for once Dougless gave no thought to equality as their horses' hooves destroyed crops and, even once, a shed. They ran into the woods, tree branches low overhead. Dougless put her head down on the horse's neck and kept going. Nicholas left the trail and went through the forest. The grounds were clear of deadfall, for even twigs were needed for firewood, so, except for the overhanging branches, their way was clear.

She never thought to question how Nicholas knew where Kit was, but she was sure he did know. Just as he had known she would come when he hurt his arm, he knew where his brother was.

They broke through the trees to a clearing and ahead, surrounded by more trees, sparkled a pretty, spring-fed pond. Nicholas was off his horse while it was still running, and Dougless followed him, tearing her heavy, long skirt when it caught on the saddle.

She ran toward the pond and what she saw chilled her. Three men were taking Kit's nude, motionless body from the pond. Kit's body was facedown, his long dark hair hanging, his neck limp and lifeless.

Nicholas was standing and staring at his brother. "No," he said, then, "NO!"

Dougless shoved past Nicholas and went to the men holding Kit. "Put him down here. On his stomach," she ordered.

Kit's men hesitated.

"Obey her!" Nicholas bellowed.

Dougless went to work at once, applying modern techniques to get the water out of his lungs. She straddled him, pushing up on his lungs, then lifting his bent arms to let the air in. Once, twice, three times. No response.

"Pray," she said to the man nearest her. "I need all the help I can get. Pray for a miracle."

The men went to their knees, their hands clasped, their heads bowed.

Nicholas knelt before Kit's inert body and placed his hands on Kit's wet head, then bowed his head, his eyes tightly closed.

Dougless kept working. In, out. In, out. "Kit, please," she whispered. "Please live."

When she was ready to give up hope, Kit coughed.

Nicholas's head came up as he looked at Dougless. She kept stroking Kit's back, lifting his folded arms.

Kit gave another cough, then another, and then he vomited water as his lungs cleared.

Dougless rolled off him, put her face in her hands, and burst into tears.

Nicholas held his brother's shoulders while Kit got rid of the water. A knight draped his cape about Kit's bare lower half, while the other men stared down at Dougless. Her hair was down, her dress torn, she'd lost a shoe and Nicholas's blood was on one sleeve, the other sleeve missing.

Kit at last quit coughing and leaned back against his brother. Tiredly, Kit looked at Nicholas's arm that was wrapped tightly about his chest. Blood trickled down Kit's bare, wet chest. Kit looked up at his men, six of them, all staring down at the Montgomery woman, who was crying softly into her hands.

"This is a fine way to treat a man back from the dead," Kit managed to croak out. "My brother bleeds on me, a pretty woman sheds tears. Is no one glad that I yet live?"

If anything, Nicholas's grip on Kit tightened. Dougless looked up and wiped her eyes with the back of her hand and sniffed. A knight handed her a handkerchief. "Thank you," she murmured and blew her nose loudly.

"The maid has saved you," one of the knights said, awe in his voice. "It is a miracle."

"Witchcraft," muttered another man.

Nicholas looked up at the man. "You call her witch again and you will not live long enough to repeat the words."

The men knew that Nicholas meant what he said.

Douglass looked at Nicholas and knew that his hatred of her was over, that perhaps now he'd listen to her. She blew her nose again and started to stand. When she stumbled, one of the men helped her. They were all looking at her as if she were part saint, part demon.

"Oh heaven," she said, "stop looking at me like that. This is a common practice in my country. We have lots of water and people are always drowning. Really, it's no miracle."

To her relief, she could see the men believed her, probably because they wanted to.

"Now, I want all of you to stop standing around and get busy. Poor Kit must be freezing! Nicholas, your arm is a mess. You two help Kit and you others see if there are any clean bandages for Nicholas's arm, and someone go see if the horses survived the trip. Now go! Scurry!"

One advantage women throughout time have had is that the little boy in men always remembers a time when women were all-powerful. They bumped into each other as they ran to do her bidding.

"You have a shrew on your hands, brother," Kit said happily. Nicholas still held his brother tightly, as if afraid Kit would die again if he released him. "Perhaps you would fetch my clothes for me," Kit said softly to Nicholas, then shook his head as Dougless started for Kit's clothes piled on the bank of the pond.

Slowly, Nicholas released his hold on his brother and started to rise, but he swayed on his feet. The loss of blood, combined with the ride and his fear, had weakened him. Dougless stood back and watched as Nicholas slowly made his way to the bank and, gathering Kit's clothes, brought them back to his brother.

Kit accepted the clothes with the solemnity of a king accepting the crown at his coronation, then he grinned. "Sit down, little brother," he said.

Nicholas took a step backward, and Dougless caught him in her arms and led him to sit down, then sat beside him. Nicholas turned and put his head in her lap.

Kit laughed. "Now that is more the brother I know." He looked up as his men came back into the clearing.

Dougless looked down at Nicholas and stroked his sweat-dampened black curls. This was, at long, long last, her Nicholas. Here again was the man she'd loved and lost.

"Do you grow onion-eyed again?"

His words, so heart-stoppingly familiar, did indeed bring tears to her eyes. "The wind," she murmured. "Nothing more." She smiled at him. "Give me your arm. I want to see what you've done to it."

Obediently, he held up his arm and her stomach lurched. The bandage was saturated with blood and his hand was encrusted, as well as his sleeve above the wrappings.

"How bad is it?"

"I do not believe I will lose the arm. The leeches—"

"Leeches! You can't afford more blood lost." She glanced up and saw that Kit was now dressed, and being weak, he was supported by the men who led him to his horse.

"Nicholas, get up. We're going back to take care of that arm," Dougless said.

"Nay," he said. "I would the two of us stayed here."

He had that look in his eye, that soft, sexy, hooded look that promised he would make Dougless glad she stayed.

"No," she said, even as she bent down to kiss him.

"A woman's 'no' pleases me much," Nicholas said softly, his uninjured arm moving up to her hair.

Their lips didn't meet.

"No you don't," Dougless said sternly. "Up! I mean it, Nicholas, get up.

You aren't going to sweet-talk me into doing whatever you want while your arm turns to gangrene. We must return to the house, clean the wound, and let Honoria sew it back together."

"Honoria?"

"She can sew better than anyone."

He frowned. "It does pain me some." He slowly, reluctantly lifted his head from her lap, but, as he moved past her head, he planted a quick, sweet kiss on her lips.

They rode slowly back to the Stafford house, and as they approached, Dougless tried to straighten her spine and her clothing. But her dress, torn, bloody, dirty, was beyond repair. Somewhere she had lost her little pearl-studded cap. As they grew nearer, Dougless remembered running past Lady Margaret without speaking and, too, practically before the lady's face she'd kicked the gate open. And now here she was, looking like something off the streets, riding astride, her skirts up to her calves.

"I don't think I can face your mother," Dougless said to Nicholas.

He gave her a puzzled look, but looked away when he saw the house. One of the knights had ridden ahead and the news of Kit's near-death had reached them. Lady Margaret and all her ladies were waiting to greet them. Dougless swallowed.

Lady Margaret hurried forward to clasp Kit to her when he'd dismounted, then she turned to Dougless.

"My pardon, ma'am," Dougless said, "for my appearance. I—"

Lady Margaret took Dougless's face in her hands and kissed her on both cheeks. "You are beautiful to me."

Dougless felt her face grow hot with embarrassment and pleasure.

Lady Margaret turned to Nicholas, glanced at his bloody arm, and yelled, "Leech!"

Douglass put herself between mother and son. "Please, my lady, may I see to his arm? Please," she whispered. "Honoria will help me."

Lady Margaret seemed to be torn. "Do you have a tablet for wounds?"

"No, just soap and water and disinfectant. Please, let me care for him."

Lady Margaret looked over Dougless's shoulder to Nicholas, then nodded.

Once upstairs in Nicholas's bedchamber, Dougless gave Honoria a list of things she'd need. "The strongest, harshest soap you have, something with lye in it, then I want a kettle for boiling water and I'll need needles—silver needles—white silk thread, beeswax, my tote bag, and the cleanest, whitest linen in this house." Three maids scurried to do her bidding.

When she was alone with Nicholas, she had him soak his bandaged arm in a long copper pan of clean water. He was bare from the waist up and, as efficient as Dougless tried to be, she could feel his hot eyes on her.

"Tell me of what we once were, each to the other."

Dougless put water on to boil in the fireplace. "You came to me in my time." Now that he was ready to listen, she found herself reluctant to talk. The Nicholas who accused her of witchcraft had no power over her, but this Nicholas, who looked at her with sparkling eyes, made her toes curl.

She went back to him, saw that the dried blood had softened away from the bandages. She propped his arm on the pan, took small sewing scissors and began to snip away the encrusted bandage.

"Were we lovers?" he asked softly.

Dougless's breath drew in sharply. "I cannot do this if you don't hold still."

"I did not move, you did," he said, then watched her for a while. "Were we together long? Did we love much?"

"Oh, Nicholas," she said and found to her shame that tears were again coming to her eyes. "It wasn't like that. You came to me for a *reason*. You had been found guilty of treason and you came to my time because Lady Margaret's papers had been found. You and I researched to find out who had betrayed you."

She began to slowly peel strips of linen off his arm.

"Did we find the truth?"

"No," she said softly. "*We* did not. I found out the truth after you went back, after you . . ." She looked up at him. "After you had been executed."

Nicholas's face was changing, losing its look of sex. He could no longer continue to discount the woman. She had known about the servants in the closet when he and Arabella had been fumbling on the table. And she had known about Kit. His heart hammered in his chest when he thought how close he had come to losing Kit. If the woman had not been there, Kit would have died.

And it would have been Nicholas's fault, he thought, his own fault and no one else's because he'd lied when she asked him about the cabinet at Bellwood. She had said that Kit showed Nicholas the cabinet a week before his death, but Nicholas had not listened. He had heard only that she spoke of Kit. His jealousy had nearly cost his brother's life.

Nicholas leaned back against the pillows. "What more do you know?"

She opened her mouth to tell him of Lettice but she couldn't, not yet. It was too soon and he didn't yet trust her enough. She knew he loved Lettice, he had wanted so much to leave the twentieth century—and Dougless—to get back to his beloved wife. It would take more time before she got enough confidence to talk to him about Lettice. But there was time now. Now there was no urgency as there had been with Kit.

"I will tell you all later," she said, "but now I must see to your arm."

Dougless continued pulling the bandage from his wound until at last she saw the deep slash. She'd never been good with bloody wounds, but years of teaching elementary school had taught her to look at broken teeth, blood-dripping wounds, and broken limbs while remaining cheerful for the child's sake. She knew Nicholas's wound needed a doctor and she also knew that now she was the best that was available.

Honoria and the maids returned with all Dougless had ordered and she set them to work. Honoria did not allow the maids to question anything Dougless told them to do. The four women removed their outer sleeves, rolled up the linen sleeves above the elbow, then Dougless had them scour their hands and arms. She boiled needles and silk thread.

The only sedative-type pills she had in her tote bag were her Librax to calm her stomach when she was worried. She wished she had good ol' Valium but she didn't. She gave Nicholas two Librax pills and hoped they'd make him drowsy.

Within minutes, he was asleep.

When everything was as clean as she could get it, Dougless set Honoria to sewing Nicholas's arm. Honoria blanched, but Dougless insisted because Honoria's stitches were fine and accurate.

Dougless wasn't sure what she was doing but she directed Honoria to sew the gash in Nicholas's arm in two layers. The inside stitches would have to remain in his arm forever, but Dougless's father had a steel plate in his leg from World War II, so she guessed Nicholas could live with some silk inside his arm. She pulled the top layer of skin together while Honoria carefully sewed it.

When Nicholas's arm was sewn, Dougless wrapped it in clean linen. She told the maids she wanted them to boil linen to be used the next day, and when they touched the linen, their hands were to be clean, very clean. Honoria said she would see to it.

Dougless dismissed all of them, sat down in a chair by the fire and proceeded to wait. If Nicholas developed a fever, she had no penicillin, no oral antibiotics, nothing but a few aspirin. She told herself she needn't worry because she knew Nicholas's future, but today she had changed history. If Kit didn't die, then perhaps Nicholas would. Would she go back to the twentieth century and find that Kit had lived to a grand old age but his younger brother died from a cut on his arm? History—or in this case the future—was different from now on.

She was dozing in the chair when the door opened and Honoria entered. In her arms was a gorgeous gown of velvet in a deep, deep purple, the color of an eggplant, with wide, trailing sleeves of soft white ermine, the little black tails sewn on at intervals.

"Lady Margaret sends this to you," Honoria whispered so as not to disturb Nicholas. "It will have to be fit to you but I thought you might see it now."

Dougless took the dress from her, touched the soft velvet. It wasn't like modern rayon velvet or heavy cotton velvet; this was all silk and glistened as only silk could. "How is Kit?" Dougless whispered.

"Sleeping. He says someone tried to kill him. Someone swam under the water and caught his leg and pulled him under."

Dougless looked away. In Lady Margaret's account found in the wall, she believed that Kit had been killed, that his drowning had not been an accident.

"If you had not known how to raise him from the dead . . ." Honoria whispered.

"I didn't raise anyone from the dead," Dougless snapped. "There was no magic or witchcraft involved."

Honoria gave her a hard look. "Your arm no longer pains you? It is well?"

"It's fine now, just a dull ache. It's—" She broke off and refused to meet Honoria's eyes. Perhaps there was magic involved. She was sent back in time, and when Nicholas's arm was cut she had felt his pain.

"You should rest now," Honoria said. "And change your gown."

Dougless glanced at Nicholas, still asleep. "I must stay with him. If he wakes I want to be here. I can't risk his having a fever. Do you think Lady Margaret will mind if I stay here?"

Honoria smiled. "Were you now to ask for deeds to half the Stafford estates, I do not believe Lady Margaret would deny you."

Dougless smiled back. "I just want Nicholas to be safe."

"I will bring you a robe," Honoria said and left.

An hour later, Dougless had removed her torn and dirty gown, as well as her steel corset, and now she sat before a warm fire, wearing a pretty ruby-red brocade robe. Every few minutes she put her hand to Nicholas's forehead. It was warm, but he didn't seem to be running more than a few degrees of temperature.

17

The shadows in the room lengthened and still Nicholas slept. A maid brought Dougless food on a tray, but Nicholas did not waken. As night fell, she lit candles and looked down at him, so peaceful on the bed, his dark curls vivid against his pale skin. For hours she'd done nothing but watch him and when she saw no signs of fever, she began to relax and look about her.

Nicholas's room was adorned richly, as befitted a son of the house. His mantelpiece had several plates and goblets of gold and silver on it, and Dougless smiled when she looked at them. She'd come to understand what Nicholas meant when he said his wealth was in his house. Since there were no banks to hold the wealth of a great family like the Staffords, all they had was put into gold and silver, formed into beautiful objects and decorated with jewels. Smiling, she touched a pitcher and thought it would be a lot prettier if her family's stocks and bonds were transformed into gold dishes.

Beside the fireplace was a long row of tiny oval portraits, all done in exquisite colors. Most of them were people she didn't know, but one of them had to be Lady Margaret as a young woman. There was a hint of Nicholas's eyes in hers. There was an older man who had the shape of Nicholas's jaw. His father? she wondered. There was a miniature oil of Kit. And on the bottom was Nicholas.

She took the portrait from the wall, held it a moment and caressed it. What had happened to these portraits in the twentieth century? Was one hanging on some museum wall with *Unknown Man* on a card beside it?

Still holding the portrait, she walked about the room. There was a cushioned seat beneath the window and Dougless went to it. She knew the top lifted and she wondered what Nicholas kept inside. Glancing at him to make sure he was asleep, she put the portrait on a shelf, then lifted the seat. It creaked but not too loudly.

Inside the seat were rolls of paper tied with pieces of yarn. She took one and released the string, then unrolled it onto the floor. It was a sketch of a house and Dougless knew instantly that the house was Thornwyck.

"Do you pry?" Nicholas asked from the bed, making Dougless jump.

She went to him, felt his forehead. "How do you feel?"

"I would feel better if there were not a woman invading my private goods."

Dougless thought he sounded just like a little boy whose mother had looked inside his secret box. She picked up the plan from the floor. "Have you shown these to anyone besides me?"

"I have not shown them to you," he said, and made a lunge for the corner of the paper, but Dougless moved away. Weakly, he lay back against the pillows.

Dougless put the plan down on the window seat. "Hungry?" She ladled soup into a silver bowl from a pan on the hearth, where it had been set to keep the soup warm. She sat beside Nicholas and began to feed him. At first he protested that he could feed himself but, like all men, he soon adjusted to being pampered.

"You have looked long at the drawings?" he asked between bites.

"I had just opened the one. When do you plan to start building?"

"It is merely foolishness. Kit will—" He broke off and smiled.

Dougless knew what he was thinking, that he'd come so very close to losing Kit.

"My brother is well?" Nicholas asked.

"Perfectly healthy. Better than you. He didn't lose enough blood to flood a river." She wiped his lips with a napkin and he caught her fingertips and kissed them.

"If I live, then I owe you my life, as well as my brother's. What can I do to repay you?"

Love me, Dougless almost said. Fall in love with me again, just as you did before. Look at me with eyes of love. I'll stay in the sixteenth century forever if you would love me. I would give up cars and dentists and proper bathrooms if you'd love me again. "I don't want anything. I just want both of you to be well and for history to come out all right." She put the empty bowl on a table. "You should sleep more. Your arm needs to heal."

"I have slept all I need. Stay and entertain me."

Dougless grimaced. "I've run out of entertainments. There isn't a game I ever played or a song I ever heard that I haven't dredged out of my memory. I'm just about played out."

Nicholas smiled at her. Sometimes he didn't understand her words, but he got the meaning.

"Why don't you entertain *me?*" She picked up his sketch from the window seat. "Why don't you tell me about this?"

"Nay," he said quickly. "Put those away!" He started to sit up but Dougless pushed him back to the pillows.

"Nicholas, please don't tear your stitches. You must be still. And stop glowering at me! I know all about your love of architecture. When you came to me in the future you had already started building Thornwyck." She almost laughed at the expression on his face.

"How did you know I planned this for Thornwyck?"

"I told you. When you came to me it was four years from now and you'd already done it. Actually you'd only started it. It was never finished because you . . . you . . ."

"Were executed," he said, and for the first time he really thought about her words. "I wish you to tell me all."

"From the beginning?" Dougless asked. "It will take a long time."

"Now that Kit is safe I have time."

Until Lettice gets hold of you, she thought. "I was in a church in Ashburton and I was crying," she said, "and—"

"Why did you weep? Why were you in Ashburton? And you cannot stand and tell me this long story. No, do not sit there. Here."

He patted the empty half of the bed beside him.

"Nicholas, I can't get in bed with you." Just the thought of being so near him made her heart beat faster.

"Do you believe I can do aught when I am so weak?" he said, his eyes half closed in tiredness.

"I believe you'd give a woman trouble if both your arms and both your legs were bandaged."

He opened his eyes and smiled at her. "I saw a . . . a dream of you. You were in a white box of sorts, water was pouring on you and you wore no clothes." He looked her up and down, as if he could see through the voluminous robe. "I do not believe you have always been so shy of me."

"No," she said hoarsely, remembering being in the shower stall with him, the "white box" of his dream. "One night we were not shy of each other and the next morning you were taken away from me. I'm afraid now that if I touch you I'll be returned to my own time, and I can't go yet. There is more for me to do."

"More?" he asked. "You know of others who die? My mother? Is Kit not yet safe?"

She smiled at him. *Her* Nicholas. Her lovely Nicholas who thought of others before himself. "You are the one who is in danger."

He smiled in relief. "I can care for myself."

"In a pig's eye you can! If I hadn't been here you'd probably have lost your arm or died from the wound. One of those idiots you call a physician had only to touch that cut with his filthy hands and presto! you're a goner."

Nicholas blinked at her. "You do talk most strangely. Come, sit by me and tell me all." When Dougless didn't move, he sighed. "I swear to you on my honor I will not touch you."

"All right," she said and felt that she could trust him more than she could trust herself. She moved to the other side of the bed and climbed up on it, for it was a few feet off the floor. She sank into the feather mattress.

"Why did you cry in the church?" he asked softly.

If Dougless was sure of one thing about Nicholas, it was that he was a good listener. He was more than a good listener since he pulled from her things that she didn't want to tell him. She ended up telling him everything about Robert.

"You lived with him without marriage? Did not your father kill him for abducting you?"

"It's not like that in the twentieth century. Women have free choice and fathers don't tell daughters what to do. Men and women are more equal in my time."

Nicholas snorted. "It seems that men still rule, for this man had all of you he wanted, but he did not make you his wife, share his goods with you, or demand his daughter respect you. And you say you chose this freely?"

"I . . . Well . . . It's not like you make it sound. Robert was very good to me. He and I had some good times together. It was only when Gloria was around that it was awful."

"Were a beautiful woman to give me all and in return I was only to give her, what do you say, a 'good time,' I would be most grateful. Do all women of your time give themselves so cheaply?"

"It's not cheap. You just don't understand. Many people live together before they get married. It's to test the waters, so to speak. And, besides, I thought Robert was going to ask me to marry him, but instead he bought—" She stopped. Nicholas was making her feel as if she thought very little of herself. "You just don't understand, that's all. Men and women are different in the twentieth century."

"Hmmm. I see. Yes. Women no longer want respect from a man, they want a 'good time.'"

"Of course they want respect, it's just that . . ." She couldn't think how to explain her living with Robert to a sixteenth-century man. In fact, now, living in the Elizabethan world, she could see that living with a man *had* cheapened her. Of course marriage was no guarantee he was going to respect her, but why hadn't she stood up to Robert and said, How dare you treat me like this? or, No, I will not pay for half of Gloria's plane fare, or, No, I will not iron your shirts? Right now she couldn't remember why she'd let him walk on her that way.

"Do you want to hear this story or not?" she snapped.

Nicholas lay back against the pillows and smiled. "I wish to hear all of it."

After she was past his many questions about her relationship to Robert, she was able to continue. She told of crying on Nicholas's tomb, of his suddenly being there and of her not believing who he was. She told of his walking in front of a bus.

She didn't get far after that because Nicholas started asking questions. It seemed he'd had a vision of her on a two-wheeled vehicle and he wanted her to explain what it was. He wanted to know what a bus was. When she said she'd called her sister, he wanted her to describe a telephone.

Dougless couldn't describe all he wanted to know so she got off the bed and got her tote bag. She pulled out her three magazines and started looking for photographs.

Once she showed him the magazines there was no hope of continuing with her story. There was an Elizabethan saying, "Better unborn than untaught," and Nicholas seemed to epitomize that belief. He was insatiable in his curiosity and he asked questions faster than Dougless could answer them.

When she couldn't find pictures to show him, she pulled out a spiral notebook, colored felt tips, and began to draw. The pens and paper caused more questions.

Dougless was beginning to be exasperated because she couldn't continue her story, but then she realized that now that he believed her, she'd have time in the future to tell him everything. "You know," she said, "when I saw Thornwyck, the tower on the left looked different. And where are those curved windows?"

"Curved windows?"

"Like this." Dougless began to sketch, but she wasn't very good at drawing.

Nicholas rolled onto his side, took the pen and made a few beautiful perspective sketches of the windows. "This is like the windows?"

"Yes, exactly. We stayed in one of those rooms and we could see the garden below. The church is just next door and the guidebook said there used to be a wooden walkway from the church to the house."

Nicholas leaned back and began to sketch. "I have told no one of my plans but you say that this was half built before I . . . Before I was . . ."

"Right. Yes. After Kit died you had complete freedom to do what you wanted. I guess now that Kit's alive you'll have to get his approval to build this place."

"I am no master builder," Nicholas said, looking at his sketch. "Were Kit to need a new house he would hire someone."

"*Hire* someone? Why? You can do it. These are beautiful drawings. I've seen Thornwyck and happen to know it's beautiful."

"I to be a tradesman?" he asked, one eyebrow aloft haughtily.

"Nicholas," she said sternly, "there are many things I like about your century, but your class system and your sumptuary laws aren't part of what I like. In my century everyone works. It's embarrassing to be 'idle rich.' In England even royalty works. Princess Diana goes all over the country cutting ribbons and digging holes for trees just to raise money for one charity after another. And the Princess Royal, well, I get tired just reading her schedule. Prince Andrew takes pictures; Princess Michael writes books. Prince Charles tries to keep England from looking like a Dallas office complex, and—"

Nicholas chuckled. "It is not so rare now that royalty works. Do you think our lovely new queen sits idle?"

Suddenly Dougless remembered having read that one of the reasons Nicholas was executed was that some people were worried that he might go to court and seduce the young Queen Elizabeth. "Nicholas, you aren't thinking of going to court, are you? You wouldn't want to be one of her young men, would you?"

"One of her—" Nicholas asked, aghast. "What do you know of this woman who is queen? Some say Mary of Scotland is the true queen and that the Staffords should join forces with others to put her on the throne."

"Don't do that! Whatever you do, don't put your money on anyone but Elizabeth." As she spoke, Dougless wondered if she was changing history. If the Staffords and all their money had been put at Mary's disposal, would she have taken the throne? If Elizabeth weren't queen, would there have been a time when England was the reigning world power? If England hadn't been a world power would America be speaking English? "Heavy," she said under her breath, mocking a young cousin of hers.

"Who will Elizabeth marry?" Nicholas asked. "Who will she put on the throne beside her?"

"No one, and don't start on me, we've already had this argument. Elizabeth marries no one and she does a super job of running the country and a lot of the world with it. Now, are you going to let me tell you the rest of this story or are you going to keep telling me that what did happen didn't?"

He grinned at her. "You gave yourself freely to a man and I came to save you. Yes, please continue."

"That's not exactly it, but . . ." She trailed off and looked at him. He *had* saved her. He'd appeared in that church, sunlight flashing off his armor, taken her away from a man who didn't love her, and shown her the true give and take of love. With Nicholas she could be herself. She never had to think about having to please him, she just seemed to naturally please him. When she was growing up she'd tried so hard to be as perfect as her older sisters. It seemed that every one of her schoolteachers had taught all three of her sisters before Dougless. And Dougless was always a disappointment. Dougless daydreamed; her sisters never did. Dougless wasn't much good at sports but her sisters had excelled. Her sisters had had millions of friends but Dougless was always a bit shy, always felt like an outsider.

Her parents had never compared her to her sisters. They didn't have to, for there were tennis trophies, horse riding trophies, baseball trophies, spelling bee medals, science fair ribbons everywhere. Dougless had once won a third-prize yellow ribbon at church for the best apple pie and her father had proudly hung it up beside his other daughters' blue ribbons and purple "best of show" ribbons. The yellow had looked strange and, to Dougless, embarrassing. She took it down.

All her life it seemed she'd wanted to please people but had never been able to. Her father maintained that whatever she did was okay with him, but Dougless merely had to look at her sisters' accomplishments to know she needed to do more. Robert had been an attempt to please her family. Maybe Robert, a distinguished surgeon, was supposed to be the biggest trophy of all.

Nicholas had saved her, she thought, but not in the way he meant. He hadn't saved her by pushing Robert down some stairs. He'd saved her by respecting her and she had begun seeing herself through his eyes. Dougless doubted very much if her sisters could have handled what had happened as well as Dougless had. All three of them were so sensible, so level-headed they would probably have called the police on a man in armor who said he was from the sixteenth century. Not one of them would have been soft-hearted enough to take pity on a poor crazy guy.

"What makes you smile so?" Nicholas asked softly.

"I was thinking about my sisters. They are perfect people. Not a flaw in them, but I just realized that perfect can sometimes be a little lonely. Maybe I do try to please people but I guess there are worse things. Maybe I should just find the right person to please."

Nicholas was obviously confused by this. He took her hand and began to kiss the palm. "You please me much."

She snatched her hand away. "We can't . . . touch one another," she said, stammering.

He looked at her through his lashes, his voice low. "But we have touched, have we not? I remember seeing you. I seem to know of touching you."

"Yes," Dougless whispered. "We have touched." They were alone on the bed, the room dark except for the golden glow of three candles.

"If we have touched, then it will not matter if we touch again in this life." His hands were reaching for her.

"No," she said, her eyes pleading. "We cannot. I would be returned to my own time."

Nicholas didn't move closer to her and he couldn't understand why he stopped. But he could feel the urgency in her. Never before had a woman's "no" stopped him. He soon found the women didn't really mean no. But now, on the bed with this most desirable woman, he found himself listening to her words.

He leaned back against the pillows and sighed. "I am too weak to accomplish much," he said heavily.

Dougless laughed. "Sure and if you believe that I have some land in Florida to sell you."

Nicholas grinned, understanding her meaning. "Come, then, sit close by me and tell me more of your time and of what we did there." He held up his uninjured arm and Dougless, against her better judgment, moved near him.

He pulled her very close to the side of him and wrapped his strong right arm about her. She pushed at him for a moment, then sighed and snuggled against his bare chest. "We bought you some clothes," she said, smiling in memory. "You attacked the poor clerk because the prices were so high. And afterward we went to tea. You *loved* tea. Then we found you a bed and breakfast." She paused. "That was the night you found me in the rain."

Nicholas listened to her with half an ear. He wasn't yet sure he believed her story of past and future, but he was sure of how she felt in his arms. Her body next to his was something he remembered very well.

She was explaining that he'd seemed able to "hear" her. She said she wasn't quite sure how it worked, but she'd used it the first day she'd come to the sixteenth century. She had "called" to him in the rain and he had come to her. She chided him for his rudeness and for making her ride on the back of the horse. Later, when she was in the room in the attic she had again "called" him.

Nicholas didn't need further explanation of this, for he seemed to always feel what she felt. Now, as she lay in his arms, her head on his chest, he could feel her sense of comfort, but at the same time he felt her sexual excitement. He'd never wanted to make love to a woman so much as he wanted to make love to her, but something stopped him.

She was telling of going to Bellwood and of his showing her the secret door.

"I believed you after that," she said. "Not because you knew of the door but because you were so hurt that the world remembered your misdeeds instead of all the good you had done. No one in the twentieth century knew for sure that you had designed Thornwyck. There was nothing left behind to prove that you were the designer."

"I am not a tradesman. I will not—"

She twisted to look up at him. "I told you that in our world it's different. Talent is appreciated."

He looked down at her, her face so close to his, and put his fingertips under her chin and held her. Ever so slowly he brought his lips to hers and kissed her gently.

He pulled back, startled. Her eyes were closed, her body soft and pliant against his. He could take her, he knew that, but something stopped him. He moved his hand from her chin and found that it was trembling. He felt like a boy with his first woman. Except that the first time Nicholas had bedded a woman, he had been eager and enthusiastic, not trembling as he was now.

"What is it you do to me?" he whispered.

"I don't know," Douglass said, her voice husky. "I think maybe we were meant to be together. Even though we were born four hundred years apart, we were meant for each other."

He ran his hand down her face, neck, shoulder, arm. "Yet I am not to bed you? I cannot take the clothes from your body and kiss your breasts, kiss your legs, kiss—"

"Nicholas, please," she said, pushing out of his arms. "This is difficult enough as it is. All I know is that when we were together in the twentieth century, after we made love you disappeared. I was holding you and you slipped right out of my grasp. I have you again now and I don't want to lose you a second time. We can spend time together, talk, we can be together in every way except physically—that is, if you want me to stay with you."

Nicholas looked at her, saw and felt the pain she felt, but at the moment he wanted to make love to her more than he wanted to understand anything.

Dougless saw what he was thinking, and when he lunged at her, she rolled off the bed. "One of us has to keep his wits. I want you to get some rest. Tomorrow we can talk more."

"I do not want to talk to you," he said sullenly.

Dougless laughed and remembered all the things she'd once done to entice him. "Tomorrow, my love. I must go now. It's almost dawn now and I must meet Lucy and—"

"Who is Lucy?"

"Lady Lucinda something or other. The girl Kit's to marry."

Nicholas snorted. "A fat lump, that."

Dougless's anger flared. "Not beautiful like the woman you're to marry, is she?"

Nicholas smiled. "Jealousy becomes you."

"I'm not jealous, I'm—" She turned away. Jealousy didn't begin to describe what she felt for Lettice, but she said nothing. Nicholas had already made it clear that he loved the woman he was to marry, and he would listen to nothing Dougless said against her. "I have to go," she said at last. "And I want you to sleep."

"I would sleep well if you would but stay with me."

"Liar," she said, smiling. She didn't dare go too near him again. She was tired from the excitement of the day and from a night without sleep. She lifted her tote bag, stepped to the door, took one last look—barechested, skin dark against the white of the pillows—and hurriedly, before she changed her mind, she left the room.

Lucy was waiting for her by the fountain and after Dougless had showered, they rehearsed their vaudeville act. Dougless was going to play the straight man, the dummy who asked the questions so Lucy would get all the laughs.

When, at daybreak, Dougless made her way back to the house, Honoria was waiting for her, holding the purple velvet dress.

"I thought I might take a nap," Dougless said, yawning.

"Lady Margaret and Lord Christopher await you. You are to be rewarded."

"I don't want any reward. I just want to help." Even as she said it, she knew it was a lie. She wanted to live with Nicholas for the rest of her life. Sixteenth century, twentieth century, she didn't care which if she could just stay with him.

"You must come. You may ask for whatever you wish. A house. An income. A husband. A—"

"Think they'd let me have Nicholas?"

"He is pledged," Honoria said softly.

"I know that only too well. Shall we start getting me harnessed?"

After Dougless was dressed, Honoria led her to the Presence Chamber where Lady Margaret and her oldest son were playing a game of chess.

"Ah," Kit said when Dougless entered. He lifted her hand and kissed it. "The angel of life who gave me back mine."

Dougless smiled and blushed.

"Come, sit," Lady Margaret said, pointing to a chair. A chair, not a stool, so Dougless knew she was being greatly honored.

Kit stood behind his mother's chair. "I wish to thank you for my life and I wish to give you a gift, but I know not what you would wish. Name what you would have of me. And think high," he said, eyes twinkling, "my life is worth much to me."

"There is nothing I want," Dougless said. "You have given me kindness. You have fed and clothed me most sumptuously. There is nothing more I could want." Except Nicholas, she thought. Could you gift-wrap him and send him to my family home in Maine?

"Come," Kit said, laughing. "There is something you must want. A chest of jewels perhaps. I have a house in Wales that—"

"A house," Dougless said. "Yes, a house. I'd like you to build a house at Thornwyck, and Nicholas is to make the plans for it."

"My son?" Lady Margaret asked, aghast.

"Yes, Nicholas. He has made some sketches for a house and it will be beautiful. But he must have Kit's . . . I mean, Lord Christopher's backing."

"And you would live in this house?" Kit asked.

"Oh no, I mean, I don't want to own it. I just want Nicholas to be allowed to design it."

Both Kit and Lady Margaret stared at her. Dougless looked at the women around them, sitting at their embroidery frames. They were also gaping.

Kit recovered first. "You may have your wish. My brother will have his house."

"Thank you. Thank you so very much."

No one in the room spoke again, so Dougless stood. "I believe I owe you a game of charades," she said to Lady Margaret.

Lady Margaret smiled. "You no longer need to earn your keep. My son's life has paid for you. Go and do what you wish."

Dougless at first started to protest that she wouldn't know what to do with herself, but then she figured she'd think of something. "Thank you, my lady," she said and bobbed a curtsy before leaving the room. Freedom, she thought, as she went back to Honoria's bedroom. No more having to entertain people. Good thing, since her store of songs was down to the McDonald's jingle.

Honoria's maid helped Dougless remove her new dress and corset (her old corset that was beginning to rust through its silk covering) and she went to bed smiling. She had prevented Nicholas from impregnating Arabella, and she'd saved Kit. All that was left was to get rid of Lettice. If she could do that, she would change history

Smiling, she fell asleep

18

What followed was, for Dougless, the happiest week of her life. Everyone in the Stafford household was pleased with her and it seemed that she could do no wrong. She figured it would wear off after a week or so, but she planned to enjoy it while it lasted.

She spent every minute she could with Nicholas. He wanted to know all about her twentieth-century world and he never tired of asking questions. He had difficulty believing her talk of automobiles, and airplanes he didn't credit at all. He went through everything in her tote bag. In the bottom were a couple of foil-wrapped teabags and Dougless made him a cup of tea with milk. As he'd done the first time he'd tasted ice cream, he kissed her soundly in pleasure at the taste.

In return for telling him of the twentieth century, he told her of his life. He showed her dances, took her hawking one day, then laughed at her when she refused to allow the lovely bird on her arm to kill. He showed her buzzards in pens that were fed nothing but white bread for days to clean the carrion from their craws before they were butchered and eaten.

They argued about educating the "lower classes." And that led to a squabble about equality. Nicholas said her America sounded violent and lonely, and Dougless wished she hadn't told him so much.

He asked her hundreds of questions about the immediate future of England and especially about Queen Elizabeth. Dougless so wished she remembered more to tell him. He seemed fascinated with the idea of sea travel and with exploring her new country.

"But you'll be here, married to Lettice. You can't go anywhere—if you're alive. If you're not executed."

Nicholas would *not* listen to her when she spoke of his execution. He had a young man's belief that he was invincible, that nothing could hurt him. "I will not raise an army to protect my lands in Wales because they are not my lands but Kit's, and if he is alive then the future I once had will not be."

She had no argument for him. When she asked him who he thought had tried to kill Kit, he merely shrugged and said it was some ruffian. Dougless still couldn't get used to the idea of a land where there was no federal government, no police force. The nobility, besides having all the money, had all the power. They judged disputes, hanged whomever they wanted, and answered only to the queen. If the peasants had a good ruling family they were lucky, but many were not so fortunate.

One day Dougless asked Nicholas to take her to see a town. He raised an eyebrow at her and told her she would not like it, but he would take her.

He was right. The peace and relative cleanliness of the Stafford household had not prepared her for the filth of a medieval town. Eight of Nicholas's men accompanied them to protect them from highwaymen. As they rode, Dougless looked at every shadow behind every tree. Being attacked by a dashing highwayman in a romantic novel was one thing but, in reality, she doubted if real highwaymen were anything but criminals.

The town was dirty beyond anything Dougless had ever imagined. People emptied kitchen slops and chamberpots into the streets. She saw adults who she was sure had never had a bath in their lives. At the corner of a bridge over a little river were tall pikes with rotting human heads on them.

She tried to look at all of it, to see the good. She tried to memorize what houses looked like, what the streets were like, the carts. If she did return to her time she wanted to tell her father what she'd seen. But she seemed to see only the bad. The houses were so close together that women passed things from the windows to each other. People shouted, animals screamed, someone was beating on metal with a hammer. Filthy, diseased children ran up to them, clutching their legs and begging. Nicholas's men kicked them away and Dougless, instead of feeling sympathy, felt herself recoiling from their touch. When Nicholas turned and saw her pale face, he ordered his men to start for home.

Once they were again in the open air and Dougless could breathe, Nicholas called a halt and tablecloths were spread under the trees, and food brought out. Nicholas handed her a goblet full of strong wine. With trembling hands, Dougless took the wine and drank deeply.

"Our world is not like yours," Nicholas said. In the past days he had questioned her on every aspect of modern society, and his questions had included bathing and sewage drains.

"No," she said, trying not to remember what that town looked and smelled like. America had many homeless but they did not live like these people did. Of course she had seen some well-dressed people in the town, but the sight of them could not take away from the stench. "No, a modern town is not like that."

He stretched out beside her while she sat and drank her wine. "Do you wish to stay in my time?"

She looked at him and between them were the images of what she had just seen. If she stayed with Nicholas that town would be part of her life. Whenever she left the safety of the Stafford house, she would see rotting heads on pikes, streets filled with the contents of chamberpots.

"Yes," she said, looking into his eyes. "I would stay if I could."

He lifted her hand and kissed it.

"But I'd make the midwives wash their hands."

"Midwives? Ah, then you plan to have my children?"

The thought of bearing a child without a proper doctor and hospital terrified her, but she didn't tell him that. "A dozen at least," she said.

Her sleeve was too tight to push up but she could feel his hot lips through her clothing. "When shall we begin making them? I should like more children."

Her eyes were closed, her head back. "More?" Suddenly, something that Nicholas had said came back to her. A son. He had said he had no children but he'd once had a son. What exactly had he said?

She pulled her arm from him. "Nicholas, do you have a son?"

"Aye, an infant. But you need not worry, I sent his mother away long ago."

She was concentrating hard. A son. What had Nicholas said? *I had a son but he died in a fall the week after my brother died.* "We have to return," she said.

"But we will eat first."

"No." She stood. "We have to see about your son. You said he died a week after Kit drowned. Tomorrow will be a week. We must go to him now."

Nicholas didn't hesitate. He left one man to pack the food and dishes, while he and the other seven and Dougless tore back to the Stafford house. They jumped off their horses at the front gate. Dougless lifted her skirts and ran after Nicholas.

He led her up to the third floor where she'd never been before, then threw open a door. What Dougless saw horrified her more than anything she'd yet seen in the sixteenth century. A little boy, barely over a year old, was wrapped from his neck to his feet in tight bindings of linen—and was hanging from a peg on the wall. His arms and legs were pinned to him exactly like a mummy. The bottom half of the bindings were filthy where he'd relieved himself and not been changed. Below him on the floor was a wooden bucket to catch excess "drippings."

Dougless could not move as she stared in horror at the child, whose eyes were half open, half closed.

"The child is fine," Nicholas said. "No harm has come to him."

"No harm?" Dougless said under her breath. If a child in the twentieth century were treated like this, it would be taken from its parents and the parents prosecuted, but Nicholas was saying that the child was fine. "Take him down," she said.

"Down? But he is safe. There is no reason to—"

Dougless glared at him. "Down!"

With a look of resignation, Nicholas took the boy by the shoulders and, holding him at arms' length so he'd drip onto the floor and not on his father, he turned to Dougless. "And what am I to do with him?"

"We are going to bathe him and dress him properly. Can he walk? Talk?"

Nicholas looked astonished. "How am I to know this?"

Dougless blinked. There was more than mere time between their two worlds. It took Dougless a while but she got a big wooden bucket brought to the room and hot water. Nicholas muttered, complained, and cursed, but he unwrapped his smelly, dirty son and plunked him into the warm water. The poor boy was covered with diaper rash from the waist down. Dougless used some of her precious soft soap to gently wash him.

At one point the boy's nurse came in and was very upset, saying Dougless was going to kill the child. At first Nicholas wouldn't get involved—probably because he agreed with the nurse, Dougless thought—but Dougless started glaring at him and he made the woman leave.

The warm water made the boy perk up and Dougless guessed that the bindings had been so tight the boy had been in a bit of a stupor. She said as much to Nicholas.

"It keeps them quiet. Loosen the swaddlings and they weep most loudly."

"Let's wrap *you* in bindings like that, hang *you* on a peg and see if *you* don't cry bloody murder."

"A child has no sense." He was puzzled by her actions and her thoughts.

"He has the brain now that he'll go to Yale with."

"Yale?"

"Never mind. Have safety pins been invented yet?"

Dougless had to improvise diapers. Nicholas protested when she used one diamond and one emerald brooch to fasten the corners of the boy's linen diaper. She wished she had some zinc ointment for his rash but didn't.

When at last he was clean, dry, and powdered (thanks to another hotel giveaway sample from her tote bag), she handed the boy to his father. Nicholas looked horrified and bewildered at the same time, but he took the boy and after a moment he even smiled at him. The child smiled back.

"What's his name?" Dougless asked.

"James."

She took the boy from Nicholas. He was already a very good-looking child, with his father's dark hair and blue eyes. He also had the beginnings of a cleft in his chin. "Let's see if you can walk." She put the boy on the floor and after a few stumbles, he walked to Dougless's outstretched arms.

Nicholas stayed with her while she spent an hour playing with the boy, and when she went to put him down for the night, she found out more about Elizabethan childcare. James's crib had a hole in the middle and the child was strapped in at night, his bottom over the hole, and once again a bucket was put under him.

Nicholas did little more than roll his eyes at her when she demanded that the child be given a proper mattress. The nurse complained and Dougless could see her point. If the child had no rubber pants, by morning the mattress would be filthy, and how does one clean goose feathers? She solved the problem by putting a piece of waxed cloth, such as rain gear was made out of, over the mattress. The nurse did as Dougless bid but she was grumbling when Dougless and Nicholas left.

Nicholas was chuckling as they left the room. "Come and have supper with me," he said. "We will celebrate the cleansing of my son." He took Dougless's hand and tucked it under his arm.

◇ ◇ ◇

Nicholas leaned back on the bench and watched Dougless playing with his son. The sun was bright, the air heavy with the scent of roses, and as far as Nicholas could tell, all was perfect in the world. It had been three days since she'd taken the boy off the peg and out of swaddling, and during those three days the child had spent a great deal of time with them. But then so had many people spent time with them. Nicholas was amazed to discover how much Dougless had got herself into in the short time she'd been with the Stafford family. Early mornings she "rehearsed," as she called it, with the fat little heiress, and yesterday she and the heiress had put on a ridiculous play while wearing ridiculous peasant clothes. They had sung a song about "Travelin' along, singin' a song . . ." and then told jokes that bordered on blasphemy.

Throughout the play, Nicholas had refused to laugh, because he knew she had done this work for Kit. She had even told Nicholas so. The rest of his family had laughed uproariously at the play, but Nicholas refused to do so.

Later, when he got her alone, she had laughed at him and accused him of being jealous. Jealous? Nicholas Stafford jealous? He could have any woman he wanted so why should he be jealous? She had smiled so knowingly that, to stop her, he had grabbed her to him and kissed her until she couldn't remember her own name, much less think of another man.

Now, leaning back against the garden wall and watching her toss a ball to his son, he felt at peace. Was this love? he wondered. Was this the love that the troubadours sang of? How could he be in love with a woman he hadn't taken to bed? Once he'd thought he was in love with a half gypsy girl who had done splendid things to his body. But with this Dougless all they did was talk—and laugh.

She had nagged him so much about the sketches she'd found while snooping in his belongings that he started making new drawings. Kit had told Nicholas that building on Thornwyck could begin in the spring.

They talked together, sang together, rode, walked. He told her things about himself he had never told another soul.

Two days earlier a portrait painter had come to the Stafford household and Nicholas had commissioned him to paint a miniature oil of Dougless. It should be finished soon.

Looking at her now, he was beginning to wonder if he could live without her. Regularly she mentioned leaving. She talked about what he must do when she was gone. She talked of cleanliness until he could bear no more, but she kept saying cleanliness was of utmost importance.

When she was gone . . . He couldn't stand to think of not being with her. Many times during the day he found himself thinking, I must tell Dougless that. She said that in her time men and women were partners and they shared thoughts and ideas. He knew his mother's last husband had often asked Lady Margaret's opinion, but he couldn't remember his stepfather saying, How was your day? as Dougless asked.

And there was the child. The child was a bother, of course, but there were times when he enjoyed the boy's smiles. The boy looked up at Nicholas as if his father were a god. Yesterday Nicholas had taken the boy into the saddle before him and the child's squeals of laughter had made Nicholas smile.

Dougless laughed at something the boy did and brought Nicholas back to the present. The sunlight was shining on her hair, but then the sunlight only seemed to come out when she was near. He wanted to touch her, hold her, make love to her, but the threat of her disappearance kept him from pulling her into his bed. Oh, he kissed her when he could, touched every part of her body he could reach. They snuggled together in the evenings, alone in some deserted nook, and watched the firelight or the stars out an open window. He touched her, held her, but they went no further. The possibility of her leaving him was too great for him to risk.

A boy came to tell Nicholas that Lady Margaret wanted to see him, so reluctantly he left the garden and Dougless and went into the house.

His mother awaited him in her private closet off her bedchamber.

"Have you told her?" Lady Margaret asked, her face stern.

Nicholas didn't have to be told what she meant. "Nay, I have not."

"Nicholas, this has gone too far. I have been lenient with the woman because she saved Kit's life, but your behavior . . ." She trailed off because there was no need to say more.

Nicholas went to the window, opened it, and looked down into the garden. He could just see Dougless below. "I would spend my life with the Montgomery woman," he said softly.

Lady Margaret slammed the window shut and glared at her son. She had eyes that could pierce a man. "You cannot. The dowry for Lettice Culpin has been accepted and part of it spent to buy sheep. The woman brings land with her and a good name. Your children will be related to the throne. You cannot throw that away for this woman who is nothing."

"She is all to me."

Lady Margaret glared at him. "She is nothing. Two days ago the rider returned from Lanconia. There is no Montgomery king. This Dougless Montgomery is no more than a fast-tongued—"

"Say no more," Nicholas said, cutting her off. "I have never believed her to be of royal blood, but she has come to mean more to me than bloodlines and property."

Lady Margaret groaned. "Do you think you are the first to love? When I was a girl I loved my cousin and I refused to marry your father. My mother beat me until I was willing." She narrowed her eyes at Nicholas. "And she was right. Your father gave me two sons who lived to manhood and my cousin gambled his fortune away."

"Dougless is not likely to gamble my fortune away."

"Nor will she increase your fortune!" Lady Margaret calmed herself. "What ails you? Kit is to marry a fat child while you are to marry one of the great beauties of England. Lettice is much more beautiful than the Montgomery woman."

"What do I care for money and beauty? Lettice has a heart of stone. She marries me, a younger son, only for my connection to the throne. Let her find another who will overlook her lack of warmth and will see only the perfection of her face."

"You mean to unkiss this bargain? You will break your betrothal?" Lady Margaret was aghast.

"How can I marry one woman when another owns my heart?"

Lady Margaret gave a derisive snort of laughter. "I did not raise you to be a fool. Keep the Montgomery woman after your marriage. Make her a maid to your wife. I cannot believe Lettice will mind that you do not come to her every night. Get Lettice with child and then go to your Montgomery woman. It was an arrangement my second husband had and I did not mind. Although he gave his woman three children and me only one and that one died," she added bitterly.

Nicholas turned away from his mother. "I do not believe Dougless would agree to such an arrangement. In her country I do not believe such things are done."

"Her country? Where *is* this country of hers? It is not Lanconia. Where does she get these games and amusements? Where do these strange implements she carries come from? She adds on a machine. She has pills that are magic. Is she from the devil? Do you wish to cohabit with one of the devil's own?"

"She is no witch. She's from—" He stopped and looked at his mother. He could not tell her the truth about Dougless. Dougless had made a remark about the household loving her now because she had saved Kit, but that it would soon be forgotten.

Lady Margaret glared at her son. "Do you sell yourself to her? Do you believe whatever story she tells you? The woman is a liar and . . ." She hesitated. "She interferes too much. She has you drawing houses like a tradesman. She has the girl Kit is to marry dressing like a peasant. She takes children from the nursery. She teaches the servant children to read and write—as if that were needed. She—"

"But you have encouraged all of this," Nicholas said in astonishment. "I was the one who preached caution when she came. You took the tablet she offered."

"Aye, I did. I was much amused by her at first. And I would be amused now, were not my youngest son thinking himself in love with her." Lady Margaret softened and put her hand on Nicholas's arm. "Love God, love your children when they are grown if you must, but do not give your love to a lying woman. What does she want from you? What does she want from all of us? Listen to me, Nicholas, beware of her. She changes too much in our family. She wants something."

"No," Nicholas said softly. "She wants naught but to help. She has been sent—"

"Sent? She has been sent here by whom? Who sent her? What can she gain?" Lady Margaret's eyes widened. "Kit said someone tried to pull him under when he nearly drowned. Did the Montgomery woman arrange to have him drowned and then to save him? Such a trick would gain her much in our family. Or perhaps she meant for him to die. Were Kit dead, you would be earl and she has you in her palm."

"No, no, no," Nicholas said. "She's not like that. She didn't even know about Kit because I had lied to her about the door at Bellwood."

Lady Margaret's handsome face showed her confusion at his words. "What do you know of her?"

"Naught. I know naught bad of her. You must believe me, the woman wants only good for us. She has no evil intent."

"Then why does she want to prevent your marriage?"

"She does not," Nicholas said but turned away. When he had first met Dougless, she had said many derogatory things about Lettice, but lately she had said nothing. Nicholas realized his mother's words were making him doubt Dougless.

Lady Margaret moved to stand before her son. "Does the Montgomery woman love you?" she asked softly.

"Yes," he answered.

"Then she will want what is best for you. And Lettice Culpin is best. The Montgomery woman must see that she can bring no dowry to the marriage. She has lied about having an uncle who is king, so I doubt if she has any relative who matters. What is she? The daughter of a tradesman?"

"Her father teaches."

"Ah," Lady Margaret said. "The truth at last. What can she offer the Stafford family? She has nothing." She put her hand on Nicholas's arm. "I do not ask you to give her up. She will stay in this house with you, or go with you and your wife. Breed with the woman. Love her. Make free with her." Her face became stern again. "But you cannot make her your wife. Do you understand me? Staffords do not marry the penniless daughters of teachers."

"I understand full well, madam," Nicholas said, eyes dark with anger. "I, more than anyone, feel the weight of my family's name on my shoulders. I will do my duty and marry the beauteous, coldhearted Lettice."

"Good," Lady Margaret said, then lowered her voice. "I should hate for something to happen to the Montgomery woman. I have grown fond of her."

Nicholas stared at his mother for a moment, then turned on his heel and left the room. He stalked angrily to his bedchamber and there, alone, he leaned against the door and closed his eyes. His mother's words had been clear enough: do your duty and marry Lettice Culpin or "something" will happen to Dougless. Even as he thought the words, he knew how Dougless would react to his marrying another woman. Dougless would not remain in his household to wait on his wife.

To lose Dougless and gain Lettice, he thought. To trade Dougless's eyes looking at him with love for Lettice's cold, calculating eyes. The first time he had met Lettice he had been taken with her beauty. Dark eyes, dark hair, full red lips. But Nicholas had been around enough beautiful women that he was soon able to see beneath her beauty. She walked about the Stafford household, her eyes on gold vessels, adding them, her mind like a scale weighing how much gold the Staffords owned, how much silver.

Nicholas had tried to seduce her but had failed. He had failed not because Lettice was unwilling but because she was uninterested. Kissing Lettice was like kissing warm marble.

Duty, he thought. His duty was to marry the woman who had more money, the woman with the bluest blood. "Dougless," he whispered and closed his eyes.

Tonight he must tell her, he thought. Tonight he had to tell Dougless of his impending marriage. He could put it off no longer.

◇　◇　◇

"You can't marry her," Dougless said quite calmly.

"My love," Nicholas said, walking toward her, his hands outstretched.

They were in the center of the maze, a place he'd led her to tell her the news. He knew she didn't know her way out of the maze and therefore she was less likely to run from him.

"I must marry her," Nicholas said. "It is my duty to my family."

Dougless told herself to remain calm. She told herself that she had a job to do and that she must explain to Nicholas why he couldn't marry Lettice.

But when the man she loved told her he was to marry another, logic fled her.

"Duty?" she said through her teeth. "No doubt it's a great hardship for you to marry a beautiful babe like Lettice. I'll just bet you're dreading it. And I guess you want me too. Is that it? A wife *and* a lover? Only I can't be your lover, can I?" She glared at him. "Or maybe I can be. If I went to bed with you, would that keep you from marrying that evil woman?"

Nicholas was moving toward her, trying to take her in his arms, but he halted. "Evil? Lettice is greedy perhaps, but evil?"

Dougless's fists were clenched at her side. "What do you know of evil? You men are all alike, no matter when you were born. All you can see is the outside of a person. If a woman is beautiful she can have any man she wants, no matter how rotten she is inside. And if a woman is ugly, nothing else matters."

Nicholas dropped his hands; his eyes were angry. "Aye, that is all that interests me. I care naught for duty or family or for the woman I love. Tearing the clothes from Lettice's divine body is all that interests me."

Dougless gasped, feeling as if he'd slapped her. She turned on her heel to leave the maze but she knew she didn't know her way out. She turned back. Anger was holding her upright but, quite suddenly, the anger left her. She collapsed on the bench, her face in her hands. "Oh God," she whispered.

Nicholas sat beside her and pulled her into his arms, holding her while she cried against his chest. "It is something I must do. It has been arranged. I do not wish it, not now, not since I have you, but it is what I must do. Were something to happen to Kit I would be earl and it is my duty to produce an heir."

"Lettice can't bave chilled," Dougless said against his chest.

He pulled a linen handkerchief from inside his slops. "What?"

Dougless blew her nose. "Lettice can't have children."

"How do you know of this?"

"Lettice was the one who caused your execution. Oh, Nicholas, please don't marry her. You *can't* marry her. She will kill you." Dougless was calming somewhat and beginning to remember what she must tell him. "I was going to tell you, but I thought we would have more time together. I wanted you to trust me more before I told you. I know how much you love Lettice and—"

"Love her? *I* love Lettice Culpin? Who has told you this?"

"You did. You told me that's one of the major reasons you wanted to return to the sixteenth century, because you loved her so very much."

He pulled away from her and stood. "I came to love her?"

Dougless sniffed and blew her nose again. "When you came to me you'd been married to her for four years."

"It would take more than four years to make me love that woman," Nicholas muttered.

"What?"

"Tell me more of this love I bore for my wife."

There was a knot in Dougless's throat so she had difficulty speaking, but she did her best to explain all that he'd said to her. He questioned her thoroughly, asking about their last days together. Dougless held on to one of his big hands with both of hers, while she answered his questions.

At last he put his fingertips under her chin and lifted her face. "When I was with you before I knew I must return. Perhaps I did not want to cause you pain when I left. Perhaps I meant to prevent you from loving a man who would not stay."

Dougless's eyes widened, tears sparkling. "You said that," she whispered. "On our last night together you said you wouldn't touch me because I'd grieve too much for you."

He smiled at her and smoothed a damp tendril of hair away from her face. "I could not love Lettice were I to live with her a thousand years."

"Oh, Nicholas," she said and threw her arms around his neck and began kissing him. "I knew you'd do the right thing. I knew you wouldn't marry her. Now everything will come out right. You won't be executed. Lettice won't have any reason to try to kill you or Kit. And she won't get hooked up with Robert Sydney because Arabella hasn't had your baby. Oh, Nicholas, I knew you wouldn't marry her."

Nicholas pulled her arms from around him and held her hands, his eyes locked with hers. "I am pledged to marry Lettice and I shall leave for the marriage in three days' time." When Dougless struggled for release, he held her hands firmly. "My way is not yours. My time is not the same as yours. I have not the freedom you have. I cannot marry to suit myself only."

He leaned closer to her and put his lips to her cheek. "You must understand me. My marriage was arranged years ago and it is a good alliance. My wife will bring property and relatives into the Stafford family."

"Will this property and these relatives help you when the axe-man removes your head?" she asked angrily. "Will you go to your death thinking how good this marriage was?"

"You must tell me all. What you tell me will help me prevent an accusation of treason."

She jerked out of his grasp and walked to the far side of the grassed area at the heart of the maze. "You'll be able to prevent your execution as well as you could have prevented Kit's drowning. If I hadn't been here, your brother would be dead and your lovely Lettice would be marrying an earl."

Nicholas's mouth twitched at a smile. "Were I the earl, I would not marry Lettice. No doubt my mother would marry me to your fat Lucy."

"You can laugh at me if you want, but I can assure you that when you came to me before you weren't laughing. Facing an executioner's axe doesn't make a person feel jovial."

Nicholas sobered. "Nay, it would not. You would tell me of Lettice? Tell me all that you know?"

Dougless sat down on the bench, at the far end from him, away from his touch. She stared ahead at the green wall of trimmed hedge and didn't look at him.

She started slowly, at the very beginning, telling him of reading Lady Margaret's papers that were found in a hole in a wall. She told how Nicholas had finagled an invitation into the Harewoods' home, where they'd met Lee and Arabella.

"We read the papers and asked questions all weekend but found out little. In the end you drew your sword on Lee and he told you that the traitor's name was Robert Sydney. We both thought you'd return after that but you didn't. You stayed." She closed her eyes for a moment. "We had a wonderful time together but then we . . ." The pain of that morning in the church when Nicholas had disappeared was still fresh. "We made love and you went back. Later I found out you had been executed."

She drew a deep breath and told him more. She told of meeting Lee and Lee's telling her of finding Lady Margaret's account of what had happened, the truth that only became known after Nicholas's death.

She told how Lettice had planned to marry a Stafford, produce an heir, and put the child on the throne of England. She repeated Lady Margaret's belief that Lettice had had Kit killed so she'd be marrying an earl instead of a younger son.

"After you married her she tried to persuade you to raise yourself at court. She wanted to gain as many people to back her as possible, but you refused."

"I do not like court," Nicholas said. "Too many people conspire against one another."

She turned to look at him. "You refused to take Lettice to court so she tried to kill you. When I met you you had a long, deep scar on your calf where you had fallen from a horse about a year after your marriage. You said someone had loosened the girth on your saddle."

Nicholas didn't speak so Dougless continued. She told him that Lettice had begun to look for someone to help rid her of Nicholas and she'd found Robert Sydney. "He hated you for having his wife on a table and impregnating her. Lady Margaret thinks he killed both Arabella and the baby."

"But I did not impregnate Arabella," Nicholas said softly.

"When you started to raise an army to fight in Wales, it was easy for Lettice to get Robert to tell the queen of your treason. Queen Elizabeth was jittery about Mary of Scotland anyway, and maybe she'd heard rumors that the Staffords were considering joining with Mary."

Dougless looked at him, at his beautiful face, his bright blue eyes. She put out her hand, her palm on his soft, dark beard. "They cut off your head," she whispered, blinking back tears.

Nicholas kissed her palm.

Dougless dropped her hand and looked away. "After your . . . death Robert Sydney blackmailed Lettice into marrying him. He wanted to put his own child on the throne, only the beauteous Lettice, the woman a man had died for, was barren. She could have no children."

Dougless grimaced. "Lee said it was all ironic. Lettice destroyed the Stafford family for a child she would never have."

There was silence between them for a while.

"And what of my mother?"

She looked back at him. "The queen confiscated all the Staffords owned, and Robert Sydney married her to Dickie Harewood."

"Harewood?!" Nicholas said with disgust.

"It was either that or starve to death. The queen gave Sydney a couple of your estates, and then someone pushed your mother down a flight of stairs and broke her neck."

She paused at Nicholas's intake of breath. "After that there were no more Staffords. Lettice had managed to wipe out all of you."

She turned to look at him. His face was pale.

Nicholas stood and walked toward the hedge. He stood silently for a while, thinking over her words, before turning back to her. "What you say could have happened once but could not now."

She understood what he was saying, that now it would be okay to marry Lettice. Anger began to swell her veins. "You wouldn't be such a fool as to marry her after what I've told you, would you?"

"But your story could not happen now. Arabella does not carry my child so Robin has no reason to hate me. Kit is alive so I have no reason to raise an army, and if Kit must raise an army you will be assured that I will petition the queen's permission first."

Dougless came to her feet. "Nicholas, don't you understand that you don't know the future? When you were in my time the books said you had died three days before your execution. After you returned the books told of your execution. History is so very easy to change. If you marry Lettice, when I return will I read that Kit was killed another way? That maybe Lettice came up with another way to have you executed? Maybe she'll find someone else to help her. I'm sure there are other men with pretty wives who hate you."

Nicholas smiled at the last. "A man or two."

"You're laughing at me! I am talking life and death to you and you stand there *laughing* at me."

He pulled Dougless's rigid body into his arms. "My love, it is good that you care so much, and it is good that you have warned me. I will be cautious from now on."

She pushed away from him. Her voice and body showed her anger. "You are thinking like a *man,*" she accused. "You think that no woman could ever really do *you* harm, don't you? I tell you all of this and you chuckle at me. Why not wink at me and pat me on the head as well? Why not tell me to go back to my sewing and leave things like life and death to males who are capable of understanding?"

"Dougless, please," he said, reaching out his hands.

"Don't you touch me. Save your touches for your lovely Lettice. Tell me, is she so beautiful that she's worth all the tragedy that she'll cause? Your death, Kit's death, your mother's death, the end of the noble Stafford family?"

Nicholas let his arms fall to his sides. "Do you not see that I have no choice? Am I to tell my family and the Culpins I must break the betrothal because a woman from the future says my bride might kill all of the Staffords? I would be considered a fool and you . . . you would not be treated well."

"You risk everything because of what people might say?"

Nicholas clenched his fists and searched for a way to explain what must be, so that she could understand. "In your time do you not contract bargains? Legal bargains on paper?"

"Of course. We have contracts for everything. We even have marriage contracts but marriages should be made for love, not—"

"We do not marry for love. We cannot. Look you about. See the wealth of this house? This is but one house my family owns. These riches have come to us because my ancestors married for estate, not for love. My grandfather married a shrew of a woman but she brought three houses with her and much plate."

"Nicholas, I understand the theory, but marriage is so . . . so intimate. It's not like signing a contract to do some work for someone. Marriage has to do with love and children and a home and safety and having a friend."

"So you live in poverty with one you love. Does this love feed you, clothe you, keep you warm in winter? There is more to marriage than what you say. You are poor so you cannot understand."

Her eyes blazed. "For your information I am *not* poor. Not by a long shot. My family is very rich. Lots of money. But just because my family has money doesn't mean I don't want love, or that I'd sell myself to the highest bidder."

"How did your family obtain its wealth?" he asked softly.

"I don't know. We've had it forever. My father said that our ancestors married—" She broke off and looked at him.

"Your ancestors married who?"

"Nothing. It was a joke. He didn't mean anything."

"Who?" Nicholas asked.

"Rich women," she said angrily. "He said our ancestors were quite good at marrying rich women."

Nicholas said nothing, just stood there looking at her.

Her anger left her and she went to him, her arms about his waist, holding him tightly. "Marry for money," she said. "Marry the richest woman in the world, but please don't marry Lettice. She is bad. She'll hurt you, Nicholas, hurt all of you."

Nicholas pushed her out to arms' length to look into her eyes. "Lettice Culpin is the highest I can hope for. I am a younger son, a mere knight. I have naught but what Kit allows me. I am fortunate he is so generous to allow me to live at his expense. The lands Lettice brings to this family will benefit us all. How can I not do this for a brother who has given me so much?"

"Lettice isn't the best you can hope for. Lots of women like you. You can get someone else. If you have to marry someone for money we'll find her. Somebody rich and not ambitious like Lettice."

Nicholas smiled down at her. "Having a woman in bed is not the same as a marriage alliance. You must trust me on this. Lettice is a good match for me. No, do not frown. I will be safe. Do you not see? The danger of her is in not knowing. Now that I know, I can save my family and myself."

"You're going to check every saddle cinch to see if it's been cut? What about poison in your food? What about a wire stretched across the stairs? What if she hires thugs to beat you up? What about drowning? Burning?"

He chuckled in a patronizing way. "I am pleased you care. You shall help me keep watch."

"Me?" She pulled away from him. "Me?"

"Aye. You shall stay in my household." He gave her a look through his lashes. "You shall attend to my wife."

It took Dougless a moment to react. "Attend to your wife?" she said evenly. "You mean like help her dress, check that her bath water isn't too hot? That sort of thing?"

Her calm tone didn't fool him. "Dougless, my love, my one and only love, it will not be so bad. We will spend much time together."

"Do we spend the time together with or without a permission slip from your wife?"

"Dougless," he pleaded.

"You can ask this of me after the way you talked about my living with Robert? At least with Robert I was his *only* woman. But you . . . you're asking me to wait on that . . . that killer! What am I supposed to do at night while you're trying to produce an heir with her?"

Nicholas stiffened. "You cannot ask me to be celibate. You say you cannot share my bed for fear of returning."

"Oh, I see, *I* can be celibate, that's perfectly okay. But you, Mr. Macho Stud, you have to have a different woman every night. What do you do on the nights when Lettice tells you no? Chase the maids into the arbor?"

"You may not speak to me like this," he said, his eyes dark with rage.

"Oh, I can't, can't I? If someone travels four hundred years just to warn another person and that person won't listen, for no reason except his own vanity, then the party of the first part can say any damn thing she pleases. Go ahead, marry Lettice, see if I care. Kill Kit. Kill your mother. Lose your estates you think are so bloody valuable. *Lose your head!*"

She shouted the last part, then rushed past him and ran through the maze, tears blinding her.

She was lost within three minutes and she just stood there crying. Maybe a person *couldn't* change history. Maybe it was predestined that Kit was going to die and Nicholas was going to be executed. Maybe it was never meant that the Stafford family should continue to live. Maybe no one could change what was going to happen.

Nicholas came to her but he didn't speak and Dougless was glad. She knew that mere words would not change what each felt must be done. She followed his silent form out of the maze.

19

For Dougless the next three days were hell. Everyone in the Stafford household was very excited about Nicholas's forthcoming marriage, and it was all anyone could talk of. Food, clothes, who would be there, what had happened at other marriages, that was all the conversation. Huge carts were packed with the goods Nicholas and Kit would take with them. With a feeling of doom, Dougless watched the preparations for the long visit. Nicholas and Kit not only were taking their clothes with them, but furniture and servants as well.

To Dougless it seemed that every item loaded into the carts was a further weight on her heart. She tried to talk to Nicholas. Tried and tried and tried. But he wouldn't listen. Duty meant more to him than anything else in the world. He would not forsake his duty to his family for any reason on earth, not for love, not even for the possibility of his own death.

On the night before Nicholas was to leave, Dougless felt worse than she ever had before. When her stockbroker boyfriend had been taken away to jail, it had been nothing like this. Only the day Nicholas had returned to the sixteenth century and left her in the church was comparable.

In the night she took her thin, silky slip nightgown from her tote bag, removed her heavy, voluminous sixteenth-century gown and slipped on her modern gown. With her borrowed robe about her, she went to Nicholas's bedchamber.

Outside his room she put her hand to the door. She knew he was awake; she could feel it. Without knocking, she opened the door. He was sitting up in bed, the rough sheet covering his legs, his chest and hard, flat stomach bare and exposed. He was drinking from a silver tankard and he didn't look up when she entered.

"We must talk," she whispered. The room was silent except for the crackle of a fire and the sputter of candles.

"Nay, we have no more to say," he answered. "We both must do what we must."

"Nicholas," she whispered, but he didn't look at her. She slipped the concealing robe from her. The nightgown she wore was outrageously revealing by Elizabethan modes of dress. Its thin straps, low neck, and clinging fabric left nothing to the imagination.

She crawled across the bed to him, like a tigress on the prowl. "Nicholas," she whispered. "Do not marry her."

When she was near him, he looked at her—and the wine sloshed from his tankard. "What do you?" he asked hoarsely, his eyes at first shocked and then hot.

"Perhaps you'll stay with me this night," she said, drawing nearer to him.

Nicholas looked down the front of her nightgown and when he put out a hand to touch her shoulder, his hand trembled.

"One night," she whispered, moving her face close to his.

Nicholas reacted instantly. His arms were around her, his lips on hers, drinking of her, taking her as he'd wanted to do for so long. The fabric of her nightgown tore away as his hands, his lips were on her breasts, his face buried in them.

"This one night for your promise," Dougless was saying, her head back. She was trying to remember what she had to do before Nicholas's lips and hands drove all thoughts from her mind. "Swear to me," she said.

"All that I have is yours. Do you not know that?" he said, his lips moving lower on her body, down her stomach. His hands were on her hips, his fingers digging into her flesh.

"Then do not go tomorrow," she said. "This one night for tomorrow."

Nicholas's strong hands were lifting her hips up and the remains of the gown were sliding farther down. "You may have all my tomorrows."

"Nicholas, please." Dougless was trying to remember what she meant to say, but Nicholas's touch was driving the thoughts from her head. "Please, my love. I will not be here. You must swear to me."

After a moment Nicholas raised his head and looked up at her, up past her lovely body to her face. His mind was reeling with the sensations of touching this woman who had come to mean so much to him, but he was beginning to hear her. "What would you have me swear to you?" he asked in a low voice.

Dougless lifted her head. "I will spend tonight with you, if you'll swear not to marry Lettice after I'm gone," she said evenly.

For a long moment Nicholas looked at her, his bare body poised over her half-nude body, and Dougless held her breath. She had not come to this decision easily, but she knew that, even if it meant losing Nicholas forever and returning to her own time, she had to stop this marriage.

He rolled off her and the bed in one smooth motion, pulled on a loose robe, and went to stand before the fire, his back to her. When he spoke his voice was low and husky. "Do you think so little of me to believe I would risk the loss of you for one night's pleasure? Do you think so little of yourself to sell yourself to me for a promise?"

His words were making Dougless feel very small. She pulled her torn gown up over her shoulders. "I couldn't think of any other way," she said as an excuse. "I'd do *anything* to stop your marriage."

He turned to look at her, his eyes dark with emotion. "You have told me of your country, of your ways. Do you think yours is the only way? This marriage means naught to me, yet it means all to you."

"I can't have you risk your life for—"

His eyes blazed. "You risk *our* life for her!" he said angrily. "You tell me o'er and o'er that you cannot come to my bed. Yet you are here now, dressed as a . . . as a . . ."

Dougless pulled the sheet over her bare shoulders, feeling like a strumpet. "I only meant to try to get you to promise you wouldn't marry her," she said, feeling near to tears.

He came to the bed, looming over her. "What love is this you bear for me? You come creeping to my bed, appealing to me like a whore. Only you do not want gold, nay, you want me to dishonor my family, to put aside what means most to me."

Dougless put her hands over her face. "Don't, please. I can't bear this. I never meant—"

He sat on the edge of the bed and pulled her hands away. "Do you have any idea how much I dread the morrow? That I dread the woman I must make my wife? Were I free, were I in your time, I could freely choose where I love. But here and now I cannot. Were I to marry you, I could not feed you. Kit would no longer give me a place to live, food to eat, clothes to—"

"Kit's not like that. Surely there would be a way for us to live. You help Kit with the estates, he'd not throw you out, he'd—"

Nicholas's hands tightened on her wrists. "Can you not hear? Can you not understand? I *must* make this marriage."

"No," she whispered. "No."

"You cannot stop what must be. You can only help me."

"How? How can I help you? Can I stop an axe-man's blade?"

"Aye," he said. "You can. You can stay by me for always."

"Always? While you live with another woman? Sleep with her? Make love to her?"

He released her hands. "So you do this," he said, looking at her bare shoulders above the sheet. "You would take yourself from me for all eternity rather than see me with another woman?"

"No, that's not it. It's just that Lettice is evil. I've told you what she'll do. Choose another woman."

He gave a smile that had no mirth in it. "You would allow me another wife? Allow me to touch another woman when I cannot touch you? You are willing to stand to one side for the rest of our lives?"

Dougless swallowed. Could she live in the same house with him while he lived with another woman? What would she do, be a maiden aunt to Nicholas's children? How would she feel when, each night, he went off to bed with another woman? And how long would he continue to love her if he couldn't touch her? Were either of them strong enough for platonic love?

"I don't know," she said softly. "I don't know if I could stand by and see you with another woman. Nicholas, oh Nicholas, I don't know what to do."

He sat on the bed beside her and gathered her into his arms. "I will not risk losing you for a hundred women like Lettice. You are worth all to me. God has sent you to me and I mean to hold you to me."

She put her head on his chest, parting the robe so her cheek was on his skin. In spite of herself, tears came to her eyes. "I am frightened. Lettice is—"

"A mere woman. No more, no less. She possesses no great wisdom, no amulets of power. If you are by me she can do me or my family no harm."

"By you?" Her hand went under his robe, touching his skin. "Can I stay by you and not touch you?"

He removed her roaming fingers from inside his robe. "You are sure you will return if I . . ."

"Sure," she answered firmly. "At least I *think* I'm sure."

He held her fingers up and looked at them as a starving man might look at a feast. "It would be much to lose were we to try, would it not?"

"Yes," she said, sadly. "Much, much too much."

He dropped her hand. "You must go. I am a man and you tempt me more than I can bear."

Dougless knew she should go but she hesitated. Once again she put her hand on Nicholas's skin.

"Go!" he commanded.

Quickly, she rolled away from him and ran from the room. She went back to Honoria's room and slipped into bed, but she didn't sleep.

Tomorrow the man she loved, no, more than loved, the man who meant so much that even time could not separate them, was leaving to marry another woman. What was she to do when Nicholas returned with his beautiful wife? (Dougless had heard so much of Lettice's beauty that Dougless would have hated the woman even if she knew nothing else about her.) Should she curtsy and congratulate her? Something like, "Hope you enjoy him. Is he as good a lover with you as he was with me?"

Dougless had a vision of Nicholas and his pretty wife laughing together over some private joke. She saw Nicholas sweeping Lettice into his arms and carrying her off to the room they shared. Would they put their heads together over meals and smile at each other?

Dougless slammed her fist into the pillow and made Honoria stir. Men were such fools. They never saw past a pretty face. When a man asked about a woman, all he wanted to know was how pretty she was. No man ever asked if a woman had morals, whether she was honest, kind, did she like children or not? Dougless imagined a beautiful Lettice torturing a puppy in front of Nicholas, but Nicholas not noticing because dear, luscious Lettice had looked at him through fluttering lashes.

"Men!" Dougless muttered, but even as she said it, she didn't mean it. Nicholas had not allowed himself to be seduced tonight because he was afraid he'd lose Dougless. If that wasn't love, what was?

"Maybe he was saving himself for Lettice," Dougless said into the pillow and began to cry.

The sun came up and still Dougless cried. It was as if she couldn't stop. Honoria did everything she could to cheer Dougless but nothing worked.

Dougless could see, hear, think of nothing else but Nicholas and the beautiful woman he was to marry. She had choices, hideous, nonchoices the mere thought of which made her cry harder. She could stay in the sixteenth century and watch Nicholas with his wife, watch them talking together, watch while Lettice was given an honored place in the family as a son's wife. Or she could demand that Nicholas give up his wife or Dougless would leave. And what would she do? How could she earn her living in the sixteenth century? Drive a taxi? Maybe become an executive secretary? She was rather good with computers. She'd been in the Elizabethan age long enough to see how well a lone woman would fare without a man. She couldn't even so much as ride two miles from the house without fear of being set upon by thieves.

And even if she could leave him, that would mean he'd fall into the hands of the scheming Lettice.

What else might she do if she couldn't leave and she couldn't stay? She could work harder at seducing Nicholas and then, after one lovely night of passion, she could return to the twentieth century. Without Nicholas. Alone. Never to see him again. She imagined herself at home in Maine, sitting by herself and thinking that she would give all she possessed to see Nicholas, to speak to him again. She wouldn't care if he were with a hundred women if she could just see him one more time.

"Women's lib doesn't cover this situation," she said through her tears. Women's lib said you weren't supposed to let your guy have affairs, so she guessed she certainly wasn't supposed to let him *marry* someone else.

It was all or nothing. To have Nicholas she had to share him, share him physically, mentally, share him every way possible. To leave him meant absolute, eternal loneliness for Dougless, and possibly death for Nicholas and his family.

Every thought she had made her cry harder. Days went by and still she cried. Honoria made sure that Dougless was dressed each day and she tried to see that she ate, but Dougless couldn't eat. She didn't care about eating or sleeping. Her mind was on Nicholas alone.

At first the other people in the Stafford household were sympathetic to Dougless's tears. They knew why she cried. They had seen the way she and Nicholas looked at each other, the way they touched. Some of them sighed and remembered their first loves. They felt for Dougless when Nicholas went off to be married and Dougless cried in heartbroken grief. But their sympathy wore thin when Dougless's tears went on day after day after day. They began to ask themselves what good the woman was. Lady Margaret had given Dougless everything but now Dougless gave nothing in return. Where were the new games, the new songs the woman should be providing?

On the fourth day, Lady Margaret called Dougless to her.

Dougless, weak from fasting and endless tears, stood before Lady Margaret, her head down, her cheeks wet, her face swollen and red.

Lady Margaret was silent for a moment as she looked at Dougless's bent head, heard the soft weeping. "Cease!" Lady Margaret commanded. "I am most tired of your tears."

"I can't," Dougless said, hiccuping. "I can't seem to stop."

Lady Margaret grimaced. "Have you no spine? My son was a fool to believe himself to love you."

"I agree. I'm not worthy of him."

Lady Margaret sat down and contemplated Dougless's bent head. She knew her younger son very well, knew that this woman's tears would wrench his too-soft heart. Already Nicholas was believing he could not do his duty and marry the Culpin woman. How would their marriage fare if he returned and found this strange red-haired wench crying for love of him? Lady Margaret had always been able to reason with Kit, but Nicholas, like his father, had a stubborn streak. She did not think Nicholas would do it, but what if he returned, saw the red-eyed face of this Dougless, and attempted to set his marriage aside?

Lady Margaret continued to look at the bent head before her. The woman *must* go. Yet why did she hesitate? For that matter, why had she allowed this woman into the Stafford house? At first Nicholas had been enraged that his mother had so trusted the oddly dressed, oddly spoken young woman enough to take an unknown tablet from her. Yet Lady Margaret had taken one look at her face and she *had* trusted. Trusted her with her life.

Nicholas had been so angry after that. Lady Margaret smiled in memory. It seemed that Nicholas had locked the girl in a filthy cell at the top of the house and she'd stayed up there, eaten by fleas, while Lady Margaret had argued with her son over the woman. Nicholas had wanted to toss her into the road, and, in truth, Lady Margaret had known he was right. But something prevented her, something inside her made her refuse to throw the girl out.

It was Nicholas who had gone to get the girl. He had been "trying to reason" with his mother (what he called his stubborn insistence that he was always right) when, abruptly, he got up, left the room, and went to fetch the girl.

Lady Margaret smiled broader when she thought of the girl's absurd story of being a princess from faroff Lanconia. Lady Margaret hadn't believed her for a moment, but the foolish story had given her a reason for keeping the girl near her, against Nicholas's strenuous protests.

Those first days had been divine. The girl was lively and amusing beyond all reasoning. Even her speech was amusing. And her actions never failed to delight, puzzle, fascinate. The girl was stupid about so many things such as dressing, even eating, yet she was clever, very, very clever, about some things. She knew more about medicine than any physician. She told curious stories about the moon and the stars and the earth being round. She had devised a short, wide chair that was stuffed with down and had fabric nailed over it. She called it an "easy chair" and gave it to Lady Margaret. She didn't know it but she had half the household rising early to hide in the gardens and watch her bathing in the fountain, using a marvelous foam on her hair and skin. In private Lady Margaret had inspected the wonders in her bag, had even used the little brush and something called toothpaste.

Oh, the girl was entertaining all right. At one point, Lady Margaret hoped she would never, never leave.

But then Nicholas had fallen in love with her. Lady Margaret had not at first cared. Young men often fell in love. At sixteen Kit had been in love with one of her ladies-in-waiting. Lady Margaret saw that the woman took Kit to bed and taught him a thing or two, and then she'd sent Kit to the kitchens where she knew a voluptuous servant girl was working. Within a week Kit had been "in love" with the serving wench.

Lady Margaret had had no such troubles with Nicholas. Nicholas had never needed an introduction to women. Over the years he had given his body freely, but never his heart.

She should have known that when Nicholas did give his heart he would give it so completely that a hundred voluptuous serving girls would not be able to take it back. At first Lady Margaret had been glad when Nicholas had shown such extraordinary interest in this Dougless Montgomery. Lady Margaret had thought that when Nicholas came back with his bride, since Dougless loved him, the red-haired woman would not be tempted to leave the Stafford household. Lady Margaret would miss the girl's humor and knowledge if she were gone.

But as the days progressed, Lady Margaret refused to see just how attached Nicholas was becoming to her. When at last Lady Margaret had really looked at her household, what she saw did not please her. Her youngest son loved the woman to the point of obsession. Her eldest son spoke of giving the girl great riches, and Kit's future wife talked of little else except what Dougless said or did.

As did the rest of the household speak of her. "Dougless says children should not be swaddled." "Dougless says the wound must be washed." "Dougless says my husband had no right to beat me." "Dougless says a woman should have control of her own money." Dougless says, Dougless says, Lady Margaret thought. Who ran the Stafford household? Did the Staffords or this girl who lied about her relatives?

And now she stood before Lady Margaret weeping, weeping as she had done for days. Lady Margaret clenched her teeth when she thought of how the tears of this one woman were affecting everyone.

But most of all, they affected Nicholas. Nicholas who said he loved her, Nicholas who talked of breaking a betrothal because of this woman who had nothing, who was nothing. Yet this woman, to whom Lady Margaret had given so much, now threatened everything in her family. Were Nicholas to disavow his contract with the Culpin family . . . No, she did not like to think what could happen.

The red-haired woman *must* go.

Lady Margaret's face set into a firm, hard line. "The runner has come from Lanconia. You are no princess. You are related to no one in the royal house. Who are you?"

"J-just a woman. No one special," Dougless said, sniffing.

"We have given you all that our house has to offer and you have lied to us."

"Yes, I have." Dougless kept her head down, agreeing with everything she said. There was nothing anyone could say to make her feel worse. The marriage was to take place this morning. Today Nicholas would marry his beautiful Lettice.

Lady Margaret took a breath. "On the morrow you will leave us. You will take what clothes you came in, no more, and you will be sent forever from the Stafford house."

It took a moment for Dougless to understand. She looked at Lady Margaret, blinking at her through tear-filled eyes. "Leave? But Nicholas wishes me to stay, to be here when he returns."

"Do you think his wife will wish to see you? My foolish son has grown too attached to you. You do him harm."

"I would *never* harm Nicholas. I came here to save him, not to hurt him."

Lady Margaret glared at her. "From whence do you come? Where did you live before you came here?"

Dougless clamped her mouth shut. She could say nothing, absolutely nothing. If she told Lady Margaret the truth Dougless's life would be worth nothing and there would never be a chance of her seeing Nicholas again. "I . . . I will provide entertainments," Dougless said, her voice desperate. "I know more songs, more games. And I can tell you many more stories about America. I could tell you about airplanes and automobiles and—"

Lady Margaret put up her hand. "I weary of your amusements. I cannot feed and clothe you. Who are you? A peasant's daughter?"

"My father teaches and I teach too. Lady Margaret, you can't throw me out. I have nowhere to go and Nicholas needs me. I have to protect him as I protected Kit. I saved Kit's life, remember? He offered me a house then. I'll take it now."

"You asked for your reward and received it. Due to you, my son works as a tradesman."

"But—" Dougless put out her hands, pleading.

' "You will go. We harbor no liars here."

"I'll wash dishes," Dougless said, pleading. "I'll be the family physician. I can't do worse than the leeches. I'll—"

"You will *leave!*" Lady Margaret half shouted. Her eyes glistened like precious stones. "I will have you no longer in my house. My son asked to be released from his betrothal for you."

"He did?" Dougless almost smiled. "He never told me."

"You disarray my household. You bewitch my son till he does not know his duty. Be glad I do not have a whip taken to you."

"This is better? Sending me out there into those . . . those people? Sending me away from Nicholas?"

Lady Margaret stood and turned her back on Dougless. "I will not argue with you. Say your farewells this day and on the morrow you will be sent from my house. Now go. I do not wish to see you again."

Numbly, Dougless turned and left the room. Not seeing anything, she made her way back to Honoria's room. Honoria took one look at her face and guessed what was wrong. She had been expecting such a thing.

"Lady Margaret has sent you away?" Honoria whispered.

Dougless nodded.

"Do you have a place to go? One who will take care of you?"

Dougless shook her head. "I will be leaving Nicholas to that evil woman."

"Lady Lettice?" Honoria asked, puzzled. "The woman is cool perhaps, but I do not believe she is evil."

"You don't know her."

"You do?"

"I know a great deal about her. I know what she is going to do."

Honoria had learned to ignore these odd remarks of Dougless's. She thought perhaps that she didn't want to know all there was to know about Dougless. "Where will you go?"

"I have no idea."

"Do you have relatives?"

Dougless gave a weak smile. "Probably. I imagine there are some six-teenth-century Montgomerys about somewhere."

"But you do not know them?"

"I only know Nicholas." Nicholas, who was now, no doubt, married. She had thought she had choices, that she could choose to stay or go, but now it looked as if her fate were being decided for her. "I know Nicholas and I know what will happen," she said tiredly.

"You shall go to my family," Honoria said firmly. "They will love your games and songs. They will care for you."

Dougless managed a bit of a smile. "That's very kind of you, but if I can't stay with Nicholas I don't want to stay here at all."

Honoria's face whitened. "Suicide is against God."

"God," Dougless whispered and tears came to her eyes. "God did this to me and now it's all going wrong." She closed her eyes. "Please," she whispered, eyes closed. "Please, Nicholas, don't marry her. I beg you, please."

Honoria, concerned, went to Dougless, felt her forehead. "You are warm. This day you must remain in bed. You are ill."

"I am past ill," Dougless said as she allowed Honoria to push her down on the bed. She barely felt Honoria's hands unfastening the front of her dress as she closed her eyes.

Hours later she opened her eyes to see a darkened room. She was in Honoria's bed, wearing only her linen gown, her hair down. Her pillow was wet so she knew she had been crying while she slept.

"Nicholas," she whispered. Married now. Married to the woman who would kill him, who would eventually kill all the Staffords. She closed her eyes again. When she awoke again it was night outside and the room was very dark. Honoria was asleep beside her.

Something is wrong, Dougless thought. Very wrong. She remembered Lady Margaret telling her she must leave the Stafford family, but there was something else.

"Nicholas," she whispered. "Nicholas needs me."

She got out of bed and went into the hall. All was quiet. Barefoot, she went down the stairs, her feet moving about under the dried river rushes on the floor. She went out the back toward the garden, following where instinct and some indefinable pull led her.

She went across the brick terrace, down the stairs, along the raised walk, and turned into the knot garden. There was only a quarter-moon and it was very dark, but she didn't need to see, for she had an inner sight.

As she approached the garden, she heard the fountain splashing, the fountain where she had showered each morning until Nicholas left. She had not been outside since Nicholas rode away.

There, standing in the fountain, his body unclothed, covered with soap lather, was Nicholas.

Dougless didn't think, used no reason. One minute she was outside the fountain and the next she was in Nicholas's wet arms, holding him, kissing him with all the desperation and fear that she felt.

Everything happened too suddenly for her to stop and think. She was in his arms; they were on the ground; she was nude. They came together with a clash of pent-up desire that made Dougless scream. Nicholas, not gently, no, not gentle at all, bent her body backward over a stone bench and rammed into her with blinding force. Dougless, holding on to his shoulders, her nails digging into his skin, put her legs about his waist, and held on.

Fast, furious, frantic, they tore at each other. Their bodies, covered with sweat, stuck together as they rose and fell together, again, again, again.

When at last they finished, Nicholas put his strong hands under her and lifted her to meet his final deep, deep thrust. Dougless cried out as the world darkened and her body stiffened as she found release.

It was a while before she recovered herself and could see again, think again. Nicholas was grinning at her, his teeth white. Even in the darkness she could see his happiness.

But Dougless was beginning to think. "What have we done?" she whispered.

Nicholas unwrapped her legs from his body and pulled her to stand before him. "We have only just begun."

She was blinking at him, trying to make her mind work because her body was trembling at the touch of him. The tips of her breasts were touching his chest and they were tingling. "Why are you here? Oh, God, Nicholas, what have we done?" She started to sit on the bench but he pulled her into his arms.

"There will be time for words," he said. "Now I will do what I have much wanted to do."

"No," she said and pushed away from him. She was fumbling about for the remnants of her gown. "We have to talk now. There will be no more time. Nicholas!" Her voice was rising. "We will have *no more time!*"

He pulled her back to him. "You do still insist you will disappear? Here, look you, we have tasted—merely tasted—of one another and you do remain."

How could she tell him? She collapsed on the bench, her head down. "I knew you were here. I felt you. And just as I knew you needed me, I know that this is our last night together."

Nicholas didn't speak, but after a moment he sat down on the bench beside her, very close, but not touching her. "I have always felt you," he said softly. "This night you heard my call but it has always been so with me.

After I left I . . ." He paused. "I felt your tears. I could hear nothing else but your weeping. I could not see Lettice for seeing you in your tears."

He put his hand out and took hers. "I left the woman. I said naught, not even to Kit. I took my horse and rode. When I should have been saying vows I was riding to you. It took until now to reach you."

This is what she had wanted, but now that it was here, the enormity of what he'd done scared her. She looked at him. "What will happen now?"

"There will be . . . anger," he said, "anger on both sides. Kit . . . My mother will . . ." He looked away.

Dougless could see how torn he was between duty and love. And now she wouldn't be here to help him. She squeezed his hand. "You will not marry her even after I'm gone?"

He turned blazing eyes toward her. "You would leave me now?"

Tears came again to her eyes as she flung herself against him. "I would *never* leave you if I had a choice, but I don't, not now. Now there is no choice. I will go soon, I know it. I can feel it."

He kissed her, then smoothed her hair back. "How much time?" he whispered.

"Dawn, I think. No more. Nicholas, I—"

He silenced her with a kiss. "I would rather hours with you than a lifetime with another. Now, no more talk. Come, we will love away these hours."

He stood and pulled her up beside him and led her into the still-running fountain, where he began to soap her with the last of her soft soap. "You left it behind," he said, smiling at her.

Forget that this is the end, Dougless thought. Forget it. Time *must* stand still for this one night. "How did you kn-know I showered here?" she said, her voice stumbling.

"I was one of those who watched."

She stopped soaping herself and Nicholas's hands stilled at her look. "Watched? Who watched me?"

"All," he said, grinning. "Did you not notice the men's yawns? They rose most early to hide themselves."

"Hide!" Her anger was rising. "And you were one of them? You *allowed* this? You let men spy on me?"

"Were I to stop you I would have halted my own pleasure. It was a dilemma."

"Dilemma! Why you—!" She lunged at him.

Nicholas sidestepped, then caught her, pulling her close to him. He forgot about soaping her as he bent his head and began kissing her breasts, the water pouring down on top of them. "I have dreamed of this," he said, "since my vision."

"The shower," she murmured. "The shower." Her hands were entangled in his hair as his mouth moved lower and lower. He was on his knees before her. "Nicholas, my Nicholas."

They made love again, as they had once done, in the water. For Nicholas it was a discovery of her body, but for Dougless, she had had months of remembering and wanting. Her hands were all over him, memorizing, remembering, finding new places she had not touched or tasted before.

By the time they finished it was hours later. The water had stopped flowing. She and Nicholas lay in each other's arms on the sweet grass.

"We have to talk," she said at last.

"Nay, do not."

She snuggled closer to him. "I must. I wish with all my heart that I didn't have to speak but I must."

"On the morrow, when the sun touches your hair, you will laugh at this. You are no woman from the future. You are here with me now. You will remain with me for all time."

"I wish . . ." Her voice grew hoarse and she swallowed. Her hand was roaming over his body, touching him. The last time. The last time. "Nicholas, please," she said. "Listen to me."

"Aye, I will listen, then I will love you again."

"When you left before no one remembered you. It was as if you hadn't existed. It was so horrible for me." She buried her face in his shoulder. "You had come and gone, but no one remembered. It was as if I'd made you up."

"I am most forgettable."

She raised on her elbow to look at him, to touch his beard, his cheek, to caress his eyebrows, to kiss his eyelids. "I will never forget you."

"Nor I you." He lifted a bit to kiss her lips and when he wanted more, Dougless pulled away.

"The same may happen when I leave. I want you to be prepared if no one remembers me. Don't . . . I don't know, don't make yourself crazy trying to make them remember."

"No one will forget."

"They probably will. What if the songs I taught you are remembered? It could ruin some very good Broadway shows in the twentieth century." She tried to smile but didn't quite make it. "I want you to swear some things to me."

"I will not marry Lettice. I doubt now I will be asked again," he said sarcastically.

"Good. Oh, very, very good. Now I won't have to read about your execution." She ran her fingertips over his neck. "Promise me you'll take care of James. No more swaddling, and play with him sometimes."

He kissed her fingertips and nodded.

"Take care of Honoria, she's been so good to me."

"I will find her the best of husbands."

"Not the richest, the *best*. Promise?" When he nodded, she went on. "And anyone who's delivering a baby has to wash his or her hands first. And you have to build Thornwyck and leave records that *you* designed it. I want history to know."

He was smiling at her. "Naught else? You will have to remain by my side to remind me of all this."

"I would," she whispered. "I would but I cannot. May I have the miniature of you?"

"You may have my heart, my soul, my life."

She clasped his head in her arms. "Nicholas, I can't bear it."

"There is naught bad to bear," he said, kissing her arm, her shoulder, his lips traveling downward. "Perhaps Kit will give me a small estate and we—"

She pulled away to look at him. "Wrap the miniature up in oiled cloth, something that will protect it over the next four hundred years, and put it behind the . . . What's the stone thing that holds up the beams?"

"A corbel."

"At Thornwyck you'll make a corbel that's a portrait of Kit. Wrap the miniature and put it behind the corbel. When I . . . when I return I'll go get it."

He was kissing her breast.

"Did you hear me?"

"I heard all. James. Honoria. Midwives. Thornwyck. Kit's face." He punctuated each word with a little kiss on her breast. "Now, my love," he whispered, "come to me."

He lifted her body and set her down on top of him, and Dougless forgot anything else on earth except the touch of this man she loved so much. He stroked her hips, her breasts as they moved together. Up and down. Slowly at first and then building faster.

Nicholas rolled with her until she was on her back and his passion rose as he entered her deeply, her body rising to meet his. They arched together, both with their heads back, then they collapsed, Nicholas on top of her, holding her very tightly.

"I love you," he whispered. "I will love you for all time."

Dougless clung to him, holding him as tightly as she could. "You will remember me? You won't forget me?"

"Never," he said. "Never will I forget you. Were I to die tomorrow my soul would remember you."

"Don't speak of death. Speak only of life. With you I am alive. With you I am whole."

"And I you." He rolled to one side and pulled her close to him. "Look you. The sun comes up."

"Nicholas, I'm afraid."

He stroked her damp hair. "Afraid of being seen so unclad? It is not something we have not seen before."

"You!" she said, laughing. "I'll never forgive you for not telling me."

"I will have a lifetime in which to make you forgive me."

"Yes," she whispered. "Yes. It will take a lifetime."

He glanced at the lightening sky. "We must go. I must tell my mother what I have done. Kit will no doubt be here soon."

"They will be angry, very angry. And my part in this won't help matters any."

"You must go to Kit with me. I will be shameless. I will tell my brother he needs must give us a place to live in memory of saving him."

Dougless looked up at the sky, growing lighter by the minute. She could almost believe she was going to be able to stay with him. "We'll live in a pretty little house somewhere," she said, her words beginning to gain speed. "We'll have only a few servants, fifty or so," she said, smiling. "And we'll have a dozen kids. I like kids. And we'll educate them properly and teach them how to wash. Maybe we can invent a flush toilet."

Nicholas chuckled. "You wash too much. My sons will not—"

"*Our* sons. I'm going to have to explain to you about women's lib."

He stood up and pulled her up into his arms. "Will it take long?"

"About four hundred years," she whispered.

"Then I will give you the time."

"Yes," she said, smiling. "Time. We will have all the time we need."

He kissed her then, kissed her long and hard and deeply, and then his kiss lightened. "Forever," he whispered. "I will love you throughout time."

One moment Dougless was in his arms, his lips on hers, and the next she was in the church at Ashburton, and outside a jet flew overhead.

20

Dougless didn't cry. What she was feeling was too deep, too profound for her to cry. She was sitting on the floor in the little church in Ashburton, and she knew that behind her was Nicholas's marble tomb. She couldn't bear to look at it, to see the warm flesh of Nicholas translated into cold marble.

She sat where she was for a while and looked at the church. It looked so old and so plain. There was no color on the beams or on the walls, and the stone floors looked bare with no rushes on them. In the first pews were some needlepointed pillows and, to Dougless, they looked crude. She was used to seeing the exquisite needlework of Lady Margaret's women.

The door of the church opened and the vicar came in. Dougless remained where she was.

"Are you all right?" the vicar asked.

At first Dougless couldn't understand him. His accent, his pronunciation were foreign-sounding. "How long have I been here?" she asked.

The vicar frowned at this young woman who was so very strange. She walked in front of speeding vehicles, she insisted she was with a man when she was alone, and now, just after entering the church, she was asking how long she had been here. "A few minutes, no more," he answered.

Dougless gave a weak smile. A few minutes. Weeks in the sixteenth century and she had been away a few minutes only. When she tried to stand, her legs were weak and the vicar helped her rise.

"Perhaps you should see a doctor," the vicar said.

A psychiatrist perhaps, Dougless almost answered. If she told her story to a psychiatrist, would he write a book and turn what happened to Dougless into a movie-of-the-week? "No, I'm fine, really," she whispered. "I just need to get back to my hotel and—" And what? What was there for her to do now that Nicholas was gone? She took a step to leave.

"Don't forget your bag."

Dougless turned back to see her old tote bag on the floor by the tomb. The contents of that bag had helped her throughout her time in the Elizabethan age. Looking at it, she felt a closeness to the bag. It had been wherever she had been. She went to it and on impulse unzipped the top of it. She didn't have to inspect the contents to know that everything was there. The bottle of aspirin was full, none of the pills she had given away were missing. Her toothpaste tube was full, not flat. No cold tablets were missing, no pages gone from her notebook. Everything was as it had been.

She lifted the tote bag, slung the strap onto her shoulder, and turned away. But abruptly she halted, then turned on her heel, and looked back at the base of the tomb. Something was different. She wasn't at first sure what it was, but something had changed.

Careful not to look at the sculpture of Nicholas, she stared at the base.

"Is something wrong?" the vicar asked.

Dougless read the inscription twice before she realized what was different. "The date," she whispered.

"The date? Ah, yes, the tomb is quite old."

Nicholas's death date was 1599. *Not* 1564. She bent and touched the numbers, trying to make sure she was seeing correctly. Thirty-five years. He had lived thirty-five years past when he was supposed to have been executed.

It was only after she had touched the date that she looked up at the tomb. The sculpture was of Nicholas but it was very different now. It was not of a young man, dead in his prime, but of an older one, a man who had been able to live out his life. She looked down the length of him, saw that his clothes were different, the longer knee breeches of 1599, instead of the short slops of thirty years earlier.

She caressed his cold cheek, traced the lines the sculptor had put at the corners of his eyes. "We did it," she whispered. "Nicholas, my love, we did it."

"I beg your pardon," the vicar said.

Dougless looked up at him and gave him a dazzling smile. "We changed history," she said and, still smiling, she walked outside into the sunshine.

She stood in the graveyard for a moment, feeling disoriented. The gravestones were so old, yet before her whizzed a car. Dougless gasped in horror at the first sight of a car. As she gasped she felt her lungs expand. For a moment she had a deep sense of everything being wrong. She felt naked and drab in her plain clothes. She looked down at her boring skirt and blouse with distaste. Her back felt as if it had nothing to support it now that her corset was gone, and her leather boots pinched her feet.

Another car went by and the speed of it made Dougless feel dizzy. She walked to the gate, opened it, and stepped onto the sidewalk. How odd to have concrete under her feet. As she walked she looked with awe at the buildings about her. Huge expanses of glass. Shop signs with writing on them. Who can read them? she thought, remembering that where she had been few people could read, so signs were painted pictures of what was sold in the shops.

How clean everything was, she thought. No mud, no chamberpot empty-ings, no kitchen slops, no pigs foraging. The people in the street were odd-looking, too. They all wore the same drab clothes as she did. And they all seemed to be equal, no beggars dressed in filthy rags, no ladies with pearls on their skirts.

Dougless slowly walked down the street, staring wide-eyed as if she'd never seen the twentieth century before. The smell of food made her turn and enter a pub. For a moment she stood in the doorway and looked. The place was obviously supposed to be a facsimile of an Elizabethan tavern, but it missed by a long way. It was too clean, too quiet, too . . . lonely, she thought. The people sitting at the tables were isolated from one another. Not at all like the gregarious, nosy Elizabethans.

At the back of the pub was a chalkboard with the menu on it. She ordered six courses, taking no notice of the waitress's raised eyebrows, and went to a table to sit down and sip her beer. The thick glass mug felt odd and the beer tasted as if it were half water.

She pulled her tote bag onto the bench beside her and began to rummage in it. In the bottom was her guidebook to the historic houses of Great Britain. Bellwood was in there and it was open to the public, just as it had been before. She looked for Nicholas's other houses. No longer were they listed as being ruins. All eleven of the houses Nicholas had once owned were still standing. *And three of them were owned by the Stafford family.*

Dougless blinked her eyes and reread the passage. The guidebook said that the Stafford family was one of the oldest and wealthiest in England, that in the seventeenth century they had married into the royal family, and that the present duke was a cousin to the queen.

"Duke," Dougless whispered. "Nicholas, your descendants are dukes."

The food came and Dougless was a bit startled at the way it was served, without ceremony, all the dishes put on the table at once.

She began to eat and kept reading the guidebook. Except for Bellwood, all Nicholas's houses were private residences and not open to the public. She turned to Thornwyck. It too was a private residence, but a small section of it was open to the public on Thursdays. "The current duke feels that the beauty of Thornwyck, designed by his ancestor, the brilliant scholar Nicholas Stafford, must be shared with the world," she read.

"Brilliant scholar," she whispered. Not the ladies' man he had once been called. Not a rogue, not a wastrel, but a "brilliant scholar."

She closed the guidebook and looked up. The waitress was hovering over her with an odd expression on her face.

"Something was wrong with your fork?" she asked.

"Fork?" Dougless couldn't think what the woman was talking about. She continued to stare at Dougless until Dougless looked down at her empty plate. There beside it lay an unused fork. Dougless had eaten her meal with a spoon and a knife. "It's all right, I just—" She couldn't think of what to say so she gave the woman a weak smile and looked at the bill. The amount —enough to buy a hundred medieval dinners—made her blanch, but she paid it.

Outside again, she didn't allow herself to stand still. If she stayed in one place too long, she knew she'd start to think, to think about Nicholas, about losing him, about never seeing him again.

She practically ran to the train station to catch the first train to Bellwood. She had to see what had changed. On the train ride she made herself read the guidebook, anything to fill her mind.

By now she knew the way to Bellwood from the train station very well. According to the twentieth-century time she had visited the house only the day before—the day when she'd heard of Nicholas's execution. The guide then hadn't been very pleasant, after all, she remembered Dougless as having set off the alarmed door, thus disturbing her tour.

Dougless bought her ticket and guidebook for the tour and when she got in line, the same guide was at the head.

In the house, Dougless, after having once thought the house was so beautiful, now saw it as bare and drab and lifeless. There were no plates of gold and silver on the hearths, no exquisite needlework on the tables, no cushions on the chairs. But most of all there were no richly dressed people moving about, no people laughing, and no music anywhere.

They arrived at Nicholas's room before Dougless could recover from her distaste of the barren house. Dougless stood to one side, looked up at Nicholas's portrait, and listened to the guide. The story was different now, very, very different.

The guide could not use enough superlatives when describing Nicholas.

"He was a true Renaissance man," the guide told them, "the epitome of what his era hoped to achieve. He designed beautiful houses that were a hundred years ahead of his time. He made great advances in the field of medicine, writing a book on disease prevention that, had it been adhered to, would have saved thousands of lives."

"What did the book say?" Dougless asked.

The guide gave her a hard look, obviously remembering the door-opening incident. "Basically, that doctors and midwives should wash their hands. Now, if you'll follow me, we shall see—"

Dougless left the tour after that, went out the entrance, and walked to the library. The librarian looked up at her and smiled. "The Stafford collection?"

"Yes," Dougless answered. To these people not twenty-four hours had passed since she'd visited this town.

She spent the afternoon reading the history books. Every scrap of information was different now. She saw the names of people she had known and come to love. They were just names in history books to other readers, but to her they were flesh-and-blood people.

After three husbands, Lady Margaret never again married, and she lived into her seventies.

Kit married little Lucy, and one book said Lucy became a great benefactress who encouraged musicians and artists. Kit had run the Stafford estates well, until he died of a stomach ailment at age forty-two. Since he and Lucy had had no children, the earldom and estates went to Nicholas.

As she read about Nicholas, she touched the printed words as if they would make him seem closer. When she read that Nicholas had never married, quick tears came to her eyes, but she blinked them away.

Nicholas had lived to the grand old age of sixty-two, and during his life he had done many great things. The books went into detail about the beauty and creativity of the buildings he had designed. "His use of glass was far ahead of its time," one author wrote.

One book told about Nicholas's ideas of medicine, how he had crusaded on cleanliness. "Had his advice been taken," the author said, "modern medicine would have had its start hundreds of years earlier."

"Far ahead of his time," the books said again and again.

She leaned back in her chair. No Arabella-on-the-table. No telltale diary about what a womanizer Nicholas was. No betrayal. No conspiracy between his wife and his friend. And, most important, no execution.

She left when the library closed, walked to the station, and took a train back to Ashburton. She still had a room at the hotel and her clothes were there.

Once in her hotel room, she had difficulty adjusting to the modernness of it, especially the bathroom. She took a shower but couldn't bear the hot water or the hard, sharp forcefulness of the showerhead. She turned the cold on, turned the water to a drizzle and felt more at home.

The flushing of the toilet seemed like a waste of water to her, and she kept staring at the big mirror in wonder.

After a room-service supper, she put on her flimsy nightgown and felt like a lewd woman. And when she went to bed, she felt lonely without Honoria beside her.

Surprisingly, she went to sleep immediately and if she dreamed she did not remember doing so.

In the morning she had difficulty with the hotel when she ordered beef and beer for breakfast, but the English, better than any other people on earth, understand eccentrics.

She reached Thornwyck by ten A.M., just as the gates were opening. She bought a ticket and started on the tour. The guide talked at length about the Stafford family, who still owned the house, and especially about the brilliant Nicholas Stafford.

"He never married," the guide said with twinkling eyes, "but he had a son named James. When Nicholas's older brother died and left no children, Nicholas inherited, and when Nicholas died, the Stafford estates went to James."

Dougless smiled, remembering the sweet little boy she had played with.

The guide continued. "James made a brilliant marriage and tripled the family fortunes. It was through James that the Stafford family really made its money."

And he would have died if Dougless had not intervened.

The guide went on to the next generation of the family and the next room, but Dougless slipped away. When she'd seen Thornwyck before, it had been half in ruins and Nicholas had shown her the corbel of Kit's face high on the wall of what would have been the second floor. Unfortunately, the second floor was not open to the public.

She opened a door that said NO ADMITTANCE, and found herself in a small sitting room furnished in English chintz. Feeling like a spy, but also knowing she had to do what she did, she went to the doorway and peeped out. The hall was clear so she tiptoed down it, thinking that rugs on the floor made sneaking much easier than noisy rushes.

She found a staircase and went up to the second floor. Twice she had to hide when she heard footsteps, but no one saw her. In Nicholas's house there were so many servants that it would have been impossible for an intruder to get to the second floor unnoticed, but those days were long gone.

Once on the second floor she had trouble orienting herself, as she tried to remember just where the corbel would be. She searched three rooms before she entered a bedroom and saw it, high above a beautiful walnut wardrobe.

She plastered herself between the wardrobe and the wall as a maid walked out of the adjoining bath. Dougless held her breath as the maid checked the bedspread, then left the room.

Alone again, Dougless went to work. She pulled a heavy chair beside the wardrobe, climbed on it, then, after three tries, managed to achieve the top of the wardrobe. She had just put her hand on the old stone corbel when the door opened. Dougless flattened herself against the wall.

The maid came in again, this time with an armload of towels. Dougless didn't breathe until the woman left.

When the door closed, Dougless turned and touched Kit's stone face. The stonework looked to be solid. She wished she'd had the foresight to bring a screwdriver or small crowbar. She pulled and tugged at the face and was almost ready to give up when the stone moved in her hand.

She broke her nails and skinned her knuckles, but she was at last able to pull the face away. A long piece of stone protruded from the back of the face and fit neatly into the corbel.

Standing on tiptoe, Dougless looked behind the head. Inside a hollowed-out place was a cloth-wrapped package. Quickly, she took it, slipped it into her pocket, shoved the corbel back into place, and climbed down. She didn't take the time to put the chair back as she hurried from the room.

She made it, without being seen, back to the tour just as the group was in its last room.

"And here we have the lace display," the guide was saying. "Most of the lace is Victorian, but we do have a very special piece of lace from the sixteenth century."

Dougless gave the guide all of her attention.

"It seems that although Lord Nicholas Stafford of the sixteenth century never married, there was a mysterious woman in his past. On his deathbed he asked to be buried with this piece of lace, but there was some confusion and Lord Nicholas went to his grave without the lace. His son James said the lace was always to be kept in a place of honor in the family, since it had meant so much to his beloved father."

Dougless had to wait for the other tourists to move before she could see into the case. There, under glass, yellowed now and worn-looking, was the lace cuff Honoria had been making for her. The name Dougless was worked into it.

"Dougless?" a tourist said, laughing. "Maybe ol' Nick didn't marry because he was a little"—he waved his hand—"you know."

Dougless spoke before the guide could. "For your information, Dougless was a woman's name in the sixteenth century, and I can assure you that Nicholas was *not* a little"—she glared at him—"you know." She stormed past him and left the house.

She walked into the gardens, and, while the other tourists exclaimed over their beauty, Dougless thought the gardens looked messy and neglected. She went to a quiet corner, sat on a bench, and took the package from her pocket.

Slowly, she unwrapped it. Touching the waxed cloth bindings, which had last been touched by Nicholas so long ago, made her fingers tremble.

The miniature portrait of Nicholas came to light, as rich and bright as the day it had been painted. "Nicholas," she whispered and put her fingertips on the painting. "Oh, Nicholas, have I truly lost you so completely? Are you gone from me forever?"

She looked at the miniature, touched it, and when she turned it over, she saw something engraved on the back. She held it up to the light to read it.

> Time has no meaning
> Love will endure

He had signed it with an *N*, a *D* over the top of it.

She leaned her head back against the old stone wall and blinked away tears. "Nicholas, come back to me," she whispered. "Please come back to me."

She sat there for a long time before she rose. She'd missed lunch, but she went to the tea shop and sat down with a plate of scones and a pot of strong black tea with milk. She had bought a guidebook at Bellwood and one at Thornwyck and, as she ate and drank, she read.

With every word she told herself that what had happened had been worth the pain of losing the man she loved. What did the love between two people matter when, by giving up their love, they had changed history? Kit had lived, Lady Margaret had lived, James had lived, Nicholas had lived. And with the lives, the family honor had been saved, so that today a Stafford was a duke and part of the royal family.

Against all that, what did one piddling little love affair mean?

She left the tea shop and walked to the train station. She could go home now, home to America, home to her family. No more would she be an outsider, and never again would she have to pretend to be someone she was not.

On the train ride back to Ashburton, she told herself she should be jubilant. She and Nicholas had accomplished so much. How many other people had the good fortune to be able to change history? Yet Dougless had been given that opportunity. Through her efforts the Stafford family was still flourishing. There were beautiful buildings standing because she had encouraged Nicholas to use his talent for designing. There were . . .

Her thoughts trailed off. It was no use telling herself what she *should* feel, because what she did feel was miserable.

In Ashburton she slowly walked back to the hotel. She'd need to call the airlines and make her reservations.

In the lobby, Robert and Gloria were waiting for her. At the moment she didn't think she could handle a confrontation. She went to stand before Robert. "I'll get the bracelet," she said, then quickly turned away before he could speak.

He caught her arm and halted her. "Dougless, could we talk?"

She stiffened, preparing herself for his abuse. "I told you I'd get the bracelet for you and I apologize for keeping it."

"Please," he said, and his eyes were soft.

Dougless looked at Gloria. Gone from the girl's face was the smug, I'm-going-to-get-you look. Wary, Dougless went to sit in a chair across from father and daughter. Lucy and Robert Sydney, Dougless thought. How much Gloria looked like Kit's bride-to-be and how much this Robert resembled a sixteenth-century Robert. Dougless thought of how she and Nicholas had changed the lives of both of those people. Robert Sydney had been given no reason to hate Nicholas, because Arabella had not been impregnated on a table. And Dougless had helped Lucy gain some self-confidence.

Robert cleared his throat and spoke. "Gloria and I have been talking and we, well, we decided that maybe we weren't quite fair to you."

Dougless stared at him, her eyes wide. At one point in her life she had looked at Robert while wearing a blindfold. She saw only what she wanted to see; she had endowed him with characteristics that he didn't have. Now, looking back at their life together, she saw that he'd never loved her. "What do you want from me?" she asked tiredly.

"We just wanted to apologize," Robert said, "and we'd like for you to join us on the rest of the trip."

"You can sit in the front," Gloria said.

Dougless looked from one to the other, puzzled, not by their words, for Robert would often apologize or do whatever was needed to get her to do what he wanted, but by the sincere looks on their faces. It was almost as if they really meant what they were saying. "No," she said softly, "I'm going home tomorrow."

Robert reached out and took her hand. "Home to my house, I hope." His eyes were bright. "To the house that will be ours as soon as we're married."

"Married?" Dougless whispered.

"Please, Dougless, I'm asking you to marry me. I was a fool not to see how good we were together."

Dougless gave a bit of a smile. Here was what she'd wanted so much: marriage to a respectable, stable man.

She took a deep breath and smiled broader, for suddenly she didn't feel like selling herself so cheaply. She was no longer the baby of the family who wasn't as good as her big sisters. She was a woman who had been transported to another time, and she had not only survived, she had succeeded in accomplishing a monumental task. No longer did she need to prove herself to her too-perfect family by bringing home an achieving husband. No, Dougless was the achiever now.

She picked up Robert's hand and put it back in his lap. "Thanks, but no thanks," she said pleasantly.

"But I thought you wanted to get married." He looked genuinely puzzled.

"And Daddy said I could be your maid of honor," Gloria said.

"When I do get married it will be to someone who wants to give to me," Dougless said, then looked at Gloria. "And I will choose my own bridesmaids."

Gloria turned red and looked down at her hands.

"You've changed, Dougless," Robert said softly.

"I have, haven't I?" Dougless answered, wonder in her voice. "I really, truly have changed." She stood. "I'll get your bracelet now."

She started toward the stairs and Robert followed her, Gloria remaining in the lobby. He didn't speak to her until she unlocked her room and went inside. He followed her and shut the door behind him.

"Dougless, is it someone else?"

She took the diamond bracelet from where she'd hidden it in her suitcase and held it out to him. "There is no one," she said, feeling the loss of Nicholas.

"Not even the guy you said you were helping to research?"

"The research is done and he is . . . gone."

"Permanently?"

"As permanently as time can manage." She looked away a moment, then back at him. "I'm quite tired now and I have a long flight tomorrow so I guess we'd better say goodbye. When I get back to the States I'll clear my things out of your house."

"Dougless, please reconsider. We can't end what we've had because of a little argument. We love each other."

She looked at him and thought how at one time in her life she had thought she loved him. Then their relationship had been one-sided, with Dougless doing all the pleading, all the trying-to-please. "What has changed you?" she asked. "How could you leave me stranded in a foreign country with no money just a few days ago, and now you're here asking me to marry you?"

Robert's face turned a bit red and he looked away sheepishly. "I really do apologize about that." He looked back at her and his face was filled with earnestness and sincerity—and also a little confusion. "It was the oddest thing. You know, all your money used to make me furious. I put myself through med school while living on canned beans, yet you always had everything. You have a family who adores you and a history of wealth that goes back centuries. I hated the way you used to play at living on your teacher's salary, because I knew you could get all the money you ever wanted if you'd just ask. When I left you at that church I knew Gloria had your purse and I was glad. I wanted you to see what it was like to have to survive without money, to have to rely on yourself as I always have."

He took a deep breath and his face softened. "But then yesterday everything changed. Gloria and I were in a restaurant and quite suddenly I wished you were with us. I . . . . I wasn't angry at you anymore. Does that make sense? All the anger I felt for your having been given everything just evaporated. Gone, as if it had never been there."

He went to her, put his hands on her shoulders. "I was a fool to let someone like you get away. If you'll let me I'll spend the rest of my life making it up to you. We don't have to get married if you don't want to. We don't have to live together. I'll . . . . I'll court you if you'll allow me. Court you with flowers and candy and . . . and balloons. What do you say? Give me another chance?"

Dougless stared at him. He said that yesterday his anger had left him. All her days in the sixteenth century had passed in just a few minutes of twentieth-century time, and during her time with Nicholas she had defused the anger of Robert and Gloria's look-alikes. Could this anger of Robert's be based on his bitterness over what had happened in the sixteenth century?

When Robert had first seen Nicholas, he had looked at him with rage. Why? Because Nicholas had once impregnated his wife?

And Gloria seemed to be no longer angry with Dougless. Because Dougless had once helped an earlier incarnation of Gloria?

Dougless gave her head a shake to clear it. *Were I to die tomorrow my soul would remember you,* Nicholas had said. Were Robert and Gloria the souls of people who had lived before?

"Will you give me another chance?" Robert repeated.

Dougless smiled at him and kissed him on the cheek. "No," she said, "although I thank you very much for the offer."

He pulled away from her and Dougless was glad to see he wasn't angry. "Someone else?" he asked again, as if his ego could stand that rejection better than her choosing to have no one rather than him.

"Sort of."

Robert looked at the bracelet in his hand. "If I'd bought an engagement ring instead of this . . . Well, who knows?" He looked back at her. "He's a lucky SOB, whoever he is. I wish you all the luck in the world." He left the room, shutting the door behind him.

Dougless stood in the empty room for a moment, then went to the telephone to call her parents. She wanted to hear the sound of their voices.

Elizabeth answered.

"Are Mother and Dad back yet?" Dougless asked.

"No, they're still at the cabin. Dougless, I demand that you tell me what is going on. If you're in one of your scrapes again, you'd better tell me so I can get you out. You're not in jail this time, are you?"

Dougless was amazed to find that the words of her perfect older sister didn't anger her, nor did they make her feel guilty. "Elizabeth," she said firmly, "I would appreciate it if you didn't speak to me in that manner. I called to tell my family that I am coming home."

"Oh," Elizabeth said, "I didn't mean anything, it's just that usually you're in one mess or another."

Dougless did not speak.

"Okay, I apologize. Would you like me to meet you and Robert, or does he have his car?"

"Robert won't be with me."

"Oh," Elizabeth said again, allowing time for Dougless to explain. When Dougless was silent, Elizabeth went on. "Dougless, we'll all be very glad to see you."

"And I'll be glad to see you. Don't meet me. I'll rent a car and, Elizabeth, I've missed you."

There was a pause, then Elizabeth said, "Come home and I'll cook a celebration dinner."

Dougless groaned. "When did you say Mother was coming home?"

"All right, so I'm not the world's best cook. You cook, I'll clean up the kitchen."

"It's a deal. I'll be there day after tomorrow."

"Dougless!" Elizabeth said. "I've missed you, too."

Dougless put down the telephone and smiled. It seemed that not only had history changed, but so had the present. She knew, felt inside herself, that never again was she going to be the butt of the family's jokes, because no longer did she feel incompetent, as if she couldn't handle her own life.

She called Heathrow, booked her flight, and began to pack.

21

Dougless had to get up very early to catch the train to London and then take a long, expensive taxi ride to the airport. The sense of accomplishment that had sustained her since she'd left the sixteenth century was leaving her. All she felt now was very tired and very alone. She'd fallen in love with Nicholas twice. She remembered when he'd been in the twentieth century and the wonder on his face as he'd touched a book of color photographs. She remembered the way he'd been fascinated with watching the taxi driver shift gears. And the *Playboy* magazine in the drawer at Arabella's!

When she went to the sixteenth century and he hadn't remembered her and he'd seemed to hate her, she had thought he had changed. But he hadn't. He was still the man who put his family before himself, and when he began to include Dougless in his family, he loved her as completely as he did them.

The boarding of the plane was called and Dougless waited until the last moment to get on. Maybe she shouldn't leave England. In England she would be closer to Nicholas. Maybe she should buy a house in Ashburton and visit his tomb every day. Maybe if she prayed enough she would be returned to him.

She tried to control herself, but the tears started anyway. Nicholas was truly and completely gone from her. Never again would she see him, hear him, touch him.

Tears were blinding her so that, as she boarded, she walked into the man in front of her, and her tote bag slid off her shoulder into the lap of a first-class passenger.

"I'm so sorry," she said and looked into the blue eyes of a very handsome man. For a moment her heart pounded, but then she straightened. He wasn't Nicholas; his eyes weren't Nicholas's eyes.

She took her tote bag from the man while he stared up at her with interest. But Dougless wasn't interested. The only man who interested her was sealed inside a marble tomb.

She made her way back to her seat, shoved her tote bag under the seat in front of her and looked out the window. As the plane began to taxi and she realized that she was leaving England, she began to cry. The man in the aisle seat beside her, an Englishman, buried his face deeper into his newspaper.

Dougless tried to make her tears stop. She gave herself little pep talks about how much she'd been able to accomplish, and reminded herself that losing Nicholas was a small price to pay for all the good she had done. But each thought made her cry harder.

By the time the plane was aloft and the FASTEN SEATBELT sign was off, she was crying so hard she didn't see what happened next to her. The man from first class, a champagne bottle and two glasses in his hand, asked the man next to Dougless to exchange seats.

"Here," he said.

She could see through her tears a tall glass of champagne being held out to her.

"Go on, take it. It'll do you good."

"You're an A . . . American," she said through tears.

"I'm from Colorado. And you?"

"M . . . Maine." She took the champagne, drank too fast, and choked. "I . . . I have cousins in Colorado."

"Oh? Where?"

"Chandler." Her tears weren't flowing as fast.

"Not the Taggerts?"

She looked up at him. Black hair and blue eyes. Just like Nicholas. The tears sped up again. She nodded.

"I used to go to Chandler with my father sometimes, and I met the Taggerts. I'm Reed Stanford, by the way." He held out his hand to shake hers, and when she didn't take his hand, he picked hers up. He clasped her hand in his. "Nice to meet you." He held her hand, looking at it, saying nothing, until Dougless snatched it away.

"Sorry," he said.

"Mr.—?"

"Stanford."

"Mr. Stanford," she said, sniffing, "I don't know what I did to give you

the impression that I was an easy pickup, but I can assure you I'm not. I
think you'd better take your champagne and return to your seat." She was
trying to be regal, but it lost something since her nose was red, her eyes
swollen, and tears were running down her cheeks.

He didn't take the glass and he didn't leave.

He was beginning to make Dougless angry. Was he some weirdo who
liked crying females? What in the world had happened in his childhood to
cause him to be turned on by tears? "If you don't leave I'll have to call the
stewardess."

He turned to look at her. "Please don't," he said and there was something in his eyes that made Dougless halt as she reached for the stewardess
call button. "You must believe me, I've never done anything like this in my
life. I mean, I've never accosted a woman on a plane before. Or even in bars
for that matter. It's just that you remind me of someone."

Dougless wasn't crying any longer. There was something familiar in the
way he moved his head. "Who?" she asked.

He gave a little grin and Dougless's heart skipped a beat. Nicholas sometimes grinned like that. "You wouldn't believe me if I told you. It's too
farfetched."

"Try me. I have a lot of imagination."

"All right," he said. "You remind me of a lady in a portrait."

Dougless was listening now.

"When I was a boy, about eleven, I think, my parents and older brother
and I came to England for a year to live. My father had a job here. My
mother used to drag my brother and me to antique stores, and I'm afraid I
wasn't very gracious about going. That is, until one Saturday afternoon
when I saw the portrait."

He paused and refilled Dougless's empty glass. "It was a miniature oil,
done sometime in the sixteenth century and it was of a lady." He looked at
her and in spite of her swollen face, his eyes were almost caressing.

"I wanted that portrait. I can't explain it. It wasn't that I just wanted it, *I
had to have it.*" He smiled. "I'm afraid I wasn't exactly sweet-tempered
about voicing my wants. The portrait was quite expensive and my mother
refused to listen to my demands, but I've never taken no for an answer. The
next Saturday I took the tube, went back to the antique shop, and put
everything I had as a down payment on the portrait. I think it was about
five pounds."

He turned to her and smiled. "Looking back on it I think the old man
who owned the shop thought I wanted to be a collector. I didn't want to
collect; I just wanted *that* portrait."

"Did you get it?" Dougless whispered.

"Oh yes. My parents thought I was crazy and said an Elizabethan miniature was no possession for a child, but when they saw me week after week
putting all my allowance down on it, they began to help me. Then, just
before we left England, when I'd begun to feel I was never going to get
enough money together to buy it, my father drove me to the antique shop
and presented the portrait to me." He sat back in his seat, as if that were
the end of the story.

"Do you have the portrait?" Dougless whispered.

"Always. I'm never without it. Would you like to see it?"

Dougless could only nod. From his inside coat pocket, he withdrew a
small leather case and handed it to her. Slowly, Dougless opened the box.
There, on black velvet, was the portrait Nicholas had had painted of her.
Without asking permission, she lifted it from the case, turned it over, and
held it to the light.

"My soul will find yours," Reed said. "That's what it says, and it's signed
with a *C.* I've always wondered what the words meant and what the *C*
stood for."

"Colin," Dougless said before she thought.

"How did you know?"

"Know what?"

"Colin is my middle name. Reed Colin Stanford."

She looked at him then, really looked at him. He glanced down at the
portrait, then up at her, and when he did so he looked at her through his
lashes, just as Nicholas used to do. "What do you do for a living?" she
whispered.

"I'm an architect."

She drew in her breath. "Have you ever been married?"

"You do get to the point, don't you? No, I've never been married but I'll
tell you the truth: I once left a woman practically at the altar. It was the
worst thing I've ever done in my life."

"What was her name?" Dougless's voice was lower than a whisper.

"Leticia."

It was at that point that the stewardess stopped by their seats. "We have
roast beef or chicken Kiev for dinner tonight. Which would you like?"

Reed turned to Dougless. "Will you have dinner with me?"

My soul will find yours, Nicholas had written. Souls, not bodies, but souls.
"Yes, I'll have dinner with you."

He smiled at her and it was Nicholas's smile.

Thank You, God, she thought. Thank You.